MW01236225

HARD CASE III
Voyage of the Damned

by Bernard Lee DeLeo (Author), RJ Parker (Publicist)
Copyright 2013 Bernard Lee DeLeo
Published by RJ Parker Publishing

ISBN-13:978-1493521685
ISBN-10:1493521683

PAPERBACK EDITION

Chapter One: Little Sister

I'm watching the faces in the press corps outside the Oakland Community Center where Samira Karim had just finished giving a talk on reformation within Islam for women. Her speech, well received inside, was in the process of being trampled on out here by reporters wishing to create the news rather than report it.

I watched my protégé Jafar stoically enduring the ridiculous question/statements from the press. See, here's how it works. If anyone in the world other than Muslims, especially Americans, ever started putting women in burkas, doing female genital mutilation, or whacking their own children, wives, or sisters using honor killings as an excuse, the media would go wild with outrage. Since Islamic extremists are doing it... well... that's okay with our weirdo media. They haven't counted on any women having the guts to speak out against the virtual slavery women endure under Islamic Law.

Samira not only speaks out. She does so in venues where she puts herself at risk every moment in public. I've gathered the West Coast Avengers together in order to make our own statement on her behalf from now on, along with our benevolent Company boss, Denny Strobert, sometimes known as the Spawn of Satan. Samira and Jafar are still in their teens, but both have seen death in the most gruesome of ways. Jafar has dealt death out in the same manner. He's my kid brother by choice. Anyone messing with Jafar or Samira messes with me, and I'm a killer — not one of those Hollywood movie types. I'll gut you and throw your body into a landfill somewhere like you're a fly on my chicken salad sandwich — and I have backup.

Then it happens. It's one of those goofy instances you wish you had planned for. One of the Al Jazeera mutts screams out whore in Arabic, rips off one of his shoes, and throws it at Samira. Everyone on the platform ducks comically like he was throwing a bomb, complete with screams of anguish – everyone but Samira and Jafar. Samira stands stoically without moving while Jafar plucks the shoe out of the air. By then, my minions, Lynn Montoya and Clint Dostiene, are standing right next to mister shoe thrower. Because of their value in undercover assignments, both are dressed like MIB's, along with Lynn wearing a red hair wig, and Clint with a goatee and his hair blond.

I smile because I can't control everything, and I take my entertainment where I can get it. Lynn gives the shoe thrower a pop right between his eyes with the butt of her Glock 9mm. He cries out like a five year old that falls off a swing on the playground, lurching backwards with hands gripping his wounded head. Lynn's unimpressed. Clint moves into the face of shoe thrower's cameraman. Lynn laughs that insulting, dick shrinking he-haw that can make men impotent in a heartbeat. She nods at Jafar who tosses the man's shoe to her. Lynn spins and whaps the guy across the face with it, before holding it up to the other media morons.

"Anyone else want to throw something at my little sister, Samira? C'mon. Step up!" She smacks the cringing shoe thrower again in the head. "How about you, pussy-boy? Want to take a shot at me? I know Samira could kick the crap out of you, but I handle all her light work."

Lynn motions for shoe thrower to come get some. "I see it in your eyes, you needle dicked asshole! Don't be bashful."

"I would rip you apart, whore!" The shoe-man gestures at Clint. He's dancing around, his hands waving vainly to express the twisted featured vitriol his face radiated. "It must be very comforting to have a bodyguard when you mouth off bitch!"

4

Clint laughs and grabs shoe-thrower's cameraman. "You come with me. Take her on, Sissy-boy. You'll find out my partner there isn't as easy a target as you think. You'll be free to do anything you can. Any of you other stooges pop in, and we'll pop you."

Clint guides the reluctant cameraman away from the scene. I have the deadliest men on earth watching the rest so I'm not worried. Lynn Montoya is the whole package – unarmed combat, no conscience, and she's as good with a knife as a gun. I can see already that without backup, the media idiot is looking for a way out. That's when Lynn decides to prompt him.

Lynn drops her hands and laughs at shoe-boy. I've worked my way down to the edges of this get together. At my size, that ain't easy. "You are so cute! I bet your mommy dressed you in burkas so in case you turned out to be a girl, didn't she?"

Even some of the other media boys couldn't keep from a chuckle at that remark. Shoe-boy exploded. He went for Lynn with death in his heart and eyes. Lynn dropped down under his attack, spinning and fisting him on the back of his head so he dropped to the ground like a head of lettuce. Lynn laughs again, clapping her hands in delight.

"You are so cute! I bet you want to be a real boy. Well, pumpkin, jump back up and let's do this before your tiny dick shrinks all the way into your belly."

Yeah, I laughed. Montoya is an artist at provocation. Dipshit should have walked away. He didn't. He jumped up, and got into a fighter's stance, keeping his rage in control. Lynn matched him with a smile. I already knew from training her that pain didn't bother her. Shoe-boy went full defensive. Lynn went full offensive. She launched a roundhouse kick to his temple that ended the fight before it began. Shoe-boy dropped unconscious to the ground in a heap. I intercepted a guy of Middle Eastern descent running at her from the blindside, catching his right arm and holding him in suspended animation.

"If you move, I'll clock you."

My informative interception made the right impression for the big guy heading their way. He's an inch taller, and motivated. He grins at me. Sucks to be him. I Gronk him. It's an expression my step daughter Alice created for neutralizing a perp. I couldn't let myself be distracted by some newbie. I had to be ready for something happening with deadly weapons. Lynn couldn't let it end like that of course. Her adrenaline's flowing. She's getting cranked up, but only entertainingly so… so far. I drag big boy along with me in case he turns out to be a person of interest when I send his picture to my boss, Denny Strobert.

"Well… c'mon," Lynn screams out while dancing around over her last dance partner. "I want all of you media hypocrites! You spit on your country, and crap on anyone who speaks out to reveal the truth about perversion. I'm sick of this shit. At least have the guts to betray your country openly. Here I am! Take a real shot, instead of backing wife beating morons who strap bombs onto their own children!"

Lynn smiled, as of course no one took her up on the challenge. She kicked shoe-boy in the ribs with disdain. "Yeah… that's what I thought. On your feet my big brave shoe thrower."

Apparently, Clint had been working on the previously 'who the hell cares' Montoya. I liked it. Sometimes when a new recruit passionately embraces their country, perceptions change as long held hidden values resurface. See, we minions of the military complex don't blindly follow directions, but we damn sure know right and wrong. We also believe there is not a more benevolent country on earth than the United States of America. Yeah, it's personal. It's great Lynn has embraced our perception.

Clint moved in then when she had no takers at all for her offer, and plastic tied shoe-boy's hands behind his back. He traded one liners with Lynn for a while, smiling at his partner. Lynn then reluctantly nodded and grabbed shoe-boy by the ear. "You're coming with us, cupcake. Make a bad move on the way out and I will make you wish you'd never been born. Do you understand?"

I watched the toned down shoe-thrower nod his head in agreement as I walked up. "I believe that's the end of this press conference, folks. Please walk away politely so my friends and I don't have to disperse you. Believe me, you won't want that."

The media walked away with the usual grumblings and the smiling promptings from two huge, dark well-dressed men, Devon Constantine and Jesse Brown. When they wave for you to leave an area, you leave the area. Casey and Lucas had walked up to take charge of the guy I Gronked. Casey plastic tied his hands while Lucas patted his groaning face. I gave Jafar the signal to escort Samira down to us.

"I liked your public attitude adjustment, Lynn." I held up my i-thingy. "Hold bright boy up until I can get a nice mug shot."

Lynn of course jerked on shoe-boy's ear to get his head up, and then posed with him, her face a smiling mask that cracked the rest of us up. I clicked one of shoe-boy's cameraman as Clint encouraged him to keep his head up or have it smacked down to the cement. The guy Casey and Lucas held up between them, stared at me with one of those death stares these clowns are so good at. Yes, we're cognizant of the ACLU lawyers all these jerks have waiting in the wings. They made the first move, which means they can be charged. Denny rings me back within moments of sending the photos. I tense up a little because he has his game face on, peering at me from my i-thingy screen.

"They're all bogus, John, including the big one not pretending to be part of the media. I wish to hell I was there instead of Washington, damn it! Give me half an hour to see if I have some people in your area for holding those guys."

"Wait one, Den." I look over at Clint. "They're all phonies. Tie the cameraman up too, Clint."

There's a slight commotion I have to wait through as the cameraman doesn't want to be restrained. Clint shows him how voltage travels through the human body when contacted with stun-gun electrodes. He gets quiet and complacent then. Casey has already frisked them, and handed me the fake ID's they did have on them. I go back on with Denny.

"Okay, we have them. We can take them over and hold them at the House of Pain if you want. Something tells me you're working on a barter system for these three?"

"Yeah, something suspicious has come up. I may if I can get the right exchange rate, John. I'll call you right back." Before I can turn and explain things to my crew, Lucas starts hammering me to the amusement of the others.

"Well, Denny-light? We heard you schmoozing with your master, the Spawn of Satan. I noticed you have the Strobert management dialect down perfectly. Do we get to play with these three, or did Spawn cut you out in favor of a deal he's going to cook up in hell?"

I hang my head to much laughter, including from my protégé Jafar and his wife, Samira. "You guys are really hurtful. At least Lynn has the class to recognize I'm doing my best to help all of you."

Lynn stayed silent with a big grin.

"Lynn?"

She shrugged. "Sorry, Dark Lord. You're in thrall to the Spawn of Satan. Lucky you, we haven't staked you through the heart... yet."

Gronked again. The laughter puzzled our prisoners to no end. "Have I told all of you ingrates I have a long memory?"

"Thank you all for your support," Samira said without prompting. "I am sorry I have caused all of these problems."

"Spawn's using you as bait, kid," Montoya said with conviction. "He lets you choose the venue, and then we rack up the targets. They can't resist honing in on you. They're dumber than a bag of rocks."

Lynn gets an energetic verbal reinforcement from her audience. Our captives are eyeballing each other with angry glares.

"Mr. Strobert never pushes me. He has tried as my Father and Jafar urge, to have me tone down my speeches." Samira pauses while looking around at all of us with that disconcertingly intense look of hers. "It is not Mr. Strobert's fault that I do this. I do it in spite of his objections. I am bait by my own doing."

Montoya, as if anticipating our captives' wish to spew out of their pie holes, spun on them, her butterfly knife click-clacking into fully extended murderous readiness. "Go ahead boys. Say something. I won't shut you up. I'll bury Mr. Pointy here right in your dicks up to the hilt."

Silence... birds chirping... horrified captives' faces. The rest of us stayed solemn. No need to reinforce a very real threat. Dev and Jesse had already shoed away the other media, and now watched for anyone approaching, while trying to edge back to hear our exchanges.

"We don't kid ourselves here, Samira," I told her. "There are interconnecting interests in most of what's going on. If you

9

thought we were blaming Denny, don't. He's the best at what he does. We minions of the Spawn keep him in line as to his requests, although my fellow West Coast Avengers think I've sold out to management." I pause as I draw some laughter. "What we really need to worry about is Lynn. She's out of control. Clint, for God's sake, take the knife away from her. She needs an intervention."

Lynn gasped in stunned outrage as my plea drew wild amusement. She finally shrugged and started giggling. She smacked Clint, who was laughing the hardest. "We have to hold our own against the boy's club Dark Lord is forming, Samira. Fight the darkness, sister... fight the darkness."

Lynn's plea even drew laughter from Samira. My i-thingy signaled the return of the Spawn. I didn't want to take the call in front of our detainees so I walked away to confront my supposed puppet master. "Yeah, Den, go ahead."

"I don't believe in coincidences, John. Whoever sent those three nabbed Laredo. I just got word earlier this morning. I tried to gather more details before letting you all know. They must be aware of Clint's relationship with him, which means our presence on the West Coast is getting on the radar of our enemies. We knew this day would come. I wish it wouldn't have hit us before we consolidated the gains we've made. I'm not dictating this. These guys may or may not know where Laredo is. Talk it over with the crew and call me back."

Uh oh. "If you can work a trade, we'll handle the exchange. It will be a trap, and many will die."

Denny nods. "That's how I figure it too. They'll make some ridiculous demand involving trading Samira. I'm sure that's what this media impersonation was. They took a shot with the intention of sending a message. Even those idiots know we wouldn't hand over Samira, but they probably have another agenda involving her being silenced. She's killing them in the press. The converts she's making overseas are even carrying her picture with them in protests against their governments. The ones behind this didn't figure on their team of fake media watchers getting taken. Let me see if they'll be enough for an exchange."

No more crap with maybes. We need to get in front of this. Laredo meant a lot to all of us, but it will make Clint mental. What upsets Clint unleashes Lynn. Since joining us on the coast, they've been invaluable, but they feed off of each other. A drone strike would be less deadly than having those two launch. "See what you can do in a hurry, Den. I have to let Clint know immediately about Laredo, and make sure he knows you're on it full bore."

"Understood." Denny disconnected.

My crew knew by the look on my face it was time to buckle up. "As usual, we have more trouble than a few dimwits with cameras and a shoe fetish. Denny got word earlier today, Laredo Sawyer was taken. He thinks these guys are part of the message we're getting sent: one, they know who we are, two, they want Samira to stop the speeches, three, they think they can barter Laredo for us to stop Samira. Denny believes they didn't know we'd have a force on hand for the speech today, and that's how we ended up nabbing the three quacks. Spawn is bartering to get Laredo in exchange for shoe-boy and his partners."

"Do these guys know where Laredo is, John?" Clint eyed our guests with a slight smile, and Lynn's engine of destruction was revving up in anticipation.

"He's gathering info as we speak, Clint. Spawn wants to get our thoughts. The exposure we've been getting in the local news these days with our legal business front may finally be causing us some problems. We were all laughing at the article in the Tribune about Oakland Investigations, Bond Retrieval and Security being listed as home for a new crew of 'Expendables' like in the movies. Notoriety will make some of what we do from now on extremely difficult. No matter what this exchange will be like if Denny can get it set up, it's going to get messy."

"Laredo's comin' home," Lucas stated. "How many get sent to hell for the homecoming will be just icin' on the cake."

"I like that 'Expendables' tag," Casey added. "So... does Spawn want Lynn to give these boys her 'Ginsu' knife demo?"

Clint gestured at shoe-boy. "Let her carve him up first while his partners watch. I'd bet a thousand bucks they'll sing like lovebirds in a cherry tree."

Casey shakes his head. "I wouldn't touch that sucker bet."

Lucas walked over to smile at shoe-boy's horrified face. "This cherry's ready to pop right now. I can tell he thinks we can't do anything bad to him, but he's not sure."

Lynn then saunters over to play her part in softening these three up, and she is very good at it. Dev and Jesse had moved in to make sure our guests stayed in place. I saw Jesse cringe as Lynn smiled her happy psycho smile as she stroked shoe-boy's face with her hand.

"Ah, he's just anxious to get started, Lucas. See, we know you three are here illegally. We also know no one but your bosses know you're here, which means no one's going to miss any of you." Lynn's face lost all joviality in a slow melt down into a narrow eyed grim promise of pain. Her voice came out in a whispery soft wave of menace. "Oh, sweetie, you and I will have such a good time. I bet you never believed those stories about people being skinned alive. They're all true, but the skinner has to be very patient. The tip of the knife can't be inserted too deeply. If the knife is sharp, you won't feel much of the slicing, but oh baby... as the air hits the raw fiber of your being when I lift the skin away, it's intense. My friend Lucas is right. When your two friends see what's in store for them they'll do anything so as not to have the same thrill you're going to have."

Lucas, Casey, and I have had to do some creative interrogating when someone needed a monster to talk. Lynn usually only has to talk to them, and they tell us everything. It saves on cleanup time. It was my turn now to fill in for Denny, who gives the monsters a little glimmer of hope. I see Jafar try to guide Samira away, but she refuses. I move over to look into shoe-boy's face.

"Now see what you've done, Lynn? The poor guy is terrified. You're supposed to give him his other option before you tell him about plan B."

Lynn gets outraged. "What other option, Denny-light? I skin him like a Thanksgiving Day turkey, and his two pals tell us everything we want to know so as not to become turkey B, and turkey C. What's with this plan B shit?"

She grins at me, because my mouth may have tightened when I got called Denny-light again. The little brat. I put my arm around shoe-boy in protective fashion. "What's your real name?"

"Abu."

I pat his shoulder. "Good start. I bet you want to know what your other option is, don't you, Abu?"

Abu gets passionate, his head nodding, while he blurts out, 'yes', over and over until Lynn has to grab his chin to shut him up. His eyes widen in shock at the closeness of Lynn's smiling face.

I take over again. "See, Lynn, he wants his option. Here's what we have for you, Abu. You tell us every detail of your life as a terrorist idiot, especially who sent you today, and we pass you up the line to our boss, who will take care of you until we check out all your great information. If you impress the boss, and all your info checks out, you get to keep your skin. If it doesn't, Lynn here gets to keep you for her very own until she gets bored. Unfortunately for you, by the time Lynn gets bored, you'll be praying to die. Any questions?"

Abu shakes his head no violently. "I will tell you."

"Wise choice." I turn to his cohorts. Lynn is entertaining them by click-clacking her Balisong knife open and closed, alternating it from hand to hand. They're impressed. "How about you boys? Want to help us out or go with Lynn somewhere secluded so she can show you some more knife tricks?"

Energetic affirmations to help from both men elicited a disappointed sigh from Lynn. I texted some questions to everyone's phone. "Good. Here's how our initial session starts. We're going to split you boys up and ask you a couple of very important questions. If the answers don't match, someone's going to wish they were never born. Clint, you take the cameraman since he's made your acquaintance already. Casey can take the big guy, and Lucas will have our buddy Abu. I texted the questions. Let's split 'em up and get this part over so I can call Spawn."

Dev and Jesse kept up a roving patrol to keep away any curious bystanders while Lynn and I stayed with Jafar and Samira. I had only asked three questions — what are your companions' names, who sent you, and where are they holding Laredo. Samira walked over next to Lynn, who was watching Clint.

"You were most impressive, Lynn. Would you really do what you threatened?"

Lynn looked questioningly at Jafar.

"I do not speak to Samira about our work at all, Ms. Montoya."

Montoya nodded her understanding, smiling over at me. "He's a keeper, DL, tight lipped, and efficient. I heard you recruited him out of a jail cell, and you watched over Samira in an Afghan cave, so how much can I share with my protégé."

That's deep. I get her drift. "You can tell Samira anything. Jafar makes his own choices. I do much the same with Lora. I answer anything she asks me truthfully, but she chooses not to ask." I turned to Samira. "You've seen a lot more of death than Lora, and I don't make decisions for you or Jafar. Be careful what you ask for, Samira. Lynn's part of our family now, but her part in what we do is geared to her abilities which are violent and horrific to most people."

Samira's countenance darkened. "I would like the truth. I have no rose colored glasses as to what we must do, and I know if any of our methods are exposed, the idiot enablers will surely put us all in prison." Samira looked away for a moment, gathering her thoughts carefully. "I am sick of being a lamb protected from the slaughter. I wish to be more, and I see in Lynn a way to achieve it. I...I admit I don't know if I can do what is required. I only know I do not wish to be shielded from it."

That's plain enough for me, and Jafar is already smiling as he must have heard similar arguments from her before. "You can answer her, Lynn."

"Let's put it this way, sister, if Abu decided silence was golden, I would have made him scream and beg to let him tell us everything we wanted to know."

"Then you would have skinned him?"

Lynn shrugged. "Like a fresh Cornish hen for dinner."

Samira's lips tightened into a thin line of determination. "I know I am not capable of that, my sister, but I understand it. Thank you for trusting me."

Lynn's countenance changed to vivid appreciation. She put her arm around Samira. "You're welcome. I'm a monster, kid. I respect your dedication. I know from what John's told me you've seen horror close up from the time you were born. That it didn't turn you into me is a good thing. If you can adjust to the fact we can't survive fighting monsters with a holier than thou perspective, you and I can still be a team."

Samira smiled up at her. "Yes. I can be Lynn-light as John is Denny-light."

You can only imagine the he-haws everyone within earshot drew from that one-liner. Gronked again. The guys led our sheep back to the fold, after comparing notes.

"Names matched, and the boss matched," Lucas said. "They have Laredo held in Belize."

Interesting. We need bargaining power. "Tell me the boss is local... please."

Clint chuckled, perceiving what I had in mind. "He's in San Francisco right now. Our buddies here know him as Manny Silva. He flew in to oversee this operation, and to handle information gathered as to how we would react to them snatching Laredo."

Holy crap. "Thee Manny Silva? Saudi Arabian mom and Egyptian father who changed his name? He's been on Denny's person of interest list for years. Rich, beyond rich, and suspected of everything under the sun. He's a wahabi believer, except of course in his life style. Well hell, my friends, I think we need Mr. Silva to step up and volunteer for an exchange."

"I agree with emphasis," Clint said.

"I'm in," Lynn echoed her man. "I owe Laredo, and I have a feeling it will be a hot exchange, DL."

"Small doubt about that, Lynn," I admitted. "I'll call Denny, but we're going immediately. Dev and Jesse can watch our guests while the rest consider abduction plans. Where's Manny staying?"

"The Mark Hopkins," Clint answered.

"We did a snatch and grab there two years ago, Dark Lord," Casey said. "Denny has a much tighter grip on things than what we faced then. Let's go get this done. You know Laredo will whine for months if we don't get him out of Belize... like instantly."

"He's pulled us all out of the soup," Clint said after the laughter died down. "He screwed up and tried to go live on the beach with the ill gotten gains from our last bad guy score. If we get him back in one piece, we should recruit him here on the coast. We need an air-wing prerogative. Hell, he's flown everything, including a Stealth. I know you fly helicopters, John, but frankly... you suck."

I connected to Denny immediately, relaying the information we'd gained without any filler. His lips tightened, and it looked like Denny wanted to come right through the i-thingy.

"Get that son-of-a-bitch, John! Don't worry about fallout. Don't worry about anything. I'll take the heat. If you can keep collateral damage at a minimum, then great. If you can't, too fuckin' bad. I'm taking a flight into Oakland first thing tomorrow morning."

"We'll get it done. I'll update you when it's finished." No use getting wordy here.

"Talk to you then, John." Denny disconnected.

I walked back amongst my brethren. "Let's get these boys incarcerated at Hotel Pain. Can you and Jess watch them for us, Dev?"

"Yeah, brother, but don't you need us along?"

I told him the facts. "Not on this trip. We may need a couple of the crew on the outside of jail."

Both Dev and Jess chortled away at that explanation.

"Understood," Dev acknowledged. "We'll head there now."

"You go with them, Samira. We'll need Jafar with us."

Samira nodded her head slightly. "By your command, Denny-light."

Dev and Jess were still laughing as they prodded our captives toward the limo. I of course was in the middle of my own roast at the hands of my one time friends.

"Can we cut this laugh fest short and go get Manny. I'd like to do this op with quiet sophistication, but my master Spawn wants him no matter what. We don't take chances. Jafar seals off all communication except ours, hacks into the hotel feeds, and we go in with badges and ID's. We find out where our boy is. Then we take him, hot and heavy. I need you to stay at the desk and make sure the hotel people don't do anything stupid, Lynn."

"Whatever it takes," Lynn answered. "Are we packing enough fire power?"

"We have everything we'll need with us," Casey said. "We're all packin', but Lucas and I have vests and MAC 10's in our trunk."

"Do the vests say anything special, Case?"

"Of course, John. We stole them from the FBI."

"We'll probably have to sew a couple together for you, Dark Lord," Lucas spiked me.

"Maybe we should take Lynn up with us and leave Denny-light at the desk," Clint suggested as we headed for Lucas's SUV.

Lucas shook his head no. "That won't work, Clint. We may need to bust in the door with his head."

"Good point."

I trailed the hyenas while considering my new role as a target of opportunity.

Chapter Two: Mission For Manny

Jafar drove Lucas's SUV up around the semicircle in front of the Mark Hopkins Hotel. Lucas, Casey, and Clint hurried out with Homeland Security/FBI badges and ID's flashing to make sure the greeters did not approach our vehicle under any circumstances. Jafar began hacking into the hotel security system immediately while Lynn and I waited outside the van. The Mark Hopkins Intercontinental Hotel is a magnificent building. The entrance gives the incredible perception of entering the magic kingdom. I know we looked very impressive, armed to the teeth, FBI vests, and grim looking faces. We meant every aspect of it.

"Everyone is on line, John," Jafar said in my ear. "You have control."

"We have the desk people primed," Clint immediately acknowledged. "C'mon in. They know who Silva is by our pictures. He's here under the name Atlee Morgan."

"On our way." Lynn and I moved to the entrance with wide mouthed guests and concierges moving out of our way. "No one touches a communication device or moves out of your sight until we have Silva, Lynn."

Lynn glanced at me with a smile. "No problem."

We reached the front desk a few seconds later with Clint, Casey, and Lucas watching the desk personnel as well as the gawkers. I held up my ID for the front desk manager to see.

I gestured at Lynn. "Special Agent Montoya will be here at the desk. I want all your employees out here from your backroom. No one touches a communication device until we have Silva in custody. If anyone tries to call out, Agent Montoya will stop them."

Lynn moved around amongst the desk personnel. She checked the room behind the desk and disappeared for a moment, returning with two other employees, and a confiscated cell-phone. "Go ahead, John. I have this."

"No casualties this time if you can help it, Agent Montoya," Clint said.

Lynn smiled, looking around at her Mark Hopkins employee companions. After Clint's statement, they eyed Lynn with growing concern. "We're going to get along just fine, aren't we, kids?"

Heads nodded in unison at the face Lynn uses on serial killers. We immediately headed up on the elevator with Jafar monitoring everything imaginable: camera feeds, random calls, and especially hookups out of Silva's room.

"Someone is on-line, but doing nothing of note, John. They are unsuspecting."

"Thanks, kid. We're seconds away from the door."

"Are they really going to use your head to get through the door, John?"

My companions enjoyed that zinger on the way out of the elevator with Jafar snorting his own self-absorbed appreciation. The Dark Lord will have to reestablish some parameters with his minions. We reached the door to Silva's suite. Clint grabbed the handle while Casey slid the room card. I charged through the door the moment it unlocked. I take the first hit on front door, narrow space attacks, because seeing me coming at you, a shooter will aim for the biggest target: my chest. One of Silva's men is quick on the draw and I get three shots in the vest rapid fire before Casey puts two right between the shooter's horns. I'm on my knees when Clint runs over Silva's second man and Lucas puts Silva on his face. Casey continues around the suite with weapon ready while I roll around on my back like the proverbial turtle in the desert.

"All clear," Casey calls out.

"Oh, get up, you big baby," Lucas orders as he walks by with Silva and gives me a kick in the shoulder.

"Call Bigge Tow," Clint orders. "Tell them we have an eighteen wheeler on its side."

Smartass comebacks elude my usual razor sharp wit. Wheezing some air back into my lungs is about all I can handle. I'm laughing on the inside though. Casey finishes me off by taking a photo with his i-thingy before showing me Denny's smiling face. I roll over onto my side with a weak wave.

"I caught a military flight out of Washington, John. I'll be there in a few hours. Are you okay? You look a little winded."

Regaining my hands and knees with a smiling Casey still helping Denny face-time with me, I give him what should be my snarly face. It probably more closely resembles an open mouthed trout. "Five... by five... Prick."

Denny laughed. "Nice work, guys. See you soon. I located my cleanup team. They'll be over in half an hour. Take the good stuff and head for pain central."

Casey puts away his phone, and starts undoing the straps on my vest. I'm not proud. I stay where I am while he does it. The guy Clint ran over is beginning to cry out in pain. Casey helps me up. "What's wrong... with him?"

"I think I dislocated his shoulder," Clint answered. "He thinks that should mean he doesn't get restrained. I showed him what pain could be."

"I have Silva's goodies loaded up, DL," Lucas said. "Are you through playing invalid enough to cart it down while we watch the bad guys?"

"I'll manage... you unfeeling wretch." I took the bags from a laughing Lucas. He led the way with Silva. Clint followed with whiney. I trudged along with the bags while Casey watched our six.

When we reached the front desk, there were no hotel guests in sight. The front desk employees were on their hands and knees with hands clasped behind their heads. One guy was curled up in a fetal position. Lynn was answering the hotel phone and taking messages. She glanced up and waved.

"Okay, kids, you can all get up now. Pete, I wrote down your messages. They're next to the phone. No one enters the room our team just vacated. Our CSI people will be by to clean up. Go about your business, except for you bright boy. You stay on the floor until all of us are gone. Understand?"

The guy shook his head violently in the affirmative.

Lynn moved around toward us. "Hi guys. You don't look so good, DL."

"We had a quick draw McGraw in Silva's room. DL took three to the chest running point before Case retired him," Clint explained. "It was an unfortunate close grouping of shots, causing our fearless leader some discomfort. May we inquire what this poor sap on the floor did?"

Lynn shrugged. "He decided he was exempt from our no communication order. I convinced him to see it our way. Let's get out of here. I think Jafar is getting worried. I bet you're going to be wearing a nice new black and blue for Lora tonight, DL."

I nodded at her while we all headed for the exit. "I'd plead for sympathy, Lynn, but these barbarians I'm leading have been ragging me mercilessly."

That got a chuckle from the barbarians and Lynn. Lynn put her arm around Silva, who was checking her out. "Hey… I think Manny here has a crush on me. Are we going where I think we're going, DL?"

Time for cross checking information. "Yep. Spawn will be arriving in a few hours, but I'm wondering if you'd like to find out where Mr. Silva here has our friend Laredo before then."

I watched with admiration as the light changed instantly in Lynn's eyes. She hugged the suddenly uncomfortable Silva, much to the amusement of my crew, especially Clint. I could tell by the look in Silva's eyes Lynn probably wouldn't even have to touch him.

Lynn shook Silva like an excited old acquaintance. "Oh Manny, did you hear that? We are going to have some fun. See, we have this great place we call the House of Pain. I have control issues, and every once in a while I have to feed my darker side. The Dark Lord here lets me have a really tough guy like you he knows probably won't ever talk about the bad things he's done that we need to know about."

"I will tell you nothing!"

Manny's statement of bravery cracked up the barbarians, and actually elicited an excited hand clap of joy from Lynn. She pinched his cheek. "That's what I'm talkin' about! My last outing was a real disappointment. Agent Dostiene and I caught these three serial killer monsters. They had been carving up women all over the country. When I got them on the cutting room table, I barely had a chance to touch them before they rattled off everything they'd ever done in their entire lives. It was embarrassing. I had to duct tape their stupid mouths just to shut them up. They needed to feel a little of what their victims felt, but it was damn difficult to keep them conscious enough for the demo."

We arrived at Lucas's SUV. Lucas opened his cargo area hatch and we stuffed our two guests inside. Clint plastic tied their ankles too, and duct taped their mouths for the trip. Lynn patted Silva's cheek. "Sorry, Manny. I'd like to talk over what adventures we have to explore together with you on the way over the bridge, but the last guy I prepped pissed himself all over Lucas's seat. I'm lucky to be alive."

"Damn right!" Lucas played along. "Don't you start talkin' to him now."

We loaded the bags in with them, and shut the hatch. I could tell Lynn's blood threatened to pound right out of her veins as she slipped into the back next to Clint. It's no secret to any of us she enjoys her work. Lucas's Chevy Suburban has three row seating, so Jafar went in the back next to Casey, and I sat up next to Lucas. We maintained a comfortable silence for the trip. Jafar phoned ahead and the big pull up door was open for us when we arrived.

Samira ran up to embrace Jafar as if he'd been gone for a month. Ahhh... young love.

"Dev, you and Jess take the kids home. Have you heard from Lora about what's on for tomorrow?"

"Yeah. Some bail bond firm in LA sent out a message that Katy Scarpatha skipped bail, and is heading our way. Jess and I have two airport escort gigs, but that's it for Friday."

"I know that name," Lynn said. "She's the one accused of being a contract killer working the Southern Coast, right? How the hell could they let her loose?"

"Probably the same way they let you loose." My zinger elicited an indignant snort from Lynn and laughter from the crew.

Lynn giggled and shrugged her shoulders. "Okay... okay... I walked right into that one. You know of course, DL, there will be blood."

"Yeah, I know. Anyway, you're right. The DA didn't have enough to make the judge hold Katy without bail because she's been very careful – no priors, just rumors. We've been following the case, but Lora wanted to wait for an offer. I'll find out what it is, and we'll see what we can do. One mess at a time. We'll get Laredo back, and then go from there. I'll have Lora text you and Jess tomorrow if there's any change in the schedule, Dev."

Dev gestured toward the back. "Okay, brother. Our guests are in the holding cell. We fed them already."

"Thanks. Denny's on the way, and he always brings a few of his Praetorian Guard with him to collect any of our temporary house guests."

As Dev, Jess, Jafar, and Samira moved toward our limo, Lynn ran up and put her arm through Jess's. "Jess? Don't you want to stay and watch my interrogation?"

The rest of us know Jesse wants nothing to do with anything Lynn does in an interrogation. He knows what she's capable of. Although he's heard us joking around about the fact she rarely has to do anything but talk to captives, Jess saw Lynn's interrogation recording of the Harvard serial killers, where she found out all details of prior murders. It was not for the faint of heart. Lynn found out how upset the recording made Jess, and immediately memorized all her really good faces of death during the video to pull out on our hapless Mr. Brown. Jesse immediately stopped walking now, and plucked Lynn's hand off of his arm as if it were a scorpion.

"Don't touch me! C'mon, Lynn... that ain't funny. I'm always right in place when you need me. Funnin' me with your monster faces is gettin' old, except of course to my supposed buddies." Jess cocked a thumb at the crew who were enjoying his discomfiture to no end. "Besides, how do I know where that hand of yours has been? I know you have those guys stuffed in the suburban's storage area. I bet you climbed in with them on the way back, and the good Lord only knows what you did with that hand?"

That cracked up everyone, except Lynn, who put hands on hips in pretend outraged fashion. "I'll have you know I only climbed in with them over the bridge, Jesse Brown!"

Jess snorted in distaste. "Yeah, I'll bet you did too. Goodnight, Lynn. C'mon, Dev, before she talks the rest of these clowns into putting me in the trunk for a demo."

Lynn watched the four as they cleared the exit, before turning to the rest of us with a big smile. "Okay, boys, the Snow Whites are gone. Let's have some fun."

"I should never have let Dev and Jess talk me into letting them see your Harvard performance."

"They wanted in all the way, John," Clint said. "Tommy said no way, no how. They could have stayed on the periphery with him. Hell, you guys handle all the fight dates, escort gigs, and most of the bond enforcement. It's great having Dev and Jess with us on a day like today though, and not have to explain a bunch of crap to them."

"Jess knows I'm only messin' with him anyway," Lynn said.

The rest of us looked at each other and then walked to the suburban in silence.

"Hey! Did you guys just shun me?" Lynn jogged a few steps to catch up with us. "Oh, I get it. The boys' club is now in session.

Open up the back, Lucas, and let me have my peeps. I need to work out some control issues."

"Don't forget what we're trying to find out, dear," Clint said, as Lucas opened the suburban cargo area hatch, revealing two wide eyed, sweating, and struggling occupants.

The look Clint got from Lynn as a reply to his reminder had the rest of us backing away from him as if he just pegged the needle on a Geiger counter. He laughed and gave her the wave off. Yep. You have to be Clint to be with Lynn. Of that I have no doubt. Lynn turned to the rest of us.

"Take off, boys. We have this. We'll let Denny know the moment I skin Manny and I have Laredo's location confirmed. Denny-light can figure out a plan of attack from there."

"Yeah, no sweat guys," Clint agreed. "It's not like we're asking her to do some housework."

Ms. Montoya launched with a deep throated growl. I removed the trunk jockeys while our two resident psychos practiced their unarmed combat skills. I was happy with Lynn's progress on that front, but she was out of her league with Clint. In seconds she was tapping out from a painful jujitsu hold. Clint released her, but kept his defensive stance. He was no dummy.

"Truce?"

Lynn poked an angry finger in his direction. "You are so lucky I have work to do."

Casey and I released Manny and his bodyguard from their ankle restraints. They groaned in audible distress as we helped them to their feet. Poor babies. I could tell Lynn was warmed up. She did knife tricks with either hand in tight lipped anticipation, which became more intense whenever she glanced over at the grinning Clint.

"Manny, my friend," Lucas whispered to a very upset Silva as he pulled off the duct tape from Manny's mouth. "If I were you, I'd forget the tough guy routine, and let us start recording everything you know right now. Believe me. You don't want Lynn to start showing you her knife tricks in private."

Manny cringed back against me as Lynn reached for him. "Do not let this woman touch me!"

"That's not exactly the way this works, Mr. Silva," I explained. "If you'd like to go with Lucas and record everything, we'll put you on Lynn's back burner while we check out your story. If we like what we get, my boss may want to keep you for future reference. If your info is bad, you get the full Monty in our suite she uses where everything is plastic coated for disposal purposes."

Lynn shot forward and grabbed Manny's shirtfront. He cried out like a lost in the woods campfire girl. "I know you're going to lie, Manny. I want you to lie. Watch this, baby."

Lynn moved her Balisong knife in a whisper soft pattern up Silva's shirt. Manny swallowed hard when the material parted along the blade, unable to hold its form against the razor sharp knife. "When you're through lying to Lucas, I'll be waiting for you. After your last few days of life with me, the seventy-two virgins will run screaming from you, not that you'll have to worry about that reception. We bury the bodies in pig guts."

Silva jutted back against me in pure unadulterated terror, his head shaking in silently negative protestations. "I...I will not lie!"

Lynn smirked while whipping around on Silva's bodyguard. Casey had already removed the duct tape from his mouth. "That's what you guys all say. How about you, honey?"

"He knows all," the bodyguard blurted out. "Your friend is being held in a Belize compound owned by Sadar Kopensky."

"Yes… yes, that is the truth," Manny affirmed when Lynn looked over at him.

"Good beginning." Clint retrieved his satellite uplinked notebook from the suburban. "Go ahead and take them through their recording sessions, Lucas. I'll get coordinates for this Kopensky's place in Belize and then buzz Denny. He'll be able to order us some satellite footage."

"Take off, DL," Casey ordered. "You need to get your chest iced up so you're ready to rock when we go on a quick vacation to beautiful Belize. You have that ugly relic of a Chevy stored in the back. Take it and go home."

No argument from me. "I'll see you all later."

"Hey… Denny-light," Lynn called out as I walked toward my old Chevy. "Clint and I want to know when we go on our honeymoon cruise on The Sea Wolf."

"Never!" Lucas answered for me. "I've heard the house cleaning horror stories from Clint, girly. You ain't ever going on board my baby."

I made my getaway with a smile as the accusations began to find targets other than me.

* * *

Lora met me at the door. I couldn't believe Samira's speaking engagement and press conference had taken place only eight hours ago. It was going to be an easy morning with eight o'clock Samira talk, twenty minute press conference, and then home to play house with Lora while stepdaughter Alice attended school. Tommy was going to handle the office until noon. So much for that planned out day.

"I heard from Lynn you took three in the chest, and Casey added a picture. What happened, you leave your Dark Lord mask at home?"

Great. Another smartass. I put my arm around her and dropped my bag inside the doorway. "I take the first hit. You know that. With me coming at them, they aim center mass – my vest."

"And when one of them goes for a headshot?"

"I didn't say it was an exact science." Lora's appearance had temporarily erased the pain from my mind. Her long red hair tied in a ponytail, she wore a red halter top, white short-shorts, and medium black heels. I looked around. "Where's Al?"

Lora sighed as she closed the door. Pulling me toward the bedroom, she began loosening the halter top at her waist. "She decided to go smartass, Dark Lord's minion, on the teacher today about a history lesson."

When she didn't add anything as we neared the bedroom, I prompted her at my peril. "Okay, what witticism did she pop on the teacher you plan on blaming me for?"

Smiling up at me, Lora opened her halter top. "They were studying the Alamo, and Al was asked what she thought the Mexicans should have done rather than lay siege to the Alamo."

"Uh oh."

"Yep. She said they should have been more patient. They ended up in a war that cost them many lives, and all they had to do was bide their time until our government gave them the United States as Congress is in the process of doing now."

I started laughing. Nothing like the truth to get you into trouble in today's public school. "I thought joining history with current events was what they wanted now."

"Very funny. Anyway, Tommy's going to pick her up from school at 4:30."

I moved my hands in a feather like stroke over her shoulders and arms. The Dark Lord was having trouble concentrating on anything other than the open halter top. "Good. Let's fight the Alamo later."

Chapter Three: The Destroyer

Lora was sucking wind like a marathon runner as she pulled on a one piece blue floral summer dress. "Hurry up, John! Tommy will be here…" she stopped talking abruptly, her lips tightening as I had already dressed in my jeans and t-shirt. "How the hell do you move like that with your chest nearly caved in?"

"A more apt question would be how did I make you cry out in something other than pain for the last half hour."

She glanced up at me with her hair hanging over her shoulders and that open mouthed sultry look she knows drives me nuts. "I don't know. Maybe you could teach it to me again."

I headed around the bed with the intention of conducting that lesson immediately. Then I heard Tommy's voice, and Alice answering as the front door closed. I smiled grimly at Lora before heading out and downstairs to greet my partner along with Ms. Detention.

Tommy gave me a little wave. My long time agent and partner is wearing his 'Shaft' outfit – black leather, black pants, and black open throated shirt. Take my word for it. If you need somebody to have your back, you'd leave Shaft in the bar, and head into the alley with Tommy. "Hey John. Heard you volunteered for target practice today. How'd that work out for you?"

Alice giggled.

"About as well as this young lady's history class comments."

"You would have said the same thing, John. I'm being brainwashed in there and you don't care."

Tommy and I laughed at that word picture. "The chances any teacher could brainwash you kid are something I don't worry about. I have a feeling it wasn't the words of your answer so much as it was the attitude you projected while saying them that landed you in detention."

Al started a quick smartass remark, but swallowed it with a giggle as Lora joined us, a big frown on her face. "I bet Lynn would have said it."

Uh oh. I'd have to be careful with this one. "You're wrong, Al. Lynn learns at an accelerated level in everything she attempts. She also adapts to any situation instantly by blending in so well her presence attracts only respect. Why do you think she's so valuable undercover. Lynn can become anyone. She speaks several languages fluently, and is proficient in math and the sciences. Lynn is not just a bad-ass. She is a well-educated bad-ass, because she knew classroom time would be invaluable for what she wanted to do. Lynn would have answered the question in a way to get her point across without provoking the teacher."

Oh boy did I have little Alice with that one. Her eyes widened as I spoke, and her mouth dropped open. I could tell Lora and Tommy approved of my Lynn lesson for Alice. Score one for the Dark Lord, stepfather extraordinaire. Did the Dark Lord know if Lynn is everything he claimed? Hell no. For all I know, she was carving her teachers up by the time she was nine.

"I probably could have figured out a better way to say the same thing," Al admitted. "I like Lynn. The way she and Clint argue is funny. They always act like they're ready to hit each other. I don't think I could do all that stuff she does. I like Mom's job, bossing everyone around."

"Hey!" Lora grabbed Alice's ponytail. "I do a lot more than boss people around, missy."

"She sure does, Al," Tommy chirped in with a big smile that turned into a wavering line of confusion with knitted brows as he turned to me. "Remind me again what exactly Lora does other than boss people around, John."

"Oh, very funny, T." Lora reacted with her folded arms, tight lipped stare of death and dismemberment. "I see you over there snorting back a laughing fit, Dark Lord!"

I immediately straightened in energetic outrage at Tommy. "How dare you insult Lora the Magnificent, you lowly dog! I will have you flogged in the courtyard for this transgression!"

With Tommy laughing and Alice giggling, Lora stomped over to grab me by the ear. "You better watch it, DL. This disrespect will not be forgotten!"

"Perhaps you could return your attention to the original target. I didn't get detention. I got shot. Beeper's groupie is in trouble for giving attitude to her teacher. So, here I am with you pinching my ear like I'm a recalcitrant child while the real culprit skates."

"Bieber! Justin Bieber!" Lora's Minnie-me imitates Lora's outraged stance perfectly. "You promised you wouldn't call him Beeper anymore."

"Did not." Yeah, I probably did. Minnie-me put a huge poster of the great Beeper on her bedroom wall. I can't help it. He looks like a Beeper.

"Did so!"

Lora and Tommy are both stifling enjoyment over our great Beeper dialogue. "Look. I like the Beeper. I'd rather listen to a chipmunk being castrated with a dull butter-knife than hear him sing, but he looks like a clean cut kid. If he can make a fortune wailing away in that claws scraping across the blackboard voice of his, then more power to him. Beep... beep."

Al's mouth is moving but no sound is coming out. I think I may have gone too far. Lora and Tommy are enjoying the moment... loudly. My few moments of being stepfather extraordinaire were ending abruptly. To describe Minnie-me as being in the grips of silent rage would be an incredible understatement. My stepdaughter had Beeper-fever worse than I thought. Her fists clenched at her sides.

"At least Justin doesn't beat people up for a living!"

Ouch. "That's true, Al. Maybe I should try to be more like the great Beeper."

I started singing Alice's favorite Beeper song 'As Long As You Love Me' which I'd heard so many times I've thought of yanking out my own eardrums with pliers. I did it of course in Dark Lord vocals, pantomiming the great Beeper's moves from the many times Al had interrupted my few minutes of TV time to show me the latest Beeper music video. Tommy was howling and he hates the Dark Lord, while Lora had lost all motor functions as she flopped around on the floor screaming in laughter. Al tried valiantly to sear me with grim faced lasers of Beeper retribution, but she lost it. The smirk turned into a giggle, which snowballed into full blown laughter while yelling 'I hate you Dark Lord' over and over. I ended it with the great Beeper twisted face, hand reaching out gesture of teen angst. I glanced around at my helpless audience with Dark Lord satisfaction. My work here was done.

"I hate you, Dark Lord!" Minnie-me yelled out one final time, smacking my arm for emphasis. "I'm going to my room and listen to Justin."

I patted her shoulder. "Okay, Al. Your Mom and I were thinking of grounding you, but listening to the great Beeper is punishment enough. Don't overdo it though. We're not that mad. Five minutes would be plenty to atone for your sins."

Al smiled in an odd way that reminded me of those kids in movies taken over by the devil. "You know of course, Dark Lord, there will be blood."

"You little snot. You just did a Lynn on me. Hey you. Where did you get that from?" I grinned as she turned to avoid my clutching hand with a little yelp and ran upstairs."

Lora hugged me. Tommy stood there shaking his head. "That was insane brother. Will Lora the Magnificent allow you out for a little bit?"

Lora growled. "He has to ice his chest, T, and don't start calling me that or there will be blood."

"What's up? I can grab an ice pack and go with you."

"Our buddy, Alexi Fiialkov has a proposition he wants us to consider. He asked if we could meet with him over at The Warehouse today. I know the deal this morning is something that has to be taken care of right away, but Fiialkov told me it would only take about a half hour. Have you received word on what you'll need to do for that?"

"No. Lynn is working on the details, if you know what I mean. When she's satisfied, Denny will take the info and see what kind of assets we can count on. I can go with you for a short time. I'll have my i-thingy with me, Lora. If you hear about anything, let me know."

"I will, John, but you should put off the Russian mobster meeting and take care of your chest."

"I'll ride over with the ice pack on. That's all I could do here anyway."

Lora hugged me. "Thanks for the wonderful afternoon and the Beeper performance. That was the best."

"Good. I'll pull it out to use on Minnie-me for special occasions."

Lora sighed as she let me go. "You might as well. I don't think Beeper's going anywhere soon."

"If you two are done activating my barf reflex, can we get going, John?"

I caught Lora up off the floor as she let Tommy get into her head and launched. Tommy, of course, was laughing his ass off pointing at her. I have to learn from my partner. Man, can he get on Lora's last nerve with relative ease. I don't know what she thought she would do when she reached Tommy, but it's good not to find out. Tommy would have fought her off with good natured effectiveness. Lora realized instantly how silly her attack was and collapsed in my arms with a big sigh.

"The Karma train is coming for you, T," Lora fired off at the unrepentant Tommy. "I will help guide it into the station if I get a chance."

"I would expect no less, Mrs. We done here, DL, or are you going to do the robot before we go meet with Alexi."

"I'll grab a couple ice packs and meet you out at the car." I kept a restraining arm around my mate while she continued to eyeball the much amused Tommy. In the kitchen I retrieved the ice packs and kissed Lora. "You let T creep into your head again."

Lora shrugged. "Yeah, I did. You have to start feeding me info on how to make his head explode."

Oh no I don't. "Sorry, dear, that's not in the Dark Lord's marriage vows. It's best not to trade one liners with him. Good Lord, you look enticing in that outfit… you little minx."

With that, she jerked away out of my arms and pulled her short shorts down while turning with provocative flair. I stared at that magnificent butt of hers pointing at me. Oh my God, did I want to leave Tommy stranded by his car for another hour. Damn it! "That's just wrong. I will be back, and night will follow. Nothing on earth will keep you safe from the Dark Lord this night."

"Oh... I'm so scared," Lora whispered, moving in such a way I had to clench my fists and leave the room with her laughter haunting me on the way out. There would be blood.

In Tommy's car, I leaned back and applied the ice packs. We rode in comfortable silence with him chortling over his past verbal victories with Lora while I enjoyed the ice pack comfort. We arrived at our favorite hangout, The Warehouse, without any thought in my head concerning the meeting. I figured if T had anything I should know before the meeting he would have already shared it.

"Hey champ!" Marla, our favorite waitress called out the moment we walked in. "What the hell? You get into a fight I didn't get to bet on?"

"Nope. Just meeting my friend Alexi for some future business."

"He's not here right now. Want one of the usual while you wait?"

"Man, does that sound good. Yep, I'll do that."

"How about you, T?"

"Not today. I'm here on business to keep the Dark Lord in line. I'll have an iced tea if you can find one."

Marla already had the Bud and Beam in front of me while listening and nodding her understanding of Tommy's request. "I'll get you some tea. You'll probably be ready to go home by the time I serve it, but what the hell? You can always claim you walked in here and ordered one."

Oh boy, did she nail Tommy. He of course batted me in the back of the head for enjoying the moment too much. "Fine! Give me a Diet Pepsi."

As Marla laughed while serving Tommy, she glanced up at the front entrance with a gasp. "Jesus, Mary, and Joseph!"

Tommy and I looked around at the two figures walking in together. One was Alexi. The other one was nearly seven feet tall with broad features reminding me of Andre the Giant. Only difference is, this guy moved like a cat. His nearly white blonde hair, white walled on the sides, stood up in a short, flat top type cut. He looked chiseled out of stone. Tommy stared at me as if I had something to do with it. He stood up and patted my shoulder.

"Time to retire, John. Don't listen to anything Alexi says."

Marla grabbed hold of my shoulders over the bar, shaking me. "Tommy's right! Don't you dare agree to anything with Alexi and that thing."

I started laughing. I stood up to greet Alexi. He's a friend. He's also a Russian mobster with contacts in Interpol. Alexi doesn't deal in drugs, human slavery, or weapons. His main enterprise is gambling endeavors of all kinds, and sticking his fingers in everyone's legitimate business. We've done each other favors, the last one was my team catching and handing over his brother's killer. We now shook hands.

"Hello, Alexi."

"John, let me introduce my new fighter, Demetrius Subotić. He upset Baatar Okoye. We have a ring name for him of sorts: The Destroyer."

I held out my hand and Demetrius grasped it with a smile. "Hello, Mr. Harding. I have watched your fights on YouTube."

Then The Destroyer decided to test me a little by squeezing my hand like it was a rubber ball. I grinned because nobody can win that game with me, not King Kong, not Godzilla, and definitely not The Destroyer. See, I squeeze back. When Demetrius started getting an uncomfortable look on his face, Alexi laughed and smacked our hands.

"Enough! Did I not explain it is unwise to underestimate, Mr. Harding, Demetrius?"

"Yes Sir. I am sorry, Mr. Harding." He wanted to rub his hand, but resisted.

"No problem. Let's get a table, and we'll hear you out. Marla? Another round for me, and whatever Alexi and Mr. Subotic would like."

Tommy had his game face on. I could tell he didn't like any of this. Once we were seated with drinks served, Tommy started off the conversation. "Where did you fight the Big O, Mr. Subotic?"

"In Nigeria. We traveled there to give him a match. Please call me Demetrius."

"So you beat the Big O on his home turf," Tommy said. "That took balls going there to fight. How'd you beat him?"

"I knocked him out in the first round. It was not a popular thing to do. We were hard pressed to get out of the auditorium in one piece."

"It was my fault," Alexi said. "I did not think Demetrius would win so handily."

I would like to see that one. I made a note to myself to get Jafar on the lookout for the video. "Very impressive, Demetrius. Call me John. This is Tommy Sands, my partner. I take it you have an idea for a fight, huh Alexi?"

"I would like to build up an audience worldwide, starting right here in Oakland. You have become the most popular fighter on YouTube, John. We will build on that in the coming months by attaining a similar popularity for Demetrius. Then, I am hoping we can get you two together in the ring under the auspices of the UFC. They want you back as soon as possible, John. I'm sure Tommy has told you. I am hoping if things go well for you in your next UFC fight, you will be kind enough to give another newcomer a leg up."

"Alexi," Tommy said through clenched teeth. "We don't run the UFC. They are looking for another opponent for John in the coming months; but no matter how we do in that fight, we can't order them to put something on the docket between John and Demetrius."

"Please, I am aware of that, my friend," Alexi replied. "It will be up to Demetrius in the ring around here to gain his own reputation. I was wondering if once he has a legitimate following, perhaps John could ask to meet him in the cage under the UFC. If that is not possible, perhaps John could fight him here in Oakland for a very big purse."

I waited for Tommy to answer, because I don't make business decisions.

"It's your call on that, John," Tommy said. "I don't think you should be fighting this Yeti under any circumstances, no offense, Demetrius."

Demetrius laughed in a booming bass. "None taken, Sir."

"I'll do what I can then, Alexi, in either venue." I stood up and shook Alexi's hand, and patted Demetrius on the shoulder. "Nice meeting you, Demetrius. I will check out your fight with the Big O. C'mon, Tommy, I have a date with an ice pack."

"Nice meeting you too, Mr. Harding," Demetrius answered.

"Goodbye, John," Alexi added.

I waved at Marla, putting a hundred dollar bill on the bar. "Thanks, Mar."

"Retire champ," Marla called out.

* * *

"That chump's bigger than Rankin," Tommy mumbled as we drove toward my house. "You'd need a tire iron and possibly a shotgun to take that guy."

"You worry too much, T." I decided to boink him a little. "Ever since we went the UFC route you've turned into a pussy."

"Maybe so," Tommy admitted. "I don't want to see you lying in bed with twenty tubes sticking out of you. You're young, John. I know you're nowhere near the age your license says. You've got plenty of money and a good business. Alexi is going to keep finding giants until he finds one that can bury you. You need to go into management, and delegate the rest of the business to your crew. Lora can direct them."

"Wow, so now I'm the pussy?"

Tommy chuckled. "No, but you are out of control sometimes. Take for instance you adding that psycho, Montoya, to the business. Are you stupid?"

Uh oh, I feel a ripple in the Force. "Lynn's a little rough around the edges, but she's part of the package with Clint. I'm working with her, and being around everyone else has mellowed her attitude a bit. She's part of a major operation we have on the horizon."

"I think I liked things better before Denny decided to make all of us his own praetorian guard. Montoya scares the crap out of Jess, and anyone else with half a brain. That woman is capable of anything, John. Hell, I thought Casey and Lucas were scary to be around until I saw Montoya in action. She makes them seem like a couple of school crossing guards."

Yep, I need to pay more attention to underlying currents in my unit. "For all of what you just mentioned, we need her, T. You don't get involved in the deeper shit we have to do, and I don't want you to. The damn politicians in Washington are selling us out, and allowing terrorist cells to form right under our noses. Denny navigates in political rough waters like a shark with chum in the water. He needed a crew at his back like no other. That's us, including Lynn. Denny flew her to Gitmo right after the Harvard serial killer bust with Clint as her second, because he had someone there we needed a few answers from. Fifteen minutes in a room with Lynn, and the guy became a part of Denny's captive terrorist panel. That boy doesn't ever want to see Lynn's face again."

"That makes two of us." Tommy gestured with his hand at me in a calming action when I was about to address that statement. "I know it has to be done. I've seen the way these assholes go after Samira. That attack on your house woke me up to the fact things have changed, and the front lines are being drawn in our own backyard. Doesn't this nightmare with getting sold out by our supposed leaders make you want to just pack it up and get the hell out?"

Never. I wouldn't tell Tommy this, but if Denny ever makes a legitimate case for questioning one of these political hyenas who has a secret agenda behind their actions, I'd take the crew, round him or her up, and introduce Lynn to them in a heartbeat. "Truthfully, brother, it pisses me off. We have laws on the books, and in the Constitution, that would handle every single thing that has happened, and ended the threats. Our governmental morons have perverted and undercut enforcement to the point we're in danger of destroying ourselves from the inside out. Our crew out here is the field dressing the nation slaps on a battlefield wound, and we don't take it lightly. The UFC fight front is a key part of our cover. I need you with me to keep it functional."

"I'm with you, John. I guess I can look at Lynn like the crazy old Aunt that shows up on the holidays. Lora, Al, and Samira practically follow her around like puppies when she's in a room with them. What's that all about? The little lesson you gave Al with Lynn as the example of learning worked real good on Al. How much of it was real?"

"I don't know."

Tommy laughed. "Yeah, that's what I thought. Are you serious about fighting Demetrius?"

"Yep. Alexi plays us straight. If I do well against the next UFC opponent, I'd consider mentioning Alexi's fighter to them. The chances of dying are less in a UFC cage than our backstreet arena, and you get to vacation in some nice spots. I'd even consider a fight with Demetrius here in Oakland before any UFC fight."

"I saw you give him the vice," Tommy admitted. "I know how strong you are, but even you didn't knock out the Big O with one punch. Besides, you handle pain well, but Demetrius looks like he doesn't know what pain is."

"He did during our handshake."

Tommy grinned over at me and nodded at the next stop light. "Yeah, he did. The UFC wants you to fight that guy who looks like Ice Cube on steroids."

"I know who you mean. He's good, and he's had a lot more UFC fights than me. They call him The Rattler."

"That's the one," Tommy replied. "He's only lost one fight by decision, and I think he got hosed in that one. That's what comes of letting it go to the judges."

"I agree." Tommy turned onto my street and stopped in front of the driveway. "Lora will let you know if I get called away on Denny business. We have a man missing, but Lynn worked her magic to find out where he's missing at."

"I'll bet she did. If I don't see you for a while, you take care of yourself, White-bread."

"I will, T. It won't take long, because if it does, we'll be in trouble. I'll tell Lynn you said hi."

Tommy's features twisted slightly in distaste. "Yeah, you do that. I need to keep on her good side, because I don't think her bad side is in this dimension."

"I hear ya'." I watched Tommy drive away, knowing we need Lynn, because like Clint says, you don't get the bad guys using Snow Whites for bait. The fact she scares the hell out of some very scary guys is just an added humorous bonus.

Chapter Four: Deadly Trap

Clint traced a finger lightly down Lynn's side as she lay gasping for breath in front of him. She shuddered at his touch, reaching back to clamp onto his hand. "You shouldn't be allowed to do that to me. I'm a scary monster. You should be so frightened around me that even touching me would give you nightmares."

Clint kissed the back of her neck. "I love every scary inch of you. Thanks to you, we may have a chance to save Laredo. I had a feeling that old dolt would let his guard down the moment he started living the high life. I hope Denny can sort the info out so we can move on it quickly. It's tough waiting for his okay, but no one does it better. He won't send us into a Belize trap."

"Have you operated in Belize before?"

"Yeah, but just once. It's like a couple of worlds existing in the same small place. In one section they have private security patrolled areas with air conditioned houses. In another section they live in thatched roof squalor. In the bad part they have all the usual things going on: drugs, alcoholism, gangs, murder, and mayhem. The address you retrieved from our helpful guest is on George Street, which also is home to the George Street Gang. One of their guys made it up into the US. He raped and killed a thirteen year old niece of a very influential man in Democratic politics, and escaped back into the hellhole on George Street. They called in Denny. He sent me down to get him. It took me three weeks to track him down. He was no fool."

"How'd you do it, Clint?"

"They wanted a statement that could not be traced back to the US. I blew up the place they did a little celebrating in and left no trace. I used an imploding device that limited collateral damage to the gang quarters itself."

Lynn squirmed around inside of Clint's arms to face him. "How many?"

"Twenty-three."

"But they were all bad, right baby?"

Clint shrugged. "I didn't ask them."

Lynn pushed away. "You monster!"

Tonto leaped up on the bed between them, a tennis ball in his mouth. He dropped the tennis ball, and licked Lynn's face as she squealed, trying to hide under the sheets. Tonto immediately growled, rooting her out with nose and paws, while Clint laughed and made room for Tonto's actions. In moments, the naked Lynn tumbled off the bedside, arching away from Tonto's cold nose. Tonto pursued, sticking his nose into Lynn's sides as she tried to turn one way and then the other, peals of laughter heralding the dog's success at finding Lynn's weakness.

"Cli...Clint! Do... do something!"

Clint leaned over the bed. With a short two toned whistle, Tonto left off his tickling attack and leaped up to be petted by Clint.

"Damn it, he slimed me!" Lynn wiggled enticingly as she recovered with overtly sexual overtones which brought Clint down next to her with the unrepentant Tonto.

"I'm thinkin' of sliming you myself. Look, Tonto's very sorry, right Tonto?"

The dog immediately rolled over, with feet in the air, and tongue lolling out of his mouth. Clint laughed, but Lynn growled. "You have me on my last nerve, Tonto, you furry wart on humanity's ass!"

Tonto peeked up at her with one eye, which started Lynn giggling. The moment she giggled, Tonto launched, only to be caught by Clint in midair. "Oh no you don't! What the hell's the matter with you, dog? Have you been teasing him, Lynn?"

"Hell no! He's a mean dog, Clint. Tonto is a very bad boy."

"You hear that, Tonto?" Clint shook Tonto's snout, but the dog seemed intent on taking up his previous tickling attacks. The phone rang as Clint wrestled with Tonto. Lynn got up to answer it, wagging her butt in Clint's face on the way by.

Lynn saw on the caller ID it was Lora. "Dostiene and Montoya residence, boss."

"I just got told by Al she wants to be like me, ordering people around."

"It is a better job description than mine, boss. Do you have new orders for the dynamic duo and their rabid dog?"

"Tonto's been getting you again, huh?"

Lynn glared over at Tonto. He sat up attentively, raising his paw. "Yeah, I thought I had him bonding to my every wish, but he was just baiting me. His master pulls the same crap on me. Every time I think I'm making progress in their training, they backslide."

"Uh huh, same here at the Dark Lord's abode. This happened faster than we thought. I sent out digitals and the most recent alias of Katy Scarpatha everywhere with BART (Bay Area Rapid Transit), the bus stations, and train stations. An agent working the desk at the Jack London Square Amtrak station spotted our Katy getting off the train. She paid cash for a ticket East using a bogus ID, but it doesn't leave for another hour. John's meeting with Alexi and his new fighter at The Warehouse with Tommy along. The only other two capable are Lucas and Casey. They're already set to meet up with Denny."

"Say no more. We'll take it. I'd love to meet a real female contract killer. I thought John already had a UFC fight coming up pretty soon."

"He does, but when Fiialkov calls, John meets. Call if you need backup. I'll locate John and send him."

"Will do. Talk at you later, boss."

"Brat!" Lora ended the call.

Lynn turned to Clint who had been listening intently. "We have Katy Scarpatha over at the Jack London train station. Want to go practice our woodcraft?"

"If you promise not to act like we're going for a stroll around the block. You're getting too cocky, babe. While entertaining, that shoe-boy thing was a risky and wrong-headed thing to do."

Montoya went from playful relaxed mode to instant eyes narrowing surprise. "C'mon, Clint, I outed those suckers better than any of you boys could have in a public place."

Clint walked over and embraced her, his obvious attraction for his true blood mate easing any angst Lynn had at his criticism. "I'm hoping we have a long road ahead of us. John intercepted that team's back up enforcement just before he would have aced you. I've been in the game a lot longer than you. I don't issue warnings just to piss you off."

Lynn returned Clint's feverish and groping embrace. "I know you care. We're not going to live forever or die in our bed, cowboy. You took off from Laredo's base across the border to take on an entire convoy. How come I get crap for a little baiting exercise, but you can play one man army without any critique allowed from me?"

Clint pinned her against the bedroom wall. "Because the convoy was the price to bring you with me forevermore. I love you. I want to ride this wave of ours beyond some rock wall. It's so good I just don't want to lose you on a whimsical fuckup."

The next fifteen intense minutes allowed the couple only ten minutes to spare before the eastbound train arrived that Scarpatha would be taking. Clint and Lynn joked and laughed on their way into the station, holding day bags for an imaginary trip. Clint spotted Scarpatha within minutes of entering the building. He also knew it was a trap. Dead silence and frightened looks graced the faces of all the people he could see. Dostiene did not reason, nor did he hesitate. He picked up Lynn under his arm and darted directly for the door. Gunfire erupted around him, as screams and cascading bullets shattered glass and ricocheted behind the weaving Dostiene and his burden.

Outside the building, Clint was on his feet, weapon in hand, and murder across his features. His first shot hit one of the couple's attackers right between the eyes as the man started to follow Clint's retreat. His second shot hit dead center mass on a gunman straightening from where he had been sitting next to a real train rider who dived to the floor. A scream to his left announced Lynn's disappearance from his side. She gutted another would be gunman, his horrified features showing above Lynn's devastating attack, while his weapon clattered to the floor. Montoya dived over the bank of seats, allowing her victim to collapse screaming, clutching at his bulging entrails.

Lynn's attack, coupled with the screams of the gunman captured the attention of everyone but Clint. His next shot splattered the brain matter of a fourth shooter, the man's last coherent moment a grim canvas of death. Katy Scarpatha, in the meantime, had played her part perfectly for the deadly trap. Seeing it shatter in an instant, she plunged a hand into her bag, hoping to clear her weapon in time to escape from the fiasco. The bloody blade at her throat stopped all motion instantly.

"Oh hell, girlfriend, go ahead and try to pull that piece," Lynn whispered in her ear. "I'll make sure that weapon pull of yours will be your last, but hey, go for it, baby."

Scarpatha froze. She retracted her hand slowly from the bag, uncomfortable with the pressure Lynn was exerting on the blade at her throat. Blood began to ooze out around the blade. Scarpatha helplessly cringed back as the first trickle inched down her neck.

"Ah, sweety, don't stop," Lynn urged. "Go for it. I'll make your neck into a gaping maw of blood. You'll have to croak out whatever crap you have to say in your final words silently. I don't give a shit. It's all good."

Clint in the meantime had reentered the building amidst screams and people diving to the floor, weapon up and ready for any out of place movement. He trekked in a shooter's crouch to Lynn and Scarpatha. "Hey, babe, ask her if that's all."

This time Lynn knotted her hand in Scarpatha's hair. "Answer Katy like your life depends on it! It does!"

"That's all... no more!"

"Duck down here and put the muzzle on her head," Lynn directed, forcing Scarpatha to the floor.

Clint grinned, as he followed Lynn's order. He was happy to see she took nothing for granted. A contract killer is not to be taken lightly. Lynn plastic tied Scarpatha's wrists behind her back. They picked Scarpatha up, propelling her around the room. Satisfied, they had done for the hit team, Clint called Lora.

"Hi, Clint, are you two in position?"

"We're better than that. It was a trap. We have four dead. Scarpatha is bound and unhurt, except for finding there are better monsters in the world than she is. It's a mess. We have our FBI ID's and we're going to need them, and more."

Lora didn't waste time. "I'll call Denny and John. Do what you can. Are you going to call your FBI couple?"

"Yep. No avoiding it. Talk when I can, Lora." Clint disconnected, and called Sam Reeves, his FBI contact.

"Oh boy, Clint Dostiene. How many dead?"

"Four, but they were all bad." Clint heard sirens in the background as Reeves groaned audibly in his ear. "We were taking a contract killer into custody named Katy Scarpatha. She was at the train station, but it was a trap to get me and Lynn."

"You got Scarpatha?"

"Yep, and Lynn took her alive."

"I'm in Sacramento. Janie and I can head your way if the police want more than a talk with me. Have them call me directly. I'll make it a Homeland Security issue. Knowing you, it probably is, and I'm sure Strobert will want to question Scarpatha."

"You can bet on that, Sam. We've already been attacked twice now, and a CIA operative taken hostage. I don't believe in coincidences. My guess is this Scarpatha may be tied in with it. Our group on the West Coast is on the radar, and we're getting hit. Denny and John thought this day would come after the attacks on John and Jafar's houses – reason being we're bringing these groups to the surface."

"I get that Clint. What you and Montoya did for us with those Harvard serial killers was... ah hell, never mind. You call, we come. I know you're on the right side of this, no matter how you got there."

"I appreciate that, my friend." Clint disconnected with a sigh of relief. Lynn watched him with a tight grip on the back of Scarpatha's neck. "Sam and Janie are backing us up if need be, and we can give the cops Sam's number. He'll cover our play."

"Good to know. Hold on to my sweetie here." Lynn gave over Katy to Clint. She checked on each one of the assassination team with care. When she finished making sure they were dead, including the one she disemboweled, Montoya walked around the room. "You can relax folks. I'm really sorry for this massive inconvenience. Please stand up. The Oakland police will arrive shortly to take your statements."

Her announcement elicited a scramble of relieved would be train riders into a milling circle around Lynn, including the station workers. Montoya held up her hands in a calming motion. "Hey! Calm down. The police will be here shortly. Follow me over here away from the bad guys."

Clint watched with grudging admiration as the crowd of a dozen people, two of them children, followed her without question, casting sidelong glances at the bodies they passed. He noticed she was busily trying to wipe off blood from her hands with a hanky in front of her. Clint wedged Scarpatha into a seat, and held out his FBI ID with both hands up as Oakland police officers approached in full armor over the shattered glass on the floor.

"I'm FBI Special Agent Clint Dostiene. All threats are over. Who can I speak to in charge?"

A Sergeant with Francona on his nametag approached Dostiene with slow deliberation. The lean, five foot eight police officer peered closely at Dostiene's ID. "What's this all about?"

"My partner and I were apprehending a contract killer wanted in connection with multiple murders when we were ambushed here in the station. We have numerous witnesses over there with Agent Montoya, who were being held hostage in the trap. I have my FBI superior's number here if you would like to call him. This is Katy Scarpatha."

"I recognize her from our briefing this morning," Francona acknowledged as he looked more closely at Scarpatha. "I'm thinking you won't want to hand this over to us locals so what do you have in mind?"

"Within the next few minutes a supervisor with Homeland Security will be calling in. In the meantime, I'll put you on with my FBI superior so your bosses won't think I'm some looney stringing you along."

Francona nodded. "That sounds good to me. This is a mess."

"Yeah it is." Clint called back Reeves and handed the phone to Francona. A few minutes later the police officer handed the phone back.

"We have direction. Agent Reeves has already talked to your Homeland Security supervisor, Dennis Strobert, along with my Captain. We'll handle the dead and the crime scene, including interviews. I'm to let you have Katy Scarpatha for Homeland Security to interrogate. Once I receive word from my Captain, I'll let you and your partner take Scarpatha."

Clint held out his hand and Francona shook it. He then took out his FBI business card, handing it to the police officer. "Thank you, Sir. That will be most helpful. I'm sorry to stick you with the aftermath of this cluster-fuck, but this is a bad one we have to move on right away."

"Don't worry about it. Can you walk me through this before you go?"

"Certainly." Clint got Scarpatha on her feet, keeping a steel grip on her arm while doing a thorough retelling of what happened as Francona trailed with markers and another officer taking pictures. When they reached the curled up would be killer Montoya disemboweled, Francona looked up from the body at Clint in surprise.

"This guy's been gutted."

"We were surprised, and my partner had to move fast and silently to protect the bystanders," Clint explained.

Francona turned his attention to Montoya, who was crouching near the kids in the witness group conversing amiably with them. Focusing again on Dostiene, he shook his head. "Man, I've never even heard of any law officer using a knife."

"She would have cut my throat!" Scarpatha claimed, raising her head so Francona could see the dried blood at her throat. "My rights were violated!"

"What right? The right to take a train station full of people hostage while setting up an ambush to kill two federal agents?"

Francona grinned at Dostiene's words. "Sorry, my compassion for contract killers is a little short today, Ma'am. Thanks for taking me through it, Agent Dostiene. Nice meeting you."

"It's been a pleasure working with you. I hope to not repeat anything like this again."

"Yeah, that would be nice. I'll just wave at you when my call comes in."

"That'll work." Clint guided Scarpatha toward the exit, making eye contact with Montoya. She said her goodbyes to the witness group and joined him, smiling widely at Scarpatha.

"Oh my. Look who gets to join us for some quality time. How you doin' girlfriend? I heard you all across the room about being unhappy with your apprehension. Clint and I will make it up to you, won't we, partner?"

Clint saw Francona answer his phone and wave. "Yep. I'm certain you and Katy are going to be BFF's in no time. Let's go. We're cleared."

"Where are you taking me?"

"Let's keep that a surprise, girl." Montoya put an arm around Scarpatha. "You don't want all the fun and mystery to get blurted out in our first meeting."

* * *

Comprehension followed by terror screamed through Scarpatha's mind. She heaved backwards against Clint's iron grip on her arm. She began fighting and twisting, dragging her feet. "You have to turn me over to the authorities!"

Katy heard an ominous click clacking sound. She felt and heard the slight swish of material parting at her jeans' crotch. Scarpatha yelped and froze as something cold and metallic caressed the skin, pausing at her rectum. It stopped there. Sweat beaded out on her face, stinging her eyes with salty runoff. Her underarms stained her blouse as every muscle tensed to hold on to its stillness. She didn't dare turn her head or speak. Scarpatha felt the whisper of hot breath at her ear. Blinking sweat and terrified tears, she heard Montoya giggle as if enjoying a humorous anecdote.

"Katy girl, is somethin' wrong?" Lynn's whisper made Scarpatha start to tremble. "I don't think you understand your position in our little game. Let me explain the rules. You don't speak, twitch, or move a muscle unless I tell you to. I don't know if you've ever had a razor sharp nine inch blade shoved slowly up your ass, but honey, it's an experience you won't ever forget. If you don't keep walking with us nice and quiet, Clint's going to clamp your mouth, and I'm going to take your temperature. What do you think, Katy girl? You want to take another shot at obeying the rules."

"Yes!" The word hissed out between Scarpatha's lips. She felt the metallic coldness move away. Katy could not ever remember being afraid. Fear seemed inadequate to describe the horror she felt now. An arm encircled her shoulders as Lynn momentarily tilted her head against Scarpatha's head with a sigh.

"I haven't had anyone to play with for a long time, and you're just the cutest thing."

Katy felt Clint's hand grip her arm, but she only moved forward at Lynn's urging. These two would torture her without mercy and without hesitation. Scarpatha glanced over at Lynn's smiling face with terrified certainty they would make her talk. She wondered if telling them the truth would save her. Lynn patted her shoulder with familiar friendliness. Scarpatha shuddered.

* * *

Denny drove by the house so we could ride together. He didn't look in the mood to talk. We were on our way to pain central, where Clint and Lynn were entertaining Katy Scarpatha. I could tell by the way Strobert gripped the steering wheel his mind was processing threads outside the range of my knowledge. I had my suspicions we were in trouble. Someone decided my West Coast Murderers' Row needed to be dealt with. None of the killers used for the train station ambush were of Middle Eastern descent. Everything during and since Samira's encounter pointed at another entity stirring up something much more than we thought.

"We're getting hit, John," Denny said finally. "I admit I didn't believe the backlash against our operations would happen this soon. If it had been anyone else but Clint, I'd have dead operatives on my tab."

Well, okay. Let's get the hankies out folks. You assemble the best. You field them. The time frame for weird happenings, or focused annihilation, doesn't always happen in a predictable sequence. "We don't have Clint and Lynn because they're cannon fodder. Dry your eyes, Denny pooh, and give your team credit for a win. I'm sure you didn't foresee multiple attacks with differing agendas under one flag. Boo hoo. Let's concentrate on the win and the info we have."

Strobert snorted his distaste for my assessment, but grinned over at me with nodding acknowledgment. "Granted, what I think of as luck is insulting. Ambushing Clint Dostiene is a job for a 'Reaper' drone, not a bunch of two bit thugs with guns. He is something else, brother, but Lynn is one scary package. She turned a contract killer into our new key to thug information central. Clint said she did one onsite impalement lecture, and they can't shut Katy Scarpatha up."

Oh boy could I imagine that. I think I just clenched thinking about it. "It works every time, Denny -no remorse, no compassion, and no mercy. Add in her impalement demo... and Lynn is like the ultimate 'fear factor'. I know something has you upset besides success. Give me the bottom line."

"Terrance Brannigan."

I leaned back in awe of that name, but only in that I would snap his neck like a rotted twig if I ever had the chance to. "Well that's just... disturbing. I guess we have the good and the bad to look at in this sequence of events. It seems we've baited the wrong fish. We've done something to piss off one of the upper echelon of chaos. You should have a big smile on your face. I don't even think about the name Terrance Brannigan. He's so far up the food chain, it makes me wonder about our info."

"Scarpatha received the details for the trap, agreed to the amount, but had a serious hacker logged on to trace the money. Brannigan fucked up. This one's tough, John. Brannigan is a billionaire purveyor of drugs, arms, and political chaos. He can buy off anyone."

"No, he can't."

Denny chuckled. "Sorry. There isn't one person in your crew I would doubt even for a moment. I meant the political

59

structure in California is in debt to this guy up to their eyeballs. He buys and sells people, especially politicians, in the background of the most dangerous agenda of all: chaos. He thrives on it."

The bright lights shine for a moment. I'm the deer in the headlights as this set of Denny insights hits my brain. "The Harvard serial killers. You think they were his baby."

Denny pulled off the road and parked. "Son of a bitch! How the hell did you come up with that, John?"

Not as hard as you think, Den. "I know you. I've learned a lot from you. Don't short change yourself. I'd bet you haven't even received confirmation from Clint yet on the threads you probably have him working on. This Brannigan is a cold blooded killer without the guts to do anything up close and personal. He throws a seed in here and there, hoping for disaster without rhyme or reason. He struck pay-dirt with those scumbags Clint and Lynn nailed. They were his perfect passion for perversity. Three psychopaths with IQ's off the charts torturing and killing in perfect harmony without leaving a trace until Clint arrived to investigate. It's only now when you mentioned Brannigan that this shit all fits."

Denny stared at me without blinking for far too long. His mouth tightened. Without another word he turned back to the wheel and accelerated toward our destination. It was another five minutes before he said anything. "It proves his only agenda is a chaotic set of games where he drives money and precious metals in any direction he chooses. He has no conscience as to countries' treasuries he devalues, or the myriad lives he destroys. This is war, John."

Now, you're speaking my language. "I agree, brother. Let's ignore the fallout and concentrate on getting Laredo out. Then we go after Brannigan. You handle the white wash while we go dark op on this guy. No more sideways slants into obscure bullshit."

Denny shook his head in the negative. "We can't play it that way. Terrance Brannigan is the most high profile entity on the planet. The reason he's able to perpetrate this crap with impunity is he owns players at every level."

"I didn't say anything about taking the prick into custody. We have the top of this particular food chain. He's not in hiding. Laredo's a priority. We know now all the incidental characters in this are a smoke screen. We can do this op with care, pluck Laredo out, and then take care of the kingfisher. Oh Lord in heaven would I like to put that cocksucker into Lynn's care for a few days."

Denny chortled for a few moments trying not to show his amusement at that vision and failing. "Good God, that woman is habit forming. Okay... you're right. I won't insult you with some two bit lecture on the danger of your whole crew ending up on an Interpol most wanted sheet."

"We protect everyone here at ground zero, hit Laredo's capture zone hard and heavy - then we work on the end of Brannigan. I've seen the entertainment sheets. He thinks he's untouchable. Forget about taking him out in some covert hit. I say we take him out as an untraceable assassination. Brannigan can be our illustration that no one is untouchable. You can't be anywhere near that part of it. We get caught and we're a rogue outfit."

Denny shrugged, his eyes never leaving the road. "I hate the plan, John. I wish I had a better one."

I don't look at this as a bad plan. Survival dictates new rules. I'll get Brannigan. I'm not sure about much other than that, but I will get him. All of these incidental attacks have his fingerprints on them, and form a picture I can recognize logically. The loose ends were mounting up before I heard his name. I'm a lot more comfortable now than before. Some folks just need killin'.

We arrived at pain central, driving in through the open big door. Clint closed it up behind us, walking over to Denny's side. "Hell of a day, guys. I worked the facts, traces, and coincidences in the series of events with Terrance Brannigan as our cipher key. Oh yeah."

"Where's Scarpatha?" Denny exited his side, looking around.

"She's in lockup for now. Lynn's getting some alone time because she didn't get to play with Katy."

"You told me Scarpatha told you everything," Denny replied.

Clint laughed. "Believe me, Denny. I didn't need a polygraph to know Katy told us everything. She starts hyperventilating if Lynn is within twenty feet of her. Lynn thought she should have taken Katy through a little confirmation process. She didn't take kindly to me overriding her suggestion."

Lynn walked out of our complex's back area, smiling and giving Clint a wave. "Hello, guys. Sorry. I needed to get a grip on reality. Something about that Katy just jinks me the wrong way. Clint probably told you I went a little mental on her, but I was just being thorough, right, Den?"

"You're golden with me, Lynn," Denny answered, putting a comforting arm around Lynn's shoulders. "The Dark Lord here went into shock at your shortcomings though. He thinks you need a time out."

Lynn smacked Denny's shoulder. "Not funny. Did Clint get a chance to tell you what he found out?"

"Not yet. We get the impression Clint's come to the same conclusion Denny and I were coming to on our way over here."

"There's no doubt about the trail, John," Clint told me, handing the file he'd made over. "I had to stick with basics once his name was added in. The asshole is behind nearly everything you can think of, including fogging up the investigation with the Harvard trio. When I show Sam Reeves what I've found, he will issue a federal warrant on him."

Denny and I traded looks Clint picked up on right away, as did Lynn. Our silence hung like the noose at hangman's tree with no wind.

"Boy, you two are ambitious," Clint said, hugging Lynn to him. "Bagging a multi-billionaire is not something to be taken lightly, but as the targets of this Brannigan's latest assassination attempts, I'm in."

"Hell yeah!" Lynn put her own stamp of approval on it. "I guess we need a priority check though. We're still going for Laredo first, right?"

"Absolutely," Denny answered. "I'm hoping we can move before Brannigan initiates anymore abstract missions with us as the targets. The Harvard connection was as eerie as I've ever run across. The money exchanged hands in more than a few places to make sure his toy serial killers were not found out. I'm glad they never came to trial. I have a bad feeling Brannigan's lawyer team would have found a way to get them off."

"Thanks to Lynn, we know where to get Laredo at," Denny continued. "I have a team of analysts going over the data about that Belize farm where Laredo's being held, gathering up to date satellite footage. I'll know the details within hours about weather and flight conditions very soon. I want this op on the move by tonight. Our best chance is to hit them quick, when they don't think there's any way in the world we can do it."

"We know you're workin' it," Clint said. "It wouldn't do us much good launching a rescue where we get everyone killed in the process? Laredo doesn't want a fast tracked suicide mission for his benefit."

Lynn moved over in front of Denny. "What plans do you have for our killer?"

"Because of your complete success with her, and the dead-bang case they have against her, I think we should turn Katy over to the locals. She will never get bail again after this last run, coupled with the ambush attempt. We'll need to launch an attack on the judge if someone lets her out after all this."

I laughed at Denny's point by point on why Katy would never get another chance at bail. I wished I shared his optimism. We now knew if a price was given, she'd be able to meet it with Brannigan's money. "I see Lynn doesn't like our contingency plans for Katy."

Denny made a gesture of understanding with placating hand motions. "We will deal with Katy no matter what, Lynn."

"As John pointed out earlier, they let me go. If this Brannigan guy can buy judges, he can certainly buy juries," Lynn replied.

"He can also make enquiries about where she is, since we are on record as having her. We're not turning her over until Laredo's here with us. Brannigan doesn't believe she knows anything about him so that works in our favor. I'm not stupid enough to think she wouldn't get word to him."

Lynn smiled. "Sorry, boss, I see what you're saying. We may have gotten our signals crossed. If I would have had to extract the info from Katy, she probably wouldn't have been in any shape for a locals' turnover."

"I didn't say this was a precision game, Lynn. Shit happens. You did well without any marks, so we hold her and give her over later. Back to business. Our entry into Belize will be by chopper. The farm on Hummingbird Highway is a little past twenty-six miles in. I want your team dropped five miles out. Leave a force there protecting the dirt road leading to the farm. I want John, Clint,

Casey and Tonto on the attack, with Lucas, Lynn, and Jafar protecting and monitoring the LZ. Get your equipment together now, and be ready to go. I'll need to put your team on a carrier wing already in position. I want the chopper going over Guatemala rather than on the Caribbean side, hence my plan to use the Vinson. I'll have a team watching your people here until you get back."

I liked that the place was way inland. I'd been to Belize on another matter, along that same route. It was open terrain with plenty of cover. "Sounds good to me. It's probably a little too close to Guatemala for Clint's liking though."

Clint chuckled. "No worries there, brother. I assume Denny isn't putting us with the fleet for a laugh. They'll chopper us in with one of those Black Horizon stealth babies that can fly us into position, and drop us off without being picked up on anyone's radar. That means we'll have the tools we need rather than making do with a couple of pistols and a prayer."

"Clint's right," Denny added. "We're not going half ass into this. I have the go ahead all the way up the chain. The only thing I won't have for you is recognition you guys even exist. This op is black all the way. The pilot will be one of ours. He's already in place on the USS Carl Vinson. The carrier strike force is in maneuvers near Guatemalan waters now. I have a C-2 ready to take you aboard the Vinson tonight. Our guy will chopper you all in the early AM. If this goes bad, there will not be a rescue."

"In other words, if something goes wrong and we get burned, we get to blast our way out of Belize. Cool!"

Denny shook his finger at Lynn while Clint and I laughed. "One more statement like that, Montoya, and you'll be swabbing decks on The Sea Wolf for the next year."

"Big deal. That's the only way I'll ever get aboard the damn thing anyway."

65

Chapter Five: Belize Black Op

We huddled at spaced intervals, watching the Black Horizon whisper away, skimming low over the land. Clint and Tonto immediately set out to check and secure our LZ. The rest of us stayed in place until their return. The humidity caused sweat to bead out of every pore, soaking our black incursion outfits with built in Kevlar armor. Within moments rain began to fall as predicted. A thunderstorm was due to hit, which would help us on our approach. By the time Clint and Tonto returned, Lucas, Casey and I had a low slung enclosed lean-to up over our computer geek, Jafar. Lynn took up position next to him without comment. Her job would be to protect him. Lucas would watch the road.

We were all on com with Jafar. He tested our communications before Clint, Casey, and I headed for our target with Tonto in the lead. Thunder and lightning began lighting up the night sky with an awesome display. Tonto took up a position slightly ahead of Clint, where he kept sight of his master while moving in a similar direction. Our pace brought us to the outskirts of the elegantly built ranch house in less than forty minutes. It was now nearly two in the morning. We spotted a single roving guard in raingear.

"This is perfect, John," Casey whispered, setting up the silenced .50 caliber M107 Barrett sniper rifle. "I'll take the guard out on his next round."

"On it." Clint and I moved rapidly while the guard was out of sight. We were in position at the front entrance when the guard appeared again. Casey double tapped him. I went over to the body and confiscated everything he had on him, including his keycard. We were blessed with the mojo working for us.

Tonto sat attentively at Clint's side. Our masks and flop hats in place, I opened the front entrance door. The assault was prearranged. Clint whispered to Tonto and the dog leaped into the house, with the two of us rushing after. Tonto crept along low to the floor once the entrance was secured. I won't bother whitewashing our incursion. It was a massacre. Our MAC 10's with silencers disturbed no one as thunder claps sounded every few minutes. The men we found died unready for what we did, and we killed everyone we found on our search for Laredo. We located him in a makeshift cage at the rear of the sprawling house. Once we confirmed where he was, Clint and I moved on while Tonto guarded access to the unconscious Laredo.

We had killed six to that point, all living in semi-military style. When we reached the last bedroom on our route around the villa, it was obvious this was the leader of the group holding Laredo. He was the only one to have a woman sleeping with him. Since we needed a bit of information to go along with pulling Laredo the hell out of there, Clint stayed in place with him while I went through the entire house once again with thoroughness. I joined him a few minutes later. The woman was already stirring uneasily in her sleep because of the thunder. Clint made her sleep much deeper with an injection once we identified her companion as Sadar Kopensky. He snored gloriously unaware of anything going on around him.

"This guy sounds like a buzz-saw, John."

"Get Tonto in here to wake him so we don't have to shoot our way into Laredo's cage."

A short whistle later, and Kopensky awoke from slumber with Tonto's maw at his throat. He screamed, which enticed Tonto to give his neck a little shake.

"Stay very still, Sadar, and shut the fuck up!" I turned on the light next to his bed when Sadar did what he was told. "Where is the key to the cage?"

"In...in the top drawer of my dresser!" Tonto kept Sadar occupied, the man's features twisted into a grimace of terror.

Clint got the key and went back to get Laredo. Tonto and I entertained Sadar until he returned with a beaten but relieved Laredo. We shook hands.

"Damn, John... am I ever glad to see you guys. I thought maybe they'd cut me loose like they did Clint in Guatemala." Laredo walked over to the bed and petted Tonto. When the dog relaxed and backed away from Kopensky, Laredo punched down full force, shattering the man's nose. He flexed his hand with a grin, watching Kopensky role around on the bed in agony, clutching his spurting nose. "Oh yeah, boys. That felt hella' good."

"Why didn't you punch him in the nuts?" I asked. "Now we have a bleeder to walk back to the LZ."

"Good point, John," Laredo answered and punched Sadar in the nuts, evoking a piercing scream. "Don't worry, I'll kick the son of a bitch's ass all the way to the LZ."

I sighed as Clint laughed. "Okay, you watch Sadar with Tonto, while Clint and I round up all his goodies. Want to find out all the money locations, and special accounts while we're gone?"

Laredo's face nearly beamed. He looked skyward for a moment. "Thank you, Lord. Leave me a recorder, and don't hurry."

Clint and I went through the now well lighted house, turning everything inside out. All of our search was accompanied by the sound of screams and growls from Sadar's bedroom where Laredo and Tonto tag teamed our unfortunate Kopensky. We found two laptop computers and a safe. Laredo loved escorting

Kopensky to the safe where Kopensky opened it with trembling hands but no hesitation. We loaded up everything inside it into the pack I carried. Next came outfitting Laredo and Kopensky in foul weather gear for our walk out. Then, I smashed the control panels for lights and communications. Last, but not least, Clint had Kopensky answer one more question.

"Who were you sleeping with?" Clint had already run across a female cartel leader when he rescued Montoya out of Mexico. We didn't want to make an error in judgment, leaving behind someone of status because of their gender. That would be sexist.

"She... she is my mistress."

"How about it, Laredo? Did you ever see a woman walking around like she was in charge here?" I didn't like the way Kopensky had answered the question.

Laredo shrugged. "I heard a woman's laughter a couple times, but this is the shithead that questioned me. The guards were all male that moved me. Did you guys run across a pockmarked face with a scar along his cheekbone? I'd like some quality time with him, brothers."

"Gee, I'm sorry." I did remember that face. "I can show him to you, but unless you're into necrophilia, there's not much use."

Laredo laughed. "I should have known with you two here in the same place. Sorry I can't help with the ID on the woman."

"I didn't find anything like a purse," Clint added. "I hate like hell to leave her."

"Let Tonto chew on his nuts for a while just to be sure," Laredo suggested.

"No!" Sadar went to his knees as Tonto moved with a growl to his side. "Brannigan... Maria Brannigan!"

Clint and I looked at each other with big grins. "Sweet Jesus, Clint, I think our ship just ported in the night."

"I remember the name from when I back-traced the info we got," Clint replied. "Maria is Terrance Brannigan's sister. How the hell did you end up with her?"

Sadar groped around for an answer, trying to come up with something he wouldn't get beaten or have his balls chewed over. His nasal presentation entertained Laredo. "She runs his South American holdings. I... I met her after capturing Sawyer. She had a list of interrogation questions to be answered. Maria gets bored easily. We had a few drinks one night and entertained one another. We... have been together since then."

"You know me, Clint," Laredo said. "I gave up everything when asked. Hell, I know pros don't stop. No way in hell was I going to get tortured for months just to finally give it up when they got creative enough. These people don't follow the Geneva convention directives or even common human decency, and they know damn well they will get the truth out of you. Oh, wait a minute... they're just like you guys."

"You look okay, brother." Clint put his arm around Laredo's shoulders after he and I enjoyed a laugh over his interrogation philosophy, because he was right, except maybe in Clint's case. "We'll go over the items you told them later. So, they mostly gave you attitude adjustments after the interrogation, keeping you alive for ransoming. Give it to me straight. Do you think the suave Sadar here could have been enticing enough for a hookup with Maria?"

Laredo thought about it. "Late thirties, uniform, his own fortune from screwing people, not hard to look at, speaks a few languages... yeah, I could see it happening. I know about Terrance Brannigan. I'm betting it wouldn't have happened if he saw it coming. I take it you guys have a lot more to add in the Terrance Brannigan category, huh?"

"Yep. I guess we need to pack Maria up for shipment. Let me check for an all terrain vehicle to make our journey fast and easy to the LZ. You'll help with that, right Sadar?" I put the Vulcan neck pinch on Sadar as he shook his head agreeably.

Fifteen minutes later, we were speeding toward our LZ with plunder and prisoners in a four wheel drive Toyota pickup with thunder, lightning, torrential rains, and a very happy Laredo Sawyer. I broke radio silence. We stayed off air unless either party had something important.

"DL on line. We have package. Coming at you in a Toyota."

Jafar's relieved voice came on immediately. "Acknowledged DL. The Cleaner states she is wet and unhappy."

That cracked up Clint and I. Lynn's official tagline was The Cleaner, much to her professed outrage. Then Lucas's voice came on. "This is Ahab. Get your asses back here before I have to put a round in the back of her head."

That pronouncement did nothing to help. Clint was helping me steer while both of us were howling, with Casey hugging Tonto for stability.

"Lynn Montoya," Laredo stated with conviction. He leaned in where his audio could be heard. "Hey cutie, is that you?"

"Yeah, cowboy, the damn boys club dropped me into this fuckin' jungle dressed in twenty pounds of equipment in the middle of a fuckin' hurricane! Help me!"

Now all four of us unbound people were howling. I finally got enough of a grip to speak. "We brought you two new toys, Cleaner."

"Well damn! Now you're talkin'. I hope they aren't as disappointing as Katy."

"Katy," Laredo repeated questioningly.

"Lynn scared the female contract killer so badly, she gave up everything before Lynn got to play with her new toy." Clint shrugged when Laredo's gaze narrowed, uncertain how to take that information.

"Did not!" The Cleaner interjected.

By then I was nearing our LZ. The torrential rains were subsiding slowly. Lucas met the Toyota as I slowed to a stop. "I would have hailed for pickup, John, but we have an incoming convoy of some kind. Jafar is trying to narrow the satellite range down to get a better look. How do you want to handle it – take them now or go to ground until they leave?"

Casey spoke before I had a chance. "I hate hot LZ's. We're rogue anyway. Let's act like it. I say find out if the convoy has any plunder. Arrrrrrrhhhh maties!"

Yeah, we're all a little nuts. In answer, Ahab, The Cleaner, and Geek-boy all started doing their crappy talk like a pirate routines. "Fine. Casey takes out the lead truck with the M107. I'll blow the last one in line with the M136 rocket launcher. Lucas, Lynn, and Jafar open up on the stopped up middle. Rules of engagement are as follows for us rogues. If these guys are delivering food, and aren't dressed in camouflage gear, we'll let them pass as the dawn patrol. If they're wearin' camo, we hit them."

I heard acknowledgement from all. We set up our trap without further discussion, leaving Tonto and Laredo to watch our prisoners. Then it was wait time. About forty-five minutes later the lead truck came in sight. They were wearing uniforms. Casey took out the cab of the lead truck, causing a flip to its side. I then blew up the last truck in the convoy, demolishing the cab and front engine section. Lucas, Lynn, and Jafar fired short bursts into the trucks in the middle, until guys were screaming out to surrender.

With Tonto called to action, we had the transporters herded into a hands clasped behind the head circle in no time, while Clint, Casey, and I inspected the shipments. Imagine our surprise when we found they were hauling an entire lab out to the estate. It had everything, including the chemicals for creating meth and anything else they wanted. It was state of the art. In the back of one truck we struck pay dirt. It was like a mobile mansion with bar, kitchen, hot tub, etc. I called Clint and Casey over to check it out. I'd never seen anything like it. While we were exploring in awe of the plumbing and gadgets, we heard a scuffling sound under the bar in back. Clint hauled out this guy dressed in a tuxedo. A woman huddled underneath with him straightened. She was about five feet, eight inches tall, auburn hair, slender, with an off the shoulder black evening gown on.

"Must be a party, DL," Casey said. "Who might you be partner?"

The guy straightened, brushing off his tux. He was a little taller than the woman, but carrying about thirty pounds too much with sparse brown hair combed over. "I am Alexander Torre. I am Terrance Brannigan's executive assistant. What is the meaning of this?"

"Do not fool with these men," the woman hissed at him without taking her eyes off of us.

"We need to move," Clint said. "You two get dressed in foul weather gear, and put on some shoes you can walk in."

"I'm not going anywhere with you men!" Alexander stated, but his companion immediately began donning a coat and digging out other shoes from a bag as Clint watched her."

I moved over and grabbed Torre by the neck. "Here's the way it goes, Alexander. You get your foul weather gear on, or I start breaking things on your body. Want a demo?"

Alexander's eyes nearly popped out of his head. He indicated with headshakes and gestures he was ready to comply, so I let him loose. He got his gear on under my watchful eye, while Casey grabbed up the computer gear in the mobile barroom.

"Let's back the hell out and I'll hit the trucks with the launcher."

We joined our group with the new prisoners. They had the surrender group on their knees with hands behind their heads. Lucas met me on approach. "I hate to say this, but we have a decision, we either waste these guys or screw ourselves."

"I'm blowing the floating lab convoy. We'll plastic tie these guys hands behind their backs and send them toward the compound after we call for pickup. I'm not going pussy on you Lucas. I don't see them causing us problems if we get the hell out of here quickly enough."

Lucas smiled. "It's all good, John. We're on a roll. No use descending into darkness any more than we already have. I'll get them cinched up, and tell Jafar to call for pickup."

After Lucas had the men bound for walking, I blew the convoy up with the M136. That display got some instant respect. They all knew they could have been in the blast zone. I faced the group and gave them their directions in Spanish when Jafar told me pick up was ten minutes out.

"You will not be set free of the ties on your hands. Start walking toward the compound. You can find something to free yourselves there and wait out the storm. Get moving now. Don't stop. Don't look around."

They didn't need much prompting. Our captures headed for the compound without a backward glance. We rounded up our transfers. Brannigan's sister was coming around pretty well, and she was not happy. She had regained her feet, soaked to the skin in spite of the rain parka I had put on her. The way she danced around in place with her hands secured behind her back was a little amusing as we waited.

"Let me go right now, and I don't have you bunch tortured and killed!"

Oh my, she gave us a laugh with that one. I saw Lynn taking an instant liking to her. She loved the ones who were so far out of touch with reality, they could issue threats like that. To her credit, Lynn didn't play or assume anything. She looked at me first. I had no objections to a small attitude adjustment. I nodded at her with a smile. Lynn worked her over without a word – nothing but well struck body shots, following the screaming Maria Brannigan to the ground. When Maria began crying and begging for mercy, Lynn held up. She gripped Maria's chin in a no nonsense shaking grip.

"I don't know, and I don't give a damn what you think. You're my bitch now, girlfriend! I'll let you know when I want you to speak. Until I tell you or ask you something, you keep your fuckin' mouth shut! Comprende?"

"Yes! Yes... don't beat me!"

Lynn laughed her serial killer laugh. She patted Maria's cheek. "Oh baby, you think that was bad? I'll show you bad. Cross me or my friends again, and I'm going to show you more about pain than you ever dreamed of." Lynn released her and stood up. She kicked Maria in the side. "You have five seconds to pop the fuck up on your feet or I start in on you again with fervor. You getting any of this, honey?"

Maria's head bobbed up and down as Lynn released her chin, eyes blinking in wide open terror. "I...I understand! Don't hit me!"

Lynn waited in silence, and she was counting. Maria made it to her feet inside the five second range. Lynn sighed with emphasis. "I was hoping you wouldn't make it. Okay... stay still and keep your mouth shut."

Maria didn't even respond verbally. She gestured with her hand in a dismissive motion. "Don't...don't hit me again."

Lynn patted her wet cheek. "Be a good girl and choose your words and actions wisely, or you get to see what's behind door number two. I'll give you a hint: it's not a Toyota."

The chopper ghosted in five minutes later. We loaded everything up. The thunder and lightning extravaganza had tailed off, but the rain pelted down non-stop. The pilot saw Laredo get boosted up and came back to grab his shoulder.

"Well, Damn! Laredo Sawyer as I live and breathe. I didn't have any idea you were the package they were picking up tonight."

The two men embraced. Laredo broke away and thumbed at his old pal. "This guy's Dutch Larkin. If I'd known he was flying us back, I would have insisted on walking. I guess they let anybody pilot one of these high tech masterpieces."

We hadn't seen Larkin when he flew us over. Six feet tall, slender to the point of emaciation, black, and possibly Laredo's age. We gave him a wave from where we had squatted for the trip back after securing our gear and prisoners. Larkin yanked on Laredo's arm.

"C'mon up front with me. We couldn't afford more than one pilot in the know on this op, so I have an open co-pilot's seat, brother."

"Oh yeah!" Laredo followed Larkin, but turned suddenly to face us with a big shit eating grin. "Buckle up children. It's going to be a bumpy ride."

Lynn popped up immediately, pointing with a warning finger at Laredo. "You make me barf, I make you bleed, cowboy!"

"Damn it, Lynn!" Laredo shook a fist at Montoya and continued into the cockpit. "Fuckin' pussy serial killers!"

Yeah, us crazies were laughing at that exchange, but our guests were understandably less amused. It was a ride in the blackness like no other to the Vinson flight deck. I didn't bother staring out a window. I knew only pitch black darkness and solid sheets of rain pounding the exterior would be all I'd see. I found a position for the first time since we left the Vinson that my chest didn't ache. It would not get easier. We had to load up the C2 with gear, plunder, and prisoners. Weather or no weather, we were flying off the Vinson into San Diego, and from there home to work this Brannigan opening as quickly as possible. Jafar is reading me. The kid cinches in next to me.

"You are concerned about moving quickly on this Brannigan, John. I see it on your face."

"You're getting annoying, kid. I had getting Laredo back as my soul purpose on this jaunt, but damn, we hit pay dirt. I'm getting ambitious."

Jafar smiled, nodding agreeably. "Yes, I see it all coming together in your head without you speaking. Lynn has assumed ownership of Ms. Brannigan. The monster can surely get Maria to speak on a person to person call for a few minutes. I will triangulate that bastard's position, and you will get him."

I did a double take at my young protégé. "Shit, that's exactly what we need to play this next round. Brannigan will be thinking to get a call from the compound area though."

"I will make sure that is where he thinks he is getting the call from."

I thought this kid needed seasoning, but I was wrong. "You forget all about the military, kid. You have game. This mission showed me more than an opening into Brannigan's demise, and Laredo's rescue. If we get Laredo to hang with us on the West Coast Avengers, you and he can take everything we do to the next level."

"Samira is pregnant. I am very happy to know you do not still wish for me to join the military. I would be proud to do so, but we already go on missions vital for our country."

"Yep. You doing a four year term in the Marines would look good on your resume, but putting Brannigan in our sights immediately illustrates how much we need you with us. It's not that someone else wouldn't have thought of it. It's that we already have a team, and you're part of it. Congratulations on your starting a family. These are scary times, but we'll do everything in our power to make them less scary."

Jafar nodded in grim faced acceptance of what he and Samira would face. "I know this job is not a safe occupation, DL. Samira refuses even my most subtle hints to step back from the speaking engagements she knows provoke the most hideous followers of Islam. I know that at least in the Marine Corps, personal retribution would be non-existent. Samira is adamant about her goal to uplift women's rights in Islam, and she will never back away. It is why I love her. She does not whine or nag me about my involvement with you. We are a good match, John."

No doubt about that. "I can't play favorites or give you special dispensation, but we'll work it out. We'll put your plan into effect the moment we touch down in Oakland. I want to be on home ground when we trace this sucker."

"I am glad we have Lynn and Clint with us. They are the missing link of scary."

Boy, is that ever true. "We only need to keep in mind our exposure. I know you can hack in and annihilate threads we don't want out there in public, but we have a presence that is gaining ground everywhere. You're our transition piece between our public and private face. I know that ain't easy, kid. You have talent. I didn't set you on this very dangerous path because I had other choices. You've stepped up to our problems without missing a beat. You handle combat just fine. The sky's the limit, but I would be remiss in pointing out as your older brother by another mother that this shit will get intense. Until now, I had no one to worry about or watch over. Suddenly, in the past year I have a wife, stepdaughter, and your family unit. I ain't whinin' about it, but I do know the unintended circumstances very well. Do you?"

"I do, John. I accept that the blame as you have taught me lies in the mirror each morning we survive to see our reflection."

I gripped his shoulder. "Yeah, little brother, it is just so."

"We have to get Brannigan, or he will surely get all of us and everything we love."

"Indeed, little brother… indeed."

Chapter Six: Brannigan

Lynn and Clint were on my ass the moment we touched down on the carrier, and started transferring our equipment to the C2.

"Hey, what's up with the kissy face moment with Jafar, Dark Lord?" Lynn didn't waste any time getting down to business. "My ears were buzzing. What are you and your little twerp plotting?"

Clint was the amusing part of this interrogation as he tried to indicate some restraint on his partner's attack without success. "Lynn! Calm the hell down. Yeah, you were part of our discussion. Jafar let me know how fast he could triangulate Brannigan's ass if you can get your Maria Bo-Peep to make a call for a few minutes."

Lynn's face drained into acceptance of what she had imagined as a slight, was an actual compliment to her skills. "I get it. Sorry, DL. I'm a little on edge. That was my first time in any kind of combat. It rocks! Instead of taking out my inner monster on shithead predators, I should have joined the service."

"But then you wouldn't have met me," Clint took the bait like a big guppy.

Lynn cast the perfect look of distain upon him. "Yeah? So what. Oh, you think my happiness was keyed to your bludgeoning your way into my life, huh? I don't think so. It probably set me back in my ambitions."

"Keep talkin' Cleaner," Clint said, walking away. "Cancel the murderous honeymoon voyage, DL."

"Uh oh." Lynn ran and jumped aboard the Clint Dostiene back express. He resisted the pest's attentions for a moment, but the pest had some form of anesthetic stinger which she subdued the Dostiene inner beast with.

The couple did elicit laughs from our group and many of the ship's crew readying our C2 flight off the Vinson. The rain had subsided somewhat, which made our launch off the carrier deck aboard the C2 less harrowing. I didn't much mind, because Laredo co-piloted next to his friend, Dutch once again. We hooded our prisoners before our next landing. Denny had another military transport waiting for us in San Diego. It took only a short time to transfer gear and people once again. We flew into San Francisco Coast Guard Air Station just before noon. We slept fitfully where possible on our flights as all of us were aware we had to hit Brannigan next. Denny met us with our drivers, Jess and Dev. Next stop was pain central.

The silent ride across the bridge gave me a chance to observe my team. I'd never served with a better bunch. It's an incredible feeling when you know you can count on the people at your back. We're a weird bunch of killers and killer support people. I knew I could count on every one of them. Over the past year as I went from a solitary, I don't give a shit street fighter, to a contradictory role as husband, father, and CIA team leader, I've had moments where like Jafar, I've wondered what in the hell was I thinking. We take life for the good and bad. If I had embraced the lone wolf life style, then yeah, I could have continued my solitary mean ass life. I wanted more, and I'm paying the piper for it, along with everyone depending on me. I'm going full out in your face, make it work mode, and God help the assholes who try to derail my train. Brannigan had moved into the number one slot of people to be erased from my life's equation. We exited at pain central with Tonto very happy to run around our complex, and Lynn took over after we closed up our building.

She waited impatiently for Jess to park our transport vehicle with the hooded prisoners. Denny stayed back, observing.

When the vehicle came to a stop inside our favorite greeting place for assholes, Lynn was ready. She practically danced in place as the rest of us waited in amused silence. We all knew Maria Brannigan's arrival would not be a happy one. Lynn played it perfectly as Maria exited the vehicle with Jess's help after he removed her hood. She saw Lynn, and all neutral emotions fled her features completely. Abject terror highlighted the initial angst at seeing Lynn waiting for her. She tried to pitch back against Jess's helping hand, but he tightened his grip against any movement away from exiting the vehicle. Lynn, of course grabbed her away from a solemn faced Jess.

"Hey, girlfriend!" Lynn hugged her as if greeting an old friend, guiding her over with us. "We have a job for you, girl! It involves your brother. I'm betting you know where he is right now, but we can't take that as our assumed fact to act on. Here's what we do. You tell me where he is right now… and honey, I mean right now."

"Lake Tahoe! He's in a cabin complex we have at Tahoe! It's near Emerald Bay!"

Lynn patted her cheek with affection. "You are so cute. Okay, I believe you, but I'm going to have to go the extra yard for my all business companions. Now… this may hurt a little, but I'm sure-"

Maria started sobbing with heartrending real tears. I'm not much on this touchy-feely stuff, but it looked real to me. "Give her the choice of door B, Cleaner."

I got the glowering features of hell on earth look from the Cleaner. "Fine! Okay, Maria, here's your big chance to keep from being tortured and mutilated. Don't take the deal, honey! I think it's a scam by this nitwit here who calls himself the Dark Lord. I'll just-"

"Cleaner!"

"Fine! Okay... Maria... stop crying before I get my propane torch out."

Maria gasped, and covered her face with both hands in a shuddering successful attempt at shutting off her sobs. Lynn put an arm around her shoulders, giving her a gentle hug. "Not the tough girl, no nonsense resistance I was hoping for, but let's proceed. I need you to call your brother while geek-boy over there traces your call, and confirms what you've already told us. I hate when this happens, but these guys have trust issues."

"I'll call! Honest to God... I'll call."

Lynn let out a big sigh, gesturing in a defeated partial wave of her hands. "That's just sick, girlfriend. You give up your own brother over a little pain. I liked you when we first met, but the thrill is gone, baby."

"Cleaner!" This was like watching a show on TV with audience interaction. Again, I got the death's head stare for a moment.

"He... I mean Terry raped me when my folks were gone on vacation to Europe. He's frightening. I still think he killed our parents."

Lynn watched Maria with an analytical demeanor. "Let's say what you're telling us could be true. It doesn't exactly jibe with the way you've been working for him. Tell us what you do for your brother."

"I audit everything once one of his enterprises springs up. I make sure of everything from the ground up is exactly like the model I've built. We only slightly vary the model, depending on the clientele. We have models for every aspect of my brother's empire. I must account for every discrepancy. You found us in the midst of setting up a lab. It was to be our distribution center for the West Coast. Terry is meeting with a group in Tahoe, who will be handling the shipments from Belize to San Diego, and the distribution from there onto the streets."

Lynn looked over at me with a smile. She knows we've hit the mother lode. None of it will be taking place after we take out Brannigan, but we'll also be able to harness this distribution network with the information we gather.

"I'm impressed. Maria's a keeper. She's motivated and ready to help." Now the knife comes out as I turn to good old Alexander, and his companion. "Gee... other than letting my good friend, The Cleaner, play with you two for a while in a manner no one on earth wants to play, what do I need you two for?"

Lynn had to march over and shut the bunch up with a face to face. "Don't over share! Keep a lid on it until the Dark Lord gets you two in a recording atmosphere. Impress him or your moments after he hands you over to me will be a bit different from what you're used to. Think hell on earth as a frame of reference."

Lynn took Maria's hand. "Now you, my little helper are in like Flynn. We'll go over here away from these others where I see Geek-boy has all his playthings up and running. You'll make contact with your rapist, and chat a while. Don't make him suspicious. Think of some points you would go over with him about on a mission like you were on. You do contact him directly, do you not?"

"Yes!" Maria cringed as Lynn had moved toward her. "He has a wooded lot inside a gated community called Cascade."

I moved over next to her. "That's the one you mentioned was near Emerald Bay?"

Maria nodded. "His lake front is on the Lake Tahoe side, but that is the one."

Oh yes I like all of this so far. I gave Lynn a wait one gesture, and walked over next to Denny. "I'm familiar with that Cascade Community, Den. Tommy and I went up there to meet with a client who wanted a neighbor checked out. Our client thought the neighbor matched the picture of a skip we had on the radar. Neighbor was having some wild parties. Long story, short, he was right. We waited at his place and took the skip when he went down to the lake the following morning. The client had to bring us in through the gate in person. Once Jafar confirms the location, we can approach by the lakeside. Maria can find out when this syndicate Brannigan's meeting with will be there, and we take them all."

I could tell Denny was less than pleased with my suggestion, but my team gave signs they were all for the direct approach from the lake. "That's the hammer approach, John. I would have preferred something a bit more subtle. Taking out Brannigan is a messy deal by itself. Handling the rest of that bunch will not be easy to hide. I was thinking of a nice chemical death like Lynn gave that clown in Las Vegas. We're cutting the head off of the snake that's been manipulating shit behind the scenes. Now we find out the guy even manipulated the Harvard serial killers behind the scenes for his own enjoyment. A quick in and out with an untraceable demise in his sleep is the best possible outcome. Even bringing him here, a possible treasure trove of info, is too risky."

He's right. We're all silent for a moment. I looked over at Maria, wondering how far we could manipulate her. Someone with unlimited funds can hire a private army to snuff us. The only reason I figure Brannigan hasn't done it is because he loves to play in the background. "I have another idea. If Maria is in line for her brother's empire, we may have a mole at the very top who could feed us info."

"You know, brother," Casey said. "You're getting a little scary. Putting the sister back out there with the Brannigan fortune is insane. Besides, Brannigan would never have a will like that. He'd be too afraid of his sister killing him, especially since he raped her when they were young."

"This was all simple until we found out how big this could be," Lucas added. "Bottom line is Brannigan has to go. I knew we couldn't leave his three minions behind, but damn, this is getting complicated. I doubt this bunch can pick us out of a lineup, and Lynn has the sister ready to do anything. Do you really think you can turn these three if we are able to put her in the line of succession?"

"If she is not in succession now, I know I can put her there," Jafar offered. "Taking out the man responsible for the attacks on Samira and the rest of us is an agreed first step. He will surely have guards with him."

"We can gas them first like Casey told me you guys did to Ahmed Quadir in Dubai," Clint suggested. "Do we have anything potent enough for doing a house that size, Denny?"

"Yes, if we can tie into their ventilation. We can't just stick a tube in there and hope for the best. Any AC unit would be mounted on a slab outside the house because it will be an add on system. Let's confirm the location, and work out the details once we have the house plans. Put out the feelers with those three, John. Take Jafar and Lynn with you. I'm sure Maria has some access to data, Jafar can manipulate. First things first though. Confirm the location."

I went over with Lynn to fetch Maria. "Do those guys we sent back to the compound in Belize have any clue about the person behind the equipment they were hauling in?"

"No, no one but Alexander and I know about my brother."

"What's his female companion's part?"

"Her name is Candice Monterro. She is my personal assistant."

"One more question before we begin – are you in line to get your brother's empire if something happens to him?"

Maria looked up at me with a stunned expression. "I... yes... but only if my brother dies of natural causes. Any suspicion of foul play, and all of his holdings will be liquidated to-"

She paused, and I had to grab hold of The Cleaner. "Go on, Maria."

"His estate would be divided up and holdings given to Hamas, Hezbollah, the ACLU, the Freedom From Religion Foundation, and the Muslim Brotherhood. My brother believes in chaos."

"No shit!" The Cleaner didn't like it. "Damn, if we don't dismantle this organization somehow, the whole world's going to have a bad day."

"At least we have the cards up on the table." I led Maria over to our setup.

A few moments later we had Maria hooked up and Jafar ready. Laredo worked a second bank of screens in our data room. I gave Maria some Valium to take the edge off for the call. Once Jafar bounced around signals to appear she was talking from Belize through her smart-phone, Maria called her brother with the outline she and Lynn had worked out of probable answers and questions. We were all listening in as Jafar supplied us with our own wireless headphones he supplied the signal to from his network.

Brannigan answered on the third ring. "I expected a call sooner, Maria."

"We had a hell of a time getting out here because of the weather. I was just now able to get a signal. The equipment has been unloaded and set up."

"I don't want to talk over an open line. I needed to know before I take a meeting with our anchor group that everything is in place. This is a big step for us. I don't want any complications."

"I understand." Maria went on to the next item on the list. "Do you still want the trucks returned to the port, rather than keep them here for a few days just in case?"

"Keep them there until the weather improves. I don't want to endanger our assets needlessly."

"Have you changed any plans about your stay after the meeting?"

"I have to fly out to the East Coast in a few days. Then I may stop down there to see how things are progressing. It's damned inconvenient not having Alexander with me. I shouldn't have sent him with you."

Maria looked at Jafar's countdown, and expanded on Brannigan's statement. "I can have Alexander on his way to you by morning. He hates it down here anyway."

That made Brannigan chuckle. "No, keep him. It will do him good to get some airing out. Don't tell him I said anything about the inconvenience without him."

"Of course not. I'm glad I have Candice down here with me."

"Are you still playing house with Kopensky?"

Maria stayed silent, gesturing her silence was part of the act.

Brannigan chuckled. "Didn't think I knew about your fling with the hired help, huh?"

It was obvious Maria did know. She played it perfectly as Jafar signaled they had confirmed the location of Brannigan.

"Do you want me to break off with him?"

"Hell no," Brannigan answered with some impatience. "What the hell do I care what you do down in that jungle. Just don't bring the cretin with you where you can be seen. Is that clear?"

"Of course. He will be running things down here anyway. Shall I call again tomorrow, or wait until you decide on whether you will be stopping here?"

"No need. Call only if you have a problem." Brannigan disconnected without a goodbye. Maria handed me the phone.

"It is as she claimed, DL," Jafar said. "Laredo will have complete coverage and plans for the house in moments. He did not suspect anything."

"Let me know when you have satellite coverage on it. I want to know exactly where their vent system is," Denny told him. "That went very well, Ms. Brannigan. We have something else to discuss with you. We do not want to harm your co-workers or you. We would like someone in charge of your brother's empire who will not pursue the same goals. The drug and arms trade would end. Any ties he's had with terrorist organizations, and home grown America haters will cease. You would be free to pursue any legitimate enterprise and lifestyle you wish. We will be monitoring you. There will be no place on earth safe for you if our demands are not carried out. Is there anything about what I've said you don't understand?"

Maria shook her head violently in the negative, glancing at Lynn, but not meeting her steady monster gaze. "I understand. Anything you want done, I will do."

Denny allowed that remark to settle in. "That's very good, Maria. We are an organization that does not play around as you will soon see in your brother's case. I will be in contact with you constantly, and you will give me weekly updates into movements amongst the circle of America's enemies your brother has fostered. The first moment I feel out of contact with you will be very bad. There will be no excuses accepted in this. Are we clear?"

"Yes... yes... it will be as you say completely."

"Do you think you will be able to convince your companions of how important their cooperation will be?"

"I know how to make them comply. I will make them rich beyond their wildest dreams, and ask each one to stay on if they would like."

Denny smiled. "That is very good thinking, Maria. I will let Lynn help you get your point across to them. I do not want any misunderstandings. One word from either of them professing knowledge of us or our intentions in the press, and we will hunt them down, torture them, and bury them alive. Lynn will explain that aspect to them. We will be partners in this enterprise, Ms. Brannigan, or we will simply kill everyone involved in the empire."

"We followed my brother's orders to the letter. I will correct the harm that has been done as if my life depended on it. I...I know it is easy to say such things here under duress, and with the fortune my brother's estate commands, I could try to cross you. I will not. I see what force you can bring to bear on me. I never thought anyone could simply drop into a place like Belize without warning, and carry out such an attack. It was beyond comprehension until now. I believe. Please... just give me a chance to carry this out as you have outlined."

Denny watched Maria's face. The pleading look she maintained convinced me, and Lynn gave me a slight nod of her head. It didn't really matter to me. I planned to kill that traitorous dickhead brother of hers, and then hunt this bitch down to the ends of the earth if she didn't make good on her promises. Brannigan's chaotic empire was as dangerous as anything we'd ever faced. He maneuvered behind the scenes backing murderers, anti-American goons hell bent on our destruction, and kept up a growing drug/weapons market. This was the chance of a lifetime. I could tell Denny knew it.

"We are then in agreement, Ms. Brannigan. While I work with my young computer expert on plans, I will let you proceed in convincing your friends of their part in this very dangerous plan of empire takeover and reformation – dangerous for them, that is."

I went over with Lynn and Maria to speak with the minions. They listened intently to what Maria told them. The promise of a fortune, and a position of power in a legitimate enterprise, presented with the passion Maria expressed helped gain their enthusiastic cooperation without threats. Maria then explained what would happen if either of them broke the agreement. Neither minion appeared surprised at the threat.

"I am like Maria," Monterro said. "I have seen what your group can do. I will always remember. Once Maria is able to shed the poisonous elements of her brother's empire, it will not be difficult to help you with information gathering. The Brannigan empire as you call it has many legitimate profitable enterprises all over the world."

"You don't look overly excited with our proposition, Sweetpea," Lynn said, grabbing onto Alexander Torre's shoulders where he sat next to Candice.

"If Mr. Brannigan somehow escapes, he will kill us all. It is difficult to get excited until he is no longer in the picture."

Lynn patted his back. "Yeah, I can go along with you on that. You're more of a show me guy. Once we show you,

Alexander, I better see some real passion for our plan, or I may have to make an adjustment."

Torre looked up with tired acceptance. "Don't worry about that. He employs Albanian killers for bodyguards. I do not doubt your proficiency in violence. If I am able to emerge from this mess alive, I will be most appreciative not having to participate in drugs, weapons, and human slave trade."

Lynn stared at the now cringing Maria. "Hey, girlfriend, how come you didn't mention the slave trade?"

"I thought you might kill us all immediately," Maria admitted, looking away.

"You are going to have some real work ahead of you when your brother gets sent to hell." Lynn turned to me. "What do you think about these Albanian guys?"

"We'll have to play this out with Brannigan first. After it's established he's passed away of natural causes, and Maria assumes his position, we'll keep track of all the rats fleeing the sinking ship. I know it's not very thrilling, but would you mind staying behind with Jafar, and begin getting a database together of Brannigan's enterprises."

"Sure, DL. Our party down in Belize was enough fun for me with the commando ops. I have a change of clothes here. I'm going to get a shower after I put these three into a holding cell."

"Is...is that really necessary?"

I answered that one. "Yeah, Maria, it is. Keep cooperating and we'll have you three out of here tomorrow. Our holding cells are pretty nice."

Lynn clucked in annoyed agreement. "That's for sure. They're more like a damn motel room. C'mon, let's get you three settled in. I'll be around later after a little nappy to find out what the big bad has going in his empire."

After she led the trio out, I walked over with Dev and Jesse. They were watching an A's game on TV in our social room. "I'll need you guys for transport and pickup late. Why don't you both take off until eight. I'll put the route on your pads. We'll take the SUV. I'll have Lynn and Jafar take care of our guests for now."

"Tommy told us about your meeting with The Destroyer," Dev said, as he and Jess got up to leave. "Jess and I looked up his fights, including the match in Nigeria where he knocked the shit out of the Big O. Do you want the good news first or the bad news?"

Jess is already grinning at Dev's choice of words. I smell a set up. "Go ahead, wise-guy, lay it on me. I can tell you two have been biding your time for the right moment. Don't let me spoil it."

"The good news is I'll be throwing the towel in thirty seconds after the fight starts. The bad news is you'll already be crippled from the waist down."

After their hee-haw together, Jess gripped my shoulder. "That guy is like the missing link, John. Dev and I haven't found the chain he's missing from though, because it exists in some hell dimension... probably where Montoya came from."

"You have an absolute solid shot again in the UFC," Dev added. "What in hell do you want to play around with that white Hulk for? You know our Oakland renovated arena's the only place you'll be able to give him a shot. The UFC won't put a nobody out there with you."

I shrugged. "Alexi called in a favor. I have you two written into my will, so don't get all sappy on me. Did you happen to figure out something I could work on that doesn't involve my surrendering before the fight starts?"

Both of them laughed at my having written them into my will. I actually do have a severance amount for them written in if something out of the ordinary happens to me. I've been dividing up all our plunder from the recent stream of idiot terrorists we've been dealing with. Jafar is getting real good at offshore accounts. My friends, Devon Constantine and Jesse Brown would be amazed at how well they'll be off if something does happen to me.

"We have come up with a plan, DL," Dev said. "Clint told us you're real good with a sniper rifle. You'll have to do Destroyer on his way into the building."

"Yeah, brother, nuke him from orbit," Jess added.

"Get out of here and get some sleep. We're leaving from here." They were still snorting amusement as they waved and walked to our exit. Man, the Dark Lord gets no respect from his minions. When I turned toward the rest of my crew, they were all watching me, including Denny. Apparently everyone had enjoyed the Dev and Jess show. They had all been cleaning weapons and equipment for tonight's Brannigan party, but were in dead pause at being able to hear the Dark Lord's projected demise. I didn't care. The aspirin were finally kicking in.

"We've been hearing about your Fiialkov opponent from your cage partners, John," Denny broke the ice first. He had been watching Jafar work the Tahoe plans while networked with Laredo in our control room. "Tommy's already planning your funeral services."

I smiled at the others, enjoying not only the prediction of my demise, but now my funeral services too. Good to know. "Same old, same old, Denny. My very loyal crew has me buried every time I fight now... the pricks."

That got a laugh. Jafar's shoulders were shaking in amusement, but he didn't turn from his laptop screen. I sat down with them at the table they were working at, and had all my gear shoved at me by prior arrangement I could tell. "Gee... guys... thanks for cleaning my gear while I had the arduous task of riding herd on the Cleaner."

Lucas came after me like a Marine drill sergeant should. "Why you little panty waist prima donna sack of shit! How dare you even hint at us cleaning your gear for you, pussy!"

"Thanks, Lucas... I needed that." I caught the cleaning kit thrown at my head.

"That's thank you, Sir, you boot camp, low life cunt!"

Casey howled, stomping around like the Delta Force prick he is. Lucas has upbraided him worse, and I can tell he's enjoying my time on the grill. "You're enjoying this a little too much, Case. I want all of you there for my cage match with the Destroyer. You can all root for him. Did Tommy tell you he tried to put the vice on me?"

That cracked them all up. Even Jafar had to stop in order to enjoy the moment.

"Tommy did it perfectly for us before we left for Belize," Clint said, imitating the Destroyer's opening mouth and knitted brow of unexpected pain. "Too bad your cage match isn't a duel of shaking hands the hardest, meat."

"I tried to teach this boot camp some manners when I first met him," Lucas admitted. "The bastard's some kind of freak – nearly crushed me with that fuckin' know it all smile on his face. John needs a good lesson. He's gettin' too damn cocky. Time for the Destroyer to give him a little perspective. Get his ass down here with us mere mortals."

I was soaking it all in. These guys are the best of the best. They can ring my ass up for their amusement any time. "Luca pulled his .45 out and aimed it at my head after I released him. He said-"

"Touch me like that again and I air your damn head out!" Lucas even got the inflection right from that moment long ago.

95

"All I remember is that damn .45 pointed at my head after Denny introduced us... ah... good times."

Lucas laughed at that one. "We sure are going to get a snakehead tonight, brothers. I don't know how it will all end up, but at least that son of a bitch Brannigan will be out of the picture. That is the bottom line... isn't it, Spawn?"

Denny grinned at his nickname. "Brannigan dies tonight. That is priority number one. I'm sure he could be interrogated for God knows how many hours on shit he knows, but that prick is too dangerous. I'm well aware of how many ways this could go sideways. His death is not one of them. If the assault team has problems of any sort the order is weapons free. I don't give a shit if we have to shoot our way out of Lake Tahoe."

That's plain enough. "We'll get it done, Denny. I don't see the gas not working. If it doesn't work quite as well as we hope, maybe nobody will miss those Albanian bodyguard assholes. I know I won't."

There was muffled agreement with my line of thought on the matter.

"Let's hope this goes down as planned guys," Denny stated after a moment. "That Belize incursion was the best I've ever seen by anyone with the complications that popped up. This is the word on that from the top: excellent. Murderer's Row lived up to expectations without a hitch on the op. We have in our hands a way to reshape destiny if tonight's gig can be accomplished without incident. Making way for a Maria Brannigan takeover by natural causes is our goal. Let's concentrate on that above all else. We can deal with the Albanian killers later. If on our way to that goal, some other entity steps in the way... well then... shit happens."

Chapter Seven: Emerald Bay Sanction

Dev and Jess let us off at a little after midnight overlooking Emerald Bay. We had decided on approaching Brannigan's house around the land tip of the shore separating Emerald Bay from the main lake which bordered his house. Only a quarter moon showed its sliver of light through the windblown clouds. We moved down through the thick forest along a nearly obscured path, night-vision goggles in place. Having allowed plenty of time to reach the target, and our movements masked by darkness as well as a stiff breeze blowing through the Tahoe area, the steep descent to the bay shoreline proceeded with tedious care. I played packhorse with our very potent gas canister. It contained a less lethal derivative of the Naloxone gas the Russians used. We had employed it with very good results for the Dubai hit. No one spoke a word.

Reaching the Emerald Bay shoreline, we struck out at an easier pace along the fingertip of land acting as a partial barrier from the lake until we were in position to cut across the undeveloped forest area to the Cascade Community development. Stepping up our pace unobserved through the dense woods, and skirting the tip of highway 89, an hour passed before the Lake Tahoe shoreline became visible. Staying along the shoreline until reaching the first houses in the development, we slowed down into stealth mode the rest of our way.

Brannigan's place arched upwards from the shore's rocky escarpment to a beautiful porch with what could only be a gorgeous vista of the lake. Lights were on inside the house. One of the Albanian guards sat on the balcony overlooking the lake. If he didn't go inside, Casey would put a silenced .50 caliber round through his head. That would launch Plan B. There would be no survivors – messy, and to be avoided at all costs. We made no noise, enjoying the hushed whisper of water stirred on the shore by a gentle wind. At nearly two-thirty in the morning, the house lights went out, leaving only the dim yellowish glow of nightlights in the main living room. The guard went inside. We began our approach to the air conditioning unit on the right side of the house.

I was damn glad to get the stupid canister off my back. With Lucas and Casey watching our backs, Clint and I found the nearest place we could start our encased gas line through the ducting. It had a camera at the tip so we could watch its progress. When it reached the center according to the plans we had, I turned on the gas. We were using Denny's calculations with exactly the amount in the canister to subdue the household. By 3am we entered through the rear enclosed balcony with our gas masks in place.

We stayed in teams while clearing the house. Lucas and Casey made sure the guards were out cold but still breathing. That was key. If the gas had been more lethal than expected, it would have been time for Plan B once again. Clint and I found Brannigan in bed with a woman companion. Clint took her picture and Brannigan's while I administered his eternity shot between his left big toe and the one next to it. We watched as his body began to convulse slightly. I double checked his vitals to make sure he was in hell before positioning him with one hand clutching his black heart, and the other grasping his companion's hand. That left only the tricky part of airing out the house until all traces of gas were gone. The venting system on high blow sped up the process. Lucas gave us the all clear from his monitoring walk through with digital meter. We locked up and left.

By 4am we were moving over the last part of the land finger forest to the Emerald Bay shoreline. An hour after that we loaded our gear into the Dev and Jess transport special, hosted by a delighted Denny.

"You guys are beginning to worry me," Denny broke the silence. "The damn missions have been flawless lately, and I don't like it. If it wasn't for the Dark Lord getting ready to have his head separated from his body to calm the waters of cosmic balance, I don't know what the hell I'd do."

"Maybe you ought to put your money where your mouth is, Spawn," I retorted, observing the unabashed mirth echoing around in the van at Denny's pronouncement. "I have ten grand says you're nothin' but a loudmouth, no account, huckster, and the Destroyer's goin' down."

More laughter, including Denny. He looked around at his companions. "How about it guys? Want a piece of the action?"

Clint shook his head no. "DL's a pain freak. I know his chest hurt like hell. He lugged the damn gas canister all over the forest tonight, and the goofball was smiling the whole time."

"Did not." I don't think I did.

"Clint's right," Lucas said. "I ain't bettin' against him. If he does win over that two eyed Cyclops he'll rag us for a solid year about it."

"I saw him get choked out by the Slayer in Vegas," Jess stated. "He croaked like a damn toad, but still won."

"He's a freak," Dev piled on. "It's a sucker bet, playing the odds against a freak of nature."

"Gee… thanks Dev." I've slipped from the mantle of Dark Lord to freak of nature.

"You're on your own, Spawn," Casey finished Denny off. "I might only put a couple hundred on him to win, but I sure don't want any of that ten grand against him. John's a cement head just like Lora keeps repeating. I guess you better step up, Spawn. You're all in."

"Fine." Denny leaned back in his seat with a big smile. "When the Destroyer gets through with him, I'll get to gloat on my own, even though he's screwin' with our UFC angle."

"That's what you think, Spawn. I need to keep our buddy Fiialkov happy with this match. You don't have anything he wants, so I'm our key to Interpol inside information. After I kick the Destroyer's ass, I'll have an extra ten grand to put in the coffers of Harding International Funds."

"Or I'll have ten grand to put into the coffers of Spawn International, and ragging privileges forever. I found the Destroyer's match with the Big O. He destroyed him. I hate to say this partner, but maybe ducking him would be a good idea."

Then it hit me. I started chuckling and nodding my head. Now I get it. There must be something on the Spawn tripwire about the upcoming UFC fight. "Okay, Spawn, I get it. What's on the UFC radar you know about that I don't? You know of course this silly game you play with maneuvering us chess pieces on the sly is really annoying, right?"

Denny shrugged comically amidst the silent smiling operatives he launched at his choosing. "Like Popeye said, 'I am what I am'. Take it any way you want, meat. Quit whinin', and let's celebrate a little."

Then Denny pulled out a big jug of Jim Beam from his bag. Now that's what I'm talkin' about. Jesse looked with a pleading glance at Devon, who smiled and nodded. He was driving. Denny produced shot glasses for all of us from a pouch in his bag. Denny poured carefully. He lifted his.

"Nice work. Let's hope our empire building goes well. Maria Brannigan seems motivated, but it's tough to gauge reality when she'll be controlling a hundred billion dollar empire."

"One thing I do believe about Maria." I sipped my shot. "She believes we'll kill her if she doesn't bring her brother's company out of the darkness. She's absolutely right. If she doesn't put our changes into effect, and divest the anti-American crapolla off the ledger, I don't like her chances."

After an amused chorus of agreement, Jess spoke up. "Hey, can't you guys shoot one of those nano-thingies into them so you'll know where they are all the time?"

"I wish it were that easy, Jess," Denny replied. "This isn't the X-Files. They would know we injected them. The technology for micro devices like you're talking about only exist in Hollywood movies right now. The power for a micro-device like that to transmit over any distance is just not out of the conception phase. We have an even more reliable way, although not quite as exciting, except to them. I plan to give Maria, Alexander, and Candice a special smart-phone with Lynn on their Fave Five speed dial. Jafar will of course be tracking them, but I plan to have the trio checking in with Lynn. You know how awkward things will get if any of them don't talk to their new BFF on a regular basis, right?"

"Shit!" Jess's one word hushed pronouncement drew more laughter. He gulped down his shot. "I'd rather have an ankle bracelet."

"Speaking of Lynn, have you made any progress on our Gulf of Mexico cruise," Clint asked. "I thought Senator Cassigan was really pushing the issue about his brother Stan's disappearance. Did you get a chance to look over the threads I put together about the past incidents?"

"The Senator involved has backed away from it, Clint," Denny answered, refilling everyone's shot glass. "He left me high and dry. Wendell had to have been warned off. I did go over your preliminary notes. I think you found the missing clue with their financial reports. All four couples that disappeared, including Senator Wendell Cassigan's brother, were in dire straits financially. They all had public personas of being rich beyond rich, but your research revealed what my people didn't find – they were in debt up to their eyeballs."

"They were taken in by a firm supposedly based in Tampico, Mexico," Clint explained. "The couples were all very rich, but not in the manner they had on display in public. This fraud oil firm, called Tampico Oil and Gas supposedly had the rights to a relatively new rig already in place which had struck an oil pocket. The buy in was twenty-five million. These couples are asked to sail from Corpus Christi to inspect the investment, all of it under top secret negotiations. This company knew which couples had yachts, and ambitions about being high finance oil company owners. The scammers are not actually without setups in the Gulf. There are literally thousands of rigs in the Gulf. Tampico Oil and Gas owns three profitable ones."

Man, I'm lost. I either had too much to drink or not enough. "How in hell do they coax these idiots out into the Gulf to be taken, and to what purpose?"

Clint grinned, because he saw complete confusion on everyone's face but Denny's. "They hand pick their targets. All four couples have relatives in Congress and the Senate. Cassigan was the first one to question the disappearances. These people are not being killed. They have had their fortunes taken by this company, and are filmed living in luxury at an estate in Cancun."

"I was able to intercept one of their sales pitches once Clint found the holding area," Denny added. "Clint deciphered enough on this front group oil company to give us a behind the scenes backer: The Sinaloa Cartel. They launder money along with every other mob syndicate endeavor you can name. This one's a beauty. I thought Brannigan might be involved in this, but if anything, I think they were rivals."

"Sinaloa now has a front company to launder vast amounts of money, while maintaining a persona of legality," Clint continued. "They have hostages against direct action by our government. All four couples' Congressional relatives are on key committees. Cassigan is on the Senate Caucus on International Narcotics Control. The other three are in Congress on Ways and Means."

"So these people we thought were hostages actually entrap more targets?" Casey shook his head. "To do what, continue making recruitment movies with them living the high life down in Cancun?"

"Yes," Denny answered. "They've been robbed of their money, but promised it back with a healthy profit if they cooperate, while living like they do have a fortune down in Cancun. They're naïve idiots, but they probably don't have much choice. We haven't located their yachts anywhere, or heard anything from the crewmembers that were aboard them when taken. I'd bet they're not in Cancun, living the high life... or living for that matter. Without Cassigan's interest, this one again gets tricky. I presented Clint's case to one of our Senators who likes very much what we've accomplished. She hasn't gotten back in touch with me yet."

Wow, the Dark Lord is not very bright this early morning. "I'm still in the breeze. Do you mean despite the warnings about everything disappearing without a trace, the ones taken still manage to entice others?"

"It's this way, John," Denny said. "Once they've been absorbed, they play off the warnings in the recruitment film saying everything about the deal is top secret to prevent interlopers from accessing data and profit margins to manipulate the market with. They're treated like royalty in Cancun, but not allowed to leave. It's brilliant in a way."

"So if I understand this right," Lucas said, "you plan on using your Senator friend as a government relative for the sting we do. She would allow us to make up a completely fictional couple related to her in some way that Lynn and Clint would fit?"

"That's it exactly. The big if is her agreeing to it. Even though she's an enthusiastic supporter, I'm not sure how she'll feel about something like this. Clint's file with made up credentials for the couple he and Lynn would play was very impressive. Jafar backed him up with an account in the Caymans where we have an operative in place to make it look like our fictitious couple has forty-five million hidden there. If she goes along with our plan, I'll have Clint put out feelers through their recruitment people they mention on the videos they've forced the hostages to make."

"I hope you're not thinking of letting this bunch attack my Sea Wolf and take us all prisoner so we can get Clint and Lynn in undercover," Lucas said.

"Are you stupid?" Denny's instant retort got a chuckle. "You guys will take these suckers by any means necessary. I would like prisoners, so we can find out where these jokers have their home base. I want you to go there and obliterate it. Yes, I will have a drone ready to back you up. This op won't be black. Once we make sure we wipe out their base, you all will be sailing full speed for Cancun. Clint and Lynn will make contact with our unfortunate would be oil entrepreneurs. We have zero info on how these people were taken, or what was used to accomplish it. The Sea Wolf is loaded. It's weapons free until the survivors give up the ghost."

"If Lynn and I can get near the couples already taken, we'll herd them someplace safe, while we take care of business with the assholes we find running the estate," Clint added. "They're actively recruiting, because I've been following up on the sites they nailed the others from. I'm monitoring the situation in case they get a legitimate prospect. If they did, we could slip into their place easily without personalizing the situation with the Senator. We would need to keep them incommunicado until we finish the op. So far, there have not been any prospects that fit their criteria. Jafar has hacked the communications. The first time the prospect questions using their boat, or any aspect of the meeting, they get dumped."

"Jafar told me how much our recent busts have netted into our retirement fund for unintended circumstances," Denny said. "We have plenty to cover this op. What I don't want is to proceed without Senator Nora Braxton's support, and confirmed drone backup. The good part of all this is the nearness to the Continental USA. The bad part is the rescue on foreign soil. If we could trust the Mexican government not to tip off the bandits, we'd be doing a joint op. No one can say how high up the cartels have infiltrated the Mexican government. All will be forgiven if you guys can achieve a successful rescue. Then we can let the hostages tell their story. We pull this off, and word will get around in congress about our success."

I looked out at the light from a mountainous gray dawn providing grainy illumination inside our transport. "We would be making some rather high ranking friends. With our increased visibility, that would be a damn good thing. We're on the offensive big time right now with taking out Brannigan and positioning a positive force behind his empire. I'd like to get those people out of Cancun. I know that Sinaloa Cartel is an entity I don't want in the oil business. They don't scare. We'd need to hurt them. If we can capture a few of the right people, we may be able hurt them financially as well as disrupting their oil plans."

"John... you're just so cute as Denny-light, I could just hug you," Lucas said, reaching out his arms, and making smooching noises to everyone's amusement.

"Lean forward another couple inches, Ahab, and The Sea Wolf will be yachting around the Bay on a daily basis with tourists, because its so called owner will be recuperating in intensive care, trying to eat whole food again."

And we had one more early morning toast to that one.

* * *

Every inch of Lora's frontal skin molded to my body, as she gripped me in a heaving, sweaty aftermath of muffled love. Knowing the Minnie-me has ears like a damn vampire bat, we were trained to harness all audio expression or endure the kid's smiling sarcasm the next morning. I blamed Lora for it, and of course somehow she blamed me. She loved my house, but the bedroom placement led to unfortunate audio circumstances if we were too unrestrained. It was all good. We were careful. Al was on the opposite side of the hall, a bedroom down the way. I know for a fact she fakes hearing noises, giggling about it in the morning, but Lora's so self conscious, she falls for it every time.

I kissed Lora's forehead. "T will be here shortly for my torture session."

The weeks since the Brannigan sanction passed with a quiet solidification of our gains. Brannigan's 'natural' passing from a heart attack in his Tahoe retreat sent shock waves all over the world, especially to anti-American nut-cake organizations, completely dependent on Brannigan's former evil empire. With Denny's suggestions through Lynn, Maria had shed all of them, plunging a few of the worst into their own chaos. Once the money dried up, so did their destructive fervor. Since Brannigan had cloaked all of his seedy puppet master operations with layers of front groups, Maria pulled the plug on them, thereby staying out of the initial raging of lunatics cut off from their feeding trough. Lynn surprisingly, loves the new duty. Maria has become her real BFF, which is a real hoot to the rest of us. Alexander and Candice do what they're told, but are relieved to be out of the illegal end of things.

"Are you having any more trouble with your chest?" For emphasis, Lora rubbed her chest against mine, the little minx. "Did you remember Tess and her husband will be visiting with my Mom for a week?"

Hell no. "Sure. I didn't think it was a big deal. I'm certain Al will love the visit. She hasn't seen your family since our first holiday together. My chest has been fine."

Lora shifted out from under me, heading for the shower. "I sure hope you have a few new tricks to pull on that Destroyer guy. I'd feel better if you were allowed a baseball bat in the cage. I wish you hadn't agreed to a match in the Oakland warehouse."

"Don't worry. T and I have a whole game plan figured out to surprise The Destroyer." I wish.

Lora spun around. "Shit. I forgot to tell you we got the ticket on Kevin Halliday. I talked to Earl. He said Halliday's still in the area, but hiding out somewhere in Hayward. They've had a couple of sightings, but not in time to nab him. It's a nice payday because the bonding company Halliday used is in LA. I talked to the agent in charge of the bond. They screwed up, and they want out from under it anyway they can."

I need to give this some thought. Nothing much impresses me when I'm considering either a fight, a bond skip, or a mission with my other sponsors. Halliday is a red flag perp. He knows me. I collected him with Tommy at Lake Merritt one time. Halliday's a psycho. He's not stupid enough to act out constantly, so he drifts in and out in the gray area where law and law enforcement mingle in weird waves of bullshit. What I remember about him was I knew I should have killed him. He had assaults, armed robbery, and beating up a couple of the women dumb enough to hook up with him. It was one of those times with Tommy, where that wasn't an option. I at least found out the women beatings charge was bogus.

Halliday's about three inches over six feet with steroid enhanced body – big brown haired head, and over enhanced body. Tommy and I approached him politely because of the public place, and festival going on. Halliday wasn't having any of it. We approached from opposite directions, so he didn't know about me until Tommy fronted him. He busted backward right into me, bounced, and got ready to rumble. I gronked him. We plastic tied his hands, and had him in my old Chevy within minutes of our trek to the car. He became verbal with the threats to our families, friends, and others. It's part of the business. We don't overreact to that bait, or at least not in a situation like we were in where everyone and his brother saw me collect him. It's just business. When Halliday told T he thought he recognized him, and payback was a bitch, I reached back and broke a couple of his fingers. He got complacent real quick, but I always knew if someone didn't cap his ass, I'd hear about him again.

"I hope we're getting a nice payday for that clown. He's not your run of the mill skip."

Lora paused before heading into our master bedroom suite shower. "Tommy and I shared info. He said you two had history. Is he going to be a problem for you?"

"Nope. He may not survive the collection process though."

Lora's eyes narrowed, and she bit off the flippant remark I'm sure tried to bust up out of her control into an audible realm. "It's that bad between you two?"

I shrugged. "I've only hooked up with him once, but I know the look all too well. I don't know what he did I'm picking him up for, but he's probably done a hell of a lot more bad stuff than they suspect him of. He makes a statement I don't like, and he's going to disappear permanently. I want him off the streets. I don't want to ignore him. I imagine you've already sent the info to Tommy. After my workout, I'll take a look around the places you've heard he's at. We'll go from there."

Lora sighed and came to grapple with me as I got off the bed. "Listen you. I know this is part of what I have to do for us to be together. I don't care what you think has to happen. I just want you back with me. Everything else I figure you make allowances for or end the threat. You've converted me into a Lynn Montoya without the capability of performing in person like she does. I... I just don't want you thinking I'm so abhorrent about what you have to do that you hesitate to do what you need to. Does that make any sense?"

I scooped her up in my arms and showed her there were no hard feelings at all as to what I needed to do, except where hard needed to be. Yep, Lora and I were soul mates – a term I thought I'd rather amputate my own arm than voice even in my head. I was a recon Marine. We adapt. It's a good thing I caught her before her shower.

Chapter Eight: Kevin Halliday

Since the UFC fight with the Slayer, we now had our own workout room after moving into my new business digs. Lora normally worked out of the house, but we had to have a place to put our two limos, and an office in case we did need to meet a client. In other words, Oakland Bond Enforcement and Escort Service received a fancy name, and a new building. Not so new, just foreclosed on, and bought up by me for a great price. It already had a storefront near 2nd and Webster, with plenty of partitioned sections. Lora had the office looking terrific and very professional. It wasn't a great neighborhood, but not bad either. Our workout area had great ventilation, and every torture device Tommy could think of for readying me to fight in the cage or on the road in a UFC match.

Dev, Jess, and lately, Jafar all pitched in to pound the crap out of me. That Tommy took particular pleasure in it was an added entertainment item for my three workout partners. Frankly, we didn't have a clue how to approach the Destroyer fight. I'd watched the videos my two scouts made for me. They pointed out this and that, but no one had hurt this guy. Then I saw it. When Subotic launched his right, he stomped a little forward with his right foot. It wasn't much, but I pointed it out to my training crew.

"You're thinking to smack his inner knee?" Jess shook his head. "It's a great idea but if he doesn't give you a clear enough shot, you'll break your damn toes arching through that cement stanchion he calls a left thigh."

He's right. "Yeah, that would be the end of the fight right there. I've been watching for something I could exploit to do damage. Man, I got nothin'. The Big O hit him flush and the guy

110

barely blinked. No one's been able to get him on the mat, so ground and pound is an unknown. The right he knocked out the Big O with nearly decapitated him. I don't see anything else I can exploit except get to his legs early. I hope when he goes to the mat for whatever miraculous reason other than to pound my head into dust, that I'm able to find a hold that will work."

Dev simply stood up, holding his hands out. "Call in sick, John. Guys duck other guys all the time. He hasn't been to the UFC yet, so it's not like he can demand it. Duck him, and let's concentrate on your UFC ranking. We can worry about Destroyer when he clubs his way into a guaranteed UFC money match."

"I hear you, Dev, but I gave Alexi my word. You guys will probably have to hide me out for a few days until the swelling goes down before I see Lora and Al."

"She'll just hunt your ass down, brother," Jess said. "I'd settle for you still being able to walk from the car to your house."

I've been getting this shit from my guys ever since back when the Slayer came to town all pumped up on steroids. It's been funny to me how I'm always the damn underdog. This time though, I see their point. They want to help me, but I'm going to have to take the lead. Tommy's staying quiet. He knows I don't go back on my word, and he doesn't have anything for a suggestion that would help.

So now, here we are, busting the crap out of me. Even Tommy acknowledges I'm in shape for it. If I get tagged though, all the stamina in the world won't do me any good. You don't come back in this sport from La-La land. I did come up with a training ploy at the end of a workout. Jess and Dev throw on me from the sides while Jafar and Tommy alternate glimpses of a heavily padded two by four as targets representing the legs of Destroyer. Dev would throw a shot at my head from the Destroyer's would be right. Tommy stomps the padded board down slightly ahead of the left leg padded board Jafar held. Good God in heaven did that hurt when I missed. With both Tommy and Jafar moving the padded boards, and tilting them in a split second's time, it was the pits. Tommy always stayed in rhythm with Dev though. Today, I broke the damn two by four. That even shocked Tommy. He threw the two padded pieces down, the lower one attached by some threads of remaining padding.

"That's it for today, John. That was damn good. Lord almighty, if you get that smack in on him, The Destroyer will be one hurtin' son-of-a-bitch."

We were all standing there, everyone's chest heaving but mine. I was sweating like a four hundred pound gypsy in a sauna room, but I felt good. I could have trained another hour after that hit. It was like that board had become some kind of a straw man for me. When it cracked, it meant I hadn't pulled back, anticipating hitting my toes on Jafar's board. For a moment, I had been so confident of the strike, I let it all go without holding back.

Jess hugged me around the shoulders. "Damn straight, brother. T's right. You bam that on his leg, Destroyer's goin' down."

"If you concentrate too much though, John, he may separate your head from your shoulders," Dev added. "We're concentrating on your strike for practice. You have to keep your head in the game on all levels."

No doubt about that. "Great ending. I feel perfect for looking around for that skip, Halliday. We have a bar he'd be hittin' in the Hayward area. Tommy and I might get lucky."

"Let's all go," Jafar suggested with both Dev and Jess reinforcing his suggestion.

I shook my head. "Nope. Halliday already knows me and T. This guy's a psycho loser. That he hasn't already come after me and Tommy is a blessing. I don't want him knowing anyone else. We'll handle this one for better or worse."

Tommy smiled. "I don't think Halliday has many romantic thoughts for you, John. The dumbass resisted at this festival we found him at. John knocked his ass out cold. We get him in the car and he starts threatening us, our families, you know… on and on. John reached back around him and snapped a couple of his fingers. That shut him the hell up… 'cept nearly crying like a baby. It was our word against his about how it happened. They knew from his record Halliday was violent as hell, so they just laughed at him. I never thought he'd be out on the streets this soon. Those idiots down in LA that bonded him are desperate. They tried to get him with a Hollywood type Dawg The Bounty Hunter wannabe. Halliday shot the crew leader, and smacked around the woman he had with him. The other two guys ran that were part of Hollywood's crew."

"Seems like all the more reason for us to go along," Jess replied. "He doesn't know the three of us. We could walk right in and take him down."

"I appreciate the offer, Jess, but I don't want any new faces in on this." Or witnesses. "We know the bar pretty well. We'll go over there early. Tommy knows the guy tending bar tonight. He claimed Halliday's been in there every night when Tommy called him."

"They don't know him from shit, and Frank didn't know he was on the run. I guess Halliday's not too popular in there. He pushes around the regulars, and screws with the waitresses. On top of all that, the clown hogs the Karaoke, sounding like gravel in a can… sort of like when the Dark Lord here sings."

I waited until the yuck-yucks subsided. "If we get there early, we'll pluck him before he gets inside. He gets one halt, and then we light him up like Christmas in Times Square. It would be just my luck, I'd get another quick draw McGraw, and have my damn chest aching for another six weeks."

"Yeah, unless he shoots you in the head, John," Jafar chirped in.

"We're going to surprise him, you tater head. Besides, the B Street Bar has a stone/cement separator between the street and the bar. We'll have our ear thingies in. I'll sit there next to the entrance. Tommy can be in the car watching for his approach. He tells me Kevin's coming, and I cut him off from the door. He gets romantic, and we gronk him."

"It seems so simple when you put it like that, John," Jafar said. "I'm sure Tommy will be real thrilled about approaching the psycho."

Tommy chuckled. "This isn't our first ticket to the bad guy dance, kid. When we face off with some of these crazies, I have my riot gun pointed right at their heads when John puts the plastics on them. We're pretty good at this. We have to be here in Oakland. When the bond companies decide to send pros after their skips, it means we're their last option."

"I could see John doing it, T," Jafar continues down the same slippery path. "Would you use the riot gun?"

I shook my head at Tommy. "That's enough of this talk, kid. We'll bring in Halliday. Believe me. If Tommy needs to use deadly force, he'll use it. See you all back here when we get through in LA at 'Torture-is-Us'."

I headed for the shower we have after our goodbyes. Twice in the past, we've had to forego our collection because Tommy had to get my back. If a target pulls a piece ten feet away when I yell halt, there ain't a hell of a lot I can do. Tommy and I have a signal. If I put my hands up in surrendering form while backing up, Tommy caps them. Then I take them somewhere no one can locate the body. There's no outcry in the public or PD about these deadly suckers. If one of them disappears, they don't issue an Amber Alert. They slap high fives and go on about their business. That's exactly how it will go down with Halliday. But yeah, twice in the past, Tommy's had to put the final touches on our hoped for collections. We're a team. We don't die for this business, but we have made more than a few murdering SOB's die for it.

See, I don't get Lucas and Casey involved in this type encounter with the everyday pickups of slime-balls like Halliday. Clint and Lynn are different, because they have real FBI affiliation. Lucas and Casey would be a problem because of CIA operating on US soil. I'm the shadow-man. I have enough deniability, and cover activities, with my fighting, that I can coast on some occasions. Even with Clint and Lynn, I don't waste their talents and possible exposure on someone like Halliday. I know I'll need them on a special case here and there, and they have to be used with care. I smiled as I stepped into the shower. I've never had the kind of comfort level I have now with this crew. We're family in a very horrific scope, in that we have levels of confrontation which continue until we're all dead. We believe in each other. It's up to me as Denny-light to deploy our resources carefully, and keep all of us alive. I don't take my responsibility lightly. I'm the one this idea of a West Coast Murderer's Row was built around. I'm ending Halliday one way or another. He's a threat.

* * *

I sat in faded, worn-out jeans, windbreaker, and dilapidated Oakland A's baseball cap as I sat next to the stanchion near the entrance to the B Street Bar. A slight breeze blew by in the late afternoon to add a slight chilling effect off the ocean. Tommy's voice in my ear provided the only input I had as I faced the bar. We kept quiet, waiting for our mark. It's boring, tedious, and we don't even know if he'll show. That's the business. I don't know what Tommy does for entertainment, but I'm going over details and plans for our Voyage of the Damned if the Senator gets on board to lend her support.

"I like your idea about the leg hit," Tommy inputs to me out of nowhere.

"Me too, if I can pull it off without breaking my toes coming across. Even I can't do much if I mistime the strike, other than gimp around hoping for a miracle. I watched the vids on the Destroyer again last night. I got nothing for a plan other than that leg strike. We both know what he'll be gunning for."

Tommy laughed. "Yeah, I think we can figure on him making you do your best defensive ploy: blocking every punch with your face."

"That's just... hurtful. I remember you being much more supportive in the old days."

"Yeah... I'll bet you do, meat. I remember you being a hell of a lot less needy. You used to walk into that dingy warehouse, mouthpiece hangin' out of the corner of your mouth, dressed in those dingy sweats, all business. You had a tight lipped snarl on your face and dynamite clenched into your fists. What the hell happened to you... you pussy."

I know he could see my shoulders heavin', trying with all my might not to start howlin'. Damn. T's on his game today. "Stifle yourself! I'm on the job here."

"What job. You ain't worked a real job in five years. You sit around looking at Lora all day either at the office or home, go out and pick Al up from school, and pretend you're a contender. What work?"

Now he's laughing in my ear, and then he's not. "Coming up on you on your right. It's Halliday in a black windbreaker and jeans with hands jammed into the pockets. If he's packin', it ain't in those pockets. He's still a block away, John. When he gets about twenty feet from you, I'll get out of the car behind him."

I stood up, with the gray hoodie I wore up over my head, leaning on the stanchion. Halliday's view of me would be partially blocked until he got real close. There would be no real confrontation or talking today. Like I've mentioned, we know how violent this guy likes to get. He proved it to those poor Hollywood skip tracers. Tommy and I would do this nice and easy, or if he even blinks, then rough and hard.

"Twenty feet," Tommy says as he opens his car door.

Halliday hears the car door and turns toward Tommy. I can't have that. "Hey, Halliday, long time, no see. Time to go back to LA."

Halliday spun again, hearing my voice. I could tell he recognized me by his features twisting into a death mask. "What the fuck you want, Harding?"

He kept his hands jammed into his pockets, so it may be we can simply take him in. Most skips don't start any dialogue first unless they've made up their minds to not make trouble. "We have your ticket, Kev. You done wrong down in LA. I have to take you back down there. It doesn't have to be hard. Kneel down and lace your hands behind your head. I'll plastic tie them behind your back. Then after a gentle pat down, you'll be going on a road trip. I'll even let you listen to your favorite music on the way if you behave."

"Your fuckin' partner got a Taser pointed at my back?"

"Yep. We're all business today, Kev. Like I said, we can avoid any unpleasantness if you drop down on your knees, and lace your hands."

"I got friends inside. I yell out, and you're going to have a bad day."

I smiled. I didn't blame him for trying that bullshit. "You don't have any friends, period. You certainly don't have any in there. We checked."

His face didn't lose any of its rage element, but he nodded. "I'm going to take my hands out. Don't Tase me."

"We won't, but if you have anything in one of your hands when it comes out, I'm going to break it for you. Take them out slow." I didn't want Tommy or me getting close to him until he was on his knees with hands laced. Use your hands to get on your knees, Kev. Then lace them."

Halliday surprisingly did as told. When he was on his knees, he laced his hands behind his head. Tommy moved to the side, Taser pointed at Halliday's face. I took each hand down behind him before locking them at his wrists with double plastic ties. I helped him up then. Putting on my Nitrile gloves, I patted him down with thoroughness. Besides the usual petty cash, false ID, and knife, Halliday had a little .32 caliber auto in a hideaway pocket of his windbreaker. I popped the clip, cleared the chamber, and put it in the plastic bag Tommy held out for me. I clapped Halliday on the shoulder.

"You did good, Kev. Name your poison for music. We have one of those cable radio hookups in the GMC we're taking you down in so we get anything."

"Country?"

"Damn it!" Tommy doesn't like it. "I knew he was going to say that. It's better than rap though. You don't go for that twangy garbage, do you?"

Halliday shook his head as I eased him into the GMC backseat. "I like the new country. You don't like rap, huh Sands?"

Tommy shrugged. "Some of it. Most of it is punk ass shoutin' about rape, pillaging, and murdering people. Never

118

thought we'd be talkin' music, but it's a hell of a lot better alternative than what we thought we'd be doing."

I shut Halliday's door and called Lora while Tommy climbed in to drive. He hates my driving. Her FaceTime features boinked into view with a look of apprehension. "You okay, John?"

"Yeah, hon. It went real good, and no damage on either side for a change. Since things worked out, we're shooting right down to LA with him. Call it in for us, will you?"

With a look of relief, Lora smiled. "Of course. I'll call if there's any problem. It would be best if you picked up one of their people on the way to drop him off after you get there. They're really upset about the agent that issued the bond on him. I think they're facing a lawsuit from the bounty hunters they hired to get him. I put the address of Lane and Sterling Bail Bonds on Tommy's pad. Talk to Jan Sterling when you get there. She'll be the one to take along. If that changes, I'll call. Have a safe trip, John. I'm glad there wasn't any trouble."

"Yeah, me too... I think. Lately, things have been going so right, it's getting creepy. I feel like ramming my head into the side of a building just to even up the ledger."

Lora laughed. "I'll have to tell Al that when I pick her up from school. I love you."

"I love you too. See ya'."

In the GMC, Tommy had found a country rock station Halliday liked, so we were ready to go. "Lora's calling ahead. We're to take one of the Bail Bond partners with us: Jan Sterling."

Tommy glanced back at Halliday before he drove away. "How come you went nuts when that crew down in LA came for you?"

"They disrespected me... and... I was cranked up. The assholes pulled up next to me in their shiny black MIB van. Three jerks pile out of it dressed in more gadget shit than you ever saw before, with those fingerless gloves, sleeveless matching black vests, and tattoos so thick on their arms they looked like sleeves. They all face me down with their arms crossed while this fourth clown starts filming. I thought I was being punked by someone."

Entertaining so far. Even Tommy's chuckling. "You got us hooked, Kev. What happened?"

Halliday looked down at his feet. "This bitch dressed in black, and long blonde hair tied back, like some kind of tattooed Buffy the Vampire Slayer jumps out in front of the three shits already posing for the cameraman. She starts pointing at me, screaming 'get on your fuckin' knees, slime-ball. We're taking you in'. I said fuck you, and started looking for a place to run. She starts Kung Fuing me with all these shouts and shit like she's Bruce fuckin' Lee. They put the damn girl on me. It was disrespectful... and I was cranked up like I said. I admit it. I threw a couple of punches, one under her ribs, and the other broke her nose. The Buffster went down, threw up, and started crying. Jesus... guys... she was tryin' to kick my nuts off and bust my knees while the rest of them filmed it and smirked. I felt so bad about Buffy sitting there holding her nose and crying, I pulled my piece. I shot the fancy steroid jerk when he started yelling orders to get me with the Mace. The guys with him turned and ran."

"I shot him in the knee, so he's down screamin' like the pussy he was. I helped the Buffster over off the sidewalk. I put the cell-phone I found in her damn Batgirl belt rig in her hand. I told Buffy to call an ambulance. Then I stole their ride to get out of the area. Shit, they probably got me down for murder now. I should never have done that crank I got. That's what messed my head up when I got out of the joint. I busted up some guy in a bar down in LA, and got booked into jail for assault. I had enough money put away to get out on bail. Then I didn't show in court, and they put the Dawg type on me. I figured they'd lock me up and throw away the key, so I hitched up here. I've been cleaning joints to make livin' money."

I looked at Tommy, and he gave me a slight shrug. "I have to say, that's a damn entertaining story, Kev. I'm glad we didn't have to take you down hard."

Halliday looked up. "Thanks for that. I learned my lesson last time you guys picked me up. San Quentin taught me everything but how to stay the fuck out of trouble. It looks like I'll be getting my second dose."

"So it was the bar-fight that Lane and Sterling bailed you out for? The way I understood it, you were arrested for everything from armed robbery to murder. We wondered how the hell anyone was stupid enough to post bail for you. Your story makes more sense, although you really messed up shooting the pretend Dawg the Bounty Hunter, and roughing up his sidekick. I'll look into it when we get you down there. I know a lawyer in LA owes me a favor."

"Damn, Harding… you mean it?"

"He means it," Tommy said, sighing. "John and I probably could have ended up in the same boat as you at one time or another. No promises, but if we do manage to help you out, there won't be any more second chances."

"Won't need one. Help me stay out of Quentin, and I'll join the damn Salvation Army. I have to put that shit behind me. Seeing the Buffster cryin' in the street after I tagged her really screwed me up. I ain't ever hit a woman like that."

He looked shaken up for real. "You probably saved her life. It was a great lesson. She may have gotten a busted nose, but she could have jumped some guy that simply blew her head off. Some folks don't learn the easy way. You're a walking billboard for that. I bet she doesn't do her Buffy act on anyone else. Those reality shows stir up people into thinking they can just run out there with a cameraman, some tats, and a scowl, and actual badass dudes will just lay down for them. I'm surprised one of them hasn't gotten killed already."

Tommy gestured with his right hand flippantly. "We have a few teams of those jokers up in Oak-Town. They increase our fee rate when a bond company sends them, and they get tanked. Then the bond company has to come get us."

"I hope the Buffster feels like it was a lesson," Halliday said. "One way or another, I'll find out where to send her an apology. I ain't sending that asshole I shot anything."

"The gun will be the toughest part. We may have to get Hollywood to recant anything he has on you with the cops. We can say you didn't have a gun on you when we took you in, but if he's pressing charges, it could be bad. My lawyer acquaintance used to be a prosecutor. Now he's a defense attorney, but he won't take hardened criminals. If he'll handle your case, I know that will be the first thing he'll tell us we have to fix for him to have a chance."

"John, they filmed it," Tommy spoke up with some excitement. "These jokers can't resist putting anything they do on YouTube."

"That's right." I FaceTimed Jafar. "Hey, kid, I need you to find any videos about LA area bounty hunter wannabes getting owned within... hold on." I looked back at Halliday.

"Three weeks ago," Halliday spoke up.

"Three weeks ago. The bond company that sent them is Lane and Sterling Bail Bonds. Their target was Kevin Halliday. Can you send whatever you find to T's iPad?"

"Sure John. Wow, this is a change. Where are you now?"

"On the way to LA. We'll collect on the bounty, but I think Tommy and I are going to stick around and help Halliday out."

"On it. I should have something sent to his inbox in the next hour."

"Thanks, kid." I disconnected and looked back at Halliday. "We need to see how bad this incident looks on video before we meet with the lawyer. Tommy's right. These people can't get enough of themselves. Even when things go bad, they'll still post the video."

"I hope it's not as bad as I think it will be," Halliday replied. "I don't know that I could have done anything else once Buffy started wailing on me. I should have let them take me in, but with that idiot filming Buffy doing her 'get on your knees' act, it really pissed me off."

I hate to think it, but I might have done the same thing. "We'll wait for the video. If we see where you didn't really have enough time to react before she went all wild thing on you, that would be a start."

"Just out of curiosity, what does the lawyer owe you for?"

Tommy barked out a laugh. "Tell him, John."

It was kind of a heartwarming story, but only to us creatures of the dark. "Chad Dubrinsky had just been let go by the District Attorney's office. He and his wife lived in a small house on Faust Avenue in LA. His little boy, Charlie, was only three. They were trying to make due on his salary alone. With the layoff from the DA's office, things were getting tight. He had to start all over, doing law clerk work in a firm downtown. Long hours on the job, and then this guy moves in next door on a foreclosure sale. He starts partying to dawn, loud music, cars all over the place, and people hanging out in Chad's yard. Chad calls the cops, and gets his tires slashed, and pictures of Charlie in his mailbox."

"By then, Chad doesn't know what to do, so he called a friend of his in a law firm up here, asking for advice. The friend gives him Tommy's number, and before you know it, we're on a road trip to the City of Angels."

Tommy chirps in, not being patient enough to listen to the version he asked for. "John and I meet with this guy, and he's a mess. He's workin' eighteen hour days, his wife's having a nervous breakdown, and his little boy's in danger. John goes 'I can fix this, but it will have to be a permanent solution'. Chad looks at John and doesn't even blink – 'I don't care if you burn him up alive, just so he never, ever puts another picture of my kid in the mailbox'. That's the kind of thing John here understands for directions."

"The guy has another wild party that night. We attend in masks. I fire the riot gun up into the ceiling, and the house is cleared out in seconds. Mr. Bad Neighbor comes charging out of the back bedroom, and John put some attitude in a one punch masterpiece that literally broke out all the guy's front teeth, and his jaw. We put him in a body-bag, carted him out to the car, and headed north. End of problem."

Halliday waited, but when Tommy didn't go on, he couldn't resist. "Ah... what happened to the neighbor?"

Tommy shrugged. "He was never heard from again. No one knows what happened to him. Chad was happy, and paid us off in installments. We figure it was still a favor though."

Halliday remained quiet for a few more moments. "You guys were going to make me disappear, weren't you?"

"Never," Tommy said.

"Never," I echoed.

"Liars." Halliday let out a deep breath and sat back in his seat.

Chapter Nine: Deadly Business

It dawned on me while we'd been riding for an hour that I still had Kev cinched up in the back. I turned around toward him. "This is a pathetic apology, but I forgot I still had you plastic tied. Turn around."

I released him from the ties. They have a plastic trigger release. Very handy, but you don't want to put two bad guys side by side with them on. That Halliday never complained or said anything put another couple pluses on his good side board with me. I like a man or woman that doesn't complain. It just means they've tasted reality with common sense. Complaining is for saps that live in an alternate universe. Sure, if you have a problem, you go and state the facts and resolve the problem with common sense arguments. Sometimes you have to get through a few cardboard cutout mannequins who think otherwise, but whining and complaining won't get you there.

"Thanks." Halliday didn't waste time with profuse thanks either – another plus. "You can turn the station to whatever you guys listen to, Mr. Sands."

Tommy immediately switched the station to the jazz and oldies station. "Thank God. I didn't mind the new country for a while, but it was starting to make me bleed out of my ears. Call me Tommy. Call John anything you like."

"Thanks T. Since I never knew my mother, you can call me son-of-a-bitch too, Kev. It doesn't bother me."

Halliday cracked up at that allowance. "Ah... now that we're at least on the acquaintance level... is there any chance we can stop for the bathroom and some food."

"Coming right up," Tommy said. "We're near Coalinga. John and I usually stop there, get gas, and get something to eat at the Harris Ranch Inn. We're only two exits away. We fill up at the Chevron Station there, hit the head, and then go on to the Harris."

"Sounds good. What kind of food do they have at the Harris?"

"What do you care, meat?" Tommy glanced back at Halliday with a grin.

Halliday leaned back again. "Walked right into that one."

* * *

Halliday's filling our tank when I come from the bathroom. Tommy's buying snacks for the road after we leave the Harris. There's an old blue Cadillac Sedan de Ville parked at the pump behind us, and Kevin's glancing at it like he wants to buy it. The owner's not around, so I figure he's in the food mart. I don't see anything remarkable about the Cad. It's ugly, and probably gets about five miles per gallon on a good day.

"Hey, Kev, thinkin' about making an offer on that Cad?"

He didn't look up. Halliday finished pumping gas, and hung up the hose while I put the gas cap back in place. "I keep hearing weird noises coming from it, John. It sounds like some kind of scuffling sound. I'm in enough trouble, so I thought I better wait until you came out. The driver's that guy in front of Tommy in the cashier's line."

I check out the line of customers at the food mart cashier's line through the window. A tall lanky, pock faced guy, wearing a dark plaid shirt with cut off sleeves to the shoulder stood nervously glancing out at us as he waited to pay for gas. He had shoulder length brown hair tied in a ponytail at the back of his neck. I don't get any particular vibes from him, but I'm also listening for the noises Kevin was hearing. There's an eighteen

126

wheeler pulling out, so I have to clear my head of that noise before I can concentrate. Then I hear it – vague scuffing sounds. Then I notice the rear end of the Cad moving ever so slightly.

"I hear it, Kev. Something's moving in the trunk. That guy looks nervous as hell. I don't know whether he's packing or not, and I don't want a gunfight amongst all these people either. He's already seen me checking him out. If I approach the food mart, he may panic. Want to take another chance on trouble?"

"Hell yeah. If the fucker's got something movin' in the trunk, I want to see what he has in there."

"Good. When he starts out of the store, walk toward him. Put your hands in your pockets. Don't make eye contact. When you pass him, body slam the prick, and pin his arms. Tommy will be close. He'll back your play. I'll clean the windshields until it goes down."

Kev nodded his understanding, keeping turned away from the store. I wet one of the station squeegees and walked around to the passenger side to clean the rear window. Halliday made a show of checking out the rear driver's side tire. All the time I'm still hearing noises from the Cad trunk, and I don't like it. I see the guy getting his receipt.

"He's coming out."

Halliday straightens, jams his hands in his pockets, and heads for the store with his head down. When he passes the guy, he turns to wrap his arms around the guys middle, trapping his arms, and slams him to the pavement. Kevin maintains his grip, wrestling with ponytail so as not to lose his hold. Tommy drops his bag of goodies to rush over next to him.

"He's got a gun under his shirt, John!" Halliday calls out, but Tommy already arrives to handle that. Tommy presses the barrel of his 9mm Glock to the guy's forehead. Lanky stops struggling.

"Let me go! What the hell's wrong with you guys?"

I'm there a split second later to plastic tie the guys wrists together behind his back. I then lift him up to a standing position. "Frisk him, T. He has something in his trunk, and it's movin'."

Tommy does a professional frisk, coming away with a .45 caliber auto from the guy's belt in the back, an ID, car keys, and a boot knife from under his pants leg. By then, we're getting a small crowd of on lookers. I held up my FBI cover ID. "Relax folks. I'm FBI Agent John Harding. Please stay back while we find out what or who is in this man's trunk."

There were gasps of shock, and Lanky looked sullenly down at his feet. He'd stopped with the outraged angle when I produced the FBI ID. Tommy handed Halliday the Cad keys, and Kevin ran over to the trunk. He popped the trunk open, his features a grim mask. He made shushing noises as he reached in. Tommy jogged over after leaving Lanky's goodies with me. A moment later the two pulled a sobbing girl out of the trunk, who didn't look much older than twelve or thirteen. Sirens wailed in the distance. I considered making minor alterations to Lanky, but there were just too damn many witnesses.

"Don't even think about it, John!" Tommy called out. He and Halliday were carefully unbinding the girl's painfully duct taped body.

Lanky let out a yelp, as I may have forgotten myself for a moment while holding his arm. I leaned in close to Lanky. "You'd better pray those sirens are headed here, shithead. If they're not, I'm going to take you somewhere quiet and pluck your arms and legs off."

Lanky looked at me in horror. Oh boy, if he knew me a little better, he'd be crying. I called the number for Clint's FBI contact, Sam Reeves. He answered with a grunt of acknowledgment.

"Oh good... John Harding. Spit it out. I know you wouldn't be calling for anything else other than trouble."

"That's just hurtful, Agent Reeves. I have a pre-teen girl we just released out of a guy's Cad trunk. I have him in custody. What details would you like? It's all yours if you want it. We're in Coalinga, but the local cops are already on their way."

That sobered him up. "Janie and I are in San Diego. What state is the license plate?"

I waited for Tommy and Kevin to escort the girl past me and Lanky. She huddled closer to Kevin as they passed us. I walked over to the Cad with Lanky, and read off the Nevada license number for Reeves.

"Perfect. A kidnapping across state lines will rate a helicopter ride to you. Can you interrogate the suspect and victim if she can help within the guidelines, and do you still have that phony FBI ID?"

"Hey... for one thing, it's not phony and you know it. Yes, I'll read him his rights and interrogate him. I wish Lynn was here."

Reeves snorted. "Yeah... I'll bet you do. Tell me where you are. I know you'll need an ambulance for the girl. Can you send someone with her to the hospital?"

"Sure. I have just the right guy. I'll talk to you when you get here. The text with this Chevron Station's address is on its way."

"Just how in hell do you people end up in the middle of these shit piles?"

"We pay attention, Agent Reeves. Tommy and I were escorting a bond skip who wanted to turn himself in down LA way. The guy noticed noises from the Cad trunk at a gas station. We investigated."

"Wow, and the guy's still alive? Give the locals my number when they get to you. Call me with the details and girl's ID as soon as possible."

"On it, boss."

"Prick." Reeves disconnected.

Man, that guy's wound a little tight. I dragged Lanky around to the GMC rear hatch, opened it, and got into my small kit for Nitrile gloves. Then I checked the guy's ID. He had a Nevada driver's license with Donald King on it. I'm not good enough with the ID's to tell when they're fake or not unless I know the perp's name. This FBI and cop procedure crap is not in my line. I sent a picture of it to Reeves along with pictures of the Cad and open trunk, and of course Donald. He tried to put his head down so I squeezed his chin until Donald got the message to keep his head up. The bystanders were comforting the little girl. Tommy walked over to me when I signaled.

"Watch this cluck while I take a picture of the little girl to send Agent Reeves."

"John. This asshole has others some place around here. The girl's name is Becky Varner. She's twelve, and she says he was selling her somewhere in LA."

I shook the Donald. "Tell us where your hideout is around here."

"I ain't tellin' you shit!"

"For the first time I wish we had Montoya with us," Tommy said.

"That's what I told Reeves. I'll have to call Reeves back and get the locals to give me custody of him. Then we go old school on him." I shook the Donald again. "We're going to have a good time together until you tell us where your hideout is. I'm thinking some place quiet, me you, a propane torch... oh yeah."

130

"You can't do shit to me!"

Tommy started laughing while I called Reeves back and told him the situation.

Reeves was dead quiet for a moment. Then he took a deep breath. "Are the locals there yet?"

I watched two squad cars streak into the station with an ambulance running a block behind them. "They're here."

"Put someone on I can talk to."

"Hold on." Tommy took hold of the Donald, while I went to meet the local PD with my FBI credentials out. A short haired, medium height sergeant with Carlson on his tag met me. "I have my FBI boss on the line, Sergeant. Can he speak with you about this?"

"Yes Sir." Carlson took the phone, and gave his name to Reeves. He handed it back after a couple of minutes in a nearly one sided conversation. "Agent Reeves says the FBI has custody in this case with it having happened across state lines. That's fine with me. We'll allow one of your men to accompany the girl to the hospital."

"Thank you, Sergeant." I walked over to Kevin, who was holding the girl's hand while the EMT's checked her over. "Sergeant, this is my undercover man, Agent Halliday. He'll be accompanying the girl and staying with her at the hospital."

"Very good," Carlson acknowledged. "Great work, you guys."

"Thank you." I made eye contact with Kevin. He gave me a nod of understanding. I went back over with Tommy and the Donald.

I was smiling. By the time I reached the Donald, he started quacking about torture. Tommy moved in front of him, and I gave the Donald a short left to the solar plexus, which halted all conversation as I loaded him in the GMC. "You drive T. When we get some place with some solitude, pull over. The Donald is in our custody now."

Moments later we were on our way. Tommy headed down Dorris Avenue toward Fresno Coalinga Road. It's a barren connection with dirt roads going off with destinations out of sight. Tommy headed down one with nothing in sight as far as the eye could see. By that time, the Donald was breathing with ragged snorts and groans.

"You... you can't... do this!"

Tommy turned once he was stopped. "Shut up, pussy. We'll let you know when to speak, and it better be exactly what we're asking for or you are going to be one hurtin' son-of-a-bitch."

Let the games begin. Damn, I wish Lynn was here. We'd already be headed over to this cluck's hideout. "We can't use the torch, T. If we have to take him back with us, we can't leave any marks."

"What about pliers?" Tommy gets right into it. He's seen Montoya work. "I bet we get one of his nuts in the jaws of victory, and the little pussy will be talkin' in no time."

"I like it! I've got the large jawed ones in the back. They're in my kit. You get them, and I'll prep the Donald for surgery."

"No... no... no..." the Donald repeated in horrified cadence while slithering into a corner of the backseat. "I...I'll tell. I'll tell."

Tommy shook his head. He was getting good at this. "That ship sailed back when we asked you nicely. Now, we have to make sure you're cooperating in good faith. You may have to do it in a high squeaky voice, but that's okay."

"I'll take you there! For God's sake... I'll take you!"

"Shut your blasphemous mouth, you..." I reached back for the Donald, but Tommy grabbed my arm.

Tommy sighed. "Think about it, John. We need to get his other victims."

I pointed at the Donald. "If you're lyin', I will cut your fuckin' dick off and stick it down your throat after we find out the truth while you're still alive. If you've killed and buried victims, we will eventually find out, and I'll come get you. As God is my witness, you do not want that. I can reach you anywhere, even a federal penitentiary. Sit up straight, you fuck! Every time you screw this recording up, I will get pay back in blood later. Are we clear?"

In answer, the Donald sat up immediately. "Anything... just ask."

Tommy nodded he was recording. I repeated the Miranda rights for the Donald and asked him if he understood his rights. He answered with a yes. Tommy stopped the recording at my signal. "Okay meat, here's what I want next. You will say you can't live with yourself anymore, and you have to come clean as to what you've done, and all the details.... and I mean all the details. You pause, and there will be blood."

I gestured at Tommy and he began recording again with picture and sound.

"This is FBI Special Agent John Harding. I have a suspect who claims he wishes to confess to crimes he's perpetrated on others. He asks for no leniency or special circumstances. He claims his name is Donald King. Is that your real name?"

"Yes... yes it is."

"Do you wish to confess to crimes you have committed without any duress, but by your own free will?"

"Yes." This time the Donald nodded with emphasis when I gestured for him to do it.

"Please proceed, Mr. King."

For the next nearly an hour, the freak recounted all he had done, including two kids' bodies he had buried in Nevada. Good Lord in heaven, if it weren't for the live kids he still had stashed, the Donald would beg to be killed for days. His death would be legendary. We made a deal with the devil, and now we'd have to pay up. I concentrated on the kids, who until now had no chance. Thankfully, Becky was the first he'd planned to sell into slavery, but as a bonus, I had the name and address of the contact down in LA. It was going to be a hot time in the old town tonight.

I called Clint while Tommy drove toward the destination the Donald had given us, which was a little outside of the Coalinga city limits off of Route 33 near the Getty Oil Reef Pumping Station.

"Yeah, brother, how's the trip? I heard from the kid you've found God."

Very funny. "It's proving to be a bit more exciting than I thought. I have a case and a name I want you, Laredo, and Jafar to tear into while I'm down working on something else. I'll send the details to your inbox. It's a human slavery ring."

"I'll get right on it. You know Lynn will want in on this, right?"

"I wouldn't want it any other way, brother. We caught a guy taking a twelve year old girl to LA for sale to an unknown purchaser. We're going to end that."

"Understood. I'll put a package together for you by the time you and Tommy get back."

"Thanks, brother. Tell Lynn to sharpen her tools."

Clint laughed. "Yeah... okay."

We disconnected, and I endured the ride to hell's half acre in silence. Tommy didn't say a word. Some things are best left unsaid. That I knew what we'd find was a given. That I knew I couldn't act on it physically was a given. That hell on earth would follow if the Donald was lying... that was also a given.

* * *

Tommy and I leaned against the GMC. I was both sorry, and elated I had not torn the Donald apart. I knew even Denny would have had a hard time covering for me, and I still had a slavery ring to shut down. After duct taping that piece of human debris to the point only his nose and mouth could gasp for air in my plastic tarp, Tommy and I went in and freed the youngsters from hell on earth. They were young girls from ten to fourteen. There were five of them. By the time we were comforting them, Reeves and Labrie had touched down and driven out to meet us at the new coordinates with an FBI CSI team, and ambulances. Tommy and I are brothers. We feel each other's darkest thoughts, moods, and desires. The only thing that kept us sane was the absolute jubilation on the faces of those kids. Someone would have to die for this. It couldn't be the Donald... yet, but I had plans for the LA slavery ring.

Sam and Janie trudged out of the hell's half acre shack toward us. The kids were all in the hospital by this time. The FBI partners had followed the tracks of the Harvard serial killers, so not much shocked them. They knew closure through my two members of Murderer's Row, Clint and Lynn. I don't know where hell is exactly, but it can't be more than a couple steps past where Lynn escorted those three. Reeves eyeballed Tommy and me with grim acknowledgement. I knew he'd still have to ask.

"How did you get King to confess on video like that?"

"Are you stupid?"

Janie laughed. Reeves smiled and held out his hand. I shook it, and Tommy a moment later. "Hell of a job. King is crying for his attorney, saying he was tortured. He says he was coerced throughout the video."

"So what? Let him go if you think the video was staged or coerced," I told him plainly. "Please let him go. Let me tell him I pray to God they release him."

Reeves shook his head. "The video will hold up. It's beautifully done. The rest of the evidence we've already gathered will cement it in. I did as you requested, and sent a formal commendation down to the authorities in LA about your helper, Halliday. It was faxed a half hour ago with my signature."

"Thanks Sam. If not for him, I doubt I would have been in time to notice the noises coming out of the Cad trunk. I think Tommy and I can help him."

"You're going to type all of this up for the formal declaration, right?"

"Oh, you're funny, Sam. We're your undercover operatives, who must stay out of the limelight, while you and the courageous Agent Labrie create the needed documents with flair and official seal of justice for this case's details."

"That'll work, John," Janie acknowledged. "We'll be running the Bureau soon if you and those two psychos working for you keep coming up with signed, sealed, and delivered cases like this."

"All the better for us."

"You two can go and collect your third party informant for his ride to LA. I hope you can get him that second chance."

"Yeah, me too. We do appreciate the help on this."

"We appreciate you avoiding a gun battle in the Chevron Food Mart," Sam replied. "I doubt even trained agents would have pulled that off."

"Ah… hello," I replied, waving my hand in the air. "Trained agent here."

"Yeah, you are," Janie said. "We'll be seeing you."

Tommy peered over at me. "I hope to hell we can get down to LA before the hotel bar closes down. I need a drink."

"We'll stop by a liquor store and pick up some Bushmills. No use taking a chance like that at a time like this. Besides, if we keep Kev with us overnight, he may not have to stay in a cell again. We might be able to get him a quick check in and release with Sam Reeves signed affidavit and our lawyer buddy helping with the details. The Lord God surely took a hand today, brother. There's no way with that semi rig going by I would have heard the noises in the Cad trunk. Without Kev there pumping gas and paying attention, those kids would never have seen the light of day. For that alone, we have to spring him."

"Agreed. Let's go collect him, and speed on down south to the Bushmills' sipping happy zone," Tommy stated, straightening away from the hood. "We still haven't had a damn thing to eat. Let's pick up some Kentucky Fried to eat on the way to LA."

"That's bad for your cholesterol, T. Sorry, but you'll have to wait until we can find you a nice salad somewhere."

Tommy chuckled. "The hospital probably has a food court or something. They'll have nutrition healthy food there to appease your sensitivity, Dark Lord. When we get to LA, you'll have to be up early. I ain't lettin' you off the hook on your training. I'm. thinking a ten mile warm-up in the indoor pool before I get you for a couple hours in the hotel gym."

"Frack!"

Chapter Ten: The Buffster

The three of us sat sipping Bushmills in our luxurious hotel room, watching the video uploaded to YouTube by the idiot cameraman of Halliday's botched capture by the Hollywood Bounty Hunters. Yeah, I don't skimp when I'm on the road. We don't huddle together in some flea bitten, bed bug infested room in the Motel Despair. I checked us in at the Millennium Biltmore Hotel. Tommy and I stayed here once before. It has indoor pool, sauna, steam room, huge room with two king-size beds, and a wonderful torturous workout room where Tommy can appease his sadistic trainer instincts. We had bought Halliday some court clothes too earlier. He needed to look nice.

I had the video playing up on the big screen using my notebook computer interface. We kicked back on the beds in comfort. Tommy and I were laughing our asses off while Halliday groaned sheepishly. This was our third time through without stopping. The three tattooed goofballs who jumped out and folded their arms in scowling menace, while the blonde pixie danced around in front of them was hilarious.

"Oh boy, Kev, here it comes," Tommy announced.

The pixie Halliday had labeled the Buffster attacked with sensational strikes from all angles. Halliday parried the potentially dangerous ones toward his face and groin with a street-fighter's savvy. She buzzed around him like a hummingbird on PCP. The Buffster landed a roundhouse kick to Halliday's ear with a very impressive leap and scream of 'ki-aihhhh'. That was it for Kev. He shot a left up under her ribs, and a right to the nose. Tommy and I hid our eyes yelling 'monster' when the Buffster went down, barfed, and started crying with heartbreaking sobs.

"Oh God… I'm doomed," Kev whispered while peeking out from the hands covering his face. "Look at her. I should be locked up."

I stopped the vid momentarily. "It was a lifesaving situation, Kev… you monster."

"Yeah, kid," Tommy added. "The Buffster's been watching too many TV shows with pixies beating up badass thugs with the Kung-Fooie. It was only a matter of time before someone hit her so hard they snapped her neck, or body slammed her badly enough to break every bone in her body. Then there's the guy who'll just tackle her, get on top, and beat her face in flat."

I started the vid again, pointing out where Halliday acted with restraint. All three stooges were pulling out Mace spray and nightsticks. "These guys would have buried you, Kev. I think you have a real case here for self-defense if we can get the gun charge dropped. You locked their vehicle up and everything before heading out of the city. It looks like you got that big tattooed guy in the fleshy part over his knee. It's not much of a wound. That guy and the Buffster have no pain tolerance. They're in the wrong business, unless they stop posing, and do more with the tools they brought. Lastly, they need a guy that's a hard core threat." A knock at the door announced my visitor, and I stopped the vid once more.

"That's Chad. I'm glad he could come over tonight on such short notice."

I let in the stocky six footer with thinning brown gray hair. He wore jeans, and a leather jacket over a black pullover shirt. He gripped my outstretched hand with enthusiasm, and hugged Tommy. "Damn! It's good to see you guys. Charlie and Rose ask about you two all the time. They have a romanticized remembrance of your helping us. Rose thinks you guys are like the

Exorcist – arrive all in black with smiling assurances, and leave the next morning, taking evil with you."

That cracked Tommy and I up as Chad shook hands with Kevin. "You're Kevin Halliday I presume. Any friend of John and Tommy is a friend of mine."

"Thank you, Sir. I hope you can help me."

"Show me what you got. I see a Bushmills bottle over there. I hope you weren't going to Bogart it all and not offer your good friend a little taste, John."

"Right this way." In moments, Chad had some sipping whiskey in hand, and was seated on the beds with us watching the video. Tommy and I tried to keep from laughing, but failed once again. Chad, however, did not lose focus even once during the show. When it was over, he smiled.

"I know these clowns. They have a running ad on a couple of late night cable shows. Oddly enough, they go by the name Hollywood Bounty Hunters as you told me on the phone. Knowing you, John, you already have their names and addresses."

Yep. Jafar supplied their life history for us along with the video. "We do indeed. The leader's name is Daniel Atkins. His crew of goofballs are: Jerry Sooner, Calvin Douglas, Sigfried Kandelus, and of course the Buffster as Kev refers to her, Kensy Talon. They're not licensed, nor do they have permission to carry anything like Mace or stun-gun nightsticks."

Chad was pleased. "Exactly. After you gave me their name, I made a few professional calls. I also made a few suggestions with the knowledge of what Kevin did to help in that kidnapping case. They were stunned to hear everything that went down since last they encountered Mr. Halliday. I can't tell you how grateful I am you called, John. This is tinsel town, my friend, and this whole deal is solid gold."

My eyes may have narrowed at that announcement. I wasn't alone. "Lay it on us, Chad. I'm not sure where you're going with this."

"Once I explained they were in real trouble for confronting anyone with force without the proper licenses, Atkins calmed right down. He only had a flesh wound, and was already up and about. The police don't want any part of it. The guy you fought with in the bar will settle for a two thousand dollar cash payout to drop all charges. My fee is I am going to license this Hollywood bunch and Kevin here. I need an investigation team that owes me. They make impressive videos, and with Kevin, they'd have someone solid instead of a bunch of cardboard cutouts and a little girl. I'll take John's check down to the bar fight guy tomorrow morning first thing, and then clear up Kevin's legal problems. A lieutenant I know read the FBI affidavit, and told me flat out if the bar-fight goes away, he'll release Kevin into my custody."

I just shook my head in wonder. Lawyers are the strangest profession on earth. Tommy was chuckling, and Halliday simply stared at Chad in awe. "You are the man, Chad. If there's anything you need other than the check, just let me know."

"Actually, there is." Chad sipped his Bushmills with a big smile. "One of the conditions to enter into this rather complicated procedure is the Hollywood bunch want to meet you and Tommy. Also, the Buffster as you call her, Kevin, wants to meet face to face with everyone in attendance, especially you."

"Oh shit!" Kevin shook his head. "It all sounded good until then. What do I have to do, let her beat me up?"

"No, no, no," Chad replied, laughing. "I think she likes you."

That stunned the kid. I liked all of this so far. It made everything less complicated for getting back to the gang in Oakland. We needed to work on the slavery ring before they got tipped we're on to them. "It all sounds good to me, my friend. I'll write you the check right now. The kid's good for it, plus Tommy will go collect from the bond place. So, you've decided to go a little Hollywood, huh?"

"Yep. Plus I need some minor investigating and shadowing done if I can get Halliday here to infuse reality into the Hollywood crew. What they need is a guy like Wolverine in the X-Men – somebody actually brutal in reality that can remind them they're cardboard cutouts good for the camera, but bad in a tough situation."

"I've knocked around all my life, and survived San Quentin," Kevin said. "I've never felt lower than when I punched out the Buffster. If not for the memory of that, I probably would have made John and Tommy take me down hard up in Hayward. She... she really thinks she likes me?"

"Ms. Talon told me you showed her she was an idiot – her words. She thought it was really sweet when you picked her up in your arms and moved her over to the side with a phone."

"I don't know what to say, but I'll do anything not to go back into jail. I don't know if I can supply what you need for your plans. I will certainly try, Sir."

Chad sipped, contemplating Kevin. "I read the FBI affidavit, and heard what John had to say about your part in saving those kids. You're aces in my book, and you'll be fine if you don't try to do too much."

"John and Tommy taught me my lesson a while back, and it's one I will never forget. I remembered it when I was dealing with the Quentin population. They don't respect shit there, but they respect action."

Chad turned solemn. "Yeah, we have that in common, Kevin. John and Tommy taught me a lesson I never forgot. Sometimes a problem crops up in your life that you don't have an answer or a solution for, and you need a pro. I have skills, but they don't cover everything. I only thought they did. John didn't need a teacher for that. It's in his nature. He decided to help you. He decided what he needed to do it, and he contacted me. I'm going to get it done, and I'm going to profit from it. That's what's involved in a real solution."

Chad finished off his whiskey, and stood up. I handed him the check I had written out. "Get some sleep guys. The wheels of justice will be rolling in your favor tomorrow. I think we'll be seeing a lot more of each other, Kevin."

Kevin shook his hand again. "I hope so, Sir."

* * *

We met with the Hollywood crew when Chad called us to come over to his office at 1pm. Tommy had tortured me all morning long, even enlisting Kevin's help in a beat down while I was on the incline machine. They threw solid body shots at me from both sides while I maintained position on the machine. Very painful. Kevin apologized the whole time. Tommy didn't.

The meeting was a circus of the weird. They arrived in full costume, which had Tommy howling, to our new arrivals' chagrin. The pixie looked embarrassed. Her nose was taped, and she sported the standard black eye remnants of having your nose busted. The leader was walking around with a cane, but he looked okay, although not happy with current events. Kevin was very well dressed in black slacks, navy blue pullover shirt, and he was of course clean shaven. He also simply looked embarrassed. The pixie walked right up to him. She stuck her hand out.

"I...I'm Kensy. That was wonderful what you did for those kidnapped girls."

Kevin grasped her hand in both his. "I'm really sorry about busting you up like I did. I just didn't know how to stop you from hitting me."

Kensy started laughing, and then she hugged him. Kevin didn't know what to do. He put his arms around her awkwardly. "If... if there's anything I can do to make it up to you, just ask."

Kensy stepped away, looking up. "Come over to dinner at my place with me."

"You don't have to do that for me. I meant if I can ever help you in any way, I will."

The Buffster's eyes narrowed, which looked a little more frightening than she intended because of her black eyes and taped nose. "Oh, you think I look hideous, so you don't want to have dinner with me. I get it."

Halliday grabbed her shoulders. "You...you look beautiful. I want to have dinner with you at your place more than anything. I didn't want you to think... oh hell... I don't know... yes, I'd love to have dinner with you."

Kensy reached up and stroked Kevin's face. "Did I even hurt you at all?"

I smiled because I saw the trapped look flash across Kevin's face. He went with the truth, which was for the best.

"I didn't like the roundhouse kick to my ear, Kensy. It pissed me off."

She laughed again, clapping her hands. Then she put her arm around his waist and leaned into him. "Okay, so how do we proceed, Mr. Dubrinsky?"

Chad was enjoying the whole Kevin and Kensy show so much, he had to take a moment. Then he smiled and gestured at me and Tommy. "These are my very good friends Tommy Sands and John Harding. They are the greatest friends in the world to have, and the last people on earth you ever want mad at you. John, Tommy... this is Daniel Atkins, Jerry Sooner, Sigfried Kandelus, Calvin Douglas, and Kensy Talon by Mr. Halliday."

We all shook hands formally, except for Kensy, who kept a grip around Kevin, but waved. Atkins spoke up first.

"What'd you think was so funny when we came in?"

Tommy smiled. "Sorry about that. I didn't expect you guys to come in wearing your costumes. John and I don't know much about Hollywood reality shows. I didn't mean anything insulting. I guess you guys have to be in character all the time, huh?"

Atkins smiled self-consciously and shrugged. "Yeah, but it was kind of silly wearing them here. We were a little on edge meeting up with you guys. We've all seen Mr. Harding fight, and we know a little bit about the crew you guys have up in Oakland. Just the little bit that's been published in the media about you guys is incredible."

"I hope your leg will be okay, Mr. Atkins," Kevin said. He gave Kensy a gentle hug. "Like I told Kensy, I didn't know what to do. I thought maybe if I didn't do something you guys would Mace me and beat me to death."

The four guys all looked at each other before Atkins led the rest of them over to shake Kevin's hand. "We were idiots. Mr. Dubrinsky has explained a lot to us about our goofy actions. You could have killed us all, but you didn't. Mr. Dubrinsky believes we need you in our crew, and I think he's right. I admit we are kind of a joke at this bounty hunter gig. You were the first real badass skip we've attempted to apprehend. We've all worked movie sets as key grips, cameramen, doing stunts, lighting and extra work. Jerry has experience writing screenplays. We're trying to make a little money, and interest a producer in a reality show set in Hollywood. Mr. Dubrinsky says he could use us to do some P.I. type detective work, but he won't even consider it unless you sign on to the idea."

"I'm in," Kevin said emphatically. "May I make a suggestion though?"

Atkins nodded. "Sure."

"If we get into something really weird or dangerous, we need to ask for help from John's Oakland crew. I know from my own experience, unintended circumstances pop up, and especially when it involves apprehensions."

"That's a great idea," Atkins admitted, turning to me. "Do you field any of your crew for consults or joint actions, Mr. Harding?"

Tommy handed him a card. "Yep. You name the job you want done, and I'll give you a figure, whether you want us to advise, act jointly, or do the whole gig while your crew acts out for the camera. My e-mail address is on the card. If you just need advice, either call or write. John and I want this new thing with Kevin to work for everyone."

"If everything else is okay, and there are no more questions, I think Tommy and I will leave you guys to it. I'm sure Chad has some plans to discuss with you all. Will you need Kevin to stay?"

"He can go back to the hotel with you, John. Now that-"

"I have an extra room," Kensy interrupted. "We'll need to start rehearsing and showing him the ropes for what we have in mind."

"Uh... okay then." I shook everyone's hand again, including the stunned Kevin. "We'll drop your bag off at Ms. Talon's place. We have the address. Tommy and I will stop by your house before we leave, Chad. Thanks for all your help. We're square."

"Not hardly. See you guys later."

* * *

When we cleared the building, we just started laughing. It continued on into the GMC with Tommy driving.

"Now that's entertainment, John. Did you see Kev's face? Are you sure it was safe to leave him there? I think the Buffster's going to eat him up like a big happy meal."

"From the smile he had on his face, I don't think he cares one way or another. That was the strangest talk of a partnership I believe I've ever heard."

"Partnership, my ass. What about starting a romance with breaking your soon to be girlfriend's nose?"

Good point. "You're right, T. Never saw that one coming. I thought when Chad was talking about her liking Kev, I thought he meant she didn't want to beat him up anymore. That was very disrespectful laughing at those guys when they came in uniform. You should be ashamed."

"They were just too cute for words. Anyway, you're right. Kev will be fine. Maybe that's how it's done here in tinsel town. I'm glad we're dropping his belongings off over at the Buffster's. We'll be able to make sure he's still alive before we head north."

"Yeah, we don't want to get all the way home only to spot his picture on the side of a milk carton."

* * *

The next morning, we're headed over to the Buffster's house, having allowed for LA commuter traffic to die down a bit before we drop off Kev's bag. We planned to leave for home right after saying our goodbyes to Halliday. It turned out that Kensey Talon owned a real nice little place located in nearby Bellflower. We parked and approached the house over the cute walkway. Halliday met us at the front door in jeans and a t-shirt. Kensey, the little minx, slipped up from behind him, dressed in only his pullover shirt from the day before. She waved at us as Kevin opened the screen door and took his bag. We shook hands.

"I'm… ah… glad you're doing okay. Tommy and I have to head back home. I will probably return soon once I find out the extenuating circumstances involved in the kidnap case. I'll give you a call."

"Thanks, John. I don't know how to thank you and Tommy enough. If you need anything when you're down here, just call me. Kensey… she… ah… well, she's very special to me. I hope to be right here."

"He'll be here, Mr. Harding," the former Buffster stated, hugging him.

"I believe her, John," Tommy said. "If you two ever need our help, you have my number. I want pictures and video of any operation your group performs down here. John and I will critique it, and let you know if it looked good. Be careful with this P.I. work, okay?"

"We will, Mr. Sands," Kensey answered for Kev. "Dan told me we'll be the romantic complication in our reality show… only it won't be complicated."

"I see that. C'mon, John, let's get going. I think Kev will be in good hands."

"I believe you're right, Tommy. Bye you two. Stay in touch."

"We will, John," Kev called out as we walked to the GMC.

"Maybe we need to add a matchmaking service onto the business."

I laughed appreciatively, nodding my head as we neared the GMC. "Good one, T. What part of the new business do you want?"

"I'll take over the videos, and use Jafar to create a full proof protocol," Tommy went along with the joke. "What part do we give Montoya?"

"The complaint department of course."

We had a great time for a full hour on the way home thinking of possibilities handled by the Montoya complaint department in our pretend matchmaking scheme for the business. I came up with the greeting where the clients come in with complaints about our matchmaking skills, and Lynn pulls out her butterfly knife, click-clacking it from open to closed repeatedly. Tommy vetoed the idea, claiming if she did that, we'd not only lose the customers, who would run screaming from the office, but there wouldn't be any need for a complaint department.

Speaking of complaints, we ran into a bit of trouble when Lora found out I gambled two grand on Kevin's rehabilitation, and another grand on expenses. She FaceTimed me into faking snores, and having my head bang against the window as I passed out from sheer boredom. Nothing shut down our office manager's claims of dereliction of duty, being spendthrifts, letting a known felon sucker us, and most importantly - not updating her every hour. I had to endure this with Tommy trying to drive the GMC while attempting to snatch my i-thingy out of my hand and throw it out the window. We tried reasoning with her, but in the end, I had to shut her off.

Tommy wasn't happy anyhow. "You should have turned her off forty-five minutes ago! If you would have kept letting her chew your balls off for another five minutes I think I would have run the GMC into oncoming traffic. I know you could tell inside of thirty seconds she wasn't going to listen to reason."

"You're not very supportive of my marital negotiating temperament, T."

He cracked up at that pronouncement. "Remember the days when I just relayed messages to you? Man, things sure were simple then. When Tess showed up, mixin' civilian lawyers with Strobert and CIA business, things went to hell quick. You did take on nearly our whole crew though during that fiasco. Things were changing anyway, I guess."

No doubt about that. "We had to change with the times, T. You know that. I had another master, and the guy who eventually gained control is the right guy for the job. We can joke about Denny Strobert being the spawn of Satan, but he's on the right side of a vast pile of shit. I was about ready to ship out to Afghanistan because of the Samira deal."

"No shit?"

"I was in, and I don't fuck my country. I'm still in the Marines. They need me more where I'm at, but at the time when that traitor was in a CIA authority position, I figured it was either ship out or kill him for a while there."

"You put together a hell of a crew now. I like that Laredo guy."

"If things go really well, we may be able to fly anywhere we need to go with him on board. He can fly anything with wings or a rotor, and he's the best I've ever seen in a combat zone. Add in that he has mad computer skills, and I can't think of a better final addition."

"I heard the guys talkin' about you flying."

Apparently, Tommy's hearing about some of our business he hasn't agreed to embrace on a need to know basis. He's my brother in all but blood, and the fact he calls me White-bread, so I shrug it off. "Yeah, I got updated every time I disappeared back in the day, along with my language skills. My flying gets disrespected by my crew... as usual."

"That's tight, John. If some of them are unhappy about your flying, it means they must have been along for the ride somewhere."

Uh oh. Past flashes streaked through my head of a couple missions where I didn't have any choice but fly us or die. "Could we just leave it at the ride was a little shaky, but since I'm here talking to you, it was a success?"

"Yeah, brother," Tommy acknowledged. "I understand. Anything you don't practice all the time as a backup would naturally be shaky."

"See, that's what I told them, T. The next mission we all went on together... they brought their own barf bags, bopping them around in front of me. Our damn pilot immediately thought he was going to get killed, because that would be the only circumstance that would put me in a position to fly our ride. I had to convince him it was an inside joke. See, Laredo would have laughed his ass off."

Tommy glanced over at me real serious. "I don't get to say this much, but I'm damn proud to know you and help you. When Tess started bonding with the CIA, I finally started to nudge some incidents together, especially with how put out Strobert seemed because he could only reach you through me. I love this damn country, and knowing guys like you, and even Montoya, would do anything to protect what we take for granted means a hell of a lot to me."

"If you hadn't latched on to me I'd be in Afghanistan right now, my brother. I've already been in the 'stans. I don't like them. When that guy died in my first MMA match, I figured I was toast. When you walked up and offered me a chance with our backstreet matches. That was the best. We've sure come a long way from there."

Tommy nodded. "I've always gotten a kick out of our bond skip cases too. They made us a hell of a lot of money, and you've certainly done a lot of good along with it. I remember what gave me the idea too. There was this nutty guy that used to round up these two huge Samoan brothers, and back their play with a shotgun to do skip traces. They made some decent money, so I ran it by you, and your whole face lit up, you freak."

I laughed. Yeah, I thought it was a kick. "I remember our first one: Javier Tolliver. He was about six feet, seven inches tall, and had to have weighed about four hundred pounds. No Mace, no stun-gun — just you and me, the riot gun, and the chance to make a couple hundred dollars. You were so nervous, I thought you'd kill him before we had a chance to have him surrender."

Tommy's hands tightened on the wheel and he wasn't smiling. Then he hunched his shoulders comically. "At that moment, I thought it was the dumbest thing I'd ever done. When he swung on you, and that short right of yours caught him flush, I was the happiest man on earth. Good Lord, that was a beauty, John. You didn't even blink. He moved while you were scowling at him, and then he was out cold on the floor of Rickey's sports bar in San Leandro. Man... what a right!"

"Then you passed out business cards while I got Tolliver to sit up while I restrained him. I thought that was the coolest thing ever. One of the lawyers from Tess's firm was in there and took your card. Funny how things play out, huh?"

"If you say so... you freak. Speaking of Lora's younger sister, have you heard anything from Tess? She's probably a big time partner in a law firm back East by now."

"She's doing real well, Lora tells me. They're coming with my mother-in-law for a visit soon. At least it won't be like the holidays just before I married Lora. That was awkward."

"I remember," Tommy replied. "Tess was still a little raw about your past relationship with her, even though she had married."

"Her husband Cal's a good guy. When she showed everyone the YouTube video of the fight I'd just been in the first time with the Slayer to go along with me being beat up a bit, that was a little mean."

"Being responsible for her getting kidnapped a couple of times can do that." Tommy sticks the memory knife in me and twists.

"Yeah, poor old Tess. She wanted to run me like a dog out of her own personal kennel, playing make believe CIA agent, and ignoring all my warnings about getting involved with me."

"Lora managed to do all those things, marry you, and still runs you like a dog on a short leash."

I walked right into that one. "Thanks for the update, you prick."

Chapter Eleven: The Horrific and the Normal

"You want to come in and say hello to my handler, T?" We had arrived from LA by nine, so although it was dark, it was still relatively early.

"I'm beat, John." Tommy waved me off. "Get out and go take your medicine on your own. Lora will probably only smack you on the nose with a rolled up newspaper a couple of times for our transgressions. I don't want to be around to witness yet another beat-down. It's depressing. Now, get out."

I pointed at him as I slipped out of the GMC. "You won't like the payback for this disrespect."

"Bad dog… bad."

He was still laughing when he drove away. I turned toward the house to find my usual welcoming party, Lora and her Minnie-me standing next to each other, arms folded over chests with disapproving scowls. Gee, it's good to be home. I shouldn't have turned off the i-thingy, but Tommy would have tortured me all the way home if I hadn't.

"Well?"

I smiled disarmingly at both of them, an innocent look of interest on my mug. "Hi, girls. Well, what?"

"You turned your phone off, Dark Lord," Alice informed me. "You disrespected the mistress of the Dark Lord. What have you to say for yourself?"

"How about if you two don't get your bullying butts back in the house, I'm going to spank them for you?"

Dual gasps, and then squeals of protest, followed by ignominious retreat into the house by both, when I set my bag

154

down to do just that. Tommy should have stuck around to see the Dark Lord in action being an alpha male. I picked up my bag and walked in. Since neither one of my female dependents could put a dint in me with anything short of a baseball bat, I was unconcerned about any ambush. I'm in a great mood, so I go on into the kitchen for a little sipping whiskey. My door greeters were sitting at the table, Lora with some wine, and Al with a soda. I retrieved my bottle of Jim Beam and a shot glass. I poured a shot, and sat down to join them. I sipped in silence with a smile while they glared at me. Al couldn't keep a straight face, and started giggling.

"We're getting pretty close to Halloween. Have you decided what you'll be trick or treating as?" I decide to make polite chit chat. "You could go as the Beeper's girlfriend… ah… Selena something."

Al growled but then shrugged rather than take the chance of launching the Dark Lord into full blown Beeper attack. "He broke up with Selena. I've been thinking of looking around for a costume that looks like that woman from 'Resident Evil'."

"That's not bad. Should I dress as a zombie then, or stick to civilian clothes?"

Al's eyes widened. "If you dress as a zombie, you'll scare all the kids to death. You'd better stick with jeans and your leather coat."

"Just so you're not acing me out of going along, I don't care. Should we have a Halloween party this year?"

"Only if I can stay up late with the adults. We should ask Clint and Lynn to go along on the trick or treating too. Tonto could be one of those hellhounds from 'Resident Evil'. I'm not sure if Jafar and Samira would come."

I'm still getting the death stare from my wife. "We'll ask them. They might have fun doing something like that. We'll hit the really fixed up places. I'll see if Della and the twins want to come."

"Yeah! That would be great. I'd have my minions along to cause trouble."

"If you two are done Halloweening, I want to go over your trip details, John," said Frosty the Snow Queen.

Al smiled at me. "I'll go watch some TV. Can I stay up until ten, Mom?"

"On a school night? I don't think so. You… oh… go ahead. I hope it doesn't take a stick of dynamite to wake you up tomorrow," Frosty relented, looking up at our kitchen clock.

After Al skipped out, Lora leaned in closer to where I was still sipping, only on my second helping. "Did Tommy make you turn me off?"

"Tommy can't make me do anything. He did belittle my manhood though if I didn't." She laughed when I told her about what Tommy thought she'd do to me for punishment. "We did real well. I'm sure you already heard on the grapevine about our rescuing those kids."

I took Lora through our encounters with the Hollywood crew, and Kevin's prior confrontation with them when he broke his future girlfriend's nose. By the time I told the story through to our finding Kev and the Buffster in each other's clothing when we left, Lora was enjoying it with much amusement.

"You've probably already heard I'm going back down there to close up that slave ring. I'm not sure how much Sam and Janie will be brought in on that one. It will depend on what we find down there. In any case, Halliday will pay us back. With Chad's legal help and agent skills, I wouldn't be surprised to see the Hollywood bunch on their own reality TV show soon."

"I shouldn't have been riding you like that, John. I'm sorry. You and Tommy did the impossible getting those girls back. I was having one of my moments where nothing pleases me. I should go lock myself in a room until it passes."

"Admitting your weakness is the first step to recovery." I had to move fast as she launched on me, only to be carted over to the counter where I proceeded to lay hands on her in inappropriate fashion until she writhed against me. "I think that about covers the field trip. Want to go upstairs and negotiate a bit more while Beeper Girl is watching TV downstairs?"

Lora moaned under my busy hands. "Anything... only let's go... now. Oh... oh God... let's go!"

Who says the Dark Lord can't follow directions?

* * *

Clint and Lynn showed up the next morning at 7am. I get up at five anyway, so it was no big deal. I usually let Lora sleep in to eight. I like making breakfast for Al, and taking her to school. It's something I never thought I'd ever experience. She loves it when I walk her into school. Al prances slightly ahead, dragging on my hand. Teachers and students fall back unconsciously out of her path as she leads the way for her private troll. I smile, wave, say hi to the teachers – nothing works. They look at me like I've arrived from Planet Zeton, ahead of the troll army of despair. Al and I are tight. She appreciates a great sight gag like dragging me along into school with her. I know it will change as she gets older, and the boys look at me with fear and loathing. I'll probably have to hide during her teenage years.

"My favorite monsters. You two must be excited." I made the understatement of the year as Lynn is beginning to worry me. She's nearly pacing in step. "No coffee for you, Lynn. Come on in. Do we need to conduct this meeting in the workout room where Lynn can use the stair-climber while we talk?"

Clint is chortling, turning away, while trying not to show humor. Lynn is staring at him with I'm sure promised retribution. She sees the two of us won't let this proceed into a death race, takes a deep breath in the brisk October air, and walks past me. I give Clint the questioning look. He pats my shoulder and follows his mate inside. He has his notebook computer with him, so I figure it's a show and tell.

"We've got them, brother. We know what port they're using, their inland routes, what safe houses they're putting the girls in, and a few of the destinations," Clint said, walking past. "Lynn thinks the longer we're wasting time planning, the more girls will be disappearing. I put Laredo on alert. He's doing real good, and understands finally that retirement just ain't a choice in our line of work."

Lynn led the way into the kitchen, grabbed a mug, shot a dagger glance at me, and poured herself a cup of coffee. Clint grinned and got his own. When we were all sitting at the table, Lynn sipped her coffee with hands holding the cup in white knuckled angst. We needed to address this situation together immediately. That was for damn sure. I figured I had until the knife started click-clacking before I was in real trouble. I looked over the folder Clint handed me, speed reading through e-mails, phone number tie-ins and financial records with growing anger. I could tell more than a few were looking the other way in different parts of the political and police hierarchy.

"I don't like this. You two have spent considerable time putting the facts together, and jawing at each other about it. I can tell. Believe me, I know how you feel. Tommy and I released those girls being held at King's hell-house. I'll let you both imagine what it was like releasing King to the FBI, but we had to. This ring we're going after will have the same parameters. If we concentrate on what we need to do, we'll be okay, but we have to keep the survivors in mind. We have the resources to find these fucks long after any blunder our judicial system might perpetrate on us. Do you understand the unfortunate circumstances, Lynn?"

To her credit, Lynn was all business. She nodded her head before meeting my questioning stare. "I understand, John. This is bad. I know the feeling those girls have – nothing will ever save them, no one gives a shit, and they're going to die in a horrific way, and be buried in some place no one will ever find them. I don't share this shit with just anyone! I want these fuckers, John! I follow your lead. We get the girls. Everything else is secondary."

"That's all I'm asking, Lynn. This will be an inexact science. I know that. We have a name. I say we go down there in force, but we stay carefully attached to this hierarchy ladder. Task number one will be freeing all prospects this asshole has in captivity. Look, we can joke about a lot of things. This ain't one of them. We'll end this ring. There will be complications though to anything outside of the law. Tommy and I did just fine getting the Donald to tell us everything. We aren't even in your dimension for extracting information. You need seasoning, Lynn, which I'm sure Clint has tried to explain to you. You need to reach back in employing your skills with the psychological nudge you have down pat. Don't make this personal. Concentrate on the mission."

"I get it, John. It's hard to reconcile this kind of operation coldly. I've found out since hooking up with Clint and all of you that I'm not quite the unfeeling monster I thought I was. I'm addicted to making things right. I know we have to be careful going about what we do or they'll bury us. We get real justice. We make them pay. You guys took out a guy so high up the food chain, I got dizzy just knowing about it. My girl, Maria, is making changes to the Brannigan empire. Tell us what you want done, John. Laredo told us Denny's already set up a private hangar now for his Huey, and a brand new propjet with money from our confiscation of ill gotten gains lately. We're actually a strike force now. That Global 6000 jet Denny got and the turboprop are nice. Laredo gave us a tour."

Yeah, that was a change. "It's hard to keep perspective when Lora's ragging me about a couple grand on the Halliday job, and we have our own private air force. That was a real sales job getting Maria Brannigan to invest in it. No way Denny comes up with the fourteen million for that toy."

"She's loving it. Remember, she has hundreds of billions. Maria and I have bonded. She wants to do good. Maria knows what we do makes a difference. I promised her if a threat pops up on the radar involving any of the dead brother's dealings, we had her back."

"I'll make sure we honor your promise." I returned my attention to the rogue's gallery Clint came up with. "How did you filter down through all these aliases?"

Clint showed me a screen of the tree he followed into Interpol's database. "They turned up originally claiming to be Kosovo refugees so as to get into Belgium. They were in fact Albanian mobsters supported by the Kosovo Liberation Army. Having done some enforcer work for the Italian Mafia in New York in the early 2000's, the four moved to LA by order of the KLA in 2011. In those early days, their tracks are easier to follow. LA has proven to be a bonanza for them. They run weapons, sweatshops, prostitution rings, and slave trade to high paying customers from the Middle East. So far, Dhamo, who is the leader of the group, stays away from the drug trade due to the huge Mexican Cartel presence. A lot of their money flows into KLA coffers."

"This is going to be a tricky business, staying under the radar," Lynn added. "That's why I was so ramped this morning. Clint doesn't like my plan much, but I'm wondering if it might be possible for me to resurrect my heiress Constance Madrid to possibly entice Dhamo. Clint found out he's not with anyone, and he's a player. Best of all, he'll be in San Francisco on Friday. We can have Constance Madrid having lunch with Maria Brannigan. Guess what else – Maria knows him. He's been trying to reach her due to one of brother Brannigan's shell companies in LA at the port authority being sold. Apparently it was one of Dhamo's shipping covers for weapons."

Okay, that is some very tight thinking there. "I love the sting, Lynn. I'd like to hear Clint's objections, but damn that is some good thinking. There would be danger for Maria because of exposure, but I could see no harm done if Dhamo disappears along with his crew when Lynn talks him into calling an impromptu meeting with his other partners. What's your hang-up about it, Clint?"

Clint smiled. "I love her. I see a dozen ways this could go sideways. Lynn wants this, so I'm on board. I will add this though. If something happens to Lynn, I will kill without mercy. If you're down with that, brother, then I'm in."

That's why I like Clint. His bottom line is my bottom line. "If the deal goes deadly, then all will be at risk, and I'll be at your side."

"That's so sweet," Lynn said, clasping her hands together. "Oh barf! I'll be fine. Once I get Dhamo in a secluded spot, he will call for the meeting, and give up everything he ever did since he was three years old."

Oh yeah. When you mate with a Lynn Montoya, you better have your priorities in a line she likes, because if you don't, she'll proceed according to her own plan. "I'll brief Denny, and then we get this sting on the road. The Constance Madrid identity works super good when you can mix it in with an intro from Maria. That is outstanding, Lynn."

Lynn elbowed Clint. "I told you John would like it. You worry too much, but I like that your hang-up about it is you love me."

"I accept it's a good idea, but I will be right next to you as the bodyguard/driver. This won't be like Al Diri. All you need to do is get him alone. Then, we ship him to the House of Pain. By the time you get done ogling him with knife tricks, Dhamo will want to go with us to kill his friends."

Lynn and I laughed at that one. Just like that, Clint was on board. "I should pretend we're still doing the attack right away, so I don't end up with Tommy torturing me until we do. T is getting to like my pre-fight workout horror sessions a little too much. I know this is tough waiting for the opportunity, but if we get Dhamo to arrange a meeting of his partners, then we take them all out with one whack. Then we get all the details."

"I like it," Lynn said. "I will of course rat you out to Tommy immediately after we get done talking."

"That's just… wrong."

Clint chuckled. "You're lucky she warned you first. I knew she'd do it the moment you confided about hiding it from Tommy. I did talk to Sam last night, and he was ecstatic about the serial killer/child predator you guys nabbed. So far he's liking our arrangement."

"As long as we're keeping them out of the darker side, I'll bet."

"I don't know, John. I think maybe we've corrupted our FBI partners," Lynn said. "We have to go. Tonto wants a day in the park."

"No," Clint disagreed. "You want a day in the park, because this is your cleanup day."

Lynn gasped comically. "How dare you. Today is your cleanup day."

Clint got up, and started toward the door. "Actually, every day is my cleanup day. See ya', John. Don't work out too hard."

Lynn streaked past me to hop aboard the Clint express just as my lovely wife joined us. She took one look at Lynn trying unsuccessfully to choke Clint and turned to me. "Cleanup wars?"

"Yep. I'm getting you two a maid service today. I don't want any 'Mr. and Mrs. Smith' house destruction wars going on at your new place."

Clint turned with his saddle mate. "I was resisting doing that, but I think it would be for the best. When I went with Laredo and Denny to help look over and buy our new air force, I was only gone for a few days. When I got back, it took me five hours to find Tonto, even with him barking."

That was an ace. Lora and I were laughing our butts off, but Lynn jumped down to try out her martial arts skills in retribution. It didn't work out well for her, except it did wake up Al, who came running down the steps to referee. Al was upset when Clint made Lynn tap out from a rear full choke.

Al pointed at Clint as he stood up, lifting Lynn to her feet with him. "Disqualified!"

Clint grinned at Al. "How do you figure that?"

"Because I'm on Lynn's side against the boys club," Al stated with arms folded over chest. She was immediately joined by Lora and Lynn on each side.

"I see why Tommy thinks you're whipped, DL," Clint decided to jab me. "It's two against one all the time here, huh?"

I sighed for dramatic effect. "It's my burden. I carry it with a heavy heart."

"Keep whinin' like that, and we'll have to change your call sign to DS for Dark Sissy-boy," Lynn replied to much laughter.

"Why don't you two go home and terrorize each other while you take Tonto to the park. No, Clint, I have not forgotten about hiring a cleaning service for The Cleaner."

"Thanks, John. I'd like her to be about late twenties, blonde, hourglass figure, and-"

Clint broke and ran for their car, beating the raging Cleaner by only a step. We watched as he avoided her, using the car as a shield until she finally gave up and got inside. Clint waved.

"Those two are funny," Al said. "Do you think they really fight all the time at home?"

"I don't think so, Al, but who knows? They love each other. Best get dressed so you're not late for school. What would you like for breakfast?"

"Just some cereal, DS. I'll pick it out when I get down."

She ran for the steps while her Mom laughed, not that it would have done her any good if I'd scooped her disrespectful butt up. I'll have to work on some new Beeper gags. I'm thinking her poster might need some artistic touches. Lora put her arm around my waist.

"You didn't do so well in the one liner war this morning."

I shrugged. It was all good. "What can I fix you, babe?"

"A couple of scrambled eggs if you have time. I'll pay you back later."

I watched her sway purposely up stairs. "You got that right."

* * *

We take Al's minions to their kindergarten class every day too. Della had Jim and Kara ready to go at the door with their lunches. We leave early enough so we can walk. It's only ten minutes and the kids get a kick out of it. Plus, I don't have to look around for a parking place. I wore my most unintimidating outfit for our walk to Allendale Elementary School: black slacks, black pullover short-sleeved shirt. I was clean shaven, and my hair's cropped close to the skull anyway. Della nodded at me with approval.

"You look very nice this morning, John. Did you scare all the kids and teachers the last time you took ours to school?"

"Yes, Ma'am." I bowed my head. "I was a bad man. They almost called the cops on me. Al forced me to walk down the halls with her."

Al giggled. "Did not!"

Della and the twins were enjoying the morning show. "You better get going then, John. Thanks for taking my two."

"Hey, we're going anyway. The more the merrier, Della. Jim and Kara lead the way until we get to the crossing corners, so I don't leave them in my dust."

Della grabbed my hand. "I heard on the grapevine you were in on that big serial killer takedown. You and Tommy were the ones to free those poor girls. You are something else, John Harding."

Small doubt about that – what is the question. "Thanks, Della. It was an all-around win for the good guys. C'mon Al, get your minions started down the road. Bye, Della, don't listen to the grapevine about everything."

Della laughed. "She's the best thing that's happened to you, John."

Okay... yeah. "Actually, I'm the best thing that's happened to her, Mrs."

My tiny crew followed me off the stoop and on to our wonderful October trip to school. The morning was overcast as most Northern California mornings. Cool breeze blew off the ocean a small ways away, cloud cover made the walk brisk, and I of course checked out the neighborhood for any problems I might need to deal with. If I see something potentially dangerous to the kids on my walk, I will fix it. I'm not much on ignoring neighborhood problems. I deal with them because I'm the best equipped person in the neighborhood to fix them.

Della and my neighbors often feed me information I need to make our habitat a safe one. By the time we reached 38th Avenue and Allendale, we were part of the morning school student escort. I was cordial, smiling, and very neighborly. The group has seen me before. The parents are uneasy, but the kids look at me like I'm Jack the Giant Killer. They sort of cluster around me, sometimes to their parents' dismay. There are a couple of young moms in the walk to the school group that eyeball me with lewd intentions even Al notices. She of course rats me out to Lora the moment she gets home from school.

Jim tugs on my wrist. "John. Is someone goin' to try and take me or Kara?"

Wow, that one surprises me. Even Al and Kara take notice of Jim's question. I go for the truth, because kids taking notice of danger makes sense to me. It's when they don't pay attention bad things happen. "Anyone can be taken if you don't keep your eyes open for danger. You and Kara need to watch out for each other, and let others know if you see strangers. After we drop you off at school, always stay inside of the fenced playground. Never go outside the school until someone you know picks you up. Does that make sense to you, Jim?"

Jim nodded. He continued on as if satisfied with my answer. Al looked at me funny. "Something you didn't like about my answer, Beeper Girl?"

"I remember when they took Aunt Tess, and you had to get her back twice."

Nailed me. "Doesn't say much about my ability to protect anyone, huh?"

"Like Mom said, she's still alive. Were you in love with her, John?"

"Your Aunt Tess and I didn't get along very well. In fact if you remember how she treated me when they visited over the holidays, that's pretty much how she treated me all the time. I cared for her, but I wasn't in love with her. I am in love with your Mom."

"That's good, because I don't want you to go away."

"I ain't going anywhere, Beeper Girl. Even if your Mom kicks me to the curb, I will always be there for you."

"She won't. I won't let her. Stop calling me Beeper Girl."

Time to put one other thing on the grill here. "I want you to watch out all the time too, Al. You can FaceTime me any time you want. If something doesn't seem right, you call me, okay?"

"I will. I'm not supposed to have my iPhone in school, you know?"

Some rules are meant to be broken. "I know you're responsible enough not to play with it during school. That is the school's reason for you not having it. You're allowed to turn it in at the beginning of the day, and pick it up later, but I don't want you doing that either. I want your i-thingy close by at all times. Many times, adults make decisions that work exactly the opposite of how they intend them."

"You've made me into a criminal, DS." Al giggled when I gave her my scary face in reply. "If the security guard finds out, I'll be put in the gray bar hotel."

One of the young moms I mentioned sidled up next to me as we arrived at the school front. I had laughed at Al's comment about being taken into custody. She seemed to be interested in striking up a conversation – not a good thing near big ears Beeper Girl.

"You're John Harding, right?" She smiled up at me while holding the hand of a little boy around Jim's age. I thought I recognized her from dropping Jim and Kara off at Ms. Abel's kindergarten class. She held out her hand. "I'm Celia Gomez. My Ricky is in Jim and Kara's class. Della told me you live on her street."

I shook her hand carefully as my entourage of kids and grownups went on to their duties, leaving me, Al, and the twins with Celia and Ricky. "Yeah, I'm John. I always drop off Jim and Kara along with my stepdaughter Alice when I don't have business outside the city. I guess you're walking the same way. I drop Jim and Kara off right at the classroom door. Ms. Abel knows I'm signed in on all three kids' adult sheet."

We continued on with Alice giving me the high sign this would all be regurgitated later for her Mom's amusement so they could both play the outrage card at my expense. Celia was dressed in skintight black spandex with a pink halter top and no bra, with a light black unbuttoned top. Her black high heels made her walk with us a little noisy. With long black hair tied at her neck inside a pink hair tie, Celia was quite the young mom. Yeah, I had noticed the rather odd mom attire for walking her kindergartner to school, but I'm not in the young mom judging business.

"Are you married, John?"

"I sure am. How about you?" I turned it back on her as we cleared the front entrance, where the security guard, Gus Minsky smiled and nodded at me. Al was listening intently.

"Yes. Ricky's Dad works days." Celia hugged little Ricky at the classroom door, straightened and handed me a small note. "If you ever need me for anything, my number's on the paper. Nice meeting you, John."

"Nice seeing you, Celia," I replied politely as she swayed toward the exit.

"I'm tellin'," Al said immediately as the twins giggled in harmony.

"No, really? I'll let you tell it. I'm sure it will be more entertaining. Kara... take care of Jim. Jim... take care of Kara."

"Okay, DS." Jim saluted, while Al and Kara laughed. The twins ran inside the classroom leaving me with the instigator.

"Good one, Al. I have some great artistic endeavors in mind for your Beeper posters I'm sure you'll like."

Al gasped. She pointed her finger up at me. "Touch my Justin and there will be blood!"

A couple of her friends arrived at her side while I was he-hawing over her Montoya like threat. They looked me over with fearful curiosity. Al gave me a final wave and walked off with them. What do you know, an uneventful October morning. My favorite.

Chapter Twelve: School Attack

I started to leave when Ms. Abel scurried out of the classroom to grab my arm. Joan Abel was a middle thirties, auburn haired beauty. She dressed conservatively, but Lora always checked her out suspiciously when she walked the kids to school with me. Today seemed to be my day for interacting with attractive women. Apparently, even a bridge troll has his day.

"Hi, Ms. Abel."

"Call me Joan. You're a bodyguard and security guy, right John? I know you do street fighting and I watched your UFC match. I need someone like you. Can I hire you?"

"Slow down a little, Joan." This is weird, even for me. "I do escort work, skip traces, and some investigative work. Bodyguard work is very difficult to do successfully if the predator is stalking you and knows your habits. Maybe it would be better if you told me a bit about your problem. After class when you-"

Joan did not release me. She looked around with a haunted look I'd seen before. "I have a teaching assistant that is covering for me while I talk to you."

She let go of me and closed her classroom door, waving at the young assistant who started her class. "His name is Carlos Rodgers. I only dated him three times. He's nuts! He started showing up here at the school, accusing me of flirting with any male near me. He...he was so nice taking me out dancing and dinner the first night, giving me a quick kiss when he dropped me off back home." Joan blushed. "I slept with him on the second date. It was so perfect. He took me down to Monterey on a Saturday. We had a nice dinner at the wharf, then a terrific drive back, where we talked about our work and listened to music. I...I invited him in, and we... well... I thought we were soul mates. I'm an idiot. It was awkward, but we barely knew each other. Then on our third date, it got very weird. He stated we shouldn't see anyone else at dinner. I had cooked for us, but our dinner was rather silent. I...I resisted his advances afterward. It just didn't feel right. He got mad and raped me. There wasn't any doubt about it, but I was afraid to report it because I had slept with him. He says if I don't stay with him, he'll blow the school up."

Uh oh. Okay... yeah, I admit I'd been listening halfheartedly to romance gone wrong up until then. I can see in Joan's face that most of what she had said was no joke. This Carlos guy streaked into my paranoia list immediately. Abel had a track record with me. Carlos did not. I don't presume guilt, but I do have a tendency to go with the facts presented by someone without an axe to grind. Al attended this school along with the Sparks' twins. Any threat like what she talked about would have launched me, but the personal connection makes it difficult to think rationally. "Tell me exactly what he said, Joan."

She took a moment, taking a deep breath, and wiping at her eyes. "He said he was sorry for his behavior, but that we were destined to be together, and he would do anything to make sure that happened. I...I tried reasoning with him, but he wouldn't listen. He... he raped me again. That's when I went to the police. They were sympathetic, but they explained the difficulty in prosecuting someone I admittedly slept with voluntarily. It was my word against his about the threats. Carlos has been shadowing me for weeks now. I filed a restraining order, but they have to catch him in the act. He's going to kill me, John! He really said he would blow up the school to get me!"

"Has he tried to get into your place, or confronted you in public? I have to ask, Joan."

"No, but he calls me constantly without leaving a message. I shut off my phone back when this happened. Now, I made them change my number, and he still got it somehow. John, I don't have any place to go. My folks are dead, and I don't have any siblings. My folks had no siblings. That was one of the things that drew them together. I always thought it was really neat that I always depended on myself. Now, I'm a joke. I see in your face you doubt me."

That's not it at all. What I doubt is unless I moved in with Joan, and shadowed every movement she made, the chances of my keeping her safe, or preventing serious harm was a two out, two strike count in the 9th inning. "This has nothing to do with you. I don't doubt you at all. I know you're scared. I know you don't have anywhere to go other than fleeing to Montana. Facing facts though is something we have to do. Are you willing to get trained in using a firearm?"

"I...I can't kill someone. I've never even fired a gun."

See, this is where I get left in the no clue zone. Whatever happened to survival instinct, or anger that your life is being torn apart at the whim of some idiot who has already assaulted you? Maybe some reality would be a good thing. "Look, sometimes survival comes down to hard choices. Do you want to survive this?"

Tears leaked out of her eyes and down her cheeks, streaking the makeup I now noticed was covering for some discoloration and swelling. "Not if I have to kill someone."

Then I hit her with reality. "But it's okay if someone else does it for you?"

She covered her face with both hands, heartrending sobs muffled with determination. "I'm such a hypocrite!"

Yeah, you are. I've been around Lynn Montoya too much lately. That guy would be in pieces somewhere already. I put a comforting arm around her shoulders. "Okay, Joan, take it easy. Give me all the particulars on this Rodgers guy. I need to know his address, and phone number if you have it. Have you made Gus aware of this guy, and given him a picture of your stalker?"

"I...I didn't even think of it. Do you think that's necessary?"

"If you have the school kids' safety first in your mind over whatever embarrassment you might feel about telling Gus."

That got her. To her credit I saw horror as she realized giving Gus the lowdown on the guy should have been her first action, even if it meant having to then meet with her boss about it. Look, I know her reactions were simply a woman, otherwise very capable, getting caught up in a horrid situation, but now the monkey's on my back. "Let me give this some thought. I'll brief Gus, and get some pictures distributed. It may be you'll lose your job or have to take a leave of absence, Joan."

Her mouth tightened. She nodded, acknowledging what might be a necessity. "I should have thought of the kids first. How will you get a picture of him, I don't have one. He lives in Berkeley."

"Wait one." I called Jafar. I briefed him quickly. "J, I need everything you can get me on this Carlos Rodgers, living in Berkeley. If you come up with a picture, can you send it to my phone?"

"Sure, John. I'll see if the school has a fax number. I'll pipe a picture to them for copying if you want to let the principal know about it."

"That's perfect. Send anything you get to my phone first though. Then I'll know to go see the principal."

"On it."

I turned to Joan. "If you want to go back to your class, I'll do some preliminary checks, and call you if I need you in the office."

After I entered her cell number, she grabbed my hand in both hers.

"Thank you!"

"We're a ways away from the thank you stage, Joan. I'll call."

Joan went back into class. Jafar called moments later. "Rodgers is an alias, John. He's wanted in Chicago for a suspected killing. He was the main person of interest in a woman's homicide he had been dating. When I ran his Carlos picture from the fake DMV record he somehow obtained, three other names popped up. His real name is Steven Vergues, and Chicago is where he's from. No bail money though, because he skipped town the moment the Chicago PD issued a warrant on him three years ago. His hair's dark now, but light before. The picture's on your iPhone, John. He works as an investment broker, and real estate agent."

"Great work, J. I'm heading to the office now. Go ahead and fax the picture."

"Will do."

I studied Vergues picture Jafar had sent. Nondescript, dark brown hair, angular unremarkable face, but his eyes told a different story. The best part of this is he's wanted. That means I can take my two monsters with me, and go pick him up. I head into the school office, only to find out I'm a little late. Vergues is there. He's interacting with the office secretary, Beth Donaldson, leaning over the counter, and smiling a very endearing smile. Vergues looks up at me as I enter. His smile goes away momentarily. When I ignore him completely and walk to the counter, he seems to relax. I wait behind him with my hands clasped as if waiting for my turn to talk with the secretary.

Vergues is about six feet tall, medium build, and about a hundred and eighty pounds. He's dressed in a dark gray, pinstriped suit and tie. He turns to study me. I Gronk him with a right to his temple that sends him flying into the wall. I'm on him in a split second, yanking his arms behind his back while the secretary screams bloody murder. Gus comes running in from his post outside the school as I'm making shushing sounds at the secretary. The principal, Deidre Lomax, ran around the counter from her office.

"John!" Gus shouted. "What the hell's going on."

"This guy's wanted for murder in Chicago. He's been stalking your kindergarten teacher, Ms. Abel, and making threats. Do you have any restraints, Gus?"

"Sure." Gus pulls out handcuffs from his belt and hands them to me.

I cuff Vergues, and roll him over carefully. He's snoring slightly, out cold. I search under his coat. He's wearing a vest, and he's also packing two colorful Colt .45 caliber automatics in a dual under the arms holster with extra clips. I look up at Principal Lomax.

"Can you get me a few small plastic bags?"

"Mr. Harding," she said my name as if it were a four letter word. "This is not the place to apprehend dangerous suspects!"

Leave it to her. Forget about my bags and the suspect is a wanted murderer, wearing a vest and dual automatic pistols. I'm the one out of line. The secretary had some common sense and did as I asked. She handed me three now illegal in California plastic shopping bags. I handed them to Gus. "Thank you. Gus, can you hold these open while I put the pistols in them?"

"Glad to." Gus was no dummy. "He was here to kill people, wasn't he, John?"

"Luckily, we'll never know, my friend." I deposited each pistol into a plastic bag along with the extra clips, using my handkerchief, before emptying out all his pockets into the third bag. I gave him a professional pat down, and I didn't miss anything. Then I stood up. I took out my FBI ID, and showed it to the very upset Principal Lomax. "This is Steven Vergues, using the alias Carlos Rodgers. I believe he was about to take all of you hostage or kill you outright before murdering Ms. Abel. I'm betting he was trying to have you get Gus in here on a pretense to speak with him about a security concern. Am I right, Ms. Donaldson?"

"Yes. How...how could you know that?"

"Because he wouldn't have wanted Gus to surprise him and interfere. He had some plan for you two in the office, but he would have taken out Gus the moment he entered the office. I'm guessing, because we won't ever know. Excuse me." I called my cop friend, Earl Taylor, who has some knowledge and connection with his partner, Enrique Rodriguez, in keeping Denny and my team in the loop with the locals. They have this particular area of the city when they're on patrol.

"John? Where you been keeping yourself?"

"In plenty of trouble as usual, Earl. Are you and 'Rique on duty?"

"Yep, we're in the squad car now. What's up?"

I gave him the Reader's Digest version. He was impressed.

"Give us five minutes. We'll come in silent unless you think there's a partner."

"No partner. We're in the school office."

I gesture at my audience. "Please stay calm. Police officers are on their way here now to pick up Vergues. I'm sorry about this unfortunate incident. Your teacher, Ms. Abel, is to be commended. She contacted me when I dropped off my stepdaughter. If she hadn't, God only knows what would have happened."

"You still should have found some other way to take him outside this school!"

"Are you mental?" Gus ain't having any of that. "If not for this man, we'd probably all be dead. I suggest you think, Ms. Lomax, before you say anything else. He has the police coming over, and he has FBI credentials."

"You forget yourself, Gus!" Lomax is pissed, and scared. Yeah, she can imagine all the bad things... now. "I'm just pointing out the ludicrous position this puts me in!"

Gus is getting ready to launch. He's an ex-cop, and a grandfather. He's black, and he's seen people in authority make stupid decisions all his life. It hasn't changed his 'do onto others as you would have them do onto you' creed, but he's been around the block. Watching anyone over him screw a good ending up, because they almost got blamed when someone acted didn't sit well with Gus. Lomax is beginning to melt down. He knows when someone is looking for a scapegoat. I intercede, because I know the game too.

"It's okay, Gus. Everyone in this room knows what kind of crap falls from the media mavens if something bad like this actually happens. We were blessed for a moment in time, where maybe God in heaven didn't want another incident with dead kids. Let's be thankful for that."

Gus clasped my hand. "Amen, brother. Thank you."

"Thanks for understanding. Lately, I'm not doing well in the communication phase of this job. We were all blessed here in this school today."

Lomax started to sob. It turned into a very awkward moment with her secretary trying to comfort her. She's not the victim here, but I know she's a civilian and she's upset. Lomax is right in a way. The media would have found a way to make her the scapegoat in some manner. School officials nowadays have to not only do their jobs, but also predict when a crazy shithead like Vergues is going to come in out of the blue for the soul purpose of committing mayhem. As I reacted less than sympathetically, Gus grinned at me.

"You must be getting used to people blaming you for everything, John."

"We won this round, Gus. No one can change that. I wish Joan would have confided in you about this clown on the floor. You would have never let him in the door."

Gus shook his head. "I'm getting dull around the edges. I expect to keep the kids safe from gangbangers foolin' around outside or a parent getting a little crazy. Guys coming in to kill, strapped with dual autos would have been a long shot for me. You playin' him here in the office was the best thing that could have happened. Who you got comin' over, Earl and 'Rique?"

"Yep. They were already in the area on patrol."

That's when Vergues woke up moaning and groaning. He looked around blearily, and focused on me. "You...you hit me. Why am I in handcuffs? Let me go or I will sue your asses to hell and gone!"

I walked over and jerked Stevie boy up in the air with his feet an inch or two clear of the floor. I had his clothing so bunched in my fist, it was beginning to shut off his air. I shook him gently while I Mirandized him, and then let him down onto his feet. I could hear Gus chuckling behind me, accompanied by startled gasps from Lomax and Donaldson.

"Do you understand these rights as I have explained them? Think carefully before answering, Mr. Vergues. Take a deep breath."

I didn't really need to tell the jerk to take a breath. He was already sucking wind. After his breathing returned somewhat to normal, I repeated the question.

"Yes...yes, I understand... damn it! Why am I being held?"

"You're carrying two .45 caliber handguns in a grammar school. What did you think was going to happen?" This guy was really playing the dumbass card through the last hand.

"I can explain that. I have a permit. If you-"

"No you don't. What you do have is a warrant for your arrest from Chicago. They plan on trying your ass for killing your last girlfriend. From what I understand, they have all the evidence they need. All they need now is you."!

"This is a mistake! My name is Carlos Rodgers. I'm an investment banker. I carry large amounts of currency, which is why I must be armed at all times."

"Save your breath. The police will be here to pick you up any minute. You won't be going anywhere but jail." I made a shushing sound as the dingbat began protesting again.

Earl and 'Rique came in about three minutes later. They both shook hands with Gus, who then handed over our makeshift evidence bags. "I want my cuffs back youngsters. Use your own."

I began to get into a position where I could disable the dummy if he tried anything, but 'Rique pulled out his piece and aimed it at Vergeus's chest. "He has a vest on 'Rique."

"Thanks John." 'Rique aimed at his head. "Okay, get your cuffs back, Gus."

Gus did so, and Earl replaced them with his own. Only then did his partner put his piece away. "Jafar sent us the whole packet on him, John. Your boy called Chicago already. They're sending people to get him even as we speak."

"He also made threats to blow up the school. The kindergarten teacher here, Ms. Abel, was the target of the threat. She will testify. Do you have people going to his home?"

"The moment we looked over the packet Jafar sent us, we sent the file to the DA while in route to you. He found a judge immediately to issue a search warrant. It's a blanket warrant, covering computers, and vehicles. We'll get everything. There will be a team there shortly to conduct it."

I saw Vergues's face when Earl mentioned a blanket warrant. "Thanks, that should turn up some interesting and incriminating material. One of the evidence bags has his car keys. It's a late model Mercedes if the fancy key-fob is any indicator. Just going outside and hitting the lock/unlock should locate it for you. I'm betting he brought a lot more lethal items in his car."

'Rique was also watching our suspect's face. "I believe you're right, considering the look on his face. You're not much of a gambler, Mr. Vergues. That is not a good poker face. Did you remember your FBI credentials, John?"

"I showed them, and I gave him his Miranda warning in front of witnesses here. I had to subdue him without warning because of Ms. Abel's informing me of him threatening to blow up the school."

Vergues laughed. "You assholes are going to be sorry you ever fucked with me."

Uh oh. Everyone looked at me. This is not good. I see that petty look on Vergues's face I don't like, dumb enough to brag about knowing something we don't. "Hit the fire alarm, Ms. Lomax, right now! I'll take custody of our suspect while you all help get the kids out of this building!"

Lomax ran over and hit the fire alarm without a question.

"Call the fire department. Tell them it's a drill, but to bring emergency vehicles. Call the bomb squad, Earl. Can I have this guy?"

"He's all yours, John. 'Rique said. "Let's go folks. This is not a drill. Let's help get these kids clear of this area. We'll hunt for his car while we're out there, John. Good luck."

"It's official. The FBI has custody of this bombing suspect. Hurry folks." I grabbed Vergues by the neck, hustling him out of the office, while calling for the pros from Dover. Surprisingly, Lynn answered on the first ring.

"Please tell me you have an emergency! I just lost a bet with Clint. I have to have the house spotless before he gets back with Tonto from having coffee at Laredo's place. I'm-"

"Lynn! I have a school bomber in custody. I don't know how much time we have, but I need you to make a play for it! I'm at the Allendale School where I take Al to school. Do you two still have the big SUV."

"I'm running to it right now, John. It will still be ten minutes. Warm him up."

"Acknowledged. I'm moving him to the corner of 38th and Penniman. " I took a deep breath while watching teachers and students rushing out of classrooms for the street with all the adults taking and guiding the kids toward adjacent streets. I called Jafar. "Come over to the school and pick up Al. We have an emergency. The kids will be milling around. Help the cops and teachers move the kids away. Stay with Al and the Sparks twins until it's over."

"Got it, John. Be there shortly."

Vergues barked out a short laugh. "You fucked with the wrong guy! You can't do shit to me! Burn, baby, burn!"

I plucked him up on his tiptoes while ramming him into the wall. "If that were true, asshole, you'd already be dead. I have a special friend coming over to help you remember what you've done and how to undo it. How you end up after she's done will be up to you. Prison will look like a picnic, and death an old friend, when she gets through with you. We have a sound proofed SUV she's speeding here with as I speak. Right now, you're intact. No kids or adults have been hurt. You have a onetime only chance to end up in the Chicago PD's hands with only prison as your punishment. Take the tough guy route, and nothing in heaven, hell, or earth will keep you from a legendary death."

Vergues's eyes are dancing around in his skull. He's beginning to have doubts. I don't blame him, because if the school blows up, I'm going to spend some quality time with my monster, Lynn, in the desert somewhere. "You... you can't touch me! I've been arrested. I refuse to answer anything by my Fifth Amendment rights!"

"The Constitution is not a suicide pact. We have an organization that handles special circumstances like this. The suspects guilty by our 'caught red handed' parameters undo their threat or we torture, maim, and kill them. Congratulations, Stevie, you've qualified for special circumstances.

"Fuck you, Harding!" Vergues spits at me. "I don't believe you. This bullshit '24' threat comic routine to scare me as if you can actually do anything like Jack Bauer is a crock! Get to it, pussy. You and I know you can't do shit!"

He's pulling the Jack Bauer card. He's watched '24', and thinks it's all fiction. Well, not quite, you piece of shit. I'm beginning to think I can handle this without Lynn, but she brings the game to a higher level: no marks. I'm thinking of taking him to an empty classroom, and breaking pieces of his body one at a time. I'll wait for Lynn though. She is becoming an expert at interrogation without marks or deaths, not that in this instance I care.

I grip Vergues's jaw in my hand. "Oh, Stevie... you know so little about the new 'Protect America' plan. We get it done. If that means cutting your nuts out and sticking them in your mouth while we question you... well... we hired people who can do it, and actually smile while they do it. You're going to meet her soon. My advice... tell me everything now. If you don't, my associate will make you tell, but she won't stop there. She will take you to a plateau of pain you thought was imaginary."

Vergues grinned inappropriately. "I have no fear of you people."

I almost let go a chuckle on that one. I clamp him by the back of the neck, so if he even squeaks I'll be able to shut off the sound completely "You will, chum. Let's go out front and wait for her."

When we get out front, I move Vergues down the sidewalk toward 38th, moving quickly through the students and adults. We reached the corner only a minute before Lynn. She stopped, and I loaded Vergues into the cargo area. I jumped in after him.

"Tie him to the backdoor on his knees, John. I'll be back in a moment. I brought extra ties in my bag back there."

I propped Vergues against the door. He struggled, so I gave him a quick solar plexus punch that rendered him quiet and cooperative. After undoing the handcuffs with the key Earl turned over to me, I fastened one hand up on the cargo framework to the left, and the other to the right. I did the same to his feet on the lower framework, which kept his knees spread. By then, my red-faced gasper was getting his voice back.

Lynn parked and slipped into the back. Man, she looked good. She had tied her long hair back tightly away from her face. With black eye shadow, lipstick, black spandex bottoms, and black halter top, Lynn made that 'Girl With The Dragon Tattoo' look like a girl scout leader. It's her face. She doesn't need her face to be a pincushion, or tats everywhere. When Lynn puts on her death mask, only Clint is invulnerable to its effect. Hell, I wanted to shoot her. She went face to face with Stevie boy, and he looked away.

"Hello, meat. I'm Lynn Montoya. Maybe you've heard of me. I cut the hearts out of a whole bunch of tough guys like you."

That got his attention. He looked back at her with his eyes nearly squeezed shut. "Mon...Montoya? That's impossible! I read you were taken by the Zeta Cartel in Mexico."

"This bunch needed a monster, so they came down and got me out. Let's not talk about me. Let me give you a little demo of what's to come. I hear you like blowing up schools with kids and ex-girlfriends inside. Well, I'm here to sign you into my ten minute reeducation camp."

"Wait! I-"

Lynn jammed the piece of duct tape she had in her hand over his mouth. "Bored now. You don't get to talk yet tough guy. I need you to understand this isn't the police department. This is hell on earth, and I'm your guide. How deeply you want to go on this journey will be up to you... but not right now."

Lynn and I moved to opposite end of the cargo area where she took out a Taser and aimed it at Vergues's nuts. The needles cut off his muffled scream. Then Lynn got into a full lotus position and began cranking up the juice ever so slowly. I was glad we had reinforced glass in the SUV, because Vergues's high pitched muffled squeal would surely have cracked it otherwise. Vergues writhed and pissed himself, which was great for conduction. Each time his jerking body seemed to indicate Vergues would pass out, Lynn dialed back for ten seconds, before starting again. His eyes bulged out at his torturer, but Lynn simply smiled. I could and have done this and worse when needed, but something's added to the mix when she does it. After five full minutes, Lynn turned off the juice.

"Okay, bad boy, stop squealing or I'll crank it up again. Go ahead, John. Peel off the tape, and see if tough guy wants to be helpful. One other thing – if the school goes boom while we're playing, you are going to have a very bad three days. That's how long I made my last bad boy keep me company until he gasped out his last breath."

It was chilling listening to her tell him what would happen. I saw in his eyes he believed her. I carefully removed the duct tape. Vergues sobbed, cried, and mouthed words with no sound for the next twenty seconds until Lynn made a clucking sound of dissatisfaction.

"Momma gonna punish!"

Vergues cried out, getting his voice back. "Wha...what time...what time is it?"

"It's nearly ten," I told him. The relief in his face was obvious. Tears streamed down his face.

"It's in the center ceiling panel above Joan's classroom! Hurry! It's set to go off at eleven!"

"I'll FaceTime you the moment I get into position, Lynn. What disables it, asshole?"

"Red wire... Green wire... that order!"

Lynn slipped in near Vergues. Her butterfly knife click-clacked into the open position. "Best start praying to whatever demon you have séances with that John disarms it with no surprises. If not, I'm going to skin you before we head for an open desert somewhere."

"It'll work! It will..."

185

I was out of the van and running full speed for the school only a block away. Earl and 'Rique spotted me. A bomb squad member, fully decked out in a bodysuit met me in front of the school. "I've got it. Follow me with your squad. Do you have side cutters on you?"

The bomb squad guy with Jenkins on his nametag handed the tool over to me from his pouch. I ran through the entrance and down to Abel's classroom. I pulled a chair out of the classroom and stood on it under the center panel. I could tell right away it had been moved recently. Jenkins took up a position next to me as his squad arrived with a containment box. I shoved the tile to the side, and spotted the blinking lights right away. It was a cake of C4, wired to a timer. I FaceTimed Lynn.

"I'm here, Lynn, and showing you the bomb." I moved the bomb to the opening, turning it until I spotted the wires. I hear Vergues scream as I held my i-thingy up so he could see it.

"Yes...yes... Red wire... then Green wire within five seconds."

"You left that five second shit out," Lynn informed him. There was another scream.

I separated the wires. I clipped the red and then the green. The timer shut off. Neato. No boom. I handed the side-cutters down to Jenkins. "Open the box. I'll bring it down."

Just like that, it was over. I watched them close up the containment box. Jenkins removed his helmet and glove, holding his hand out. I shook it.

"Thanks for trusting me with this."

"We all know you, John. I didn't know you disarmed bombs along with throwing bombs in the cage."

I laughed. "It helps to know the sequence. That took a lot of guts for you and your crew to come in, not knowing if you'd get

186

blown to hell and gone. By the looks of that C4 cake, we would have been spread out over the block in tiny pieces."

Jenkins nodded, as he turned to follow his team. "It would have been quick. See ya'."

I stood on the chair again, straightened the panel into place, and then put the chair back where I had found it. I went into one of the bathrooms and washed my hands and face. Yeah, I may have sweated a little. I FaceTimed Lynn once again. She smiled at me from my i-thingy.

"It's done, Lynn. I'll be there shortly, as soon as I can clear things with the PD."

"Take your time, John. Bad boy and I are bonding. He's telling me all about the bad things he's done, all of it being recorded."

"That will help. How's he look other than pissing himself?"

"We'll have to take him with us for a time."

I heard Vergues start to cry, and Lynn's soothing voice telling him he was a good boy now, that we just had to get him cleaned up. Lynn came back on. "Stevie is a little emotional right now."

"You're the best, Lynn. That was quite an outfit you had on. Did you change that quickly before you came over to the school?"

Montoya chuckled. "No. I was waiting for Clint to get back. We were watching the foreign language versions of 'The Girl With The Dragon Tattoo'. I decided to play dress up for him. How'd I do?"

"That was the first movie I thought of when I saw you. Nice choice. I have to ask Clint later what he thinks. Be there in a few."

I slipped out the side and to the street. It took me a few minutes to find Jafar, Al, and the twins. Al cried out and ran into my arms. "It's all over, Al. Did you call your Mom?"

Al nodded. "Jafar hooked us up. We thought the building would explode like in the movies. How did you get the bomb out, John?"

"The guy who put it there told me exactly where and how to do it. Lynn talked him into being very helpful."

"You mean scary Lynn?"

"Yeah, he needed to see scary Lynn first. She's back to nice Lynn now. She and I have to get our bad guy in shape to turn him over to the police. J will stay here with all of you until they decide whether to close the school as a precaution or not. I'll see you at home later, because I think they'll probably close up. I love you, Al."

Al hugged me with all her might. "I love you too, DS."

"You little Beeper tool! J, call me if you need me."

"I will, DS."

All of my minions were laughing at me as I shook my finger at Jafar, and headed over to the police line. Earl waved and came over. It looked as if they had everything under control. I saw 'Rique questioning Joan Abel, and the bomb squad going back in with their dogs.

"Are we ever going to see Vergues, John?"

"Give me about an hour, and I'll turn him in good as new, complete with a confession."

Earl lowered his voice to a whisper. "That guy who says torture doesn't work is out of his fucking mind."

"No doubt about that, brother. There won't be a mark on him though. He may be a bit mental for a while because he's really, really sorry about what he did. Will you still be here, or should I drop him at the station?"

"We'll be here. We're going to close the school. This will be a media circus soon."

"Meet me at the corner of Penniman and 38th, Earl. Give me about forty minutes. I'll stick Vergues in your car with all the info we dug up. Then you can take him anywhere you want. He should be all ready for the Chicago pickup. He's a changed man."

"You want a parade or the key to the city, John? You deserve it."

"Actually, if that woman over there with 'Rique hadn't faced off with me this morning, my stepdaughter, my neighbor's twins, and hundreds of others might be in pieces all over this block. I had the easy part. I again introduced a fake monster to a real monster. After that, it was just a matter of snipping two wires, and finding him a change of pants."

"Amen to that, but someone else would have played around trying to get that clown to surrender in the office. You tuned him up, and pissed him off so much he revealed something he didn't want to reveal. You had a good day, my friend."

I grinned. "I had monstrous good fortune. Be back in forty minutes."

Chapter Thirteen: Evil Empire Threads

Lynn and I found a store on MacArthur Blvd. I bought jeans and underwear for our repentant sinner. After letting him clean up at a service station, we had Vergues back at the school corner with a few minutes to spare in Earl's handcuffs. Lynn patted Stevie's cheek, which caused a tear to run down his face.

"You be good, Stevie. Make sure they lock you up and throw away the key. If you don't, and they let you out, we'll find you no matter where you are. That would be very bad, wouldn't it?"

Stevie nodded in the affirmative until Lynn had to grab his chin. He cringed. "Yes, Lynn. Yes, Lynn!"

I helped him out of the SUV and into Earl's squad car. I handed Earl the key for the handcuffs along with the USB drive with Vergues's confession. "It's all there, including two other murders no one knows about. If you can keep me out of this, I would appreciate it. We're on the trail of something big down in LA, and any notoriety would be bad. I'll call my FBI contacts. They'll get in touch with you about an ongoing investigation cover story, and the FBI being overjoyed to help local police capture a deadly killer."

"That sounds great, John. You're really getting good at this government lingo."

"That's me, Earl. I've always had a dream. I wanted to be a bureaucrat."

* * *

I called Sam Reeves.

"John Harding. What have you done now?"

"With Lynn's help, stopped a school bomber. Want to hear the story?"

That perked him up. He called his partner over, and put me on speaker. "Janie's here. Give it to us."

I recited what happened in detail, leaving out only the interrogation description. I repeated the advice about how to handle the media. "I just dropped him back with the Oakland PD. I gave you Earl Taylor's number a while back as part of our local contacts here. There's not a mark on Vergues, and Earl has his complete confession, including two murders no one knows about. He did it across state lines. Chicago is picking him up tomorrow on the first murder charge."

"That's damn good, Harding. This is very strange. You know that, right? You've become some kind of lightning rod for trouble. The jury's out on whether you're somehow creating this shit, or simply in the right place at the right time. What's with the anonymity on your part?"

I ignored the lightning rod remark. "We're pursuing the slave ring in LA. I don't want anything messing that up. You two can have this whole thing. Tell them the FBI worked undercover on this."

"We'll take care of it. Thanks for this. How in hell does Montoya... oh, never mind. There are a lot of kids and adults alive because of that teacher, you, and Montoya. Nice work."

"Thanks. I'll let you know if there is anything you can use on the LA sting."

"Good luck." Reeves disconnected.

Just like that Lynn and I are free and clear of this. I got in the van. "Your friends from the FBI will be handling publicity and police about our part. I'm going to get Jafar and the kids. They're closing the school down for the day."

"I need to have the van cleaned professionally," Lynn said. "I don't want cranky to come home and get a whiff of fear and loathing permeating the cargo area. Thanks for letting me in on this, John. It really broke up my day. I bet Reeves is wondering how the sky could be falling everywhere you go."

I grinned, and stepped out. "Something like that. Great idea about the cleaning. I'm putting off the inevitable, but I know Tommy will be hounding me shortly about our workout schedule. Nice working with you, Dr. Venkman."

Lynn laughed, and waved me off on my 'Ghostbusters' reference. "See ya'."

* * *

Into my third hour of training, I was phoning it in, and Tommy noticed. Knowing the details of my morning, he pretended not to notice. He called a halt to my special training item with the boards before I ended up breaking everything in my foot. I didn't make any excuses, but for the first time in a while, I was running on empty. The lightning had struck one too many times. Dev, Jafar, and Jesse also played pretend with me. I think they were tired of kicking my ass. Tommy could not let it end with only a halt.

"Since we all know John's timing today was so far off, that if he had been fighting the Destroyer, we'd be planning his funeral now, so let's quit while we're ahead... ahead of John anyway."

"Thanks, T. I'll be on the ball tomorrow."

"Oh, you think you're done for the day, white meat? I don't think so. I'm giving these other guys a break from the joke this training session has become. You need some downtime though too. I think five miles on the incline of solitude is in order."

Everyone laughed at the unfortunate downtime Tommy boinked me with but me. Lora was in the front office with Al. She kept her close for the day after Jafar and I arrived with Al and the twins. I gave Della the short story. We agreed God works in mysterious ways, and let it go at that. Tommy and the guys left. He knew I would do exactly what he said before I quit for the day. Then with only a mile left on my five mile, thirty degree incline, hell finish, Satan's Spawn arrived. He smiled and waved. I kept silent because my sneaking hunch I had been right about hitting my stamina wall was pretty close. I saved what little breath I had for the finish. The day's journey came to a blessed end at last, and I leveled the incline, walking off a mile to wind down.

"I have to admit, after the morning you had, I never expected to see you torturing yourself in here."

"That's because you don't know Tommy very well, Spawn. I believe the torture part is finally over." I shut down the incliner, and stepped off, toweling away the rivers of sweat. "Lynn was incredible today, Den. You're about as good as I've ever seen, but Lynn is a close second in interrogation. Watching the two of you work one of these pricks together is like watching and listening to a great opera conducted by demons from the seventh level of hell. I'm impressed. Lucas and Casey are impressed, and they are never impressed. If we can stay out of prison, we may do a hell of a lot of good."

"So you're embracing this torture for penance, huh?"

"Partly. Mostly, I was going over in my head everything we've been doing. This interrogating outside the law is habit forming, and I already had the habit. I'm coming to grips with the fact I'm addicted."

"It's always best to face up to what's right under your nose, John," Denny replied. "We've been over some rough territory. We catch these jokers red-handed. We're not interrogating Cinderella. I know you think I've made deals that should never have been made. You're probably right. That's all over. We joke about it, but we are the forces of darkness in this fucking land."

"We have backing now - people in power who have been watching what we have accomplished. Brannigan's evil empire turned to the light has everyone in Washington going nuts. They want to run the empire through us controlling Maria. That won't be happening. We've been given Carte Blanche to watch dog the shadows by any means necessary by men in positions who can make problems disappear, and can't be bought. I sold us as a package. I...I've been seeing Maria."

Yeah, my mouth dropped open. "Leave the fucking gun, and take the cannoli... this is too much. You did not just tell me you're dating. Why would you tell me that? Oh, I get it. You want us to think you've come in from the dark side. Forget it, Spawn. There are no givebacks once you've signed with the Devil on the dotted line in blood." By this time Denny is howling in laughter. He liked the 'Godfather' line. "Besides, I thought you were dating some gorgon from the Greek underworld. I don't need to ground you, do I?"

I must have struck a nerve because the Spawn of Satan is trying to breathe with tears running down his cheeks, and here I am without a camera to record this frightening event. "You, the dreaded Spawn, and Maria Brannigan with a hundred billion dollar empire, together against all logical thought, and... and shit... it's the end of the world. We're doomed."

Lora and Al hear the commotion, jogging back expectantly together from the office. They watch Denny having a laughing fit, looking at me in wonder. I walk over within hearing range to shoo them away. "Denny's having a moment. Go back in the office."

"We better get you home, Dark Lord. You look like you're on your last leg."

"Gee, thanks, Lora. Three hours of torture followed by a five mile cool down on the incline take their toll. Who knew?"

Denny was finally gaining control as my two girls left together, and I closed the door behind them. I walked over and got out a couple of shot glasses and my medicinal bottle of Jim Beam. We sat down together at our small table and chair break area. I had added a Bud from the refrigerator to go along with my shot. It had been a long day, and ending it doing my Oprah impression needed something to dull my senses with. I poured. We toasted and sipped. I followed mine with half a Bud.

"Good one, John."

"Let's go over this. So Brannigan was the key to the kingdom, huh?"

"That about sums it up," Denny replied. "I didn't mean to get involved with Maria. It seems real, but for all I know, it's just an added layer of what she thinks of as protection from certain death. When I received word from Jafar on what was going down at the school, I thought maybe we'd all gone around the bend of cosmic chaos. You have a lot to lose, John. I know that bothers you; but for the first time ever, I think we actually can have something beyond the job. Is it safe? Will there be casualties? I don't fuckin' know."

I shrugged, and sipped some more. "What you've built here isn't perfect. We kept attacking. We didn't regroup, take a break, or consolidate our gains. We attacked. That's how we got Brannigan. The results are spectacular. Always before, someone would stop us just when we had momentum on our side. By the time we'd take the next step, it was too late. Tommy and I took a chance on that kid, Halliday. He kept his eyes and ears open on our trip to LA, and suddenly we're busting a murdering kidnapper while gathering info on a slave ring. Who knows whether somehow Brannigan didn't make a move putting Halliday on our radar on the chance he might kill Tommy and me?"

"I'm glad you're seeing what I'm seeing, John. Hesitation has been our weakness for decades in the Company. As far back as when I recruited you, we'd make valuable inroads, and then piss them away. When I agreed to meet with Maria, she surprisingly had nothing but good things to say about Lynn, and the real friendship they were building. Man, that item of conversation was really out there. I figured she would be the hardest dynamic to keep in line. That wasn't the case. After she saw how easily we took down her brother, it gave her hope. Until then Maria figured anyone could be bought, or would turn against their country for money, or could be threatened into compliance. She knows better now, and she wants an active role in it."

In his words, as always, Denny has somehow mixed business with pleasure. I can only wonder if his mission in seeing Maria involved only securing her help, or he was in fact attracted to her. One can never tell with Spawn. "You've briefed Maria on the sting Lynn wants to set up in San Francisco then?"

"She loves the plan. Maria believes without a doubt Dhamo will meet with her. After explaining some plausible reasons as to why the Brannigan empire divested itself of their part in the port authority, Maria will excuse herself, leaving the I am sure infatuated Dhamo alone with the most dangerous date in the Western Hemisphere."

Nicely done, Spawn. I refilled our shot glasses. "No question whatsoever about that particular fact. I think it would be wise to allow Clint and Lynn to take over the scenario after the illustrious Ermer Dhamo thinks he's won the interest and possibly the heart of Constance Madrid."

Denny nodded. "That would be my choice, but there are a few new complications beyond tricking the love-struck Albanian

I'm here to tell you about. I wonder how many other weird threads we'll find with ties to the former Brannigan evil empire. You mentioned Halliday. It's not as farfetched as you think. Talk about monsters – good Lord, was there anything Brannigan ever did that wasn't evil?"

Denny might have a point beyond what we already knew to be true. "You're thinking about the school bombing, aren't you?"

"Brannigan lived the long view. He wanted us dead, John, and out of the game. He wanted it done without any tie to him like all the rest of his chaotic plots. Remember, it didn't matter to him if every single device worked. His thrill involved the manipulation and activation of his plots. That one of them would eventually work and end us was simply like winning a chess game."

It bothers me a little Denny probably knew about Brannigan for quite a while, and that I understand it. The right time in this goofy business means everything. He's happy now because we can attack on our own schedule – me too. Then something more sinister struck me about this getting close to Maria dating game with his mention of new complications. "Do you think this Dhamo in San Francisco might be one more Brannigan thread showing up?"

Denny stared at me for a moment before sipping his shot. "That you're asking me that means you've already considered it. Yeah, I think it's a trap, because of the convoluted new info I got. Dhamo headed from LA in a boat. The key will be if Dhamo tries to get Maria and Lynn to both go with him somewhere... in a car... up to his room... anywhere no one will be around. If he just lets Maria leave without suggesting an alternative, then I believe it will go down just as we plan. It will spread ourselves a little thin, but I think we need to act in a worst case scenario mode on this. Lynn and Maria will both have trackers on them. We can cover anything inside the hotel with Clint and Lucas. We'll use two vehicles on the outside ready to go. You and Jafar will have our mobile command post. I'll take Casey with me to cover the boat. Devon and Jesse will be fine for any backup tracking. We'll have constant communication. If this is a trap, I want it sprung on my terms. Spotting his crew will be the tough part. I don't want them in position to screw us. Hopefully, a couple of them will be with the boat."

"You think Dhamo is here to kill Maria? How would that have ever been considered by Brannigan. His sister ran… oh… you think he knew about Maria knockin' boots with his South American drug boss: Kopensky. So, because of that hookup, Brannigan decided he wanted a death in the family."

"I do indeed. Maria told me her San Francisco trip was planned on the books before we took out Brannigan or moved on Kopensky. We won the chess match with the master, because he had no clue we would not only go through that setup at Samira's conference, but also get Kopensky's name. Never did he figure we'd streak down to get Kopensky, and free Laredo. Dhamo might have had it in mind to make a deal with the sister, but then Maria began selling off the evil empire, including Dhamo's port interests. I think he's decided to play out Brannigan's death in the family wish."

"Does Maria know?"

"That hurts, John."

Yeah, right. "Does Maria know her brother may have wanted her dead?"

"I don't even know if that's true yet. I'm guessing. If I told her, she might give away the whole operation. Dhamo's takedown would be messy."

"It's nice to know you're not letting romance get into the way of your role as the Spawn."

"Very funny." Denny finished off his shot, and poured another. "I care about Maria. She knows who I am, what I do, and she's okay with it. I wish there was another way to do this on Friday, but we need Dhamo alive. I want that damn Albanian Mafia shit shut down before they're importing nukes through the Port of Las Angeles. Yes, I'm a cold hearted son-of-a-bitch to allow Maria to again be put into danger. They want her dead. If we get Dhamo and his crew, the last Terrance Brannigan thread that knows of the evil empire, and Maria's connection to it, will be dead. From then on, she's just an heiress with a hundred billion dollar fortune."

He had a point there too. Those shots went right down to my toes and shot back up into my brain. The Spawn has me at a disadvantage. What's to argue about anyway? We're going to cover all our bases, and he's right, Maria will be safer if we close down the Albanians. "I can't argue with your logic. I've been wondering if maybe we're playing this the wrong way. He's coming up here by boat. Why don't we take him at sea before he even gets here?"

Denny smiled. "We would have, if I had received any warning. Dhamo didn't take any chances. He arrived last night with his three partners from LA. Instead of San Francisco, they parked it at the Berkeley Marina. Dhamo's staying at the Double Tree right at the Marina. Jafar only got tipped to his landing because he's had all of Dhamo's holdings in LA on a watch list. It was under the radar when it left LA, but when it docked in Berkeley, it triggered a notification. Jafar hacked into the Marina security cameras. Dhamo brought the guys closest to him. It doesn't change anything except it's more likely to be a trap."

Not much doubt about that. "They're planning on taking Maria and Lynn on a one way boat ride. All Dhamo has to do is get the drop on them outside the hotel, and have the boat fired up and ready to go. Do you think Lynn's cover of Constance Madrid is blown?"

"It's possible. We know now Brannigan probably had his hand in on a couple of things that happened in Las Vegas. With the connections he has there, it would not be a stretch to picture him following up on any and all who had contact with you, especially after Al Diri died mysteriously. He would have passed the info on, but I'm not sure Dhamo would be a party to it."

This could work. "If we never want the Albanians to surface, what better place would there be than to take them on the boat?"

"None," Denny answered. "It's a chancy trip though from where Dhamo makes his move to the boat. It's a messy one, John. We can't find out all their way stations in LA for the kidnapped girls without taking one or more of them alive."

"There is a thread of insanity winding through Washington D.C. that will eventually obliterate us," Denny went on, staring at his shot glass. "That thread throws open the borders to criminal mafias from all over the world, potential terrorists, and illegal aliens subverting our economy. Most of the crap we can't do a damn thing about. We are going to stop Dhamo."

Yep, Denny better take a cab tonight. "I believe you. I hope this thing with Maria works out for you. Maybe it's not too late to have little Spawns."

I got another laugh from him on that line. If there was any way to make this parlay come out right, Denny would find it. I held up my shot glass to toast the real master.

* * *

Ermir Dhamo stood up as he saw Maria Brannigan walk into the barroom with a blond haired beauty he knew would be the infamous Constance Madrid his partner had warned him

200

about. He was over six feet tall, late thirties, with his hair cut to light brown stubble, and his beard cut to match. Maria Brannigan, dressed in a black strapless evening gown extending to slightly above her knees, held out her hand to Dhamo. He grasped it with both of his.

"It is good to see you, Maria. I appreciate very much you meeting me here. I thought perhaps we could walk along the pier. It is beautiful tonight, and far less cold than San Francisco. I am so sorry for the loss of your brother."

"Thank you. Ermir, I'd like you to meet my very good friend, Constance Madrid. Constance, this is Ermir Dhamo."

Lynn smiled slightly – a vague, but enchanting upturn, with eyes brightly intent on Dhamo's face without blinking. She held out her hand to shake Dhamo's strongly. "Maria tells me you have business dealings to discuss. Would you rather I wait at the bar?"

She turned, gesturing at the very plush bar, her form fitting midnight blue, draped back, and thigh length gown moved along her body as if it were her skin. Dhamo hesitated, and then shook his head.

"Please join us. Our business will not take long." Dhamo looked up at the bartender for only a moment, and a waitress was at his side an instant later. "What will you ladies have? I would like some champagne. Will you join me?"

After the champagne was served and toasted, Dhamo turned to Maria. "We have known each other a long time. Why did you decide to divest yourself of your brother's port assets? They were very profitable."

Maria leaned forward with serious intent. "It was not an easy decision. I had come to notice many of my brother's holdings worked at cross purposes, and sometimes in actual competition with each other. I no longer wanted anything under my control of a questionable nature. I am sorry this has caused you problems, Ermir, but I had to act in my best interest."

Dhamo leaned back. "It is then a done deal?"

"I'm afraid so. I hope we can remain friends, and possibly be involved in a future business dealing we can both agree on."

"Yes, of course we can. This has been but a minor setback for me because of the suddenness of your divestitures. We will make other deals. What of you, Ms. Madrid? Have you any interest in the business sector?"

Lynn leaned forward, one hand supporting her chin as she answered. "Unlike my friend, Maria, I have no interest in that area. I do have a team of pros who handle my holdings, and I monitor them closely, especially their results."

Dhamo chuckled. "That is very good management. Delegating to competent people is a must. I imagine they don't last long with you if they are incompetent."

"I can make them last for days," Lynn answered cryptically, enjoying the look of sudden tension on Dhamo's face. It was at that moment Lynn knew her Madrid persona was blown. "I make them account for everything they've done, so the rest of my managers will know what to correct."

"Ah... yes, of course. Errors must be gone over with great care to prevent further damage," Dhamo replied, his features relaxing again into a smiling countenance. "Why don't we let the champagne chill while we take a walk along the pier? We can come back after a refreshing stroll and dine together."

Maria clasped Dhamo's hand momentarily. "I really should be going, Ermir. Perhaps you could keep Constance company. I'm sure-"

"Maria... we see each other so rarely," Dhamo interrupted. "Please... let us walk together and talk of old times. I have many stories that will delight you involving your brother. He and I were very close."

"Stay for a while, Maria." Lynn patted her friend's shoulder. "Perhaps your appetite will improve after the walk."

Maria nodded. "Very well. I'm certain I have a few stories that will interest you about Terry too, Ermir. He was a very complex and many times bewildering man."

"Excellent." Dhamo stood up, and his two guests stood with him. "Your brother was very generous to causes he believed in."

"Yes, Terrance Brannigan often supported causes he believed in." Lynn grinned up at Dhamo as they walked out of the barroom. "Anything that was anti-American, traitorous, and harmful to our citizens, your Terry gave generously and often."

Lynn's blunt comment had the desired effect on Dhamo. His mouth dropped open slightly as they cleared the exit in the direction of the Berkeley Marina nearby. Maria laughed, furthering Dhamo's confusion.

"It is the truth, Ermir," Maria said. "My brother made a fortune beyond anyone's imagination, because he lived in the United States. He was a genius, but a perverted one. Terry spent small fortunes trying to destroy the very country that made him one of the richest men in the world."

Dhamo's features took on a cunning look, listening to Maria as they walked. He began looking around as they approached the pier, the many boats an impressive sight under the cloudless night sky. "It surprises me you would talk so openly now, Maria, but you never hinted at such a thing when Terry was alive. It does not however surprise me that you would hold such an opinion, Ms. Montoya."

Dhamo had been reaching under his coat as he spoke. He leaped sideways away from the women while pulling out a silenced Glock 9mm. Lynn grinned, seeing how much time it took him to pull it, and the elaborate holster pocket inside his jacket she glimpsed. Two hands grabbed Dhamo's wrist, while a very dark arm curled around his neck. Only when Dhamo's voice and breath were shut off, did Clint twist Dhamo's wrist to the breaking point while extracting the weapon. A minute later, Dhamo's hands were plastic tied behind his back.

"Damn, Clint, he was like in slow motion. I could have done a vasectomy on him by the time he pulled that thing. Hey, Lucas… I think he's turning blue."

Lucas eased up on his hold with a grin. A limousine rolled along next to the group. "His three partners are on the boat. Spawn and Case are watching them, so if you'll look after our prize here, Clint and I will help round up our new addition to the West Coast Avengers' fleet."

Lucas released the gasping Dhamo to Jesse Brown, who had emerged from the passenger front seat. "Do I have to ride in the back with Cruella Deville, Lucas?"

That question drew laughter and a slap on Jess's shoulder by an outraged Montoya. Lynn ducked down and pointed at the laughing Devon Constantine behind the wheel. "I see you in there chortling away, Dev. I thought we were buds."

"We are, Cruella, get in."

"No knife tricks before we get him on the boat, Hon," Clint piled on.

"Definitely no cuttin' while I'm in the back," Jesse added. "Can we drop you somewhere, Ms. Brannigan."

"No, but thank you, Jess." Maria had been laughing with the rest of them at her new BFF's roasting. "Have a good trip."

"I thought you had my back, girlfriend," Lynn called out after her as Maria walked away. "Shove him in, Jess, if that's not too much to ask of your sensibilities."

"Yes, Ms. Deville," Jess replied while stuffing the still gasping Dhamo into the back.

Lynn slipped in next to Dhamo, patting his leg. She closed the rear door. "We are going to have some fun. I already took my seasick pills, so you don't have to worry about me being uncomfortable while we're going over the details of your slave ring down in LA. We're going to need... well... like everything."

"I will tell you nothing!" Dhamo had his teeth clenched and his shoulders hunched as if already expecting a blow.

Jesse patted Dhamo's shoulder. "Take my advice, partner. Tell us everything before you get on that damn boat with Cruella. My friend, Dev, will record it. Cruella will get it out of you. Save yourself some pain, and spill it."

Lynn threw up her hands. "What the hell, Jess? Are you trying to ruin my cruise? Wait until he hears all the details from the voyage's entertainment director: me. We're going old school on this sea cruise, especially since Lucas is flying with Denny, Jafar, and Case. I'll only have the Dark Lord and Clint with me. They don't give a shit if the boat gets a little bloody."

"You'll get nothing from me! I demand to be able to call my lawyer!"

Dev and Lynn laughed appreciatively, but Jess leaned back with a heavy sigh. "Bon Voyage, meat. Sucks to be you."

Chapter Fourteen: Force of Arms

We had eyes on the boat. It wasn't in a perfect spot, but the fact Dhamo's three partners were on board made up for it. After giving over responsibility for Dhamo to Lucas and Clint, The rest of us concentrated on the boat. Jafar actively monitored the entire area around us, and the likely exit out of the Double Tree. Clint and I cleared all potential sniper nests. I knew Denny didn't want to take these guys in a firefight. The boat could get damaged enough to be unusable for our decoy LA trip we had decided on.

"It is all clear, John. Lucas and Clint just took Dhamo. They're securing him now."

"Any ideas yet?" Denny asked.

"Let's throw the kid in the water next to the boat. He can splash around like he's drowning. Then we'll rush 'em when they come out to shoot him." We could always count on Casey to add the comedic touch. Jafar was looking at him unhappily.

"I was the bait last time. Let John be the bait."

"He's too damn big," Denny entered the conversation more for laughs than anything else. "Besides, John took the first hit in the hotel. He has a fight coming up."

"A little swim won't hurt him." Casey eyeballed me with a big smile. Prick.

"That water's like ice, you pelican."

Casey continued without compassion. "It has that real nice and easy low fantail entry to slip up on. You'll be banging them around in seconds. They won't know what hit them. Besides, you were Marine Recon. I thought you guys were tough."

"Oh, I get it. Delta's the baddest outfit on the planet until they have to get their feet wet, huh Case?"

"Are you going to get on with this, DS, or whine the rest of the night?"

"Damn it!" My toes were curling up in protest before I even got my shoes off.

"I'd say shoot it out and the boat be damned," Denny said. "Unfortunately, Captain Ahab wants to be admiral of his own fleet. That means there will be hell to pay if the shootout gets a little wild."

"Oh no... we can't have that. It's okay though if I freeze my ass off, just so long as the boat's okay for Admiral Ahab."

"I think you have outlined the situation perfectly, John." Casey pushed me toward the end of the pier. "No use in putting off the inevitable. Let's go. Man up."

* * *

By the time I reached the Dhamo's boat in my boxers, I was one cold reserve Recon Marine. I clung to the low fantail, slipping inch by inch up on the platform, listening intently. I could hear them conversing about whether to send someone in to check on Dhamo, but that was vetoed by the other two. I peeked inside the well-lighted interior. Man, it was nice inside. One had his back turned to me. The other two were facing me. All were seated with no guns in sight. That would make sense because they figured to simply collect two women for a forced cruise.

It was over in seconds. I launched in through the open back, grabbing the guy with his back to me and ramming him into the one facing him. That left only the one on my left. He went for a gun in the cabinet next to him. An overhand right dropped him straight to the deck. In seconds, I was in the midst of my two other stunned boaters. I pretended it was ground and pound time. By the time Casey and Denny leaped aboard to help, with Clint and Lucas right behind them, the three Dhamo partners were no longer a threat.

"What the hell, John?" Lucas is staring at me, his hands on hips. Then he gestures at the deck and the groaning crewmembers Casey and Clint were securing. "Did you have to get blood on my deck you big ape. You call yourself a Recon Marine. My God! In my day-"

I wasn't having any. "Shut your pie-hole, Ahab. I took this ship by force of arms. I claim it as is my bounty for my very own. Am I right maties?" Arrrrrhhh..."

The rest immediately began gesturing and talking like pirates in Ahab's face. A good time was had by all. Denny handed me my clothes. I went into one of the three swank heads on board and showered. That was heaven. By the time I came out, Jess and Dev were guiding the very reluctant Dhamo on board with Lynn trailing them. Jess and Dev also were hauling the big equipment bags we'd be taking with us. Jafar was last on board with two more bags. Clint ran over to Lynn, showing her the video of my claim to the boat at Ahab's expense with Jafar, Dev and Jess looking over her shoulder. The four of them were laughing their asses off in moments, with Lynn pointing at Lucas.

"You...you have to save that for Lora. Oh... my... God! That was a classic ace, John. Ahab... you got served, and I can't think of anyone more deserving."

"You'd best watch that mouth of yours Cruella," Lucas retorted. "I want my fleet in top condition. I hold you personally responsible for it to be spotless when you bring it back to its home port next to The Sea Wolf."

"Blow it out your ears, Ahab. John's captain of this prize. How come you didn't have any clothes on, Cap."

"He had to do a sea approach," Clint explained.

Lynn's eyes widened. "Damn. You let them talk you into getting into the bay? No wonder you didn't take any crap from Ahab. I'm glad you and Clint are piloting this cruise. I'd let you bunch do your own interrogating if I had Ahab yapping at me all the way to LA."

Lucas tried to hold his Captain Ahab glowering look of outrage, but lost it, chuckling and nodding his head. "You got that right, Cruella. I'd have you shipshape by the time we pulled into LA." He looked around at the interior of the over fifty foot Aicon Flybridge yacht. "Man, this is a beautiful boat. I wish I was piloting her down the coast."

Lynn put an arm around Lucas's shoulders. "You're piloting The Sea Wolf on my honeymoon cruise, Ahab. You'll be my personal valet, because otherwise, I'm afraid you won't be able to recognize the master cabin after a few days."

I think I saw steam literally blow out of Lucas's ears. He whipped around, clamping Lynn's arms to her sides, and lifting her right off the deck, propelling her squealing toward the fantail. "Don't like the bay temp huh, Cruella? I think a little immersion therapy would be in order."

"Clint!" Lynn screamed out, realizing she couldn't do anything with her legs or arms to prevent what was happening. "Get Ahab, or the next time you get me, you'll need a pill to get it up!"

That threat amused Ahab along with the rest of us. He let her down. Lynn rubbed her arms plaintively. "I'm going to be bruised for weeks, you wanker. That wasn't funny, Ahab. I thought you were really going to throw me in the damn bay."

Lynn put a hand down in the water, yanking it out with a shiver. She looked back at me. "John, you are one big dodo for letting them talk you into doing a polar bear in the bay. I bet it was Case, wasn't it?"

"Of course," I admitted. "It did work, and now I have my own nifty boat. My toes will probably fall off tomorrow. You have a very strange look on your face. What's up?"

"I'm thinking I probably won't have to bloody up the boat after all. I think using Lucas's immersion therapy idea on these quacks will probably be all we'd need for info gathering."

"Now you're using your head, Cruella." Lucas put his seal of approval on the idea. "Hell, waterboarding was always a cleaner method."

The looks of horror on our Albanian mobsters' faces were an indication we may be able to get the location of their slave dens more easily than I thought. "I like it."

Lynn crouched down to look at the Albanians. "Yep. I bet if I cut one up a little, and we drag his ass along for shark bait, the rest of them will want to help us out willingly."

"This is insane!" Dhamo didn't like anything that was happening. To him and his partners, what they had seen so far must appear unreal as hell. "You have us in custody! We must be surrendered to the proper authorities! You cannot simply torture us!"

Jess walked over and put a hand on Dhamo's shoulder. "It's a long way to LA, pal. I hope you wise up before Cruella drags you behind the fantail with your intestines hanging out."

Denny gave Devon Constantine a slight nod. Dev continued the ploy. Of course we all knew it wasn't a ploy, but Denny liked the looks he was seeing the Albanians were trading back and forth.

"Jess and I clean up after Cruella, Dhamo... you moron. We don't even stay to watch what she does," Dev added. "We're not like you guys though. Most times if Cruella gets the info before she gets her knife out, you get a quick ending or prison. I doubt you bunch will ever see a prison, but man, take my word for it: there are things worse than death."

"How can you people do this!" Dhamo was trying to get up. Casey helped him the rest of the way.

"We have a volunteer for the tow line," Case said. He tousled Dhamo's hair. "He would have been my first choice anyway."

"Mine too." Lynn smiled, patting Dhamo's cheek. "He thinks this is all a game we're playing for our own amusement, which in a way is true. Once I gut him, and we're towing him ever so slowly along in the water, Mr. Dhamo here will be an object lesson his buddies on the deck won't ever forget."

I could tell Denny was satisfied with the progress.

"Let's get off, and let them get started," Denny said. "We'll see you guys in LA. You have the satellite hookup, so send anything you have to Jafar. If we can hit those places the moment you reach port, so much the better. Any info you get on the way down will help us cordon off the areas we'll be hitting."

"We've done this route before. With the current in our favor, we'll make LA in about two days," I replied. "I don't want the guys to miss anything when we're trolling for Jaws, so we'll wait for first light before questioning them. Lynn will have targets a little while after that for you guys to confirm. If you find out they're lyin', give us a call, and we'll ask them a little less politely."

"Oh, wait a minute, Dev," Clint said, stopping the group as they were getting off. "You and Jess better let me know what Tommy wants done with his pug while he's with us. We don't want him to miss his training."

"Yeah, brother!" Dev and Jess were enjoying that offer. Dev pointed at my scowling face with enthusiasm. "We'll have T map out exactly what he wants John doing while out at sea. How long can he stay in the water without dying?"

Clint rubbed his chin thoughtfully. "Quite a while. It's probably pretty warm all the way down... maybe fifty to sixty degrees. I figure he could do an hour in there."

"What!?" Okay, this was not funny, although everyone else was laughing except for the Albanians. They still thought they were in the Twilight Zone, which in a way, they were. "I'm not being tortured. What is it you want to know? I'll tell... I'll tell."

"Don't be a pussy, John," Dev told me. "You have to be ready for The Destroyer. Tommy will know exactly the right regimen for you in the water. Maybe Clint can hold the boat steady while Cruella beats on you."

Oh, they were really getting into it now. I grinned. "You remember what happened to Van Rankin when he tried to tap out on me, Dev."

"Bye, John." Dev turned immediately with Jess a heartbeat behind.

Clint was still laughing as the rest of our compatriots cleared the boat, but Lynn looked confused. "Wow, you sure turned Dev's water off. What was that about?"

"Dev and Jess train John. They're his sparring partners. Tapping out means the same as with us fooling around with holds. I watched John's UFC fight with Rankin. Poor old Van wanted to tap out, but the Dark Lord twisted him away from the referee's sight and snapped his neck. I think Dev and Jess probably don't want to test out the tapping out after too many smartass remarks."

Lynn turned to me. "Damn, DL, you killed that Rankin guy on purpose, huh? What was that about?"

I shrugged. "He was blowing kisses at Lora in the audience."

Lynn got a big laugh out of that answer. "Definitely... a killing offense."

"We'd best get moving," Clint said. "You want to drive for a while, John?"

"Sure, but don't think I've forgotten about you butting in to offer training suggestions, you prick. Cast off the lines."

"Are you stupid? I didn't just fall off the turnip cart yesterday." Clint grinned at me. "The moment those lines come off, you hit the gas, and I hit the water. I don't think so."

Damn it. "Fine, I'll cast off. Start up the diesels. You gangsters get down on the deck. Show them their lovely parting gift when they don't comply instantly to orders, Lynn."

Cruella reached into an equipment bag and pulled out a special eighteen inch long nightstick. She fired off an arc. "You boys don't move fast enough, I massage your balls with this. Any questions?"

Dhamo dived immediately to the deck.

"Good boy," Lynn complimented him. "Okay, I think we're ready, but give me a minute to put on some boating clothes."

"Sure, I'll warm up the engines." Clint went forward while Lynn took some clothing into the main cabin.

I watched the guys on the deck. It didn't take a mind reader to know our Albanian Mafia representatives thought we were not only nuts, but that we would do exactly what we threatened. They were eyeing each other, wondering which would pop first. I knew without a doubt Dhamo would tell us everything by morning. Having to cruise along the rest of the night, thinking about being shark bait with your intestines hanging out would make for a very bad night.

The diesels kicked on in a low roar with the usual clanking reverie. Lynn emerged from the cabin dressed in jeans, blue hoodie sweatshirt, heavy socks and tennis shoes. She gave me a little wave. "Cast off, ye landlubber!"

"I thought you agreed I was Captain," I reminded her.

"That's only if I'm not on board, ye varmint! Cast off I say, or feel me lash!"

That was good pirating. "Aye, Captain."

I went out to cast off, looking up at the night sky, the harbor marina filled with boats, the lights on shore. I knew this was not supposed to be a pleasure cruise, but we were going to have some fun when we weren't scaring the crap out of our guests. This was one part of what we do. On the flipside of the same coin we were about to take a voyage along one of the most beautiful coastlines on earth. I planned to lock our Albanians down for the night, and sip a couple up on the fly deck as we coasted along on our way. After that damn night swim to take the boat, I figured I had that and more coming to me. With the lines cast off and secured, I gave Clint a wave we were set. I stayed where I was, enjoying the view, as he steered out to sea. Holding tight to the railing at the bow, the jaunt out of the marina was a good one.

After we reached the beginning part on our route, Clint used the already plotted course entered into the navigation unit for returning to LA. He gave Lynn a quick course on shutting down the boat if anything happened while he and I took care of our duties as prison guards. We gave each one a chance to stretch, use the bathroom, have a little to eat and drink, and whine about their treatment. One warning from Cruella was all it took to curb the complaining. Clint and I then secured the Albanians in suitable manner that they would have needed someone to parachute on board to get them loose.

"You thinking what I'm thinking, DL?"

"I am indeed, brother. This boat is well stocked with sipping whiskey, and mixes. I'm not having a mixer. I'm having a sipper."

Clint agreed. "That's golden with me. Hey, Cruella? What would you like to drink? DL and I are going to sip an adult beverage up on the fly deck while we put the boat on slow cruise. We need the Captain here to come up with a name for our new boat."

"You call me Cruella one more time, pork chop, and... and... oh hell, just bring me a glass of wine."

Clint looked at me with knitted brows. "That's the first time she ever asked for wine. Do we have any wine?"

I went back to the bar. "Yep. There's white or red."

"Go with the red," Clint directed. "I'll get the Jim Beam and our glasses."

It was only five minutes later we were all up on the luxurious fly deck, cruising at a few nautical miles per hour. I wanted to savor these moments tonight. I toasted my companions. "To more moments like this."

"Amen, brother," Clint said.

We sipped with the breeze in our faces, and it was good.

Lynn reached over and popped me playfully on the forehead. "I bet that went right to your toes after the sea attack, huh DL?"

"Correcto," I replied, pouring another.

Lynn sat up. "I figured it would be pretty obvious soon, and this is a perfect time to share it. I'm pregnant."

She stated it in such a matter-of-fact manner, it took a moment to register. Clint dropped to his knees, enfolding the laughing Lynn in his arms. These two must have been planning this behind the Dark Lord's back. Lynn hugged Clint with all her might. It never seemed possible these two would ever reach the marriage stage. Now, they went and skipped right to the kid stage. I sipped my whiskey, simply enjoying these two monsters sharing at least the most touching moment of their lives. The incongruous fact Lynn could walk down right after announcing she was having a baby, and cut the heart out of a trussed up Albanian made this scene so surreal as to be unimaginable... for most people. For me, it seemed just about right.

I reached over and clasped Lynn's hand. "Congratulations. You know you didn't have to come with us. Clint and I could have handled this."

"What, and miss announcing it here in a setting like this? I couldn't think of a more beautiful place to tell Clint. It's a boy, by the way. I'm not much of a mystery fan. I needed to know, so I could get my head around it."

Clint stroked her face. "You're amazing. Did the doctor say anything about possible complications?"

"Nope. All the inner parts are working fine. I'm not far enough along to have an amniocentesis test done yet. I missed a period, and checked right away. I'm only about five weeks along."

"Between now and our clearing up this slave trade mess, with my next fight tacked on, you'll probably be into your third month on the honeymoon cruise at the rate pork chop here is setting up info on our prospective hit."

Clint took my jab with a grin. "You forget we're still waiting on support from Senator Braxton. She's being very careful, in spite of Denny garnering some very important figures at our back thanks to recent successes. The whole op is ready to go with or without her help. Denny already received a guarantee for drone support when we hit the home base. We're playing hard to get right now, letting the hook float for the time being. I'm figuring you and I will go in and light up the target, once we make initial contact with the Wolf. I'll even make sure you have a wetsuit this time, John."

"Gee, thanks."

"I don't like that our honeymoon cruise hinges on the Dark Lord surviving his fight with that damn yeti," Lynn said.

"They write John off all the time," Clint replied. "He'll be okay."

"Thanks, brother."

"Besides, Denny said if he gets killed, we'll train Dev to fill in."

I listened to the two of them yuck it up over Clint's ace. "Good one."

"I don't like the name of this boat: Tirana. What the hell does that mean," Lynn asked.

"It's an Albanian city the mobsters down below seeped out of. That's our next order of business." Clint filled our shot glasses. Lynn refused his offer of more wine. "I think we ought to go with your cage name: The Hard Case."

"Nope. I'm christening it Lora. Tommy already thinks I'm pussy-whipped, so that will really piss him off. Besides... I am pussy-whipped."

When we finished laughing at that one, Lynn leaned over and patted my hand. "I heard from Lora that you're flirting with the young moms on the way to taking Alice and the Sparks' Twins to school. Want to confirm or deny that accusation?"

"I have a couple of the aforementioned moms flirting with the Dark Lord. I do not flirt back, but Lora's Minnie-me rats me out as if I do anyway. She gets a kick out of her Mom nearly going mental, trying to figure out which one it is by Al's description."

"I'm never letting Clint walk the boy to school."

"Huh?" Clint nearly spilled his shot. "You don't trust me?"

"You're weak, and I'm vulnerable to violent action. It would be too dangerous."

Clint chuckled. "Okay, I can understand that reasoning, but I think being a mommy will round off your edges a little. I'll probably have to fight for time on your schedule with my kid."

"It's neat listening to monsters talk about being mommy and daddy monsters."

"Think of it this way, DL," Lynn pointed out. "The kid won't be afraid of monsters in his closet. He'll be afraid for the monsters in his closet. He'll be warning them off." Lynn pantomimed her son huddling on the bed pointing at the closet. "Clint junior will be like 'don't come out of there if you know what's good for you, or my Mom will slice you up like sushi'."

That was funny. "Yeah, I can just imagine the PTA meetings with you two in attendance."

The satellite phone rang next to me. It was Denny. He cut right to the chase. "Forget about turning over those four. Jafar found a property out in the desert owned by those maggots. Case and Lucas went out to investigate. It's a burial ground. We called in the local PD with cadaver dogs. They've dug up eleven bodies so far, even with it being night."

So much for the lighthearted night cruise. "What would you like, Den?"

"Never to see that bunch walk the earth again. The cops have issued an all points for them, but they have no clue where they are. Make sure they never find out. I don't want those bastards getting three hots and a cot for the next twenty years while this chicken shit state wonders what the hell to do with them."

"Understood. We'll call you with the other info if Jafar doesn't already unearth it."

"Talk to you then."

I looked at my fellow monsters who had been listening in. "Let's get the info, and put them down if it checks out. That sound okay?"

"That works for me," Lynn replied. She held up her wine glass. "I'll have a bit more, cowboy. The kid won't care."

* * *

I got up at five, and nearly ran into Clint. He grinned with a wave.

"Time for the prisoner's last meal, partner."

"Yeah... boo hoo."

Clint laughed. "That pretty much describes my feelings. You know Cruella is secretly hoping they won't tell us anything."

I stuck out my hand, and Clint gripped it. "Great news last night, brother. Lynn is one hell of a woman. She'll never be saddle broken, but she'll have your back forever."

"That's how I see it." Clint shook his head. "I'm going to be a Dad. What universe can that be true, Uncle Dark Lord?"

"Right here in River City, partner. You have the house with the picket fence and a hell of a dog. Now you have the final piece to the puzzle coming soon. How's the master cabin?"

"Oh man, that is nice. Although I haven't been allowed to see it, I hear the master cabin on the Wolf is even better."

"It is indeed. Let's go take care of the dead men, and then have coffee up on the fly deck."

"Oh yeah." Clint led the way.

* * *

Lynn paced in front of our Albanian mobsters with impatience. She had a full night's sleep, her hormones were raging, and she knew these guys couldn't pay back in full for the horror they had caused. "Okay, boys, here are the facts. Take them any way you want. We've found your burial ground in LA. I won't sugar coat it for you. That means the death penalty. It's Davy Jones' locker for the four of you."

Of course the howling, moaning, and denials went into hyper drive, which we had anticipated. Clint went down the line, stun gunning each one of them into silence. They were not happy boys, but we weren't conducting this exercise to make them happy. Lynn waited for a few moments while they vibrated and writhed on the deck. Then she began to methodically kick each one of them until they got the silent message to kneel in line quietly.

"Now that I have your bullshit out of the way, let's get started with the deal. If we immediately get all the information about your operation, slave houses, and drug deals, we'll take you four up on the fly deck. We'll put you in comfortable chairs with the sun and the sea to guide your miserable monstrous asses to hell peacefully. If we don't get what we want, or you lie, I will skin each one of you alive. Then we will bait you behind the boat, letting the salt water make you scream, just before the sharks arrive. This is not a court of law. We know all of you are guilty. We've found your killing grounds. What? You turds think we'd just let you walk if you told us everything? Forget it. Easy death… unimaginable death? Take your pick, because I will get started in the next few minutes no matter what."

She had them. They believed her. I could tell they wanted to beg for their lives, but when Lynn stares at you with the easy death/unimaginable death face, you get the message she doesn't give a crap what excuses you have for what you've done. Save your breath and decide. They decided to go out with the sun in their faces. It took a bit longer to find out if what they gave up was the truth, but Jafar mapped it all out before noon. Lucas and Casey confirmed the information without tipping off the bad guys. It took longer than anticipated with cementing in the facts given us by our Albanians. It didn't matter. Whether our mobsters died in the sun or the clear night sky really wasn't all that important.

Once we found out they had given us everything involved in their slave, weapons, and drug trade, we then moved on to the financials. We had Laredo standing by in Oakland. Once we relayed the info to him, he transferred all the Albanian money in offshore accounts into our private holding funds. With that final exercise, Clint and I transferred the Albanians into their final seats. Then the outrage began.

"You are all common thieves!" Dhamo spat on the deck as he was placed in his seat.

I picked Dhamo back up, smashed him face first into his own spit, and then swiped up the residue with his face. I had to use his body for a mop as a final clean up, but his buddies got the message. We could play a while longer if they wanted. After reseating Dhamo, I grabbed his chin as blood, sweat, and tears trickled over his face.

"You have anything else to say? One more word and we put you on the towline anyway, so just speak or shake your head no."

Dhamo shook his head no, clamping lips and teeth tightly together, looking down at his feet. The rest were seated quietly. It was a beautiful night. The boat rocked gently. The three quarter moon looked awesome, and the stars were spectacular. Clint administered their guide potion into hell. We didn't stretch it out. We were anchored far enough away from the coast, it would take a long time for the bodies to miraculously make it to shore anyway, but we took precautions. Clint and I stripped them, and cut them open before tossing them into the ocean. We stayed where we were until the bodies gathered a finned audience before leaving.

The three of us once again took up our positions on the fly deck that night. I was happy, because we'd been too busy with the prisoner handling for Tommy to get through for training directions. Tomorrow would be hell in the water, but today was a day without torture for me or the bad guys, and only one slight attitude adjustment at the end. I told Clint and Lynn about how many fingers in the pie Brannigan actually had, including the Harvard serial killers.

"It's a shame we weren't able to take Brannigan on a sea cruise," Lynn said. "Why is it Denny's having us continue to LA? With all the locations zeroed in he could turn the operation over to the locals and FBI."

"He doesn't want the treasure trove of info those clowns probably have all over the place getting trampled on and lost," Clint answered. "We have to get into port tomorrow too. I've been monitoring messages and texts our deceased Albanians have coming in. I passed the codes over to Jafar, so he's taken over the receiving end on all of them. I'm sure Denny saw what I saw. There's another bigwig in the mix, probably the guy running the operation down there. Jafar was on to him before we even started on these guys this morning, so I didn't mention or ask. I let them ramble. They named everyone but that guy."

We had a conference call before the interrogation with Denny while Lynn was still sleeping. The Spawn was on top of every angle as usual. "Denny wants this Ardian Shala brought in hard, and without any official witnesses. Jafar found his residence, so he's first on the hit parade. Maybe we'll take him with us when we sail The Lora back to its new home port."

"You're taking the first hit when we go after Shala, right DL?"

"No, Cruella, I was thinking we'd lead with your butt this time covered by Kevlar. It's a much bigger target."

Clint couldn't save me. He was rolling on the deck, incoherent for the moment while Lynn launched. She couldn't get near me, and I didn't spill a drop of my Beam. I knew I could miss a training day.

Chapter Fifteen: No Mercy

"Tell Tommy I'm getting the hell out of the water! There're sharks!"

I had been in the damn ocean for nearly forty-five minutes, changing strokes as Tommy ordered with Lynn as the relay torturer. I could tell she was still thinking about the butt comment from the previous evening.

Clint was on deck with the sniper rifle. "Man up, DL. I'll get them before they get you."

"Sharks attack from below, you pelican!" I saved my breath. I know my lips were turning blue. I'm starting to think Tommy wants me to swim all the way into port. Clint's laughing at my 'Crocodile Dundee' name calling.

"Okay, Sissy, you can come out of the water," Lynn says.

I drifted back toward the fantail, and hopped on board over the shallow fantail. My teeth were chattering. Good Lord was that water cold. Clint threw me a thick robe from the clothing we'd found on board. I hit the showers instead of trading one-liners with my jovial pirate companions. They had enjoyed my training way too much. I could tell Tommy had been studying strokes. I always figured Tommy swam very well. His knowledge of varying strokes proved it to me. I taught his kids how to swim like fish, because of my expert status. Tommy mixed in the right strokes for strength and endurance. When he had me switch to the butterfly stroke; that was a killer, especially the length of time he had me do it.

I walked up on the bridge where Clint was driving. Lynn was right next to him getting a lesson on the controls, gauges, and navigation. "Did Denny pick us out a dock?"

"Yep," Clint answered. "He wants us to come in hot at Dhamo's normal docking point."

"No shit?" That adds a degree of difficulty to our porting in LA. "He does realize there may be people around expecting to see the Albanian Sopranos, right?"

"He has Casey and Lucas scanning the docking area with great vision all around that we're coming in on. Denny suggested a rather neat approach if we get a greeting party, which seems likely since the big boss has been trying to unsuccessfully reach the Albanians. Denny thinks Lynn and I should walk nonchalantly off the boat. When confronted, we tell them we bought it from Dhamo."

I sat down. Maybe the long training session had dulled my wits. "What in the hell would that ploy accomplish?"

"Denny thinks that Shala will meet the boat," Lynn announced, giggling at my open mouthed reception of that piece of info.

"Oh… my… God… our ship is porting in more ways than one." My mind's racing now. No assaults on well-guarded villas coupled with an opportunity to cast off right back out to sea with the kingpin. "Good Lord, could that possibly happen?"

"We're attacking, DL," Lynn replied. "When we attack good things happen. It makes sense Shala doesn't have a clue what happened between Dhamo and Maria. He knows communication at sea unless he wants to get onto a regular channel would be risky. In other words, Shala doesn't suspect anything, John. Dhamo normally docks at the Esprit in the Marina Del Rey boat docks."

"If he arrived standing at the dock awaiting our arrival we could do pretty much anything we wanted, including Lucas and Casey taking him before we even pulled into port. We'll have to dock, stay incognito for a while, and then wait for Mr. Big to make his angry appearance," Clint added. "If he doesn't know what the hell is going on, he will be pissed. You can bet he's tracking our GPS signature, thinking he's being dissed."

"How far are we away?" This was so good.

"We're about half an hour out," Clint replied.

"Well, okay then." This puts all of this in a different happy perspective. "If we can get Mr. Big, it means Lynn can make him her bitch, which means we can visit all his holdings with him fronting us. Man, that would be much easier than attacking each one of these holes. Now, let's talk safety. We want as few people in front as possible. I can cover you with the sniper rifle during the meet up to give Case enough time to get into place too."

"Clint and I can take down these assholes by ourselves unless he brings a small army," Lynn said. "The first one that talks after we give them our cover bullshit gets put down hard. We can adlib from there."

Clint shook his head. "John's right, Prego. We need to do this in a careful manner with backup."

"I don't think I like pet names about my condition, especially when they sound like you're calling me a spaghetti sauce. Okay, careful will be how we do it. We don't want to wait until these mutts start drawing guns. Then we'll end up without any prisoners."

"So, you'd rather get this Shala, and have him escort us around to his holdings, John? If there are multiple sightings of him in our hands before he goes skinny dipping, there might be complications."

"I see what you mean, Clint." I paused, trying to think like Denny, gave up, and called him. "We're almost in port. I thought it might be good if we had Shala out front letting us into the bad places. Clint pointed out it will make for more sightings with him in our hands. I have to defer to the master on this."

"No chances on that asshole," Denny answered. "Take him at the dock for a day cruise. Take his buddies with you, dead or alive. They've uncovered seventeen corpses. Jafar in tandem with Laredo has hacked his mainframe, so I'm not as concerned about missing data. Shala has only one holding area for his kidnapped girls. We have it zeroed in. If things go right on the dock, I'll give over everything but the girls to the FBI and locals to hit. We'll take his holding pen. Everyone in there dies - no deals, and no mercy. I'll work with some contacts to shelter and nurse the girls until we can return them home or help them get back to their lives. Laredo confiscated enough money to repair everything but their minds. I'm sure Shala will add to the pot."

I looked at the grim faces of my cohorts, and figured Denny was right about that. "We'll call with updates, Denny."

"We don't know when Shala will be in, or how he's coming, so Case and Lucas will be on line with you at all times. I'm sure we can give you at least a ten minute heads-up on his arrival. We'd take him before he gets to you, but it will be a much cleaner snatch if the three of you can take them aboard, and then disappear."

"Ten minutes would be fine."

After Denny disconnected, Lynn smile at me. "Does this mean an extra ocean training session? I figure you can go swimming just before Shala does, and warm up the sharks for him."

"Tommy won't know we're not in the middle of the mission." It was lame, but I had to try.

"He'll know," Clint replied.

"Damn it! You two can be really hurtful."

227

* * *

"Did you really call Tommy?"

Clint laughed. He and Lynn were cleaning the railings and fantail, dressed casually in jeans and pullover shirts, although Lynn's were jean short-shorts. Casey had called in Shala's arrival a few minutes before. They were playing the parts of new boat owners. "No. He called me, but it was funnier letting John think I actively ratted him out. Did you see his face when I handed him the workout Tommy outlined to me?"

"He was one unhappy Dark Lord. I would never have gotten into that water. Those damn sharks looked like they were measuring him for a snack. Tommy had him going for a hell of a long time." Lynn stopped wiping the railing. "I don't want a damn boat if I have to wipe it down constantly."

"Jesus, Lynn, you've only been wiping it for about three minutes. You do know that babies take a lot of upkeep. There's tons of laundry, changing diapers, a few baths a day, bottles to wash, and you have to do it all on nearly no sleep."

"I thought once the Mom pops the kid out, the rest is up to Dad."

Clint moved over to run a hand up the back of Lynn's thigh as she leaned against the railing, letting it come to rest on her hip. "I'll be there for you... right behind you."

Lynn giggled as Clint demonstrated the movements he planned to be right behind her with. "You're not very well informed, cowboy. There is no sex after the kid arrives. Check your manual."

"I'll check your manual." Clint enveloped Lynn with both hands working inappropriate endeavors in front.

"Hey, you two!"

Clint slipped off to the side of Lynn as he turned to face their new visitors on the dock. The one out front of the other two was Ardian Shala, a little under six feet tall, thick brown hair, clean shaven ruddy complexion, and stocky of build. The two men with him were both over six feet, heavyset, with buzz cut black hair, and mustaches. All three wore suits as if they had come over from a business meeting, complete with ties and shined shoes. Clint gave them a little wave.

"Hi guys."

Lynn turned, leaning provocatively against the railing. The three men switched their attention to Lynn with more than passing curiosity. "You guys are sure all dressed up for the docks. Is something wrong?"

"Yes. We would like to know where the owner of this boat is," Shala stated. "Is he on board?"

"Oh... you mean Mr. Dhamo? He sold the boat to us at the Berkeley Marina. He told us about the berth it had here at Espirit. We decided to take her out for a spin to LA. It was a gorgeous trip along the coast."

Ardian Shala's mouth gaped open for a moment. "That... is impossible. He could not have sold you The Tirana!"

Clint looked at Lynn in surprise, before returning his attention to Shala. "We have the papers and title, Sir. Come aboard. I have them on the bridge."

"Very well, but it was not his boat to sell. He could not have done such a thing. Lead the way. I would look at these papers of yours."

* * *

I put away the sniper rifle, and picked up my MAC 10. The moment our guests were aboard, I slid down behind them from the fly deck. I made enough noise to invite a quick turnaround.

Clint and Lynn moved in opposite directions for their weapons, leaving the firing range and arming themselves. Shala and his men went for their weapons until noticing they were staring at the MAC 10. They raised their hands. Truthfully, they should have drawn on me. This meet up would not be going well for them.

"What is the meaning of this?!" Shala was of course outraged. He turned to look over his shoulder in the direction of where he had last seen Clint and Lynn. Clint was off to Shala's right holding another MAC 10 on them diagonally with Lynn covering them from the opposite side. "Do you know who I am?"

Lynn giggled. "I can't believe he pulled the 'do you know who I am card'. Hardly anyone does that anymore. Yeah Ardian, we know who you are. You're all under arrest. Get on your knees, hands clasped behind your heads!"

They didn't move fast enough, so Lynn zapped the one nearest her with her stun-gun. Our models are like cattle prods, only stronger. The guy hit the deck in a writhing ball of anguish.

"That was your last warning. Get on your knees or I put you on your backs!"

Shala and his still standing minion dipped onto their knees with hands clasped behind heads. "You three will pay for this outrage in blood! I am Ardian Shala. I can have you and everyone you love dead inside of twenty-four hours!"

"Gee, Dark Lord," Clint said. "I think he really means it. Whatever will we do?"

Lynn was already plastic tying the one she had stunned after stripping him out of his suit coat and tie. Clint did the other two quickly. We then helped them up and onto the plush seating together. I took pictures and sent them.

"I mean every word I say!" Shala hissed that line out between his clenched teeth, his face a new very strange shade of red – angry red, pissed off red, murderous red. "Let us go or die!"

"Holy cow," Lynn said, standing in front of the men with her hands on hips. "I almost don't know where to start. Clint, we should take a break and think about this while DL does his training session."

"Oh, you are so funny, Cruella." Not even a little bit. Clint thought it was funny though. Prick. Confirmation came a moment later on the pictures I had sent. Denny called.

"You have the right guys, John. The two with Shala are his long time enforcers, Rudi Dabulla and Filpa Kraja. That Shala showed up with those two meant he really planned on showing Dhamo how pissed off he was. It also means no one has a clue about Dhamo and his boys."

"Thanks, Den. Get back to you shortly."

"Well, Denny-light?"

"They're the real deal. I'll go steer us in the direction of the open sea. Let me know which one you want to skin first."

"We're under arrest!" One of Shala's buddies, Kraja, is beginning to get a bad vibe about what was happening to them. "You must take us to jail, where we will be allowed to contact our lawyer."

"Rats!" Lynn sighed. She walked over to run a finger over each one of their cringing faces. "He asked for a lawyer, guys. We're cooked. Our hands are tied. It doesn't matter that they've been running a slave ring, drugs, and illegal weapons center. Now we won't be able to find out anything about the burial ground of innocents they've been filling."

"We know nothing about what you speak of," Shala stated. He's beginning to lose his outrage after hearing he and his men are going on an unasked for sea cruise. "This is a misunderstanding. Do not leave this docking area."

"Did you hear that, DL? You can't leave the dock."

"Yeah, Cruella, I heard." I started the engines while Clint cast off, and then steered The Tirana out to sea. I didn't stop until we were about three miles out. The sea was a little choppy, but the sun was out – another beautiful day for a cruise. I found a nice spot. We had decided on dealing. Lynn didn't want to mess up the boat, so she was going to do a quick slice and tow. Clint and I agreed. We figured it would only take one demonstration.

I went back with the group. "As you can see, we're rule breakers. We have a deal for you, since none of you will be seeing land again. If-"

The howling started immediately. They yipped and yapped about rights, arrests, lawyers, and Shala even pulled out the Geneva Convention card on treatment of prisoners. It was a riot. Once we had gotten as much entertainment value possible from the doomed mass murderers, Lynn shut them up with our high tech cattle prod. I went on.

"If you tell us everything about everything, I'll confirm it with our land force. If you all are truthful, we have a nice view and a hot shot for each one of you to take your final peaceful step into hell. The good part is it is very pleasant and painless. The bad part comes if you tell lies or refuse to be helpful. Then my associate, Cruella Deville, does what she does better than anyone."

Lynn gave me a dirty look before making her knife whip around a few times in a terrific click-clacking exhibition of a master with the butterfly knife. "Watch this guys."

Lynn lightly moved the blade tip up the guy's shirt closest to her. The material separated as if it were tissue paper. "I name my knives. This is my skinner. I can take the outer layer of your epidermis off with this so the skin peels away in my hand like saran wrap. Let me show you. Clint, if you would be so kind."

Clint threw Ardian Shala on the deck in front of his two mates. I held his feet, while Clint secured his upper body. Lynn did a wonderful impression of a surgeon concentrating with great care on a patient. She ran that damn tip along Shala's body from his neck down. His shirt and undershirt parted over his struggling body in a separating wave of material. It fell away, revealing his naked, heaving chest. A thin, red line left an illustration of Lynn's expertise. She smiled up at the two still seated men.

"See, I even left a marking line for my first cut. Watch carefully, boys. I'll take a nice little swatch off of old Ardian. You cannot believe the pain when the air hits, and we pour a little salt water over it."

Lynn gagged Ardian with a piece of duct tape, and pulled on surgical gloves. Then she proceeded to cut a three inch square off of the muffled screaming Shala, his head arching up and down, side to side. With utmost care and rock steady hands, Lynn separated the thin skin layer off in nearly a perfect square. She held it up for Shala to see proudly. He passed out. Kraja started to speak, but Lynn waved him to silence.

"Patience, bubby, I haven't gotten to the really neat part."

I revived Shala with a little ocean water. He became conscious in a frantic state of readiness to do anything Lynn wanted him to do, but he was the example both for his compatriots about what was in store for them, and proof Lynn had no problem whatsoever carrying out the chore. I handed her the small bucket half filled with salt water, as I remained across Shala's legs. She smiled at Ardian and then at Kraja and Daballa.

"Here it comes, kiddies." Lynn poured the salt water over Shala's skinless middle area. He bucked with his head banging up and down on the deck without letup. The keening whine of muffled agony went on without letup behind the duct tape. Cruella sighed contentedly. "Now that's how it's done. Want a taste?"

"I will tell you everything I know... everything!" Kraja was sincere.

Daballa stared at the writhing Shala still in stunned silence at Lynn's performance. Lynn waved a hand in front of his face.

"Hey, Sweet-pea, you still in there? How about it? Want to be helpful?"

Daballa met Lynn's questioning stare with utter horror. He nodded.

I quickly cleaned Shala's wound, and put an analgesic salve covered pad on the wound and taped it on. Compared to what he had been experiencing, it was pure bliss. He gasped. He sobbed. Lynn straddled him with her death face.

"Okay, I know your cohorts here are going to be very helpful. I need you to convince me you are too, or the bandage comes off, and your buddies get to watch me make you into a science project. What'll it be, before I get bored and reintroduce you to my little friend, Mr. Skinner again?"

Shala was convinced. "I... I tell everything."

"Good boy. Here's what we start with first. You give me all your off shore account numbers, and I'll have my transfer team make sure you're being helpful."

I smiled. Even facing what Lynn had in mind for him didn't get Shala immediately reciting account numbers I would be recording with his directions for access. Mr. Skinner made his click-clack appearance.

"Bored now. We need another demo. I-"

"No! I will tell you!" Yeah, Ardian's face had the look of someone ready to tell.

It took nearly an hour to finish getting his accounts and access tricks, including the actual transfers with Jafar and Laredo working in tandem. We hit the jackpot. His accounts totaled nearly seventy-five million dollars. By the time we had everything done with the accounts, Ardian was done. He talked for the next hour about everything under the sun, allowing his cohorts to fill in spots with him. It was the stuff of nightmares. We stuck to our original bargain after sending the information to Denny, and getting final confirmation. Shala gave us a few new leads to keep watch over in the future, and a very helpful connection to the Sinaloa Cartel I'm sure Denny received with much enthusiasm. The disposal of our blasphemous cretins, guilty of atrocities no human being should be guilty of performing on innocents, were recycled without incident. We did demonstrate just how blasphemous we cretins working for the innocents could be. That would have to be our silent satisfaction as we watched the shark recycling unit at work.

We docked at Dhamo's docking space once again. Denny, Lucas, Casey, and Jafar were waiting for us this time. They came aboard for a meeting. Denny wanted a quick debriefing before laying out plans for us concerning the site where Dhamo held seven women awaiting shipment to buyers. All of them were under eighteen. I had made coffee, and we all sat down with cups in the spacious cabin area. I recapped our events since last seeing them. It wasn't pretty, but Denny wanted to know the details of how our interrogation worked with Shala. Yes, we keep track of the most efficient ways we could get needed information. In this case, the disposal method would be considered seriously in future operations.

"Damn, girl, you are good," Lucas said. "I like the way we don't have to risk anyone witnessing anything concerning the info gathering or the disposal."

"The House of Pain has been a mainstay," Casey added, "but it was always messy. We have the Marina nearby to park The Lora. We'll need some armament added. It's not as friendly to alterations as The Sea Wolf, but we can probably add a machine gun nest, and have a couple of hand launchers aboard."

"I'll take care of it when we get her back up north," Denny replied. "Let's move on the warehouse they have the girls in tonight. I've let Sam Reeves know about our other targets. He'll coordinate the hits on them with the locals. The holding area is located in the middle of the East LA projects. It's watched and manned by a gang calling themselves the Zombies. Nothing fancy. We hit them, collect all on scene data, and take the girls with us. I have a backup team who will take care of them after rescue. No one knows about our hit. As far as the FBI is concerned, we've found drug and weapons depots with connections to the Sinaloa Cartel. Our hit will be passed off as a gang war."

"What kind of guards do they have in place, Denny?"

"In daytime, three," Denny answered. "At night, they have two, John. I'm figuring silenced sniper rounds for them, MAC 10's inside for the rest. Jafar has the layout."

Jafar handed printouts to each of us. They came complete with 3D pictures of the warehouse building from all sides, and a breakdown of the floor plan inside. "I highlighted their probable holding area. It has partitioned offices I believe they would use for the girls. Up front is where Lucas and Casey said the heat signatures and noise are coming from."

"They're pretty lax, John," Case said. "After Lucas drops the guards, you, Clint and I can go right at them, while Cruella goes for the back where they're held. You have a fight coming up. Want me to take point?"

"Considering the makeshift training Tommy came up with for me while at sea, I'd rather have an excuse to take the time off on the way back. I'll lead."

"What training you talking about?"

"You should sail back with us, Lucas," Clint said. "Tommy has DL in the drink for a hell of a long time, including shifting strokes. It's brutal."

"Clint and I throw chum in the water until the sharks start gathering," Lynn added. "Then DL hits the water, and out swims them for almost an hour."

That description was well received. "It's not as funny when the sharks do start joining the training session for real. Clint lets them rub against me before he even goes to get his rifle. Anyway, I'll take point. We'll hit them at 2 am when it's less likely they're still moving around. Are you sure it's safe to let Lucas try and get two guys at once, Case?"

"Oh, real funny, meat. I think I'll talk to Tommy about some in the water strokes to add, and I'll come along for the ride. You need to be agile in the water, and I think dodging a poking grappling hook would be just the exercise addition needed to get you into top form."

I ignored the enthusiastic approval of Lucas's plan. "Tommy would never try and pull that on me." I could see on their faces, especially Denny's that they knew as well as I did Tommy would embrace any new torture addition without a moment's hesitation. Damn it! Me and my big mouth.

Chapter Sixteen: The Darkness Works

We considered flash-bangs thrown in to disrupt the inside crew, but figured it too paramilitary for the gang hit façade we were hoping our rescue would look like. We dropped Lucas off where he had the high ground with line of sight on the guards he had already picked out during the recon he and Casey had done. Jafar monitored all communication, both ours and theirs. Denny drove us on a slow direct approach. The two guards popped up from where they lounged at the entrance as our lights bore down on them from up the street. Both bodies pitched backwards with their heads pulped.

Denny speeded up his approach. Before the SUV came to a halt, we piled out of it, masks in place, weapons ready. I tried the door. It was unlocked due to them believing they had it guarded. I led the way in. Shots rang out almost immediately. Bullets chipped the cement at my feet, and I felt one clip my leg as I started weaving. So much for the big target ploy. Clint and Casey fired bursts from behind me with their MAC 10's, as Lynn ran for the back of the dimly lighted warehouse.

I spotted the room off to the left with two dead men in front of it. A third man exited the door as I reached it. I plowed into him, tearing him off his feet, and back through the door he had exited. Three more were in the large entertainment room. It was apparent we hit them a little early. One of the men fired wildly, peppering his own guy I had gripped in front of me with 9mm weapons fire. Two more bursts from behind me silenced all gunfire. I threw down my human shield and raced for the back with Casey and Clint behind me.

* * *

Montoya ran in a zigzag pattern toward the rear warehouse area lodging the girls they hoped to rescue. She concentrated totally on the shadowed area ahead, ignoring the gunfire erupting behind. Her thoughts jumped from the single entrance door ahead to the growing life inside her. She smiled, thinking of her unborn son - just like everything else in my life, this will be tough to explain, kid.

The door ahead slammed open against its hinges, disgorging two men with what looked like AK47 rifles. The lead one pointed his at Lynn a split second before his head turned to pulp. Montoya dropped to one knee and fired three rounds into the second man, as Lucas's second shot from the position he had taken at the warehouse entrance took out a third man emerging from the doorway. No other attackers revealed themselves as Montoya again continued on to the doorway. She went left through the doorway, rolling into a firing position.

"Drop it, bitch or I blow her fucking head off!" A shadowy, hulking figure held a squirming teenage girl in a headlock with his head next to hers.

Montoya fired without hesitation, her hollow point round slightly disturbing the girl's hair as it passed a millimeter from the side of her skull. It smashed into the man's forehead, opened like a flower, and turned his brain into jelly. His corpse pitched backwards, pulling the girl with him, his last grip loosening as she fell on top of him. Seeing no one else other than the girl's screaming companions, Lynn ran forward and scooped up the girl into a comforting embrace. She retreated with her to the wall near the door, awaiting backup while scanning the room for other targets, her Glock at the ready. Lynn made soothing noises to the sobbing girl in her embrace thinking again about her impending motherhood - your Mom did good on this one, kid.

* * *

I ran by two guys with half a head and another with three dead center holes through his chest. Inside the room, girls were screaming and sobbing. The only enemy I saw as Clint and Case bracketed me was a guy with an extra hole in his head. Clint spotted Lynn with a girl in her arms, and raced over to cover them both. It looked like a very good day until a guy popped up all the way on our left where there were filing cabinets and debris strewn around. I charged him because he had an AK47 in his hands he was bringing to bear on us.

I blocked the burst, my momentum keeping me on track right through him. I saw stars, galaxies, comets shooting through outer space. My vision honed to the asshole's face, his AK47 burst unable to stop my charge, but rapidly driving me into the gray, grainy seepage of unconsciousness. A split second later I bulldozed him into the wall behind us, where he and I banged into it with force enough to send his AK47 clattering to the floor. Then, I had my hands around his neck. I perched atop him as we slid to the floor, the darkness descending through my single minded purpose with a vengeance. The last thing I heard was the sweet reverberating crack when I sent my last bodily commands to limbs which soon seemed no longer a part of me.

* * *

I was drowning. I gasped, spluttered, choked, and coughed as I imagined my cold, lifeless body descending to the ocean's murky bottom. A big dark hand smashed across my face as I blinked, Lucas's grinning skull coming into focus.

"He's okay. Get up, you big pussy! What the fuck? A recon Marine eats AK47's for a snack between meals! Tommy's right. You need toughening, boot-camp. I think an hour and a half in the water might get you tuned for the fight coming up. Otherwise... maybe we can forfeit."

I rolled to my side, as darkness receded, Lucas's insults beginning to draw laughter from the audience watching my recovery into sanity. "I...I'm right here... you no good... rotten... lifer asshole! You... you and me... you prick!"

I got up on hands and knees with Lucas howling right over me, laughing so hard, his annoying barking laugh drowned out everything around me. I took stock of the little things, like sharp pains or weakness in the limbs I methodically motored for damage. The darkness receded. I grinned, seeing my victim's sightless eyes staring at me in the horror of death, knowing where his road to the afterlife lay. Lynn knelt next to me while I maintained a solid knees and arms posture with the floor, putting a comforting arm around my shoulders.

"Jesus, DL, you took a load that time. Thank you."

I nodded, because talking normally wasn't going to happen for a while yet. Sounds were beginning to flow slowly back into my perception. I could hear Casey making jokes to our kidnapped girls, which from their sporadic laughter must mean he was a hit. Clint offered me a hand up which I took without comment, but with much appreciation. I breathed in carefully and back out while taking stock of my standing position. I kept my hands on knees, still a bit foggy, but improving by the second. A team of half a dozen men and women dressed as doctors and nurses catered to the kids we had found, leading them out with a wide berth around us. Denny played guide, directing traffic. It looked to be a good night in spite of a couple of minor pitfalls.

I straightened, enduring the last wave of dizziness the absence of breath over a space of time causes. It felt fine when I flexed my arms, twisting slowly in each direction to detect any rib issues. I had reinforced my usual Kevlar coating, hoping to pad it enough so as not to end up incapacitated and unable to fight The Destroyer. By the feel so far, I had padded it adequately. The girl I assumed was the one I had glimpsed in Lynn's arms momentarily before I opted for human target status, ran over to Lynn before she was ushered out of the building. The girl sobbed, hugging Montoya. A softening of features I had never seen before flowed over Lynn's hardened lines. She stroked the girl's hair, whispering I'm sure the assurances of common decency and compassion. The girl nodded solemnly, wiping at her eyes before turning toward the nurse waiting for her. Lynn stopped her. Clint, sensing Lynn's intent, handed over a notepad and pen. Lynn gave the clairvoyant Clint a little slap of gratitude. She then scribbled on it and pressed the paper into the girl's hand. That elicited a smile and small wave as the girl allowed the nurse to guide her away.

Denny walked over as the last of his medical team left with the girls. "That's a wrap on LA, except for what Jafar finds laying around the warehouse here. The kid's been screening your calls too, John. He says that Kevin guy's been trying to reach you. What Kevin guy?"

I told the Halliday story for them, complete with Kevin's interpretation of his meeting with the Buffster, Kensy Talon. My audience ate up my pantomime of Kevin dealing with Kensy along with the aftermath. "I'll give him a call now if Lucas is all done calling me names. He's mad because I won't let him have The Lora for his fleet."

"That was mutiny. You should have been whipped with the cat-o-nine tails," Lucas proclaimed. "Your latest sissy act confirmed you need stern guidance to get you back on track."

"Throw all the hissy fits you want, Ahab. I took The Lora by force of arms. I can't wait until we take the Wolf out for some more action in the Gulf. I want to see how she holds up under heavy fire."

"I'll lash your pansy ass to the bow so you can take the first hit."

I laughed with the rest and walked off to the side with my i-thingy on. Kevin answered on the first ring. "Hey, Kev, how's your new career doing?"

"Mr. Dubrinsky is a great guy. He has everything filed and legal, John. We've already filmed the pilot episode he sold to a producer interested in an LA based reality show spotlighting our bond retrieval agency. We've been doing shadow work for him too, checking out insurance fraud cases, and leg work. I...I'm sorry to bother you, but I need your advice. Dan wants to film us taking in an ex Hell's Angel named Les Tavor tonight. He got a tip Tavor would be meeting a dealer outside the Hotel Erwin near Muscle Beach at midnight. We'll be filming it as a segment with all the shadows and low light. I think it's a bad idea."

And then some. "I think you're right. I thought you bunch were going to do things like Chad outlined for you. That seems to be going well if you already have a pilot show done. Didn't he squash this Hell's Angel idea?"

"Dan didn't tell him, and I'm under orders not to discuss it with him. This Tavor guy jumped bail on weapons and drug charges. Kensy's supposed to take lead again. She says she won't do anything stupid, but the Buffster has a little adrenaline junky in her. Hell, Kensy's not even healed up from jumping me. Another thing... I'm in love with her."

I smiled. This goofy gig had all the signs of a disaster. Kev was smart enough to know it, but loyal enough to go along with it. "I'll help. You caught me at a good moment. I'm down in LA now. Did you get Kevlar for all your goofy friends like we talked about?"

"Yeah, I... shit John... you mean it? You're really down here? Dan's going to get us all killed. I was just hoping for some advice."

"It just so happens, some operations we're involved with went real well. We're all done, and I don't want you and the

Buffster hurt or killed. Go ahead and do whatever the hell it is you have to do. We'll set it up for you, but don't proceed unless you hear from me things are okay."

"Thanks, John. I won't forget this... ever."

"If my plan works, this apprehension will go very smooth. It will be your job to make sure that Dan guy knows it was a setup, and you would have all probably been killed doing it for real. You did say Tavor is an ex Hell's Angel, and not an active member, right?"

"Definitely. Tavor was banned because he got his club in trouble, and was skimming money from some of their operations. They'd kill him if he shows up on their doorstep."

"Good. I'll take a look at this and call you later."

"Thanks, John. Would... would you consider being my best man?

Well damn. "That serious, huh?"

"Yep. I'm going to ask her to marry me if we live through this dumbass stunt."

"I'm in. Once we get you through this, call and let me know where and when."

"I hope Tommy can come too."

I chuckled. "Believe me - Tommy wouldn't miss it for the world. Remember not to move on this unless I give you the go ahead."

"I won't."

* * *

"That's the story." I finished telling my crew all about the Tavor mission.

"I've got him, John." Jafar looked up from his notebook computer. "I have an address for his alias in East LA. I tracked his cell-phone calls. He's with his girlfriend."

Clint cuffed our youngest member on the shoulder. "Damn, kid, you're scary good."

Jafar smiled. "I learned from the best, you and Laredo. Are you all going to do this?"

"It means a cruise on The Lora, our new pleasure craft, so I'm in," Casey said, grinning at the death stare he got from his partner, Lucas. "Force of arms, Admiral Ahab, force of arms rules."

"I'm in," Lynn seconded the mission. "I want to see the Buffster in action after I tune up her projected collar."

"I go where my son's Mom goes," Clint stated, which naturally led to absolutely shocked congratulations, with Denny leading the way.

"This is incredible." Denny hugged Lynn. "What the hell did you volunteer to charge the holding area for, you goof?"

Out came the butterfly knife she calls Mr. Skinner. It whips over her wrist a few times in expert fashion before ending up in attack mode. "I'm a working Mom, Boss. Want a demo?"

Denny laughed, his hands in placating form. "No thank you. I'm just saying that if you want to take a break from the active end, you can."

"A monster is not what I emulate, it's what I am. Do I sometimes feel compassion? Yep. Do I want to go on extended leave? Nope. Clint knows me, and he damn sure knows how to keep me." Lynn molded into Clint's embrace, her eyes as she looked into his momentarily, saying everything there was to say about the subject without a word. "We know the risks. We know the danger. You and John formed something up North no one in his right mind could imagine, Denny. It's hilarious in some aspects:

monster daycare, assassins are us, drop off a toy for the Marines Toys for Tots and pick your own sanction for Christmas. Yeah, I know if Lucas hadn't blown the head off two of the kidnapper gatekeepers I wouldn't be standing here. Yeah, we all know if John hadn't rushed that asshole popping up with his AK47, maybe a couple of us wouldn't be breathing. We are what we are. There may be tragedy ahead, but I can't think of anyone I'd rather share it with than you guys."

Lucas walked over and hugged Lynn. He placed a Marine Corps pin in her hands. "I've carried this since 'Nam. Give it to your son, and pass it down, or whatever. I'm making you a recon Marine. You're the best at what you do, young lady – ain't no doubt about that."

We all saw her tear up as she hugged Lucas back after looking at the pin. "Thanks, Pappy, I'll try to make sure you never regret giving it to me." She wiped absently at the tears trickling down her cheeks, chuckling with a shrug. "Sorry… it's the hormones raging. Let's go help the Buffster."

* * *

Les Tavor screamed in horror as Lynn cut a thin line down his naked body from neck to groin, blood welling up, as he lay bound on The Lora's low fantail platform. Clint and I had him in a death grip. He wasn't going anywhere. Lynn smiled and waved.

"Hi, sweetie! Guess what? We bundled you up here because we have an acting job for you. It involves a little bit of playacting you won't like, but I'm sure once I explain the awards to you, everything will be fine. Let me introduce my team. We're the most deadly nightmare you could ever imagine having. If you do what we tell you, then all you get is some time in jail. If you don't, we'll feed you to the sharks, either now, or later when you don't do what we ask. Any questions so far?"

Tavor saw he was out to sea in the middle of what he figured was nowhere. It didn't take much imagination to figure he was in trouble, especially since I Gronked him the moment he answered the door at his girlfriend's apartment. We could have done it with a Taser, but we wanted him feeling that right I put upside his temple. It had swollen a little, but hopefully wouldn't show during filming. I could hear muffled amusement behind us as the rest of our crew enjoyed entertainment where it was offered.

"Wha...what do you want?"

Lynn detailed for him what he needed to do to make us happy. He didn't like it.

"Who the fuck are you people?! You can't just-"

Lynn kicked him overboard off the fantail platform. It was near dusk, but enough light illuminated the waters we figured the sputtering Tavor would see why bleeding in the water offshore was a bad thing. Lynn bobbed him up to the surface on our tow line so he wouldn't drown. Tavor begged, pleaded, and offered to do anything in order to get out of the water. Then the fins showed up as Lynn kept him bobbing against the boat.

"Oh baby! I think our bait here is attracting some attention."

One of the sharks brushed up against him. Tavor screamed.

"Anything! I'll do anything!"

Clint and I tugged him out of the water just in time. A shark bumped the boat's fantail, teeth showing. We of course didn't give a crap whether the shark got him or not. If the shark got him, there would be no video episode. If he did what he was told, then Tavor would go through the California justice system. No matter what, he'd be on our list. I hate unintended circumstances, so we would be monitoring him. I'm thinking by the look on his face I won't have to worry about Les. He seemed ready to do anything not to touch the water again. He had already seen we didn't mind doing anything we needed to for persuasion.

"Don't! Don't put me back in the water! What is it you want me to do? Tell me! I'll do it!"

Lynn hunched down, peering into his eyes doubtfully. "I don't know, John. What do you think?"

I played the bad guy in this one. "He's not missing any pieces yet. How will we be sure he thinks we mean business? Let's dangle one of his legs until Sharkey grabs something."

Instantly, Lynn had knife in hand. "Right or left?"

"The show... the show won't be right! Keep me whole! I'll make your friends stars!"

"He's right, DL," Clint said. "We better let him do a take in person. The Buffster won't look very appealing if she's taking down a guy with one leg."

"Yeah! That's right! I'm wanted... right? I'll make her look good!"

I shrugged. "Okay. Let's head back. It will be a catch and release day today. We'll hold onto you until it's time for your performance. It better be so good, I'll want to applaud at the end, or you'll be going for a night swim."

* * *

We all watched from our comfy stretch limo I rented for this momentous occasion. I served the champagne, even to Les. He was staying with us while the Hollywood Bounty Hunters did their low light, staged arrival with the guys jumping out impressively from their action van. Kensy Talon, better known as the Buffster, rushed to the front, dressed all in black leather. Our boy Kevin strode uneasily after her, dressed in matching black leather. With their cameraman shadowing the stealthy approach to the meeting spot, we listened to their dialogue while kicking back in comfort.

"She is so cute! Oh my God, I don't watch TV much, but if this program makes it I will definitely tune in," Lynn said. "You outdid yourself on this one, DL. If the Hollywood crew ever needs the pump primed for a show count me in."

Les had been guzzling the champagne. I had refilled his glass a couple of times. He was getting paranoid again, even with the reassurances we'd given him. "Look... I get what this is. If...if I mess up a line or something, you guys won't put me on the boat again... will you?"

Lynn turned to stare at him. He immediately switched his attention to his feet. "Look, Punky Brewster, all you have to do is go out there, and make the takedown look real. Growl a little bit. Make a few hand gestures of defiance. Let the Buffster wing it from there. From the looks of her, she couldn't hurt a fly anyhow. Protect your nuts, give up, and let them cuff you. Don't make me have to come out there and stop the scene, Les. If I do, the sharks will be the least of your worries. You've been doing real well. Now you're starting to annoy me, and that's a bad thing. If I get cranky, your chances of ever seeing a jail cell or another day on earth go right in the toilet."

Les drained his champagne and nodded energetically. "Growling. I can do growling, and then go with the Buffster's lead. No problem. I'll throw in a couple of bad guy words, and grunt a couple of times in pain."

Lynn smiled and patted Tavor's cheek. "That's better."

"They're almost ready, Les." I opened the limo door for him. "Skulk along down the sidewalk and then approach them looking big and mean."

"I got it. I won't let you down." Les dived out past me, took a deep breath, and jammed his hands into his pockets with a scowl in place.

"Perfect, Les. Go for it." Man, this was entertainment.

We monsters watched the proceedings with nearly childish enthusiasm as the forces of darkness and light met up on the sidewalk in front of the Hotel Erwin. The tattooed Hollywood boys spread out in impressive form, muscles flexing, with the lead couple of Kensy and Kevin moving forward to confront the hulking form of Les Tavor. Jafar pointed our audio pickup perfectly.

"Les Tavor!" The Buffster called him out as the group confronted their target. "We're from Hollywood Bond Enforcement. You missed your court date. Get on your knees, hands clasped behind your head. Do it now!"

I've got to hand it to Tavor. He looked up with a stunned expression, playing along.

"It's a mistake. You… you have the wrong guy."

"You're Tavor," the Buffster reaffirmed, as the rest of the crew moved into a semicircle around their target. "Don't make this a hard takedown."

"We need popcorn next time," Lynn whispered. "Damn, John… this is so good. Les is a natural."

"After the last minute coaching you gave him, Cruella," Lucas pointed out. "I'd be more willing to give kudos to the director."

Lynn laughed as Tavor retreated, his hands up in placating form, growling impressively.

"You assholes don't know who you're messing with! Get the hell away from me." Tavor grunted with attitude, his hands coming up in fighting form.

The Buffster launched with a sidekick to Tavor's midsection, bounced off, hit the sidewalk on the rebound, and cried out in pain gripping her right leg. Kevin Gronked Les with a perfect right cross that put Tavor on the sidewalk out cold. The limo erupted in laughter. We were howling. Every time we tried to focus on the scene, Kevin's horrified mug while holding his injured Buffster sent us back into spasms of hilarity. It was incredible. Then I spotted the real life drug dealer we'd forgotten Les was meeting with.

I was out of the limo in a split second with I'm sure most of my crew right behind me. I didn't bother with anything fancy as the guy gawked at the movie making extravaganza taking place in front of him. He came with two enforcers. I bowled into him full force, taking him to the cement with attitude. Clint, Casey, and Lucas put the enforcers down so fast their features didn't register anything other than surprise.

I made shushing noises to them. "We're filming here. Stay quiet."

One of the enforcers thought he needed to illustrate his badness. "Let me the fuck go! I-"

Lynn smashed him right between the horns with her Glock handle. "Shut the fuck up during filming or I will cut your dicks off! Understand!"

They had no idea what the hell Lynn was talking about but nodded without comment. We watched across the way as Kevin held the injured Buffster in his arms. It turned out to be only a slight hurt on the fall, and they ended the scene with their perp in cuffs. When I was sure the scene was over, I came over to check on our prop bad guy, Les. He was just coming around from the snooze Kevin had administered. He focused on me with horror.

"I...I didn't mean it! I would have-"

"Relax, Les. That was perfect. We're square. You did really good. You do understand the rest of our deal, right?"

Les nodded. "No mention of any of you. No claims of innocence, and absolutely no sharing of this scene other than reinforcing it was real... and... I'm on your radar."

I grinned reassuringly at him. "Yep, you have it just right. Keep it that way, and you don't ever have to meet up with my crew again. I'm sorry the actual scene got a little violent."

"It's all good," Les assured me. "I should have gone down quicker. I...I'm not experienced with this acting stuff."

"I understand, buddy. You take care now. Straight and narrow for you, or we will find you."

Tavor looked away. "I'm done. When I get out of jail, I'm through with my old shit!"

"Good plan. I hope you stick to it. The alternative won't be to your liking."

Les turned to meet my gaze. "I understand. You people are one fucking scary bunch."

I chuckled. "You don't know the half of it, Les. If you did, the next time I saw you, you'd be a priest or a Salvation Army member."

Les nodded. "My act's done. Who knows? Maybe I can be a movie bad guy."

"See, now that's the kind of thinking I like to hear about."

"Hey... thanks for the champagne. It helped."

"Straight and narrow, Les... straight and narrow."

* * *

I checked on our drug dealer and his enforcers. Lucas, Clint, and Casey had already disarmed the three banditos. They held them in reserve in case the scene needed more on screen time. I could see Lynn over making friends with the movie crew. They had seen our takedown of the three interlopers. Jafar and Denny were together in the limo running names and faces, so the rest of us walked over to the impromptu movie set.

"This show is a hit!" Lynn was excited as the rest of us joined the group. They were making sure everything filmed okay, because they could correct small errors easily on the scene. Lynn patted Kensy's shoulder. "You are so cute. I like your fronting the group, but you need to switch to weapons rather than physical interaction, kid. Listen more to Kevin here. He's been around the hard knock department, and he loves you. Take my word for it. That kind of advice is what you give credence to."

Kensy smiled with a pained expression. "Kev warned me not to do it. He told us everything was set. I need to learn how to listen. I watched those 'Kick-Ass' movies too many times, and forgot real life doesn't always emulate Hollywood."

"That's a start, young lady." Lynn patted her shoulder. "Even with your slight attack problem, with Kev finishing off the bad guy, it added tension and realism. Your producer will eat this up. John told us how you and Kev met. It was a little like when I met my partner, Clint."

Kevin perked up. He had been eyeing Lynn with the uneasiness of a guy who knew he was in the presence of a cold blooded killer. "Really?"

Lynn nodded, and sighed. "Yeah. He was assigned to find out who was slicing and dicing serial rapists. He caught me tuning up one of them."

"Oh." Kevin exchanged wide eyed looks at that simple declaration.

"Now, I'm having his baby, so hang in there you two. Rough beginnings may take extra work, but you two look great together, don't they, Clint?"

"Very entertaining," Clint spoke up from where we were keeping hold of the banditos. "I like the matching leather outfits. I agree with Lynn. This show will be a real hit if you stay within the guidelines John's friend gives you. I love the chemistry between the two of you. Just be careful with what you try to do."

Daniel Atkins walked over then. "We could have handled Tavor."

Casey laughed. "You couldn't handle a fart in the wind, partner. John kept you bunch from probably getting gunned down in the street." Casey gestured at the drug dealer and his two goons. "These guys were packing heavy heat, and you can bet they weren't going to lie down and put their hands behind their backs on command. We all had a good time, and it worked out, but if you're going to continue leading, Dan, you better get a clue."

"He's right, Dan," Jerry Sooner agreed. He and his other mates had been looking over the three banditos. "We would have been killed. Hell, Kev scattered us in seconds by himself. I think we really can make the big time with this show, but we have to stay alive to do it. Thanks for all your help, Mr. Harding. We should have run this by you and Mr. Dubinsky before setting it up. Thank God Kev called you when he did."

"I'm always around for a consult. Just call my partner Tommy or I if my friend Chad wants a second opinion." I clasped Danny boy's shoulder. "I know you want this gig to work, but you need to think things through or you're going to blow it for everyone."

"I want us to be more than pretend," Dan replied.

"You might do just that if you take it slow. It's not bad theater to get the bad guys in on it where possible. When you find them, see if they'd like to playact a bit before giving themselves up. Hell, if your show does well in the ratings, some bad guys will want you bunch to take them in. They like the spotlight as much as anyone. Figure out your bottom line and how much it would take to sweeten the pot if they're receptive to giving up with a little playacting."

"You're right. Maybe we could buy a little safety. I'll be more careful about picking jobs too." Dan held out his hand and I shook it. "Did you guys really think the show rocked?"

"You had us all riveted in place, and the humor was low key and hilarious, especially Kev's face when his precious Buffster hurt herself."

That drew more laughter, with the Buffster hugging the cringing Kevin. Kensy suddenly turned to Lynn, gripping Lynn's left hand in both of hers. "Wait! I know you now. I saw you protecting the Afghani girl that speaks out for womens' rights. You had a wig on. You really shredded that guy who threw the shoe."

Lynn pointed a finger at Kensy. "Do what I say, not as I do, you little brat."

Kensy laughed. "I hear you. You're bigger than I am. I bet Dan would love for you to do a guest appearance. We'd break viewing records."

Lynn smiled. "You're beginning to annoy me, kid."

"Think about it, Lynn. If we get the right opportunity, you'd be the badass ringer that shows up and rocks the bad guys' world."

"Kensy's right, Ms. Montoya," Dan agreed, being respectful, because he knew who Lynn was. "You would be an instant hit, with fans of the show calling for more appearances."

"I'll think about it, but you bunch have to stay alive long enough to make the show a hit. I admit it's kind of fun thinking about something as whacky as that, but my boss Denny's head would probably explode if I ever got that kind of notoriety."

"I thought John was your boss." Kensy looked confused, as did her companions.

I turned that question away. "That part is another gig, Kensy. We have to go. We'll take the drug dealer and his buddies with us for the time being. Take Tavor in, and treat him with respect. He's a bad guy for now, but he played his part real well. He might be a good consideration as an addition to your crew - a bad guy turned from the dark side, when he gets out of jail."

"Damn! That's good." Dan looked over at Tavor with a different perspective. "Ex Hell's Angel, turned from the dark side – I like it!"

Maybe I should have been in the movie business. The Dark Lord, agent to the stars.

Chapter Seventeen: Preparations

I swam the Bay water with pissed off determination. Not only had my boat, The Lora, been confiscated by Tommy, Devon, Jesse, and Jafar, I was now being tortured next to her on a daily basis. The assholes fished, brought aboard dependents, partied, and made sure I was miserable – all in addition to a barrage of full contact ending exercises using my board striking ploy. The last couple of weeks since we had made shark bait out of the drug dealer and his friends due to unexpected crimes we found out they were guilty of, the guys were making my days hell on earth.

After long periods of time in my inadequate wetsuit shell, I batted the pokes I got from my sadistic training crew almost instinctually. Naturally, this made for constant stress in the water, because any poke getting by my guard, caused an intake of seawater, along with the resulting choking spasms while getting my breath back in the midst of a redoubled attack from all hands on deck as punishment. Consequently, I was in the best shape of my life.

Some added problems cropped up after our return to home base. My Russian mobster friend, Alexi Fiialkov had been fired as The Destroyer's handler and agent. The same Middle Eastern contingent that had handled my former foe Abdul, The Terrible - The Syrian Slayer, bought out The Destroyer's contract at Subotic's insistence. As is his way, Alexi said nothing about the setback. I know he doesn't want a war with Subotic's new owners. It did place a shadow over the process now, because the new backers would probably buy their way into controlling the refs, as well as the judging panel. It's all exciting to me. I had my crew with me no matter what. I'd be prepared. That Subotic thought I'd be a stepping stone to taking my place on the UFC docket was just business. Losing Alexi from the mix did not bode well. We had other operations depending on our continued fraternization. Besides, I liked Alexi.

I plodded into the last realm of my ocean torture, letting thoughts of my present day logistics and enterprises keep me occupied. At least I didn't have to do 'The Bump' with some Bay Area sharks this session. I'm an admitted idiot. When I get bumped, I want to get me a piece. It's both my plus side thinking, and my minus side thinking. If this shit with training is stuck in Tommy's head, I will end up ridin' a shark like they do in those island type places. Then I notice it. With my excellent peripheral vision, I see Tommy sneaking into position for a hurtful strike. I grin and wait like a big shark. Tommy leans too far over, lances at me, and I don't block the strike – I grab it. Rolling with the striking pole I see Tommy's look of stunned anguish as he lets loose of the pole, and loses his balance. Oh yeah!

Tommy hits the water, and comes up in sputtering panic mode. Then it dawns on me. Tommy can't swim. I approach him carefully. Tommy's a big guy, and rescuing panicking big guys in the water requires caution. His hyper moving arms and feet are keeping his head up for gasping breaths, but he's stunned. I hold my hands up in placating form.

"I'm right here T! Focus, brother. I'm with you. Relax on your back! I got you!"

Hearing my voice, the panic leaves Tommy's face. He knows I'd die before letting anything happen to him. He lets himself go, arching into a back position. I move in immediately and balance him. "That's it, brother! Relax. The boat's right next to you. We'll have you out in a second."

Realizing what was happening, Tommy had all hands on deck ready for extraction. They had him on the low fantail of The Lora in seconds. I thought well okay, a shortened training episode from hell. Wrong. As I tried to follow Tommy up onto the fantail, the ungrateful prick bops me in the forehead with gasping admonition.

"Where... the fuck do you think you're going, meat?"

My short lived ray of hope was squashed in an instant. Damn it!

* * *

I came out of the shower, feeling marginally better. The guys were all fishing with pretty decent results by the looks of our ice chest. My sparring would of course be the next part when the pirates I sailed with finished their fishing time. Tommy glanced up at me with a grin. I pointed at him with attitude.

"Why the hell didn't you tell me you couldn't swim? Where's your life jacket?"

The guys laughed, but I didn't plan on this being a he-haw. "I want to know right now if you other three dodos know how to swim, and how well."

"My people don't swim," Jesse answered.

Devon laughed, but raised his hand. "I can swim real well. I guess I'm the exception to Jess's 'my people' comment."

"My people don't swim either," Jafar added to more laughter.

"New rules aboard this boat – life jackets for all. Even expert swimmers panic when they hit the cold ocean water in this area, especially when land is out of sight. Shit, Jess, if your big ass ever fell overboard, we'd have to tow you back to port."

More laughter.

"That was one quick grab and roll, John," Tommy said. "You may hate this training ploy, but a reaction time like that after being in the damn ocean ice water is hell of impressive. I'm beginning to like your chances against the Destroyer. If we can get your secret leg strike working more than seventy percent of the time, it's going to be a long night for Subotic."

"I feel uncomfortable with you getting optimistic, T. Next thing will be you saying I can knock him out."

"I said I like your chances. I didn't say I'd lost my mind. Tell the Dark Lord what his chances of knocking out Subotic are guys."

"Sorry, John, not happenin'." Dev shook his head. "Jess and I saw the Big O hit him flush on the nighty-night spot. He didn't even blink. Subotic has one of those skulls made of iron. Stick with the leg strike."

"And whatever you do, brother, don't let him hit you." Jess porked me, knowing I block far too many punches with my head.

"Your ground game is as good as anyone I've ever seen, but we don't know how well Subotic does on the mat. No one's taken him there yet," Tommy added.

"I have watched his YouTube fights many times," Jafar spoke up for the first time. "He has cement stanchions for legs, John. His opponents try to get him off his feet, but cannot do it. Plus, he punches downward with horrible power."

"The kid's right," Dev said. "He can knock a guy out with either hand striking down. If you try a takedown, you'll need to drive him into the cage first, so he can't unload on you."

At least we're talking out my future demise. "Let's head back and get the mat time in."

"This boat's great, John," Tommy replied. "It's even better because you took it off Captain Ahab. At least we have a craft we're allowed to use."

"If I'd known you guys were going to turn my life into a living hell with it, I'd have blown it up."

"You know this is great training," Tommy replied. "Besides, Lora has her name on it. Even Ahab can't take it away now. It's a beauty. We'll obey your lifejacket rule though."

"Doing ocean cruises when you can't swim seems a little odd to me."

"I don't need to do any swimming with my pole in one hand and a beer in the other, John," Jess informed me. "Hell, you swim well enough for all of us, but lifejacket it is from now on. I didn't like watchin' T floundering around out there like a harpooned tuna."

Laughing at the conversation while keeping an eye on his notebook computer, Jafar kept typing in broken spurts of frenetic finger movements.

"What the heck are you into, J?" I moved over to get a look at his screen. After a moment I wasn't smiling anymore. "You have the big fish on line. Damn."

Jafar glanced up and nodded. "Clint, Laredo, and I are taking turns playing our Sinaloa Cartel oil scam gang. They like the money we've been flashing due to our recent acquisitions. They're hooked. I doubt they believe any law enforcement agency could have the financial accounts we have in place. The questioning now from them is more on a personal basis with our cover couple. Clint's handling that. I feed in suggestions when I see something he can use. This is the fishing I've been doing. We let them play out on the line a little, and then draw them back tight."

"Are you guys any closer to getting an invitation at sea?"

"Done deal. We haven't set a date, because we're playing hard to get. Clint wants them begging us for a meet up. Not having a deadline really helps. We're monitoring their activity closely, because we don't want anything happening to the people they have already taken."

"Man, that's good work, kid. It looks like Ahab will have to leave port for a change, instead of sitting on the Wolf at the dock, shining the railing with one hand, his deck chair with the other, and shining the deck with his special waxing slippers."

"You really got him good taking over The Lora, John," Jess said. "He hates seeing us heading out to sea every day under your flag instead of his. I think he makes sure he's on board The Sea Wolf early so that he can monitor us when you're getting taken out to be tortured by Tommy."

He's right. "Yeah, the prick always has a smile and wave for me when we leave port. You guys holding up fishing poles and beers always brings the frown back though. I don't understand why he doesn't just come along. Casey's usually with us to pour salt on the wound, but I think Suzie's reigning in our mate Case a bit. He has to appease his woman. Take us in, T. Let's get the rest of this crap done so I can pick up Al from school. I'm going to break a couple boards today, boys."

"With your defense, Dark Lord, you'll have to if you plan to make it out of the first round."

Boinked again. "Gee, thanks T. You'd better leave the pole poking to your fellow ingrates here. I'm thinking if you don't, you really will need a lifejacket."

"We're done with the poles," Tommy replied with a wave off for me. "We'll be using bean bag guns from now on."

"I'd rethink that statement if you don't want to eat that bean bag gun, partner."

* * *

Alexi waved at me from his seat at the far end of the bar. I nodded while saying hi to my numerous police acquaintances in The Warehouse Bar. Marla tended bar. It being a Friday night, she had her hands full, but a big smile and wave for me.

"I'll put your usual by your partner in crime at the end of the bar, Champ."

"Thanks, Marla. It'll sure go down good tonight after that sadistic session Tommy put me through today."

"He needs to if you want to live through that fight tomorrow night with Bigfoot."

I nod appreciatively as my police department buddies enjoy Marla's sendup of my prospects in Saturday's late night matchup. "I have a more optimistic view of my chances than all of you do apparently. No hard feelings when I knock the prick out in the first ten seconds, right?"

By the immediate ongoing laughter, you'd have thought I told the joke of the decade. Damn. I need to work on my bar presence. I should walk into the bar with a glowering menace all over my features like my old buddy Van Rankin used to do... before I killed him in the cage. Maybe that would get me a little fan consideration. I shook hands with the smiling Alexi Fiialkov.

"It is good to see you, John."

"I figured when you called you must have gathered all the ins and outs of this fight tomorrow night, my friend. I'm sorry Subotic wasn't smart enough to stay away from that conclave from the Mideast. I bet the new Al Jazeera America network is happy though."

Alexi chuckled. "Yes, they are quite pleased. While no other network can televise an illegal betting fight forum in the Oakland warehouse, Al Jazeera will do it anyway with no fear of retribution. I admit to having planned on exploiting that very fact. The Mideast group is well connected, and capable of carrot and stick tactics I no longer pursue. They reached Demetrius through religion, pulling the infidel card. Demetrius is a devout Muslim. I tried to explain religion and this fight game have nothing to do with each other, but his family and friends have been pressuring him to have nothing to do with unbelievers."

"I'm surprised you didn't yank the rights for using the renovated fight building." I toasted Marla while sipping the double she'd placed in front of me. I chased it with half my beer, and enjoyed the feeling right down to my toes.

"I have a contract with them for overseas rights. I do not cut my nose off to spite my face. Your fight tomorrow will be profitable. I wanted to meet with you here, because my contract with them allows for their choosing of the referees and judges with stipulation they have certified credentials. I will look closely at them, but money is a very unruly participant in the process. I was allowed to make a valid recommendation for referee. I chose our very capable Jack Korlos. Whether they accept my choice or not is unknown. I will fight their bringing in of a ringer, and I've told them so in no uncertain terms."

That's good news. "Listen, Alexi, if I can get Jack as a referee, I don't give a shit what kind of ringers they pick for the judges. We both know if the fight by some miracle goes the distance, I ain't getting any decision. At least if Jack's the referee, I won't have some asshole stopping the fight every time I get a strike in."

"Good. I am happy you do not look at this through rose colored glasses. You will not win a decision, but no force on earth can get Jack to play this out any other way than the up and up. It is the main reason I hired him exclusively. He is an honorable man."

"You got that right." If I lose, it won't be because Jack Korlos screwed me. I threw down my shot with real optimism. Marla was watching as I finished off my beer. She replaced both. "Good Lord, Alexi, I hope you can pull that off. I'll owe you one."

"If you allow me to continue to have your ear for future ventures, that is all I ask."

"That's a no brainer. I'm sorry Demetrius turned out to be such a naïve idiot."

Alexi took a large gulp of his own drink. "Yes... it was an oversight mistake I will never allow to happen again."

Boy, if I was that Mideast contingent, I'd be very careful about anything with a thread back to Fiialkov. When you deal with him straight up, he's a good business man. If you break contracts with him, he never forgets, and he has contacts that can haunt someone he doesn't like forever. Even we don't know how he infiltrated Interpol, but his connection has come in handy. When someone can upstage Denny, the Spawn of Satan, you can bank on them being more powerful behind the scenes than in front of them.

"Jafar told me you're feeding logistics to him about our upcoming voyage. I want you to know we appreciate the help."

Alexi nodded. "It is a small thing, John. I have interests at cross purposes to the gang fronting for the Sinaloa Cartel. If your team is successful in its endeavors, I will proceed with acquiring some oil interests in the area. I have held off, because the cartel makes honest business pursuits nearly impossible. I would not be surprised if they are allowed to continue, they will eventually develop a pirate force out in the Gulf of Mexico. I have word of your new boat acquisition. It is a very fine craft, but an extremely uncomfortable training tool."

He got a chuckle out of me on that one. His sources were right on as usual. Alexi had eyes on everything, even us supposedly clandestine people. "Tommy is doing his level best to get me ready to fight Subotic, including using me as shark bait. The guys have a great time taking the boat out while Tommy tortures me."

"As well schooled as I am concerning your training, conditioning, and preparation, I'm afraid I will be refraining from making a wager on your fight tomorrow night, my friend. I do however wish you all the luck in the world."

I finished my Bud and Beam. "I wouldn't turn down a little luck."

"True, but that is a bloody poor sport for relying on luck, John."

"Amen to that."

* * *

My Oakland PD friends Enrique Rodriguez and Earl Taylor worked the door security for the fight. They waved me over as the line of people paying top dollar for this throw-down began doing catcalls and shouting out mean, hurtful stuff about my chances in tonight's bang-a-rama. The folks who like me can't afford the entry fee on a night like this. This bunch had lost money on me in the past, and had a few favorites lose to me in violent fashion. I waved at them while walking with my entourage of Tommy, Devon, Jesse, and Jafar. Lucas, Casey, Clint and Lynn would be watching the fight too, but from the audience. It never hurts having some of the most dangerous people in the world around if things got a little out of hand.

I spotted tonight's masters of ceremony, Jim Bonasera and Ray Alexander. They both had their cordial smiles pasted in place to welcome me. Ray stays back because he knows Tommy hates his guts, and I'm not real fond of him either. That he's lost a small fortune betting against me always brings a smile to my face. Jim Bonasera at least had always given us an even break in the past. They used to run everything until a slight miscalculation led to them being owned by Alexi Fiialkov, along with their enterprise. I at least knew they fronted for Fiialkov's interests rather than the Mideast contingent.

"Good to see you, John," Bonasera said. "We have locker rooms and everything since the last time you fought here. It was one of the keys to continuing with foreign broadcasts of the fight from our location. I'll guide you back."

I looked around in amazement. "Our own locker rooms? Well... okay Jim... lead on. Hey Ray, aren't you going to give me your usual blessing?"

Alexander's face twisted into a mask of discontent. Then he grinned. "Sure. You're goin' down tonight, pug!"

"Thanks, Ray. I hope you bet lots of money on The Destroyer. I'll feel better if I lose that way, knowing you recouped a small portion of the fortune you've lost betting against me."

My crew laughed, except for Tommy. My partner smiled at Alexander's smirking mug. "One day I'll see you out on the street when no one else is around, snake. If you see me first, run."

Ray was going to fire off some cheap thug remark, but his better sense kicked in. "No need for any remarks like that, Tommy."

"Remember what I said, Ray."

I put an arm around Tommy. "C'mon partner, I want to see my new locker room."

The old warehouse had gone through another upgrade since I had fought here last - fresh paint, more plush seating outside the cage, increased lighting. They even had a huge monitor on one wall showing UFC fight highlights. Yep, my old dank arena was gone - no more rattling sheet metal walls, or the ever present odor of blood, urine and desperation. Things change. No use getting maudlin about the place I could possibly get my brains beat out in. Besides, I had a locker room.

Bonasera led us through the contingent of well-heeled fight fans. Actual waitresses were serving cocktails from a brand new sports bar area near the monitor. It was hard to dislike what the old arena had become. I glanced back at Tommy. We grinned at each other. We'd come a long way, but only in terms of furnishings. My friends Devon Constantine and Jesse Brown were looking around wonderingly in the same manner as me and Tommy. They had thrown hands in here too when the place wasn't much more than a big shed with the only additive a filthy blood stained mat for the ground and pounders. No matter the flavor of the night, it was good to be home, my ass on the line, and friends at my back.

I explored the new locker room like a kid on his first trip into a comic book store. The guys shadowed my movements because they were just as impressed. "This is so nice. I want to make sure I don't mess it up by getting blood on the floor. Maybe you guys should plastic wrap me on the way to the shower."

Tommy grabbed me, with the other guys laughing at my admonishment. "Listen, Dark Lord! You're going to win this fuckin' fight! If you lose and I have to look at that asshole Ray Alexander's face gloating, I'm going to kill him on the spot. Do your part to keep me out of prison."

I grinned. "There's no use in sugarcoating this for you, T. We knew the time might come when I'd get carried off the mat or out of the cage. We have a plan. I'm not afraid. I go out there and trade pain with the Destroyer, just like I did with Dev and Jess here. That's how it's done. We have Jack Korlos for the referee. Asking for much more than that would be upsetting the cosmic balance, brother. Tell you what, if I lose, you can drag me along off the fantail of The Lora for a while. That'll put a smile on your face."

Tommy hugged me. "I love you, you pathetic white bread son-of-a-bitch!"

I hugged him back. What the hell. We might as well make this into a soap opera. It ain't going to matter anyway. I'll either make our plan work or The Destroyer was going to have a very good night. "I love you too, brother. How about you helping me with my gloves, and we'll take up this 'Days of our Lives' episode after the fight."

Tommy pushed me away as our buddies laughed. "Let's do this! It's going to get ugly, but we ride the Dark Lord wave right into the rocks guys. No mercy – we'll bust him up in our corner if he doesn't stick to the plan. Kid, you got your Taser, right?"

Jafar smiled. "Yeah, T. Let's light him up in between rounds if he slacks off."

Tommy shoved my gloves on in place, checking my hands and movement. "He's ready. Let's warm the prick up."

Okay, I didn't expect that, but there I was before the fight of my life, blocking strikes from all sides. A good time was had by all... except me.

Jack Korlos ducked into our side of the newly added locker room. "Hey, kid, it's time for your punishment. I hope you've been saying your prayers every night."

"Yep. Every night, Jack. Can I say how great it is to have you refereeing the fight?"

He pointed at me. "You don't know the half of it. Those assholes want to make me a rich man if I help them out on the calls. Yeah... that'll happen."

"I'd make you rich just to call it straight up, but I wouldn't insult you like that."

Jack rubbed his chin. "I don't know kid, maybe getting paid extra for doing my job wouldn't hurt my moral code much."

We all howled at that one. I pointed back at him. "You get your bonus even if they cart me back here on a stretcher."

"See you on the other side, kid." Jack walked away.

"What do you think he meant by that, John?" Jess was staring at Jack's exit.

"Ain't nothin' Jack can do now. It's nothin' personal, Jess. It's just business."

Chapter Eighteen: Just Business

When given all the parameters of this match up, I admit I was juiced. I marched out with my crew toward the cage, sucking in the boos, waving at the crowd with real passion, and enjoying a moment that either worked well, or was a precursor to death or maiming. I embraced it all, because Subotic wasn't going to make it out of this faceoff without pain. He'd proven he could take it. I'd proven I could too. Now we get to see the other side of pain together.

They played the Marine's Hymn for me, which I gotta' say always stirs my soul. I had on plain black trunks and my black ring robe with 'Hard Case' on the back. We had been sanctioned as the challengers even though this was our home turf... of course. We entered the cage area first. Man, I loved this shit. Everything on the line, and hell on the other side for the loser. Then we had a little drama. One of the crowd had one of those voices that suck the oxygen out of the room. He did do that for a moment.

"Hey Pussy! Marines suck dick!"

Uh oh. Sometimes, there's just nothing you can do but watch. Lucas pounded over to the guy's seat in what seemed like seconds. Lucas picked that boy straight up in the air and body slammed him. There was a slight disturbance as his buddies reached for Lucas only to find Casey, Clint and Lynn. The small melee ended quickly. Lucas picked the guy up off the deck and explained the facts of life to him concerning disrespecting the Marine Corps. I thought the guy took it well, considering his feet never touched the ground during the lecture. Surprisingly, the crowd got the message that tonight was not the time to shoot your mouth off before the action. I pounded my fists together pointing at Lucas who smiled and waved. No one disrespects the

Marines in front of us... no one. Then The Destroyer made his entrance, decked out all in midnight blue.

The original theme from 'The Exorcist' built up gradually to a crescendo as The Destroyer stalked with his handlers toward the cage. I caught a glimpse of his logo 'The Destroyer' in red dripping letters. It was hell of impressive. That creepy music even gives me the chills. I'm enjoying the hell out of it until killjoy Tommy bops me in the back of the head.

"Would you try... just once... not to dance at your opponent's music, you idiot!"

I smiled at Tommy. "Holy crap, T, I thought you loved me. What the hell?"

My guys started busting up, forgetting where we were or what we were doing. Subotic's contingent, having entered the cage, looked at us as if we were nuts. Demetrius Subotic, The Destroyer, looked every bit as stunningly huge as the time I'd met him over at The Warehouse. I could tell his new handlers had coached him into a new glowering and sullen cage presence. He stared across the mat at me, looking like he wanted to rip my head off. Frankly, that is what he's supposed to do, so I smiled and waved at him, receiving another bop on the head from Tommy.

"Hey... what the hell was that for?"

"Take a lesson from Bigfoot over there and put your game-face on, meat!"

I immediately crossed my eyes, and let my jaw hang open while tilting my head. "How's this?"

Even Tommy couldn't hold out on my new game-face. I saw Subotic and his crew jawing back and forth heatedly as my bunch laughed their asses off. They probably thought I was making fun of them, but who cares. It wasn't like Subotic was going to pound me with less enthusiasm if I acted like less of a clown. The crowd of course booed at our enjoyment of the moment. I waved to the crowd as Jack Korlos entered the cage. The arena quieted. Jack used the new overhead audio gizmo to announce each one of us. I pointed out we were being projected onto the monitor over the bar. I jumped up and down as Jack announced me, doing a Carl Weathers impersonation from Rocky, pointing at Subotic with pumping arm in a 'I want you' fashion. The crowd rocked the house with boos. Tommy and my guys stared at me in stunned surprise.

A guy can't even have a little fun in the cage anymore. "What?"

Dev grinned. "Your Apollo Creed imitation sucks."

"I sure hope that guy doesn't crush your head like a grape, Apollo," Jess added.

Jafar waved me off. "You are dead to me."

Tommy patted my shoulder. "Jack wants you, Apollo. Best get your ass out there before the judges rule it a forfeit."

Jack was indeed waving us together. Subotic was nearly half a head taller than me, and I didn't want to think about how much he outweighed me by. He and I exchanged loving glances while Jack recited the rules. We acknowledged our understanding. We did a quick touch of the glove, and Jack waved us back. The strangest feeling washed over me as I glanced around at the sports bar edition thinking, man, a nice cold one and a double Beam would sure go down nice right now. My reverie earned a third head slap.

"Daydream on your own time, Apollo!" Tommy followed our crew out of the cage.

"Damn, Tommy, you've already hit me more than I planned on letting Demetrius hit me." I waited for Jack to do our ready warning, while listening to the crowd roar building to a deafening audio force. He waved us together with a quick 'get it on'.

Demi surprised the hell out of me by plodding toward me, stopping, and trying to kick me right in the nuts. It's possible even his handlers were uninformed as to how many back alley brawls I'd been in. My new ocean honed reflexes came into play early. See, numerous fighters, brawlers, and bond skips had tried kicking me in the nuts. I have a sweet countermove for that particular ploy. I roll dive to the side on my back, and kick up with my right leg, catching the kicker's offending limb right behind the kneecap. I practice it constantly, because it also works with most front kicks. It would have paralyzed another fighter.

Demi had never been on the mat before. He headed there now, flat on his back. I rolled up over his face with the lower half of my body, launching a full power left hook under his rib cage. I heard the crack, just before Demi clocked me with a right from his back that sent me to la-la land for a moment while I rolled with the punch. I shook the cobwebs in the dead silence of the arena, seeing Demi scramble roll to his feet. I saw the pain in his face when he tried putting weight on the kicked knee leg. After a taste of that damn right of his, I decided to use caution. I knew two things now: he would have trouble firing out with his left because of the rib crack, and the only thing that right leg of his would be good for was questionable support.

Tommy and the boys realized the facts too as I came up on my feet. They were cheering like hell amidst a very quiet crowd. Demi's corner crew foamed at the mouth, insulting Jack for allowing illegal blows and kicks. Jack smiled, but kept his head in the game. He knew who had tried an illegal kick. Demi looked more confused than hurt, but I had news for him: it was going to get even more confusing for him. I circled to his right, inviting his left strike while peppering him with right jabs. My jabs with either

274

hand are like trip hammers. If you don't block them, you won't have a face left by the third round. The Destroyer concentrated for the moment on moving in order to loosen his right leg stiffness while keeping his hands up.

When I had his attention on my right jab, I smashed a kick into his good left leg just under the knee. He went down, because his right leg wasn't ready for any action or full support yet. I leaped in smashing rights and lefts into his head. The scouting report was right. He could take a punch. Well, okay then, time for a little variation. I revved back and roundhouse kicked him above his ear as he pushed off the mat. He blinked and dropped down again to his knees. My left leg sidekick smashed into his chest, driving him again flat on his back. I went into full mount with hammer blows to his head with both fists. Incredibly, the Destroyer turned in the midst of my barrage, continuing upwards while bucking me off. Man, this boy could take a lickin' and keep on tickin'. I spent the rest of the round repeatedly attacking his good left leg until Demi had no choice but to start lifting it every time he saw me move as if I were going to strike it.

The round ended with me backing toward my corner while watching Demi. I had no plans to be an overconfident idiot. I could hear a woman's shrill excited scream directing me to kill him. I grinned. Although I didn't look around, I knew it had to be Lynn. On my stool, the guys worked me over with ice packs and towels, but we all knew the Destroyer had made a big mistake.

"Never would have figured he'd do that," Tommy stated. "He must think you're some boot camp newbie never seen the street before, John. That was damn disrespectful."

"That right he hit me with was bad, T. I can sure understand the Big O going down under that one."

"You hit him with blows that would have sent any other human into the promised land," Dev said. "I'm glad you backed off and went for the kicks."

"John, you gonna break your damn hands hittin' that clown in the head," Jess added. "He can't move much now. Best turn his face to mulch with them jabs from hell of yours."

"And do like you said. Don't let him connect with that right. You cracked his rib, didn't you?"

"Yeah, T. He won't be able to hit me with a full force left, but God only knows how potent his half force left is. Use the Taser on me if I'm stupid enough to trade shots with him."

"I will too." Jafar chuckled as he gave me another sip of water.

"Oh shit! Be on guard. That corner guy on the Destroyer's left just shot him up with something in the leg you smashed and his arm while the judges called Jack over. He didn't see it."

I stood up. "Don't worry about it, T. Unless they have a formula to instantly heal a rib fracture and damaged knee ligaments, Demi will still be plodding. Besides, there's no rules against shootin' up in here. If any of the cameras caught The Destroyer doing needle triage, it could hurt his chances of ever fighting in the UFC. I doubt he's thinking about that now."

"Don't get careless, Dark Lord."

"At some point I may have to, T. Remember, I can't win a decision here."

"Better to still be alive, brother," Dev called out as I advanced into ready position.

Yep, it looked like Demi got an upgrade. His vitamin shots couldn't make his right leg work any better. He was favoring it as he got off his stool. The skin looked a little stretched, so it was swelling. If I couldn't knock him out, I may have to break something on him. Jack probably had orders not to stop the fight under any circumstances other than imminent death. He did the ready, set, and go. Demi and I went to work.

The Destroyer had conceived a thoughtful plan. He knew his power, his reach advantage, and the fact he could probably take my best punch, so he moved forward swinging short power punches into my arms, shoulders, and hands I covered my head with. Demi hit my left hand block so hard I almost knocked myself out as it bounced off the side of my head. I wasn't standing there like a big stationary punching bag either. I bobbed, weaved, smashed blows into his face and rib area, and generally let him chase me around. Then he threw a right pile-driver, I barely rerouted by ducking into the danger zone, while ripping a right hook right on the button of his sore rib. All the needle medicine in the world couldn't keep him from pulling back. That's when I smacked him behind his good left knee with a kick I've broken two-by-fours with. I didn't break anything on Demi, but the kick definitely broke off his attack.

I threw jabs into his face as he backed away. I had no plans to get caught off balance going into full bore attack mode yet. He tried a kick with his left, but nearly went down. I dropped and leg whipped his left before Demi could pull it back. He crashed to the mat on his right side. I jumped up and drop kicked his exposed left leg. It was a beaut. Demi dropped on his back in agony, but the damn round ended before I could stomp him. I didn't bother backing away. If he ever got to his cage handlers it would be in a crawl. I saw Lynn four rows back screaming for blood. Clint was trying to settle her down with Lucas and Casey laughing and egging her on. The rest of the arena was very quiet. I sat down on my stool.

My guys held ice packs on both shoulders and upper arms where Demi had been trying to beat them off my body. I sipped from the bottle Jafar held for me while watching The Destroyer get helped onto his stool. "He ain't going to be as spry off the stool for the third round."

Tommy nodded as he toweled off my face and rubbed some goo in. "They'll stick him with another cocktail, but you really did some leg damage on him."

"That boy can sure take some punishment," Jess said.

"He nearly made me rip my own head off when I blocked his right."

"We saw that," Dev replied. "You need to keep moving back to his right like you did after cracking that left rib of his. It shortens the distance he can arc that right. Do you think you can take him down?"

"I don't know, Dev. Going for the takedown would really be chancing a haymaker."

"The reason I ask is because he won't be able to get his left arm up because of his cracked rib. If you could wrap around that damn right of his, and lock him up in a triangle choke, he couldn't do shit with his left to bust it up."

Tommy shook his head. "I don't like it. That sucker's hands are fast, cracked rib or not. We've all seen his punching power down on the videos. If he stuns John, and gets into a full mount, we'll need a priest for last rites."

"I'm wondering if he'll try taking me down this round. He has the power, and he knows I'm going to work his legs."

"Damn, John," Jess exclaimed. "Don't let that boy take you down. If he looks like he's going to try it, bring out the Dark Lord and do the robot or something. Make him laugh. Do something!"

I laughed at Jess's suggestion. The warning buzzer sounded. I got up, taking stock of my shoulders and arms. They were hurtin'. I concentrated on The Destroyer's journey to his feet. He looked across at me while testing out his aching knees. I glanced back at Jess and started doing the robot. It was so good, even Tommy laughed. Jess had to turn away. He was howling, and shaking his head. I kept it up until Jack gave us the ready sign. I even got some laughs from the audience. When I looked back at Subotic, I knew he was going to take me down. I had a plan for it, but I didn't know if I could pull it off. See, no matter how fast you are, to do a takedown you have to duck your head at some point with your arms reaching outwards. The head is exposed for a split second.

No way was I going to try a flying knee on him. If I got trapped under him, I'd be toast. It would have to be a perfectly timed front kick right on the button. It wouldn't end the fight or anything, but it might discourage him from trying the takedown again. He covered up pretty well when Jack motioned for us to get busy, looking as if he had every intention of doing the strikes with his arms, forcing me back. I figured the takedown would come if I moved to kick at his damaged legs. Instead of the kick, I stomped his left instep. Oh baby did the pain flood his face on that one. It's downright nasty doing that to a guy with slow moving legs. I was real broken up about it. I feinted a roundhouse right, and instead stomped his instep again.

Demi had enough. He made as if to move back, and then dived forward for my legs. My left front kick caught him perfectly. It snapped his chin up like someone had hit him with a baseball bat. He staggered up stunned, and my roundhouse right kick hit smack dab on his hurt rib. His hands dropped, covering his ribcage. I hit him so hard with a left hook, I figured the force of it knocked out three people in the front row. Demi blinked, raised his hands slightly, and moved back. Then he did a maneuver I wasn't expecting. He backed up against the cage. It made it difficult for him to go after me, but it made my kicks more dangerous to launch because of his reach. Demi nearly flattened me with a right, when I moved in and stomped his left instep again. I only partially blocked it. The birdies sang, and the grainy aura of knockout land descended on me in a rush. I knew better than to stop. I threw jabs until only the birdies were serenading me. The round ended, and I backed away.

"Where the hell did you pull that front kick from?" Tommy patted my shoulder while taking out my mouthpiece. "You guessed the damn takedown right on the money."

"Yeah, but he nearly sent me to the grave when he backed up against the cage. That asshole is phenomenal. I've Gronked guys with half of what I put into that left hook I hit him with. That pisses me off!"

"Calm the fuck down." Dev gripped my chin. "You always knew there'd come a time when even you couldn't Gronk a guy. Fight smart. Keep doing what you're doing. Worst case scenario... we lose on a crooked decision. The UFC will watch the vids and come up with the fact they fixed it. Don't be a big girl about this winning shit!"

I shook loose of Dev and looked at Jafar. "Tase me, bro. I'm going in to mix it up this round."

Jafar's face melted into slack jawed disbelief. "John... don't do that. Why...why would you do such a stupid thing?"

Tommy took one look at the stare I was aiming at Demi, and pulled Jafar back. "He's nuts now, kid. Don't bother trying to talk sense to the meathead."

All quiet on the Western Front. They iced me, and fixed my boo-boos. The warning buzzer sounded. I stood up. I admit it. Sometimes I'm not as smart as I should be. I'd worn Demi down for sure. He was gimping, but stomping a little as the drugs took effect that they'd injected between rounds. His corner crew smiled out at me. Then the obvious facts of the matter hit me. The Destroyer was going to stay away from me, only taking a shot if he could get a clean one sending me into the Stratosphere. They had a win. All Demi had to do was survive. I glanced back at my crew, looking grimly across the way. Dev met my grinning look and smiled. He saw it. I turned back and waited. The round was going to be a little different than The Destroyer's crew thought.

Jack did his usual readying motions. I played the relaxed, overconfident dolt. The moment Jack made his engage movement, I streaked across the mat, and snapped a flying right leg side kick into Subotic's head right between the eyes. He slammed into the cage behind him, and dropped face first onto the mat. Demi wallowed around trying to get up when I drop kicked his damaged rib as if I were kicking a fifty yard field goal. I didn't follow through on the damage I did there. I waited until he rolled toward his damaged side. I snaked up under him, trapping his right arm up, and locking around his neck from behind in a perfect triangle choke he couldn't raise his left to tug at. Then I showed him my strength. He winced, gagging as I kept tightening. I whispered in his ear as Jack hovered near us.

"Tap out now or die."

Demi tapped out. Jack flung himself in to save the kid, thinking I would kill him anyway. I released him and rolled away. The Destroyer's corner rushed out, but Dev and Jess met them in a one sided punch-a-thon, where half his entourage were unconscious before Jack's security force arrived in mass. Tommy was with me as I regained my feet. He yanked off my gloves, and put a towel around my shoulders.

"Dark Lord, you are one bad mother fucker!"

"That was one great ending, brother. I'm going over to that damn sports bar over there and get me a double Bud and Beam. Care to join me?"

"Hell yeah! Then we get you showered and head over to The Warehouse. You and me are going to get plastered, including the kid here."

Jafar nodded with excitement. He gripped my arm with both his hands. "I...I was afraid you would do something foolish... and you did... and you still made it work! Praise Allah!"

I laughed. I hated wondering what would have happened if Demi hadn't tried the initial nut kick. I hovered over him, as the medical crew on watch that night decided not to move him because of his ribs. Smart move, because I know I did more than crack them with that last kick. Demi held his hand out to me. I grasped it in mine as I knelt next to him.

"Thank you for not killing me."

"You, my friend are one tough dude. I don't want a rematch."

Demi grimaced as the medical team put an inflatable vest in place. "I should not have listened to my handlers about the beginning. I am afraid my legs will never be the same."

Bummer. "That may be true, but if you ever need a job outside of the cage, give me a call."

The Destroyer grimaced as they finished cinching him up. "Thank you, John."

"Get well, Demetrius."

I stood up away as they made ready to transfer him onto the portable stretcher to shift him into the ambulance. I spent a few moments thinking about what would have happened if his nut kick had disabled me for all time. Yeah, I'm not all that sad about his poor old legs. I made a mental note to myself if he ever came at me again as an adversary, I planned on shooting him.

Jim Bonasera and Jack Korlos boxed me in for the formal announcement. Ray Alexander was nowhere to be seen, and Tommy was looking around for him too. Bonasera made the announcement to the crowd about the decision everyone in the arena already knew, and Jack held up my arm. There were a few scattered cheers, especially from my representatives in the audience. They had seen a hell of a fight, so mostly there were very few boos.

"Hell of a fight, kid," Jack told me. "That counter move when he tried to kick you in the nuts was a real gem."

"Thanks, Jack. Without you refereeing the fight, I wouldn't have had a chance. You're getting a bonus for straight up doing your job."

"I won't turn it down. See ya'." Jack helped his security crew guide Subotic's crew out of the cage area. They were not a happy bunch. Dev and Jess had rearranged a few faces.

I headed for the bar. Yeah, I was still in my fighting togs amidst an angry crowd, but I also noticed my crew falling in at my back. Lynn was pumped, and it was not a good idea to front me with her dancing around at my back. I reached the bar without any interference. For one thing, me heading anywhere will give someone pause. Me, with my crew at my back was a no brainer.

I reached the bar, and folks, I had an entourage when I reached it. "Bud and a double Beam, bartender." He hesitated, looking off into the hinter land of no answers. I waved my recently gloved hand in his face. "Hey, a little service here, and get my friends anything they're drinking."

The kid snapped out of it, placing a double Beam and a Bud chaser in front of me first. Oh, my goodness gracious, it tasted good. "Thanks be to God."

The rest of my retinue ordered too with Tommy arriving to put money on the bar.

I drained the double Beam, and pointed at it while I slugged down half my Bud. Oh, good Lord in heaven, it's the little things that put a smile on a human being's face. Then the reason you don't drink amidst an enemy audience became apparent. Ray Alexander showed up behind me with a bunch of Middle Eastern suits with him.

"We're appealing the fight, Harding!"

Tommy and I busted up laughing. They can dress the pig up in an evening gown and makeup, but it's still a pig. Apparently, these idiots thought because they paid to have an old, shitty backstreet warehouse rebuilt, they could tie up decisions in court, and make appeals to imaginary street-fighting grief counselors. Ray was sweating. He knew this whole business was illegal. I figured old Ray was up to his eyebrows in debt, and he took a big hit tonight.

"Best explain to your buddies how the illegal fight game works, Ray. You kiddies can appeal anything you want. Review the tapes, picket the warehouse – hell, call the cops. You have some watching the doors now. You guys lost. Now, run along. You're beginning to bore me."

I didn't look away. My people were armed, but I didn't want any shootouts. It was then, Alexi Fiialkov arrived with a small army of his warehouse security people.

"What is this I am hearing about appeals, Ray? You will appeal nothing. Get out of my sight while you can still walk!"

Fiialkov waited until Alexander hurried away before smiling and speaking to the suits still looking outraged. "You men have lost. I am sure your revenue from the overseas showing has made you much money. Pay off your debts from wagers made, and leave. Cause me any more trouble in my business, and I will show you my less cordial side. Am I clear?"

He didn't wait for an answer. Alexi made a gesture and his men surrounded the suits for imminent departure. The losers left without further comment. Alexi smiled at me, and exchanged nodding acknowledgements with my crew. "No shower, John… just a quick Bud and Beam, huh?"

"Yep. How'd you do tonight?"

"Oh… I did very well, my friend. I now own part of the holdings those gentlemen who were just here represent. It will be good to have some knowledge of their inner workings, will it not?"

Well damn. "Yes it will. Thanks for sorting this out for us. I think it was about to get messy."

"Ray is as you know… an idiot. He was probably stupid enough to guarantee Demetrius would win. He's not worth killing, but those men may have other ideas. I will leave you to your celebration."

"Goodnight, Alexi." I turned back to the bar. I heard the click-clack of Lynn's toy resuming its former position somewhere on her person. She sighed.

"Damn it. I thought for a second we'd have a little fun." Lynn turned to Clint. "I'm all tensed up. Let's hit the streets and look for some trouble."

"We're going to The Warehouse with John, my dear," Clint replied as the rest of us laughed. "I'll buy you the best wine or champagne they have."

"I need to kill something. That fight fired me up. No offense, Dark Lord, but I didn't like your chances."

I downed my drinks. "I'll get a shower and see you all out in the limo."

"Lucas and I are coming with you, partner," Casey said. "We'll make sure there aren't any more poor sports waiting to do a Psycho scene on you in the shower."

"That's a good idea," Tommy said. "See you outside."

I nodded and started toward the locker room. The drinks had numbed the ache in my arms and shoulders. "Hey, you guys like my robot tonight?"

"Oh man, that was the best," Lucas said. "I thought that Bigfoot guy was going to have a brain freeze."

"I even saw Tommy laughing," Casey added. "You know we didn't come along with you to help hold your towel, right?"

"Yeah, when Denny didn't make it tonight, I figured something was up. You guys didn't want to slap it on me before the fight. I appreciate that."

"The Gulf cruise starts next week, John," Lucas said. "They're shipping the Wolf to Texas tomorrow. Denny has a crew to go over it, and rearm our more potent weapons."

"Damn. I hope I can get back in time for Halloween. I promised Al we'd all get dressed up to escort her and a bunch of the kids around trick or treating."

"If you think I'm puttin' on some clown costume or something, you're nuts," Lucas declared.

"Nope. We're sticking with the classic look for you. You'll be Captain Ahab. I just need to saw your leg off and find a good peg."

Chapter Nineteen: Oil Rig

At The Warehouse Bar I got an ovation as I walked in. Earl and 'Rique came up to shake hands as I waved gallantly to my real fan base.

"We have the whole end of the bar cordoned off for you, John." Earl gestured at the bar, where my lovely wife Lora awaited in a short black, plunge necked dress that nearly gave me a stroke.

Lynn giggled, peeking around me and waving at Lora. "It looks like a short celebration for you, DL, but a very long night."

I couldn't speak yet, so I simply nodded. As I walked toward Lora, it dawned on me she could come up with the nicest wardrobe surprises of any woman I'd ever known. Marla met me near where Lora wrapped her arms around me.

"Everything is on the house tonight, Champ. Your buddy Alexi already called. I guess you made him rich. I got five to one odds, so I made a nice piece of change too."

"Sorry, John," 'Rique said. "Earl and I stayed away from the betting tonight. That damn guy was humongous."

"Actually, we were pretty conservative on our betting too," I admitted. I looked down the way at my friends. "Did anyone bet on me?"

Everyone looked down at the bar. "Can't say I blame you. How much were we in for, Tommy?"

"I put us in for twenty grand at four to one, so we did okay. We also got twenty-five large for the fight. I guess I'll have to hire Marla to get the final bets in. Did you watch the fight, Lora?"

Lora shook her head. "You know I don't want to see John get his head kicked in, Tommy. Just because he didn't this time doesn't mean I wanted to watch it."

"I was telling Lora about it before you got here." Marla served our drinks. "We pirated it off the Al Jazeera broadcast. That Destroyer guy ain't human. I didn't think anyone could take that kind of punishment."

"That was what we thought," Jess spoke up. "We figured John would break his hands on that guy's head."

"It was Dev that suggested the triangle choke." I gave credit where it was due while sliding half my Beam in smooth as silk.

"I'm not taking any credit." Dev pantomimed my sidekick to the amusement of the entire bar. "The Destroyer comes out for the round, all happy because he just needs to survive for them to win a crooked decision. John here plays the over confident sap until Jack Korlos orders them to engage. The Dark Lord streaks at the very surprised Destroyer, and launches a full bore sidekick to his forehead. The Destroyer slams into the cage and drops face first before DL delivers a field goal kick to his already hurt rib. Since I read lips, I was watching real close. John snakes The Destroyer into a triangle choke, makes him gag, and whispers 'tap out or die'. The big bad tapped out."

Wild applause greeted Dev's very entertaining rendition of the last fight moments. It was all good to me. I turned to our audience. "Then The Destroyer's crew rush out to cause trouble. Dev and Jess clocked at least four of them." I lifted my Beam double. "Here's to Tommy, Dev, Jess, and Jafar, the best damn corner crew ever."

Everyone toasted us at my prompting. I had a nice buzz on and feeling fine. The aches had receded, and the birdie chirps from The Destroyer's head blows had diminished to only a few whistling reminders. The closeness of Lora drove me wild. The adrenaline, testosterone, or whatever was raging through me. Then a gang of idiots flowed through the entrance like acid rain on a four leaf clover. They had guts walking into a cop bar. The leader, a six footer with short black beard and immaculately dressed walked up into my face. Before he could do me European style closeness I put a hand in his chest.

"That's close enough, buddy. My wife's here and I don't want her to get jealous."

The bar erupted in laughter, but to his credit, my incoming nitwit smiled. "I am sorry to disturb you, John Harding. We would like to speak with you outside where it would be quieter."

I'm intrigued. "Okay... I can spare a few moments. You do know if you try any crap on me I will rip your head right off your neck, right?"

That statement got his intention. He backed away with hands up in placating form. "That is not our intention, John Harding."

"Okay. You and I go out and talk. Any of your entourage moves, and my crew will take them out. Agreed?"

He hesitated, but shook his head in agreement. "Of course, we are not here to cause trouble. I wish to make you an offer I would like held in secrecy. I would of course also like your manager, Mr. Sands, to hear our offer."

Tommy shrugged. "I'll listen."

I patted Lora's hand and walked out through the side entrance with Tommy. Our negotiator followed us after making a gesture for his mob to stay put. Outside, he held out his hand. Tommy and I shook it.

"I am Athan Kalif. I am one of the shareholders in a business group contracting the fights in Dubai, and manage The

Syrian Slayer. Our fighter, Demetrius Subotic, whom you defeated fairly tonight, also is under contract with us. We do not wish to be at odds with you and your manager, Mr. Sands. Alexi Fiialkov, thanks to your unexpected win tonight, has a sizeable interest in our corporate enterprise. He would like for us to be better acquainted."

I traded confused looks with Tommy. I think I was getting the gist of it. "Seems okay so far. Tommy and I are independent contractors. Knowing a connection like yours, with ties to the UFC would be very helpful, especially when a fight card happens in Dubai. I assume you would like our consideration in fighting other fighters under contract to your corporate group."

Kalif looked relieved. "Yes, that is exactly it. We have a very good piece of information our new associate, Mr. Fiialkov, told me would be very useful to you. We have been paying protection money to the Sinaloa Cartel to allow unrestricted access to our oil platforms in the Gulf of Mexico. Mr. Fiialkov thinks you may be able to end the Cartel's extortion."

Okay, now I'm really zoned in on this. "I may have a contact that can help with that. What information can you give me for pursuing an interdiction with the Cartel?"

"During our last run in with them, we were able to electronically tag the vessel they used in their latest extortion run on us. We know which platform they're using to carry out their forays into the Gulf. We would have given the information to your government, but we were afraid they would do nothing, and the information would be leaked about our involvement. The Cartel owns so many people we were unsure how to proceed. Mr. Fiialkov told me your contact is beyond reproach, and if the Cartel's pirate base can be destroyed without repercussions dealt to our group, you would be the one to give the information to."

"You have come to the right place, Mr. Kalif."

"Good." Kalif handed me a small flash memory card. "The information and pictures of their platform are on there. They murdered the crew that obtained and sent the pictures, and blew up their boat. They believe they are still safe there. The same vessel we tagged has made numerous runs from the platform since those pictures were taken six months ago."

"What do we have to do for our part in this bargain?" Tommy knew it was important, but he knew this guy wasn't here to be a Good Samaritan."

"We would only ask special consideration for Mr. Harding to fight one of our contracted fighters, if we are able to get another UFC fight program in Dubai soon."

I held out my hand. "Done deal."

Kalif shook my hand. "Excellent. I will let you return to your celebration. Congratulations on a very intense fight. I have fired Demetrius's fight crew. Their idiotic plan was a disgrace. When we fight again here in Oakland, there will be local judges and referee – Mr. Korlos if he is available."

"Good choice, Sir. Nice meeting you. I will keep you informed through Mr. Fiialkov of our progress in this other matter."

"Thank you. Goodnight."

Tommy and I watched Kalif go back inside.

"Is that the same deal Jafar was working on when we were training on The Lora?"

"Yeah, it is. This may be the safety factor we needed. The location of their extortion racket complicates matters. We were hoping for a base that could be hit by a drone. We can't do that with even an abandoned oil platform, let alone a working one."

"I'm glad things might work out for you brother. Let's get back in. You're bringing me down, Denny-light buzz-killer."

"Very funny. I hope they don't heal up Demi for a return match in Dubai. I figured if I ever had to face him again it'd be with a gun."

"That would be my suggestion," Tommy replied, leading the way back inside. "If the UFC takes a close peek at tonight's fight vid, I doubt they would sanction Subotic. My guess is it will go viral on the Internet though with people clamoring to see a rematch."

Just what I need. "Maybe I could get Jafar to attach a virus to anyone clicking on it.

Tommy chuckled. "That would also be my suggestion."

Inside, Denny was sitting with Lora at the bar. The Spawn of Satan can sense any vibration in the Force, good or bad. "It was all good, guys. Enjoy the drinks. We're eating shortly, do get your buzz on now. I am."

Denny wisely hopped over on a stool next to Tommy, while I took the one in between my bride and Spawn. I turned first to Lora. She grabbed my hand and kissed it.

"Take care of business. I already know you're going away shortly."

"True. Tonight, however, will be one of legend."

"No can do, Dark Lord. Al will be coming home with us."

"You'll just have to be quiet, or I can seal off your mouth if you prefer."

Lora's features achieved that wanton look of anticipation I love to see. "Okay... but gag me. I don't want that smartass daughter of mine playing me tomorrow morning."

"Whatever it takes, baby," I whispered. "One piece of business, and then it's just you and me after I get a little sustenance."

"No hurry. I'm here all night. You want short time, Marine?"

Oh Lord have mercy, did I want a short time tryst. "You're killing me, Lora," I whispered with intensity. She leaned in against me, her hand seeking out how much she was killing me.

"Oh my! It feels like you may have to double the gag tonight."

I grabbed her shoulders carefully, because whatever I'd been experiencing tonight was shooting through me like a shot of adrenaline. "Calm down. Nothing on earth is going to stop our private celebration. Let me talk to Denny for a moment."

Lora smiled slowly, leaning back as I released her. "I'll be here."

My hands tightened into fists. It was going to be extremely difficult keeping the upcoming meeting of wild animals quiet... but exquisite in silence. I felt up to the challenge. Turning to Denny, I saw him smiling as he kept his eyes on the bar while sipping his drink. "Those gentlemen you probably noticed out here run the corporate bunch with an in to the UFC. They contracted The Slayer fights and rebuilt the old warehouse here. Tonight they lost a chunk of their operation to Alexi. He sent them here with this nice piece of the Gulf of Mexico puzzle."

I handed him the memory chip. "Guys died getting that to this new partner of Fiialkov, Athan Kalif. Run it with Jafar, and double check everything with Laredo and Clint. It could be the most cloaked trap of all time, or a straight forward trade, with business profit at the back of it."

Denny took the memory chip and held up his shot glass. "As usual, I missed not only a hell of a fight, but one very productive connection to our Cartel problem. This is why we do this, John. Interconnecting entertainment threads, law enforcement, and a boat all our wishes can come true on."

I drained the double Beam Marla set in front of me. "This is all good, but we have to be careful. I trust Alexi Fiialkov implicitly, but his job is to direct windfalls to us, not interpret them. I'm with you about moving fast and furious. It's the only way we've stayed ahead of the game so far. We have a week to work this, Denny. Let's be careful and do it right."

"Agreed. This has been one hell of a night, John. I never thought-"

"Harding!"

I dropped my head in buzz loss. It was the Big O... of course. The parade marched down Main Avenue with all the brass, woodwinds, and drums wildly setting the tempo of job well done, but then a canker-sore of monumental size halted it. By the time I recovered and looked around, I started laughing. There was the Big O with Lynn's knife at his throat, my crew covering his men, and the Oakland Police Department corralled momentarily by Earl and Enrique.

I stood up and walked over where Lynn was chastising the very astute Big O. "This is not a good time for you, idiot!

"You will have to fight me now, Harding!" The Big O talked around the very sharp blade Lynn held at his neck. "You cannot duck me any longer!"

I waved Lynn off, and grabbed Big O by the ear. It shocked him. By the time he realized I had him, he couldn't do anything without losing his ear. I yanked him toward the parking lot with everyone who knew me trying to intercede. I waved them all off. "This ain't about all of you. Me and O are going to negotiate out in the parking lot. I'm sick of his crap." His bunch were in good hands. The O had pissed me off for the last time. Even Lora stayed inside. She knew this was not about her in any way, shape or form. Any interference from her would be counterproductive.

When we reached the side lot, I released the Big O. I waved him on.

"Listen asshole. I'm sick of you and everything about you! You ain't getting any shot at me except right here... right now. Come get some."

The Big O rubbed his ear while giving me the wave off. "I do not fight for free. Your tricks will not work on me. I could have beaten The Destroyer. I was cheated!"

I laughed. "He kicked your ass you big pansy. Tonight... I kicked his ass. I've been drinking. I've been celebrating. You want a piece, come and get it, or get down on your knees in front of everyone, and beg for mercy!"

Oh baby, did I have him. He looked around at the silent audience of barkeeps, police officers, and deadly killers. The Big O had crossed the line, and by his features, he knew it. He stripped down to his waist, and held up his hands.

"I will kill-"

I was done talking. It didn't matter what the hell he intended to say. I Gronked him with the left hook I thought should have knocked out The Destroyer, and at least three people in the front row in tonight's fight. The Big O shot backwards unconscious into the crowd. I waited while he remained snoring on the pavement. I signaled my crew to release his guys. They stumbled over, some a little worse for wear. Jafar nodded to me, meaning he had already catalogued them.

"I guess O was waiting for the referee to give him a start. Take Big O, and get the fuck out of here. We have all your names, addresses, and pictures now. Pray to God you don't show up on our radar again. It will be the last anyone ever sees of you." Man, was I sick of that guy. His entourage got him up and on his way. Jafar picked up his discarded clothing and handed them to one of his guys. Earl Taylor came over.

"We took a vote and decided we didn't really see what just happened."

"Thanks Earl. The Big O's been yanking my chain for too long. The idiot showing up here made me mental."

"Just a warning though, 'Rique took a vid of it and uploaded to YouTube already."

"Damn it!" I looked over at Earl's partner. He and a small group of PD were watching and laughing at something on his iPad. I bet I knew what it was. 'Rique glanced up at me, and waved.

"C'mon back in, John," Denny said. "We'll sip one more and get that sour look off your face."

"That will take at least two, but you're right." My gang filed in around me as I walked back to the side entrance.

"Why didn't you throw that left at Bigfoot?"

"I did, Case. He smiled and scratched his head like a mosquito had bitten him."

"No shit? Don't fight that guy again."

"I'll tell you one thing: I'm through fighting anyone tonight." Lora was waiting for me of course when I stomped back into the bar. "Sorry. That couldn't be avoided."

She smiled. "Will he live?"

"Yeah, but only because there were too many witnesses. We're going to have a couple more." Marla brought over my pick-me-ups with a grin.

"That was entertaining, Champ. I'm glad I upgraded the security cameras. Don't worry, I didn't upload it."

"My buddy, 'Rique beat you to it, Mar. Thank you."

Tommy, Dev, and Jess moved to a semicircle around us while Denny and Jafar conferenced, probably concerning the chip. My other cohorts were gathered around the very popular 'Rique, watching the recently uploaded Big O downfall.

"Hell of a left, brother," Dev said. "You blew off a nice payday there."

"We would have had to give eight to one odds, Dev. The only thing we might have gotten is a nice upfront fee."

"John's right," Tommy agreed. "Too much risk, and no gain, especially with a UFC shot on the horizon."

Jess laughed. "I don't know, T. It didn't look like there would have been much risk."

"I didn't mean the outcome. I meant we can't afford another dead guy. DL here is having too many control issues.

That statement got a big laugh, including from my wife.

"I told the guys about our new Dubai connection," Tommy said. "Is it possible to have a match without a side mission?"

"Possible, T, but unlikely." No use in pretending Denny wouldn't tack something on. "I wouldn't mind a return to Las Vegas."

"I vote Vegas," Lora chirped in.

"I'm with Lora. That arena at the Mandalay was like going off world," Jess agreed.

"The accommodations anywhere we go are fantastic, but I agree with Jess on the Mandalay Bay arena," Dev added. "I vote with Lora. By the way, Jess and I want in on the Voyage of the Damned we've been picking up signals on."

"Sorry, Dev, that cruise is booked. I need you guys here with Lora and Tommy. I'm having Samira stay with Lora until we get back. I want you guys all on a hotline with Lora while I'm away."

"I didn't want to go anyway," Jess said. "I don't mind a boat with you swimming alongside it and me holding a fishing pole. Dev's been watching too many war movies lately. We'll keep everyone safe here."

Dev chuckled, smacking Jess on the shoulder. "Okay, brother, we'll keep everyone safe on the home front, but I'm teaching these two how to swim while you're gone."

"Get someone to film it, Dev," I urged. "I want video evidence of those lessons."

"I tol' you, my people don't swim," Jess reiterated his position on swimming.

"I am your people."

"Not anymore."

We were all laughing at Jess de-blacking Dev when the rest of the crew came over.

"Tomorrow's Saturday, DL," Lynn announced. "We're all leaving for Tahoe. Clint's finally making an honest woman out of me before the cruise. We'll take a couple stretch limos with drivers. We'll pop down to Carson City and pick up a marriage license. Lucas is the best man, Lora will be my bridesmaid, Al will be my flower girl, and everyone else will be family. It'll be a couple days up at a first class hotel with gambling and meals."

"Wow!" That actually sounded like a hell of an idea. "We're in."

Denny Buzz-Kill chirped in with one caveat. "It will have to be a working jaunt for our computer geeks. We'll need Clint, Laredo, and Jafar continuing to solidify our plans."

"Agreed," Clint said. "We also have to iron out some things for the honeymoon cruise. For one, I need to know who wants to volunteer to clean up after Cruella Deville onboard ship."

And then the fight started.

Chapter Twenty: Battle Stations

We were indeed a strike force. This mission incorporated Laredo and our new air wing, the recently purchased Global 6000. Laredo even came up with some nonsense quote for over our audio system to make it seem like we were those 'Criminal Minds' guys. I had co-piloted because I was the only one with flight experience. It wasn't as nice as being in the back with my team. Laredo's funny though, and he was good company. Besides, he let me fly for a while, so that I could practice some maneuvers while we had our travelers belted in. My flying practice only lasted until Lynn threatened to rush the cockpit and slit both our throats. I made a mental note to confiscate all weapons before takeoff from now on.

Denny and Jafar, who had flown ahead with The Sea Wolf, met us at the Corpus Christi Airport where we said goodbye for now to Laredo. Jafar drove our equipment van to the harbor where we boarded The Sea Wolf with Lucas threatening us all in the usual manner of torture, maiming, and death if the boat got even a scratch on it.

After stowing our gear and showing the newly married Dostiene's their master cabin, we checked out the supercharged twin diesels which made up the power to added weight ratio. Yes, Lucas, and I were checked out on everything of a mechanical nature aboard The Sea Wolf. To the unknowing, the Wolf appeared to be a slow moving, unwieldy pleasure yacht, but she could really move. With flip out fifty caliber machine gun nest on one side, and an XM307 25mm grenade airburst gun capable of firing 250 rounds per minute from its own flip out nest on the opposite side, we were one potent cruiser. We also stored for easy reach a hand held XM25 25mm airburst grenade launcher and my .50 caliber M107 sniper rifle – all of this in addition to our own personal weapons. Once well away from port, we'd try them all out

We had a date to meet in utmost secrecy with our oil conglomerate representatives from Tampico Oil and Gas at coordinates opposite Tampico, Mexico, and beyond either the USA or Mexico's territorial waters. Lucas captained the Wolf out of port the moment we finished the preliminary checks, and had our equipment stowed. This being October, we kept an open line to home base in Corpus Christi, where Denny kept us apprised of weather patterns, or anything out of the ordinary forming. At the moment, the skies were clear, and temperature in the mid-eighties. Because of our speed, and a slight chop in the water, Lucas got an earful from Lynn about making the Wolf cruise more comfortable. He laughed in her face. That led to a warning when she got queasy, Lynn planned on disgorging the contents of her stomach all over Lucas.

Somehow, Lucas managed a more stable journey while cussing out Lynn nonstop for miles. We did not run across anyone once out beyond twelve miles. Maritime law was a tricky deal. Every country staked out their territorial waters, but the limits changed depending on whatever was going on at the time they decided to enforce something. Mexico had in the past confiscated fishing vessels and equipment off the Baja Peninsula for what amounted to be extortion money. We would know exactly where we were, and it didn't matter who stopped us. The Wolf would not be taken by rogue government authorities acting like pirates or real pirates working the questionable waters in the Gulf.

It had always been our plan to get in place a day ahead of our scheduled meeting for the express purpose of plotting where we were, and who became interested. There was no doubt the Cartel had informants everywhere at the Corpus Christi harbor. We had disguised our equipment so as not to seem like anything more than a crew going aboard for a lengthy voyage. Clint and Lynn, dressed accordingly, gave off the vibes in attitude of a couple used to being served, and did nothing to load the Wolf. We thought our playacting was done very well, but only time would tell. If our targets even had a bad feeling about us, they'd blow off the meeting.

The signal Kalif had given us was being watched, but we didn't depend on it. If it worked out, that would be great, but if it didn't, we had to be ready. If they even for a moment suspected us to be a ship full of special ops agents, we'd be toast. Denny would warn us of anything incoming, and we had drone backup from Fort Benning. We liked our chances of freeing the captives, and ending this Cartel projection into the Gulf. What we didn't know was whether they would buy our cover. If they ignored us, we were screwed.

As we neared our chosen coordinates, the newly wedded Clint and Lynn did a comical rendition of the Titanic's bow scene with Lucas piping out the movie theme song over our incredible audio system. Who says monsters can't have a little fun and romance? The only bad part at this point in the mission is we can't fish and have a few cocktails. We planned to take turns like we did when we went after the Somali pirates. Mostly though, this op had to be dealt with in deadly serious terms. After we reached our baiting area, Lucas put us on cruise to troll the scene in a wide circle route.

We quickly went over our armaments and testing, going over each weapon with Lynn. She practiced diligently as we tested our pop out nests and targeting. Lucas and Jafar kept watch for anything on our military grade radar system. When we were certain Lynn had all the basics down, we showed her our M107 sniper rifle. We placed floating targets in the water, showing her the difficulty of targeting moving objects from a vessel. Lynn then took Jafar's place with Lucas while he practiced. There would be no newbies on this mission, at least in theory. After our practice session, we adjourned to the cabin.

I went over the weapon Denny had procured for helping us in taking live prisoners: an electronic pulse rifle capable of disabling all communications and electronics. It was actually a state of the art launcher with a heat seeking guidance system. Once launched, the missile would burst over the intended target, discharge, and float downward. This was to be its first usage in actual combat, because the people on board our target vessel would not be talking to anyone. Of course, Lucas objected to frying all the electronics on a potential addition to Admiral Ahab's fleet.

"You guys sure know how to show a girl a good time," Lynn said. "This cruise has everything: mystery, danger, and badass weapons – all in a luxurious romantic setting. I want in on all future pirate actions, shipmates."

"I'm certain Denny has no intention of excluding you, babe," Clint replied. "There may be some difficulty after this one until you become a Mommy."

Lynn sighed. "Yeah, we'll have to tone my participation down slightly until Clint junior grows up a little, and we see if he has any monster genes. Besides, I want a little girl too."

"You two procreating is starting to frighten me," Lucas commented to much laughter. "Hey, kid, did Samira allow you to know the gender of your offspring yet?"

Jafar brightened up like a hundred watt light bulb. "We are having a daughter. Lynn and Clint's son will of course not be allowed anywhere near her."

More laughter. Then we received incoming from Denny. Jafar had the satellite notebook propped on his lap. He hit the on button for our fifty inch screen, piping the Spawn into our conference channel. Denny smiled out at all of us.

"Having fun kids? The banditos are heading your way. I trust you have all studied their craft. I'm relaying real time satellite data to Jafar now. They have fourteen crew members. We need prisoners as you know; but if it gets ugly, the hell with it. Nuke 'em. The EMP launcher will take out everything they have but small arms. I still don't want them raking you with machine gun fire. If Ahab survived, I'd end up staked out in the desert praying for death."

"You got that right. I'm going to feed you every slug I find embedded in my baby," Lucas said.

I chuckled at that threat, knowing it probably wasn't quite an empty one. Lucas would certainly whine about every hit to the Wolf's hull. "We'll hit them with the EMP at distance, and follow up with the sniper rifle until we get a surrender. If they even look like they're going to open up on us with anything big, Casey will rake their deck with the fifty."

"Good. We have a great thing going. I don't want risks taken needlessly. We know where their rig is. This sea battle is so we can cut off communications, disable their major weapon, and make the assault on the rig easier. The prisoners are important for the info they have on the Cartel operation in the Gulf. If we attack the rig quickly enough, I'm hoping they won't get any messages to where they're holding our happy go lucky oil profiteers. That's all I have for now. I'll watch for anything weird. There's a Reaper in the air on supposed maneuvers right now, but it's armed, ready, and in striking distance. Captain Blood out."

"What's with the Captain Blood sign off?"

"It is from our last pirate adventure, Lynn," Jafar replied. "We would finish doing something horrendous to many pirates. Then we would come back in here, call Captain Blood, and talk like pirates. It was very entertaining... except for the pirates."

Lynn smiled, but remained silent. Then she shook her head. "And you guys think I'm a monster. So... you monsters wasted a whole bunch of poor helpless Somali pirates, gathered around for a Johnny Depp love in, complete with Arrrgh's and Maties – all in an official murderous report to Captain Blood."

"Well... it seemed a bit more appropriate before you dissected it in such crude form, Cruella," Casey retorted.

I waved. "Battle-stations, maties, we're about to make a whole bunch more pirates unhappy. What'll it be, Case? You want the fifty in case they don't comply, or the M107 for getting them in the mood to comply?"

"Damn! Ah... hell, John, we have time. Let's switch off."

That's too much like playtime. "I don't think so, Case. Even with Jafar doing spotter duty, it would take too much time. One lapse and we could eat some kind of rocket launch."

Casey nodded. "Yeah, you're right. I love the M2 fifty. With it, I can sight in to take out single targets anyway in case Jafar spots more imminent threats than you can handle safely, John. Let's go over the plans we have on their boat in case I have to disable it."

"Hey," Lynn exclaimed, "do we get to swing over onto their boat with blades in hand?"

Clint hugged his bride and kissed her on the forehead. "There will be time enough for the blades later, Hon."

"Just so you weasels don't leave me out of this party."

"Fat chance of that," Lucas replied, "and no, I wasn't referring to your butt."

Lynn gasped. She jutted an accusing finger out at the smiling Lucas while her husband had to clamp both hands over his mouth. "You're lucky you're a geezer, Lucas."

* * *

We used the stationary mount for our EMP launcher as our target vessel came within range. They had made overtures, announcing they were nearing our position, which we acknowledged. We also knew from Athan Kalif they always fired on the vessel they approached without warning, and they aimed to make casualties. Well within our M107 sniper rifle range, Casey launched the EMP load. It burst over them, and descended as programmed. In moments, their boat was dead in the water. We already knew their electronics keyed into not only navigation, but engine control. Then Jafar and I went to work.

"They are manning their 20mm gun mount, John! It is high on the craft though."

"Take it out, Case."

"On it."

Casey's controlled bursts obliterated their 20mm gun, and the three guys trying to get it into firing position. "Oh yeah! I'm glad I picked the fifty."

"Very nice, Case! That was their main mounted weapon. Now, we wait."

"A man with a rocket launcher has come up on deck, John." Jafar read off the numbers going into a calculation for wind, speed, direction, and pitch.

I had been scoping for targets, so I saw the man come on deck. To his credit, he came up with the express purpose of firing quickly. He made it into position, turning toward us, when I fired a short burst that blew his head off. Then I sighted in on the launcher, and turned it into an unusable piece of smoking trash. My shots had everyone on board the vessel hiding rather than trying to fire something at us. Then I went to work. I nicked off pieces close to the crew hiding, getting real time shots of their positions from Jafar's link up to Denny. When I didn't get any hands waving in the air, I began executing by guess the underlings. After they realized my armor piercing slugs could shred what they were hiding behind, the arms started popping up with at first hesitation. When they realized no more shots were forthcoming, the crew raised their hands while standing. Yep, in this case, firing until they were killed would have been a better choice.

Lucas moved us closer while watching our surrendering crew with I'm sure one hand on the throttle, and the other ready to veer away at a moment's notice. I had to look for an example to set. My illustration of intentions made a move to lower his hands and walk toward the boat's bridge. I blew his head off, spraying a couple of his fellow crew members with his brain and skull matter. No one moved after my illustration. When we came abreast of our target, Lucas issued orders in English and Spanish.

"On your knees, fingers locked behind your heads!"

I blew the head off one more as there was some hesitation. We weren't there to accommodate hesitation or anything else for that matter. They dropped to their knees, faces up, and fingers clasped after my demo. By prior arrangement, Clint, Lynn, and Jafar boarded the craft. They rapidly plastic tied each crewmember with Casey and I watching their backs. Lynn did some butterfly knife tricks for their amusement. They were not very appreciative, but Lynn seemed to enjoy it. I knew one thing: they weren't going to enjoy what follows. All messing around was over. We locked horns with our captives immediately.

"Who is in charge here?" Clint asked. Getting no answer, he continued. "Let me put it another way. Whoever is in charge better stand up, or we'll just gut you, and throw you all overboard."

A guy in the middle of our detainees noticed everyone looking at him, and figured it would be stupid to pretend any longer. At least the guy didn't insult our intelligence. He stood up, keeping his hands clasped.

"I am Hector Manos. We were to meet with Adrian Bantos and his wife Mariah. This is an outrage! We are here to direct negotiations for a proposed oil contract deal."

Clint was not to make this into a play on words with these guys. "Here's the deal, Hector. We know about your Cartel affiliations, your extortion racket in the Gulf, and the prisoners living on your Fantasy Island property in Cancun. We're the pros from Dover sent to end all of your enterprises out here in the Gulf. How we go about doing it will depend on your helpfulness. One thing we won't be debating with you is your survival. You assholes will not be living through this."

Clint paused while the howl went up of fear, protest, and threats as usual. In this particular instance we had decided prior to engagement about how we wished to proceed. We would see it through no matter what if we didn't get immediate capitulation to our demands. Lucas had anchored us. He jumped aboard our doomed capture to inspect the engines, and see if it would be possible to make the vessel runnable with Jafar's help on the electronics. If we could motor in near the oil rig aboard the Cartel's boat with the Wolf backing the play, our takeover would go far more smoothly. Lucas and Jafar adjourned together below decks. We all waited in place, letting our captives whine about injustice and their rights as murderers. Twenty minutes later our shipmates emerged with grim features. Jafar stayed with Clint and Lynn while Lucas came back on board the Wolf.

"No go, John. They had too much of the system computer controlled without mechanical bypass like the Wolf has." Lucas didn't joke around. "I'd like to give you more than one option, but the only one I'm seeing is you doing a sea approach. The only other option is a frontal assault after using the EMP launcher. If the rig is active, we may cause something real bad if the controls are not shut down safely."

Lucas laughed as I let my head bang down on the deck where I was positioned with my M107. "Damn it! I knew when I saw you and Jafar's faces I was screwed. What do you think for distance? A hundred yards would be enough, right?"

Lucas clapped me on the back. "Good one, John… a hundred yards… sorry. You know what we'll need to do."

I straightened, taking a deep breath, while watching Lynn messing with our captives. "We tow their boat after we try to reboot as many things as we can. Please tell me a mile will probably be enough."

"That would be my assessment. We go at night after making this Hector guy call home, and explain there would be a delay before returning due to a glitch in the computer system. They don't have another boat to send, so his excuse should be accepted without question."

"Oh boy. A mile of ocean at night, followed by only God knows what when I get to the rig. Most rigs only get people aboard by helicopter, and hoisting them up in a basket from water level. I sure as hell hope these pirates have a better access because of their main purpose."

"We're going to need some real good detail from these guys. We could abort this, and isolate the rig until we starve them out."

I don't think so. "Yeah, if we want to write off our Cancun hostages. That would be another way for us to lose all goodwill for our rogue adventures."

Lucas nodded, smiling a little. "We knew the moment they were running this damn pirate base off an oil rig we'd be in deep shit. I have an idea you might like though if you're able to secure the LZ aboard the rig. It won't save you a mile swim and a one man boarding though."

"Lay it on me, brother, this damn gig is turning septic."

"If you can ascend to and secure the landing zone, we could have Laredo fly out with a water-winged chopper, fitted with some damn weapons. He can land near where you start your approach, and then wait with us until you give word the LZ is in your hands."

"That's a terrific idea... if I can somehow manage to get up on the platform." Boy, I'm imagining all kinds of bad. Laredo landing with an assault crew if I can command the LZ would be the way to go, but it all hinged on me getting from an easily accessible lower platform up to the LZ. "You're right, Lucas, we have to proceed that way. Bad part is we won't be able to use blasting type weapons on the rig. You call Denny to get Laredo ready for launch. I'll go over with Casey and extract the info we need."

"On it. I wish there were another way, brother."

I grinned. "Yeah, me too, Lucas."

* * *

Lynn had silenced our captives by cutting Hector's right ear off. Any whimper or sound from the captives elicited a visit from Lynn waving Mr. Manos's ear in their face - very effective for captive crowd control. Casey had trouble keeping a straight face.

"You are a very sick puppy, Cruella."

Lynn clucked a bit, while waving her ear hand around. "Man up, Case! It's going to get a whole lot more gross before we're done. Ain't that right, boys? Imagine what part I'm going to cut off next."

She always comes up with something different. Lynn is the end zone of interrogation. Hector was still sobbing, lying on the side opposite his bleeding and missing orifice. Clint pressed a bandage with adhesive against his open ear hole. Hector's crew already seemed more than ready to help. Lynn had put on the mask of crazed serial killer, her eyes a molten font of fast moving sadistic twitches and tight lipped grins.

"Look, Clint! Still no takers. Let the cuttin' begin! There's my bitch right there!" Lynn kicked one of the crew over to his side. "Bring him over and strip him, boys! We need a demonstration!"

I shook my head, because in seconds we had more information flowing our way than we could handle. Casey settled them down while Clint held off the crazed Montoya, and I mean she made Freddy Kruger look like an altar boy. I helped Casey situate the now very helpful crew of pirates so we could begin our taped interrogations. They were both time consuming and entertaining; because when Lynn put on the bored serial killer mask, she had a tendency to start cutting things: articles of clothing, hair, exploratory nicks in various places. Lynn grabbed one of them by the hair, studying his face from inches away, and then tracing a line around his eye socket with the tip of her knife.

"You've got pretty eyes. I want one!" He screamed and Clint grabbed her wrist just in time. I'd say it was an act, but with her it's damn hard to tell.

"We're almost finished, baby. Jafar's checking out what we can. Remember, we made a deal with these guys."

Hector gave us everything: his account numbers, his Cartel affiliation, and a list of wrong doings where we could give some surviving relatives closure. They had murdered the yacht crews as we suspected they had, torturing them in front of the boat owners they now held in Cancun. The reason behind the helpfulness of the Cancun people became clearer to us. Hector and his crew also filled in every detail of the oil rig's frame work, and access points from the lower platform. I had been correct in assuming they kept easier access to the main platform of the rig from the water, because of what their main objectives were. Using our own schematics of the oil rig, we were able to get a clear picture from the crew where the remaining personnel were located.

We had good news on two fronts. The rig was idle, and it had a skeleton crew on it maintaining lighting and utilities. Having separated each of Hector's crew for individual interrogation when questioning them about the oil platform, we were told the number still on board was sixteen. If I could hold the main platform, Laredo could pick up my team at a specified time after I got into position. He would only be minutes away from the oil rig. Sixteen rig workers with me keeping the landing zone safe would not have a chance against my team unless they had a self-destruct mechanism. I figured on Lynn and Jafar in charge of the Wolf. Neither were trained in assaults like this one. Lynn did well on the warehouse rescue, but that had been unavoidable because of the girls we were rescuing. She was not happy after we had disposed of our Cartel murderers with a hot shot, and at sea burial. We consolidated our plans in the Wolf's living area.

"Is this some kind of insult? I did fine flushing out the guys for Lucas to pop at the warehouse. Why the hell am I getting benched with the kid? Hell, you're letting Lucas go, and he's a geezer."

After the laughter died down concerning Lucas's age status I kept it simple. "You're part of the team. You do what you do best, except in special circumstances. This assault is what we do best. The four of us have extensive experience with repelling from a chopper. Doing it in the middle of a hot LZ at night is something you'll need more training for. Jafar keeps our communications and mission status in constant updates. You'll be steering the Wolf in because I want Laredo out of there immediately after the guys hit the platform. Then we move through the structure until we can account for all sixteen workers. We know where their communications station is. I will take that out first before the team lands unless I freeze my ass off or get eaten by a shark."

"You poor baby," Lucas nailed me right away. "Big tough recon marine still whining about a little swim in the pool before action. I'm not even going to allow you to play the Marine's Hymn before your next pantywaist fight. I think 'Kum ba yah' or maybe 'Tiptoe Through the Tulips' would be better theme songs for you to consider. We'll have to change the lettering on your robe from 'Hard Case' to 'Sissy Boy'."

Even the formerly outraged Montoya was having a good time with the geezer's sendup of my male status. "If there are no more comments about my man card, I'm thinking after I take out the com center, things get tricky from there. Unfortunately, we don't know how much danger there is even with the rig idle. Hell, on an active oil rig, the workers can't have anything electronic outside of the living quarters due to the danger of triggering explosions. There's bound to be some fumes or pipes that we can't afford to spray with machine gun fire, or anything else. That's what makes it a perfect base for the Cartel's pirates. Hector told us the only weapons are on board the ship we just took over. Even the bad guys on board have only clubs and knives."

"Denny's working this on the backside through channels, but for the time being, we need to do as little damage as possible. He's going to put a team on board, after we find out how many of the survivors are just maintenance workers, and how many are murderous Cartel scumbags. Until we get those people out of Cancun, it's possible we can use the workers on the rig to keep it viable until someone from the Mexican Government confiscates it."

"There's a half dozen bad guys on board the rig, according to our former cruise guests," Lynn said. "I hope the regular oil rig workers have sense enough to go along with this no shooting allowed assault. It will be tedious enough sending all their pictures, DNA, and fingerprints to Denny before we head for Cancun. Hector said his Cancun bosses checked in once a week unless something special happened, and they called in two days ago to warn about our proposed meeting. We won't have much leeway getting to the people being held."

"I wish Hector had known the specifics about Cancun. He didn't have much more than what we already knew," Jafar added. "Once you have secured their com center, I will block all out-going communications from any hand held electronics they have, John. At least it's in the living quarters."

"That will be another key to Cruella being ready to steer the Wolf in close, so you can do just that." I exchanged the usual deadly stare-off with Ms. Deville. I won yet again as she grinned. "Anything else?"

"Yeah, Sissy Boy, I want to know when you're getting into the water," Cruella boinked me but good. "I need to take some pictures and video during the launch."

Chapter Twenty-One: Night Swim

With The Sea Wolf anchored a mile from the rig, Clint helped me with my pod I'd be towing along behind me to the floating platform. Yes, we had the smiling and filming Lynn with her digital camera. She had the spotlight from it on us while the rest of our mates enjoyed the start of my mile approach. Yeah, there're really no compassionate partings amongst us monsters. We interact on the same level as surgeons in a combat front do. If we can make each other laugh, we do. Like them, what we do doesn't always come out well. What the hell's the use of getting maudlin about what we have to do? I enjoy the hell out of it. What would bother me is this bunch hanging around like I'm already dead. They know I can do a mile over the water in my sleep. Once I get on board, they know damn well what I can do once I get on the main platform.

"Hey, Sissy Boy, get some fish for breakfast tomorrow morning before you go," Lucas munched on me some more. "Oh hell, I forgot, you're already whining about that little mile to swim. A real Recon Marine could dive down, get dinner and breakfast for us, all without missing a beat starting the mission. Shit! Instead of a Recon Marine we got you! Okay... try to get to the rig before daylight."

Even I was howling. When I could speak, I waved him off. "Thanks, Lucas. I needed that. Doing a single-handed takeover of an oil rig with no dischargeable weapons really had me worried."

"Get in the water, pussy, and quit delaying your mission... damn it!"

How could I fail with back up like that? I dived into the churning surf without any further pokes at my manhood. After making sure my equipment pod was strapped to me comfortably,

315

I made contact with the GPS transmitter on board the Wolf for my bright, divers' digital Navimate GPS wrist display screen. I already had the rig's position programmed in. Since I would not be approaching the rig underwater, I had on a full wetsuit with mask, buoyancy compensator, snorkel, weight belt, and fins. Emergency air I packed in a small Spare Air cylinder strapped to my compensator in case I had to go under for some reason. My equipment pod could be submersed out of sight with its own buoyancy adjustments. I adjusted everything so no one would see me or the pod, except for my small black snorkel, and my black wetsuit hood covered head.

Inside the equipment pod, I had a state of the art meter for reading hazardous explosive fumes. My Stryker 380 crossbow would be my only weapon other than the old Kabar bayonet I'd had since the Marines. I also had duct tape and plastic restraints. The team would all have Stryker 380's when they came on board. Only Lucas would also have a MAC 10 in case we had to drop the pretense and risk an explosion. The deceased Hector had explained only one man would be on watch in the communications center. The rest would be in the living quarters. The man on watch also did a walk around once an hour, including the lower platform.

The overcast night provided very little light. It can be disorienting when moving through water in darkness without being able to glance up at a skyline, but my GPS screen helped with the weird feeling of not knowing up from down. The taste of salt water in a choppy sea can kick in anyone's gag reflex, but the trick is to keep moving, and concentrating on your destination while keeping your snorkel up above the chop. It wasn't long before I had no frame of reference other than my GPS screen as the Wolf was no longer in sight. Nearly a half hour later, I could see the lights on the oil rig. I'll admit that sight made me feel a bit happier. I noted the low ship dock on the right side of the rig as I closed to within a hundred yards. Hector had told the truth, added on ladders provided access all the way to the upper deck.

I slowed my approach to a crawl, airing up my compensator slightly while pulling my mask and snorkel down around my neck. I pulled the waterproof night scope out of my zippered compensator pocket. At nearly one-thirty in the morning, there was no movement I could see, but the bulwark of pipes and framing made it difficult to be sure. I didn't want anyone glancing over to see the glowing eye of my scope, so I did my scanning in short intervals. The low boat ramp made it easy to get my pod up out of the water. I tied it off, opened it, and stripped off my wet suit and gear.

With my all black Kevlar clothing, thin black mask, and black no-slip shoes, I would be very hard to see. I put on my night vision headset with com gear. Slipping into my pack, I heard the noise of someone descending toward me. This was not in the plan. The bad news was he's a half hour early on his walk around. The good news is he should also be the guy in the com center. His destination could only be the boat ramp I was standing on so there wasn't much left to do but wait with my Kabar near the ladder.

The guy didn't even look around until his feet touched the ramp. He stood about six feet tall with heavy black beard, coveralls, hardhat, and foul weather coat. I had an arm around his neck and my Kabar jammed against his kidney the second he cleared the ladder. "Keep silent and you live. Nod if you understand."

He nodded.

"Get on your knees, and then on your face, using your hands full out in front." He did as he was told. I plastic tied his wrists and feet. I helped him sit up. "You the guy on watch in the radio room?"

"Yes... who are you? It is very dangerous for you to be here. You don't know who you're messing with. The Sinaloa Cartel runs this rig. Their guys will be coming back soon."

He spoke with a Southwest Texas accent. If I had to guess, I'd say this guy might be able to help me. "No they won't. Is everyone in the living quarters?"

"Yes, but-"

"How did you come to work this gig?"

"I answered an ad. I've worked oil rigs before. I didn't know what they did here until it was too late. These Cartel guys will cut your heart out and eat it." He looked around. "How the hell did you get out here?"

"What's your name?"

"Gary Cantler."

Time to break radio silence. "DL to the Wolf. Come in."

"We read you," Jafar's relieved voice answered.

"Run this name – Gary Cantler – oil rig worker."

"On it." Jafar came back on line a few minutes later. "He's an oil rig worker, but he's been missing for nearly six months. No priors except a DUI five years ago."

"Start the party. I'll have the landing pad ready."

"Will do."

I took the plastic ties off of Cantler, and then shouldered my pack with the Stryker 380 strapped to it. I picked up the explosive gas meter. "How dangerous is an idle rig like this if weapons are fired on board?"

"You don't want to do that, partner," Gary replied. "There are always stray fumes on a rig like this. Even the bad guys don't bring their weapons off the boat. They mostly have knives and clubs. Can I buy a ticket off here and back home with you?"

"If everything goes right, we may have you stay only a little longer until the Mexican Government takes it over. Okay... lead me to your communications room."

The rig was a maze, a tinker toy looking nightmare. Gary knew his way around though. In short order we were in the communications room. I noted the helicopter pad was just as our schematics outlined, on a platform above. "Can you temporarily disable the com gear without me having to wreck this place?"

It only took him ten minutes to pop up with a handful of parts. "This will do it."

"Do you know who the Cartel guys are?"

"Sure, everyone does. We don't mess with those guys. Three of us objected to being stuck out here incommunicado. The next morning, they were gone, only not back to the States."

I had an idea how to make this a bit less thrilling. "Gary, could you go in the living quarters and get the rest of the regular workers out on the main platform?"

Gary brightened. "Maybe. The Cartel guys bunk in together. They know we don't have any way off the rig."

"Go for it."

Gary jogged out of the com room and I followed. He entered another complex, gesturing for me to stay put. I did, with crossbow in hand, and Kabar within reach. It took maybe twenty minutes before Gary had led the rest of his compatriots out on deck. "That's the last of them. They're excited about getting the hell off this rig."

"Get them over there on the other side of the rig and come back. I have a nice bonus for you if you can lead my team to the Cartel boys. By the way, would they hear a Stealth helicopter?"

"I don't know," Gary replied. "What's it sound like?"

I grinned. "One's approaching from a hundred yards out behind you."

Gary turned startled at the nearly noiseless approach. "Damn. Believe me, if I can't hear it from here, they won't from where they're bunked at."

"Get your friends over in the safety area, well away from here."

Gary left to take care of it. By the time he returned my guys were repelling down on the pad. Laredo moved away from the landing pad. "Stay here. I'll bring my team over."

I glanced at my explosive gas meter. It wasn't picking up anything, but I still didn't want to test it out, even in the crew's quarters, which was supposed to be explosive proof as far as electronic gizmos. I waved at my crouching team of cold blooded killers.

"Hi guys. I have a guide down into the bad boys' bunks. Maybe we can take the whole bunch for questioning aboard the Wolf."

"Damn, boy, I may have to make you a Marine again," Lucas allowed, although somewhat reluctantly. "What's the firing danger?"

"Bad, according to my contact. The meter reads good, but I'd rather not chance it. Let's go with the crossbows. I'm hoping you don't have to fire Lucas."

"That makes two of us. Denny sent a few men with Laredo who know how to keep the rig safe since you still have the

320

maintenance men alive and well. He'll bring them on board the moment we sort out the locals. Let's do this."

Gary led us through the crew quarters to where our six Cartel guys were sleeping. A few were stirring uneasily, noting unfamiliar noises. Then, we were on them, and no amount of anything helped. One frosty dude jumped up with a knife he kept under his pillow. Clint put a crossbow bolt through his shoulder, while Casey and Lucas tumbled the rest out of their bunks. The Stryker 380 at close range had passed right through the knife wielder's shoulder without striking bone. The impact and shock put him back on his bunk in agony, clutching the wound. Clint tied a pillow case around Mack the Knife's wound, and secured him.

This is the way it ought to be, the plan coming together without firing a shot. We plastic tied our prisoners, who were already threatening us with annihilation if we didn't give up. Oh boy. That's going to be a tough sell. My team was already kicking the Cartel guys' asses up on deck without even bothering to brandish weapons, except for Lucas. There were as alluded to by Hector only six of them.

"On your knees, hands behind your back," I shouted out to them. "Make a fuss, and die now!"

They did as told. By then, Lynn had inched the Wolf up near the ramp. Jafar helped her dock it, and let me know our ride was safely secured. We were still absorbing warnings of doom from the Cartel motley crew. I allowed Gary to take his friends back inside the living quarters, explaining they might have to stay a while until we organized a relief crew. They were happy to be alive. I called Laredo down for a landing. Three men in oil rig gear followed Laredo off the platform.

"Good to see you, John. I heard Lucas made you swim to the rig from Texas."

"If felt like it. Are you staying?"

Laredo nodded. "Denny told me he wants one person anywhere near the com center. That would be me. Did you have to nuke it?"

"That was another good thing. I had a rig worker disable it rather than destroy anything. I'll go get him. He has the parts to make it operational again."

"That's a relief. I want to set up an operations base here for now until you get those people in Cancun safe. If we can get clearance, Denny wants me to fly them back to the states from here unless he can get a Coast Guard Cutter to rendezvous with The Sea Wolf. Any objections to sailing back by and dropping them off if everything goes well?"

"Actually, that sounds almost perfect. I'd rather transfer them to the Coast Guard though." I introduced myself to Denny's oil rig management team and took them with me to the living quarters. I brought Gary back with me. He and Laredo hit it off right away.

"How'd we do with the funds from Hector and his boys?"

"Pretty well for underlings," Laredo replied. "Hector made the largest donation to the West Coast Fund."

"Gary helped me big time getting this done. I'd like to work fifty thousand into a tax free fund somewhere for him."

Laredo smiled at the stunned Gary. "Consider it done. Bring your parts along, Gar, and let's get this rig's com center back working under new management."

"You bet."

"We'll be casting off for Cancun with our new informants."

Laredo's features twisted comically. "Damn. I thought maybe you had all the info you needed. So, Cruella Deville will be playing entertainment cruise director again, huh?"

"She's the best, and we need some insight into communications, guards, and layout of the place. One of the guys we just ditched told us three of the ones we just captured have been to the complex in Cancun. Thanks to Lynn, we took this rig without blowing it up or losing a single person good or bad in the process."

"You're right, John. Besides, I hear now she has her act down so well, she doesn't even hardly lay hands or knives on them."

"It will be interesting to see her with a baby."

"Maybe in your universe that will be interesting. In mine, we're provisioning for the apocalypse."

Okay, that was funny. I waved as I turned away. "See you when we get back with the hostages."

"Tell Clint the bet's still on Cruella croaks him in the night."

* * *

The Wolf put out to sea again with our new set of guests with Lucas at the helm. This after complaining about nearly everything from roughing up the boat's side while picking us up to Clint getting blood on the deck while doing triage on the guy he put a crossbow bolt through. We all took it in stride because we didn't want to show any disagreement between crewmembers. Ahab calmed down once he was again at the Wolf's helm.

I took a hot shower while the captives were entertained by the cruise entertainment director. Lynn had decided to warm them up while Jafar fingerprinted and took pictures of them for Denny. By the time I got out of the shower and dressed, our guests were avoiding eye contact with Lynn. She kept moving from one to another with her monster face, studying each one, tilting their heads, and turning them as if figuring out which side view was best. When the one Clint had shot a crossbow bolt through saw me again, he began demanding better treatment. The grim part was, we all recognized this clown from Hector's description. He was their lead torturer, the one who had conducted and participated in the killings of all the crewmembers. We had not told him his buddy, Hector Manos, bought a quick death with detailed information about what they had all done, especially the complainer, Gabe Medina.

I waited silently, listening to dead man rattle off demands for lawyers, arrest warrants, and even claiming he had diplomatic immunity. I could tell Cruella wanted to cut out his tongue, but I kept shaking her off when she turned to me. The other guys were having a hard time keeping a straight face. Finally, Jafar returned from the bridge with ten sheets of updates from Denny. Five of them had to do with Medina. I turned to Lynn as I pointed out confirmation on Hector Manos's identification of the three in our group who had been making regular trips to Cancun. Medina wasn't one of them.

Lynn turned to Medina, crouching down with a look that would have frozen the blood of anyone with eyes. I could tell Gabe was impressed. She pointed a finger at him. "We're not going to mess around with you Mr. Diplomatic Immunity. I've been listening to your shit since we left the rig. You are going to be an object lesson to your friends here on how to be helpful. You can't be helpful, so it sucks to be you."

Cruella turned to Jafar. "Remember that chum I asked you to save in the refrigerator? It's in the large sealed plastic bags."

"Yes," Jafar replied with grim purpose, because he had read what Medina had done. "I will get it at once. Shall I have Lucas come to a stop?"

"Yes, please."

Lucas slowed the Wolf down to an idle. I had an inkling of what Lynn had in mind. This would not be a pleasant demonstration. After reading what Medina had done, I didn't care what she had in mind for him. I doubted whether we would have much to worry about getting the five survivors to talk. See, in the Gulf of Mexico there are a wide range of sharks. Lynn didn't care one way or another if we attracted the right kind or not, or even if they showed up. This was a demonstration of what we planned to do. Jafar brought her a large plastic bag full of chum from our fishing off the boat. She went back and dumped it into the ocean off the fantail. The rest of us monsters manhandled the Cartel boys into a kneeling position near the fantail.

Nearly half an hour later as Lynn released bag after bag, there was a churning in the water. Lynn clapped her hands. "Showtime! Strip him boys. We don't want his clothing to get caught in their teeth. Put a life jacket on the prick so he doesn't sink."

Clint and I stripped the screaming Medina. We forced a flotation vest on the very vocal Gabe, and held him while Lynn click-clacked Mr. Skinner out. She made a shallow but bloody incision from his groin to his neck.

"That'll do it. Throw out the bait."

Clint and I threw out the screaming Medina into the ocean. It was quite a show as they nudged him. He screamed. He splashed. He begged. Sharks really have no compassion for anyone. In his case, neither did we. Our planned for sequence went on for longer than even we expected with poor old Gabe screaming to the last before he disappeared from view. A ragged flotation vest popped up a few minutes later.

Lynn spun around on our guests with passion. "Okay, ladies! That was the demo! Who wants to go next? C'mon, don't be bashful. What? No takers? Well, I'm afraid it doesn't work that way. We need to know everything you know about the Cancun estate where the hostages are held, or the Dark Lord here is going to let me cut pieces off of each of you to stir up our shark buddies before we toss you in to feed them. Please don't talk! I'm going to cut chunks out of you for bait until the cows come home, and the sun is high!"

Cruella moved to drag another victim out to be stripped. I played my part.

"Hold on, Cruella. We have to give them the alternative."

"Sissy boy!" Cruella turned away, but not without a quick grin to let me know she boinked me.

"Give us all your information about Cancun along with the personal accounts you assholes have accumulated. Impress us with not only that, but bad things you all have done since childhood. We want everything. If you don't impress me, I let my enforcer prep you for the ocean and the sharks. Believe me! You won't like that option. If you bunch impress me, we'll sit you up on deck to watch the sunrise and give you all a happy shot into hell. What'll it be?"

The decision was unanimous, but Lynn of course showed her displeasure with my alternative. She went at our very upset and willing informants with grim entreaties.

"Don't tell him anything, kids! Screw the big cluck! Let me show you a new horizon of death. It will be so intense, you'll be glad when you're dead, you rascals you. C'mon, take a walk on the wild side!"

Clint corralled her to the bridge with Lucas. Casey and Clint then watched the prisoners while Jafar and I began the tedious question and answer sessions with each one separately. I could tell that bothered them. In the meantime Lucas resumed course to Cancun. We mostly allowed them to talk at first. I compared what they said with the sheets Denny had forwarded, and the information we'd already learned. By the time we were done, we had a candidate for our next phase.

326

Chapter Twenty-Two: Cancun

He was resigned to death, and by the sheet on him, and his own cohorts' description of his duties, Joe Valois was in charge of handling the targeted couple's delivery to the Cartel's estate. The way they worked it was Hector Manos took over the couple's yacht with his own men, while the hijacked crew was taken back to the oil rig. Valois would come on board the captured yacht, smoothing things over, emphasizing the need for absolute secrecy, and all would be explained to them by their soon to be fellow partners. In Cancun, a limousine would meet them for their enthusiastic briefing by the other couples held at the Cartel estate. They were filmed and interviewed in a picturesque setting, drinking umbrella drinks, and excitedly discussing an oil partnership with the others.

Reality would come later, when the couples were taken to a closed off video room with large screen HD TV. On screen they would watch each of their yacht crew tortured hideously by Gabe Medina and killed by the other butchers. After that illuminating experience, their cooperation in slowly draining their accounts was guaranteed, along with acting as dupes for the Cartel to give glowing endorsements. Joe didn't know it yet, but he was going to buy his worthless life. We took Joe's comrades up on deck as promised after dawn, and fulfilled our part of the deal with them. They were then stripped and fed into the chummed water. It didn't take long. Joe watched in horror, believing he had not impressed us enough, and he would be fed to the milling sharks alive.

Lynn put an arm around his shoulders. "Want to maybe live through this, Joe?"

Valois turned pleading eyes toward Lynn, unwilling to believe she would save him for anything other than special torture. "Did I not tell you everything? How can I live?"

"We're going on a rescue mission to free those couples at the Cancun estate. My partner Clint and I are the ones who have cultivated this whole thing. You'll deliver us to the Cartel just as you did the other couples. As I understand it, you take the couple by limousine directly from the dock to the estate by yourself. Correct?"

"Yes! It is just so. I can get you both in without a problem. It is well guarded though. They have a dozen guards I know of. We are always passed into the compound. No one stops us. You would be treated like honored guests with me as your guide. The rough stuff does not start until after the videos they take of everyone together when we arrive. The estate has a beautiful jungle setting around its walls."

I liked this as well as Lynn and Clint seemed to. "How big is the limousine they send for you at the dock, and is the glass well tinted?"

Joe's eyes widened. He was a smart one. He had changed sides already. "It is a huge stretch limo meant to impress. Yes, you can get your team inside. You will have to force the driver to do your bidding. He is simply a driver. His name is Alto Balos. Once we are inside, I can do my usual escort job while Alto takes the limo to where the garage is. Alto must be the one who opens our door for us."

Lynn patted his cheek. "I'm beginning to like this guy. Do you usually stay overnight when you deliver people?"

"Yes, I stay overnight." Joe smiled. "I always have my overnight bag. You would like me to carry something other than a change of clothes, huh?"

"I'm thinking a couple of MAC 10's, extra clips, and a few flash-bangs," Clint said. "We'll isolate the hostages, and then get the party started. How many couples do they actually have in there?"

"Six."

"That's more than we know about or have seen on the bait video," I told him.

"They only use the Americans when doing their commercial video. Once we enter the estate, I am always to take the people directly to where the couples are all sipping drinks around their huge, beautiful indoor pool. There is soft music, lowered lighting, and a tropical theme all around the pool area. The attendants who seem to be waiters are armed guards. There are four of them by the pool."

"Do you sit with us, Joe?" I'm wondering if Clint can get at the bag while having drinks.

"Yes, I stay with everyone until the videos and interviews are over."

"Are the guards spread around the pool, or near the tables," Lynn asked.

"They remain close to the tables and lounges to serve. They are very casual, because no one has ever done anything at the estate. The brutal slaying of the yacht crews on video from the oil rigs, coupled with a show of force after the showing is all it has ever taken to keep the hostages in line."

"How about a way to go from the garage to a higher vantage point," Casey asked. "If we could get the geezer up in a spot with the M107, he might be able to pick some of them off, and guard our exit from the garage."

"I heard the geezer remark, prick!"

I looked toward the bridge. "Damn. The geezer has ears like a bat. What about it, Joe?"

"There is a stairwell access to the decorated catwalk that borders the estate," Joe replied.

"Sounds like we have a plan," Casey said. "Is there ever any problem with the authorities when you come into port?"

"Not at our dock. There is never any interference at the docking area from the authorities. They are all paid to ignore Cartel business."

I planned on Denny reinforcing that if he could do it without tipping anyone off. "Okay, what do you have to do in order to let them know you're coming with the people and their yacht?"

"I just text them when we get close to port. They make a few calls. We hook up at the dock, and then I text them again. They send Alto in the limo."

"Why am I getting a bad feeling about this being so straight forward after that perfect op on the oil rig," Casey asked. "That in addition to the Dark Lord's uneventful mile swim in the dark is giving me the creeps. I think I feel a disturbance in the Force. The Dark Lord has sucked up and used all our luck. The cosmos is working against us."

I naturally launched into the outraged Dark Lord's troll like voice. "How dare you question the Dark Lord?! You who are mere minions of the Dark Lord will do as you're told or feel my wrath!"

We all got a laugh out of my channeling the Dark Lord. Joe stared at us like we were insane of course. Lynn gave him a little hug. "Don't let this worry you, Joe. Stick with us. We'll save the innocents, kill the bad guys, and put you somewhere the Cartel will never find you. Now, there's just one more question we need answered. Will that big cheese guy who runs the estate, Edwardo Godinez, be there?"

"He is usually there, but stays in the background until after the people are forced to watch their crews murdered."

Lynn sighed. "We're going to need him, Joe."

"Yes, Ms. Montoya."

* * *

We docked in Cancun without incident or questioning authorities in the spot Joe told us was Cartel protected. He texted our arrival as we tested communications with Jafar who would be our command center aboard the Wolf. I left him with a MAC 10.

"Do not allow boarders kid. That's an order. Fire at will, and get the hell out of here. You shoot very well, and Lucas says you're a natural at the helm. Don't worry about us. We'll take to the jungle until we can get a pickup from Laredo. Make sure Denny is on through every phase."

"I understand, John. I hope the Force is with you, Dark Lord."

"Good one, kid. See you in a while."

The limousine arrived fifteen minutes later. Joe asked to be allowed to speak with Alto the driver alone, and bring him to meet us near the Wolf. I had no objections to that. Lucas took the M107 up to a spot where he could monitor the discourse. That limo would either be leaving with all of us or not leaving at all. Alto walked with Joe. He was wide eyed terrified, but understood United States operatives would be involved. That in itself put his life in danger with the Cartel.

"He understands this will get done, with him dead or with him alive," Joe informed us. "Alto is a good man with a family. He drives. He does not participate in Cartel business. Alto may need relocated with me and his family."

I nodded. "Done deal. He'll have to stay out of sight until I can arrange for such a transfer. Right now, we will be over loaded as it is going back to the oil rig, or to meet the Coast Guard. I'm hoping my boss will do an at sea transfer after we get into international waters. You have my word we'll come for Alto and his family."

The negotiations done, we loaded aboard the very beautiful stretch limousine. As intended, it was very impressive. After over half an hour, we arrived at the gates to a splendid jungle surrounded estate. The gates opened as we arrived without incident. The courtyard gleamed with newness and money. Alto stopped where he should, hopping out immediately to open the door for Joe, Clint, and Lynn. Although Clint dressed casually, Lynn wore a red off the shoulder mini-dress no one could mistake as casual. Joe escorted them inside. Alto hurried around to take control of the limo and drive us into their spacious garage. Then it was business as usual for us. I told Alto to stay in the limo, and if he didn't, I would take that as a sign he had decided to commit suicide. I recited it in Spanish to make sure he knew if our op didn't end well, I would end him.

* * *

Lynn gripped Clint's hand with fervor, her whole countenance alive with the estate's look and feel as Joe guided them through. Clint managed the speculative prospective investor as if born to it. He smiled and grimaced, his eyes taking in everything of note, trying successfully to be the objective balm to Lynn's groupie type behavior. When Joe led them into an indoor pool area with a tropical motif, Clint had little difficulty acting stunned at the overwhelming grandeur. The hostage couples sipped by poolside in loungers, or together at the ornate table.

They welcomed the newcomers with fervor and smiles pasted on their faces.

Clint smiled, waved, approached, and shook hands with everyone, making calculations as to the waiter/guards and positioning. "Wow, honey, this is really nice."

Lynn acted bursting with excitement. "This... this is so awesome. Even the secrecy seems fine now, babe!"

They sat at the table with the other hostages they had just met with Joe, who was talking nonstop while setting his bag down near Clint. The pretense ended in seconds. Clint gripped the fully loaded MAC 10 in Joe's bag, bringing it up into targeting form, and wasting the four waiter/guards with double hits from the weapon set on semi-auto. They never had a chance. Lynn grabbed up the other MAC 10 while Clint threw a flash-bang in the direction of the pool area entrance. The explosion quieted the screaming hostages.

"Move all the way back into the corner, folks! Do it now!" Lynn reinforced her order with slaps and kicks while Clint watched their backs. "Move it, Joe! Help me herd these slow pokes back there behind the potted bushes!"

Valois helped Lynn in maneuvering the terrified people into the corner, where they had solid masonry at their backs, and huge potted plants in front.

"Stay quiet! You'll all be going home shortly if you don't panic!" Lynn made sure she saw acknowledgement before turning to join Clint at the front. "Go on, cowboy. I'll look after the Bo-Peeps. Nice shootin' by the way."

Clint grinned. "It's what I do, Cruella."

He kissed her, sealing off what would have been a vocal chastisement. Then he was running for the blown apart entrance. Clint smiled as he heard the M107 firing. He knew every shot meant a dead Cartel guy. There were four shots before he reached the mangled entranceway.

* * *

Lucas let me know he was in position. Jafar acknowledged we were loud and clear, and he had no visitors. That was our code for Denny holding off all interference. Casey and I were at each side of the garage door, ready to move. Clint's flash-bang signaled they had handled the meeting. We waited, watching Lucas pick off the Cartel guys on the high ground. A few armed guards ran out of the estate entrance. They died the second they cleared the door as Case and I moved toward them, firing short bursts.

We threw flash-bangs through the front entrance, the explosions heralding screams from guys on the other side with blown eardrums. We carry those ones that are not target friendly. They make the ears, nose and even the eyes bleed. I didn't even turn when someone died right behind us, knowing Lucas still commanded the high ground. I charged through on point with Casey firing behind me. The plan was for only one prisoner. There were no takers left at the front. Two more flash-bangs went off, letting us know where Clint was. The plan was search and destroy. We threw flash-bangs at every unsecured location, moving toward Clint with careful advances. He was to hold position once the pool area and side access points were secured.

"I have four in the pool area and three more in the access halls dead, DL."

"Geezer took out five if I counted the shots right and he didn't miss," I added.

"Prick!" Lucas's one word confirmed my number.

"We got two going in," Casey said, "and four dead I finished at the entrance."

"Damn. I thought Joe said there'd be a dozen," Clint said. "I took my shoes off for the count and I'm coming up with eighteen so far."

There were brief chuckles at Clint's counting remark, including Lynn. "Still no visitors back here, DL," Lynn said. "I asked Joe about the count. He said they have a rotating staff, so six of them may have been coming in to relieve six."

"I'm betting Edwardo is hiding under his bed. Ask Joe if he knows where Godinez's suite is here."

"One moment, DL." Lynn came back on a minute later. "His lavish lodging is first hall on your right past the entrance, and all the way down. I asked, and Joe said there are no other ways to get in other than the hall. He says Edwardo didn't want windows or any other way someone could get in and do him in his sleep. His entrance is reinforced."

"Thanks, Lynn. Hold steady. I don't want Lucas to move, so it will take us other three a while to clear all the rooms."

"Will do. Our rescued people are unhappy at all the noise. How much leeway do I have in operating my complaint department?"

Laughter.

"Please don't kill them, Cruella. We've come so far to get them out alive."

"Okay, Sissy Boy, but you'd better get a move on or I may have to conduct a demonstration, and you don't want that."

I sighed. "Let's go boys or we won't have anything to show for this mission but DNA samples."

Our room to room search revealed nothing. We were thorough, collecting all computer drives along with anything else interesting. We worked from the opposite end of the estate to the other, ending with Godinez's lodging. I tried the very impressive door. It was locked. "Hey, Edwardo, we're here, buddy. Come on out."

No answer.

"You do realize while we may not be able to knock your door down, we will blow the wall adjacent to it into dust."

No answer. I shrugged at Casey. Clint and I moved far down the hall and Casey set the charge on the left wall, which was nothing but a wall. Casey ran back with us. We ducked down. The charge blew the wall to smithereens. In comical slow motion the reinforced entranceway fell inward in a single piece. Edwardo was lying in a fetal position against the wall with a machine pistol next to him.

"I don't love this guy, Case, so if he tries to make me pay for taking the first hit shoot him in the head. We'll tell Denny he got hit with a stray."

Casey smiled. "I was wondering when you were going to get tired of that first hit shit."

"Pussy," came the pronouncement in my ear from the Geezer.

I ran down the hallway straight at Edwardo. He didn't move. I kicked the weapon off to the side, and put my MAC 10 barrel to his head. "Hi Edwardo... can you hear me now?"

Casey and Clint bracketed me while I knelt on Godinez, making sure he didn't have any surprises. He was out cold. I flipped him on his stomach and plastic tied his hands behind his back. I handed Clint my MAC 10 and shouldered my buddy, Edwardo. "Let's get the hell out of here while our hostages are still alive. I'm glad Edwardo here has more than one vehicle. We have a big load. Bring our guests out, Lynn. We're heading to the garage."

"On it."

Casey and Clint kept in front, having collected Edwardo's computer drives. We all paused by the entrance until Lynn escorted the hostages out along with Joe. One of the women was crying, clinging tightly to her angry looking husband. I shook my head at Cruella.

"What? Oh... you're unhappy about crybaby here. Get over it. Hey, DL, look at the rest of them, all cooperative and quiet, right Joe?"

Joe looked down. "Yes, Ms. Montoya."

"You get the limo with Alto driving Lynn. We'll ride in front with one of their other cars."

"Don't you want to treasure hunt? Let's wake Eddie up and I'll get him to tell us where his valuables are."

"We can't, Lynn. I'd like to, but we need to get out of here. Our escape without a trace window is closing."

Lynn patted Edwardo's cheek where his head rested against my back. "Later, Amigo."

* * *

At the boat dock, we loaded our cramped cargo. We came up with enough money to give Joe and Alto so they would have no trouble getting out of Cancun. I gave them a number to reach us, and cautioned they would have to ditch everything, including credit cards, cell-phones or any other gizmo the Cartel could trace. Lucas left port in our crowded Wolf, and we called Denny.

"We'll be in International waters shortly. All hostages are accounted for and well. Godinez is also on board."

"That's what I want to hear! I have a Coast Guard Cutter on its way to you." Denny gave us coordinates only fifteen miles further. "Damn fine op, John! I'm sure Lynn will find out all the really great information Edwardo knows, so I'll leave you to it. I'll handle the oil rig aftermath. Take the scenic route home to Corpus Christi. If I can be of service, just ring me up. Captain Blood out."

I glanced over at the smiling Lucas. "I won't even say anything to crimp this ending."

"You better not. I'm with Casey," Lucas replied. "We'll have to lay low for at least a year to build up our karma. We've caused a major disruption in the Force."

"Agreed."

* * *

It wasn't long at all before we transferred our happy to be rid of us guests to the Coast Guard. That left us with but one more loose end to deal with before the honeymoon pleasure cruise began in earnest with fishing, and adult beverages. Edwardo was sitting comfortably in the living area, his sullen face a mask of discontent. After the transfer, Lucas moved us to a spot a few miles further on and cut the engines. The ocean, tranquil and gorgeous, with wispy clouds drifting above, made for a rather incongruous setting for this last segment of the mission. I came down into the main crew area, and sat down opposite Eddie.

"When am I to be transferred?" Eddie wanted to get some place where his Cartel lawyer could buy his way to freedom. "I am a Mexican National. I demand to be released!"

Lynn giggled. "Oh, you're going to get released, Eddie... just not the way you have in mind."

Eddie didn't like her tone. "Who is this bitch to talk to me in such a way?"

Jafar immediately got up shaking his head. "Oh boy. Let me know when you need me to record, John." He went to join Lucas on the bridge.

Lynn sighed happily, taking a seat next to Eddie, and draping her arm around his shoulders. "You know, Eddie, one of the most beautiful creatures on earth is a shark: sleek, fast, unstoppable, and very dangerous."

"Why are you telling me this, you stupid bitch?" Edwardo turned away.

Lynn looked across at me. "Oh my!"

I stood up. "Let's get him stripped, guys. We're all out of chum. I wish we didn't have to use the lifejacket. I noticed pieces getting stuck in our disposal units' teeth."

* * *

Casey, Lucas, Jafar, and I were fishing leisurely off the fantail, while Lynn and Clint sunned on the foredeck. Soft strains of music drifted to us from our wonderful audio system. We had decided on Captain Morgan rum as the sipping pleasure for this fishing session, our moderate intake of spirits lulling us into happy contemplation. I leaned back further, with another small sampling of my rum - Voyage of the Damned, my ass.

The End

Made in the USA
Lexington, KY
14 June 2014